Before she coul[...]
Brad whisked t[...]
and pressed his lips against hers.

His kiss was warm, liquid, sensitive and when he drew away Shane was trembling all over, completely aroused. His masculine fragrance clung to her nostrils and her heart beat wildly.

"You're beautiful, Shane," he whispered in her ear.

Suddenly his arm encircled her body, his fingers wound through her long gleaming hair, and with a single fluid motion they fell breathless on the blanket in a passionate embrace. She lay crushed beneath him as he kissed her, swept away by his strength and the strong waves of desire that flooded and weakened her. For a long time she clung passively to him. Then something inside her burst and she responded with her own fiery passion. She opened her mouth wide to his kisses; she wrapped her arms around him and tore the buttons off his shirt. It was then she knew how much she really wanted him, that she would follow wherever he was leading.

He drew away and gazing down at her glowing green eyes and moonlit hair, slowly unbuttoned the lacy bodice of her dress...

The Dance Master

The Dance Master

Norma Harris

POPULAR LIBRARY

An Imprint of Warner Books, Inc.

A Warner Communications Company

POPULAR LIBRARY EDITION

Copyright © 1986 by Norma Harris
All rights reserved.

Popular Library® is a registered trademark of Warner Books, Inc.

Cover photo by Dan Wagner

Popular Library books are published by
Warner Books, Inc.
666 Fifth Avenue
New York, N.Y. 10103

Ⓦ A Warner Communications Company

Printed in the United States of America

First Printing: August, 1986

10 9 8 7 6 5 4 3 2 1

For my beautiful daughter
JERI GAILE
who
lived it,
loved it
and
left it.

Acknowledgments

My deepest gratitude to the following persons for their contributions to this book:

My husband, Leonard, for his research and constant devotion to my work. But most of all for his love. Also, my daughter, Jeri Gaile, who graciously shared the most intimate details of her professional life.
A huge thank-you to my secretary, Ann Clark, who toiled constantly to prepare the manuscript and who gave so much of herself.
Special thanks to my two agents, Jay Garon, along with his New York staff, and Allen L. Greene of Los Angeles, both of whom supported me from the beginning. You have such good taste!
Accolades to my editor, Kathleen Malley, whose intelligent suggestions and clever ideas colored much of the final draft. And last but not least, Tom Grant and Francine Kessler of Los Angeles for their help.

I treasure each and every one of you!

BOOK ONE

The Audition

Chapter 1

The traffic on Broadway had finally wakened, snarling and angry. Alexandra zigzagged her way across Fifty-eighth Street through the horns, the catcalls, the strident whistles, all the agitated simmerings of bored and brazen truck drivers, workmen and cabbies.

"Hey, baby, some great legs."

"Where'd you get the knockers?"

Ignoring them, she reached the curb, sidestepping a fresh wad of pink chewing gum smeared on the pavement, and moved at a hurried clip.

From the corner of her eye she noticed the drugstore and bounded over. Inside, she weighed herself for the fifth time that day. Ugh! She grimaced at the spectacle. How depressing! One hundred twenty-eight.

Still shivering from the chilled April air, she removed her blue cashmere coat and let it drop to the floor, watching as the scale pointer dropped back. One hundred twenty-six. Mentally she subtracted the sum total of her leotards, her wool leg warmers, her tights and leather boots, deducting another three pounds. It put her final weight at 123. Damn! Still too much. Well, what difference would it make? All the starvation dieting in the world wouldn't remove her natural curves and healthy bustline.

Ah, well, she sighed, grabbing her things and opening

the door to a waiting taxi. Maybe it won't be so bad. The great Richard Caligari might break tradition and choose her. After all, he was supposed to be different, a maverick, a true dance innovator. Maybe she'd inspire him. Maybe he'd see beyond the configurations of her sexy body, choose her, choreograph and create new ballets on her. She laughed at the notion. "Beauty and the Breast," "Movement for Mellons," "Sleeping Boobies."

Well, to hell with them all, she decided, settling herself inside the taxi and giving directions. And to hell with all those who had decreed in their ignorant wisdom that all ballerinas should be tall and slender, with short torsos and flat chests. She, Alexandra Irina Romanov, with all her purple mountains majesty, with all her fruited plains, would give this audition everything she had, and if that didn't suit the great Caligari, she'd simply kill herself.

Dorsey Childs, now finally awake, was coming off the 'Ludes. The beautiful naked son of a bitch lying next to her was still out of it, working on another hard-on—in his sleep, for God's sake. Jeez! He was hornier than she was.

She suppressed a giggle, planted her elbow in the pillow and boldly observed him. Lean, with beautiful thighs and calves, hard chest and muscular shoulders. No different from other male dancers, she thought, except for that gorgeous hard-on now swelling between his thighs.

She closed her eyes and lay on her back, trying to recapture the time they had spent together last night, trying to recall the floating sensation of those special moments when he had taken her in his arms and buried his face in her neck; the incredibly soft texture of his polished skin, so smooth, so warm and inviting against hers. Then, later, the awful feelings of doubt, of shame, of guilt, of needing her father to hold her instead. And sleep—finally a long and healing sleep.

She recalled with pleasure the young man's strength last night, the heat of his well-muscled body against hers as his arms wound around her back and crushed her hard against his chest. She remembered his long, articulate fingers as they explored the softness of her thighs, vibrating against her nub, the moist interiors of her vagina. A shiver of lust ran through her, and she was instantly transported to the beginning of their wild encounter.

They'd found each other yesterday in advanced ballet class, and within two short hours, still sweating from the workout, they were ripping each other's clothes off in a cheap motel room. They'd shared nothing at the beginning, including their names, and had simply started to roll naked across some filthy carpet in a frantic search for sexual release.

She had lain beneath him, flat against the hard floor, trapped in his arms, yielding to the impudence of his wet and probing tongue. He licked the hollows of her throat, let his wet tongue glide along the curves of her tiny breasts, where he sucked her nipples until they ached.

Breathless, she pushed against his chest with her palms, but he laughed at the weakness of her gesture, pressed down harder, covering her mouth with more kisses.

Strange noises poured from the depths of his throat and for a moment she quickened. Who was this stranger, this unknown madman? But her fears soon vanished as his fingers gently parted the moist folds of her vagina and slipped inside.

His fingers felt good, and as he fluttered the tips, they watched each other's eyes, egged each other on with filthy words and obscene sexual gestures. And when she was wet, frantic, he grabbed her muscled thighs and wrapped them around his tiny waist.

She sucked in her breath as he rolled the tip of his hardened organ along the soft hairs and moist lips of her opening. Then she froze when he pulled her even closer and thrust himself inside.

For Dorsey he was the perfect lover. Strong, virile, a stranger with no past, no present, no future—only now, here in this room. There were no superiors, no one to intrude or tell them what was right or wrong. They were equals in equal need, and their coupling satisfied her every desire.

She writhed beneath him on the itchy carpet. Bare buttocks, spread-eagled thighs, mouth gaping, spine and pelvis arching, she met his every vulgar thrust. And when she could no longer bear it, when the friction and heat drove her mad, she screamed out, "Daddy," and collapsed in spasms beside him.

Now she needed a cigarette and let her arm drape lazily alongside the bed, feeling blindly around for her leather ballet bag. Discovering it, she plunged a spidery arm deep into the bag's interior and groped around for her pack of Camels. Shit! She couldn't find them.

Frustrated, she rolled her rail-thin body out of bed and sat bare-ass, squatting on the floor, pulling the bag wide open and peering inside. One by one she removed the contents: toeshoes, safety pins, tights, makeup, pills for all occasions, rice cakes, vitamins, hairbrush, sewing kit, Elmer's glue, but no goddamn cigarettes. Well, fuck it, she decided, and popped a shiny black amphetamine in her mouth instead.

Standing, she straightened her spine, stretched her arms and felt her long, blond hair graze her bare buttocks. With both hands she reached behind and coiled her hair into a ball, pinning it all on top of her head. Then she entered the bathroom and, after relieving herself, turned on the shower and stepped inside the spray.

She felt beautiful today, confident, absolutely sure Caligari would notice her, would pick her from the rest. And why shouldn't he? Everyone called her the golden girl of ballet, the prototype, a perfect specimen. She was young and pretty, with pale skin, startling blue eyes and bee-stung lips. But most of all she possessed the perfect ballet body —slim, long-limbed, with short torso and perfectly formed round head. A little too thin, her father had always said, but his damned opinions hardly mattered anymore. They had stopped mattering a long time ago, in fact. Now she tried never to respond to his wishes.

It hadn't always been that way. The tensions between them had begun a year before her mother's horrible death five years ago.

She shivered, pushing back the dreadful memories of *that* incident. Then, closing the faucet, she stepped from the shower and briskly toweled off.

"Dorsey? Where the hell are you?" The strange male voice was strong, demanding.

"In the shower, you imbecile."

"Why? Where the hell are you going? Come back to bed and bring the 'Ludes." Then he sang playfully, "I have something special for you. Come and see it."

"I already ha-a-ve," she sang back, mocking his exact melody. "But I can't now. I have an appointment . . . with my aunt," she added quickly.

She had lied to him—deliberately. She didn't want to remind him of Caligari's audition, which he'd obviously forgotten about. She couldn't risk his tagging along with her for the hell of it. Unlike him, she had no job and needed to concentrate on her dancing. She knew his type. All cock and ego. If he came with her, he'd try out just to prove he could, and he'd only distract her. She couldn't afford that. No! The audition was far too important to waste on the likes of him. On the likes of anybody, for that matter.

The voice, as usual, was strident, nagging, demanding. It fired off like a speeding bullet and ricocheted down the narrow hallway.

"Shane? Shane! For God's sake, where the hell are you? Get your damn ass in gear or we'll be late."

Shane held her ears against the assault and answered sweetly, "Almost ready, Mom." The smile which accompanied the words was feral, closer to her real feelings.

She rolled her long, coppery tresses into a tight French

twist, pinning the thick ends on top of her perfect oval head, then dusted her cheeks with pink blush.

How she hated the way her mother intruded into her life, saying "we" this and "we" that. What nerve! It was, after all, *her* audition, not Simone's. She was the one who would sweat and strain for Caligari. She was the one who would suffer the pain, the blisters, the bleeding toes, the flopsweat and anxiety, the terrible feelings of rejection and letdown, not Simone. Certainly what had happened long ago to Simone had been terrible—awful, in fact. But she had to live her own life now, not her mother's dead dreams.

She wrapped a pink satin pointe shoe in soft cloth for protection and slid it into the opening of the doorjamb. She shoved it close to the hinge. Quickly she opened and closed the door sixteen times. That would soften the shoe's hard exterior, rendering it more pliable and removing the loud clunk which always sounded when new shoes hit the floor after high jumps.

With both slippers softened to her satisfaction, she sat on the tattered bedspread, massaging the bindings until they were malleable. Though she hated using new shoes for an audition, she had no choice. All her others were dreadful, too beat-up to support her legs in pointe work. And when a friend from the School of American Ballet sneaked her a free pair of Freed's yesterday, she took them gladly—not just because she needed them, but as an omen.

"Shane!" the bullet fired again. "For Pete's sake, shake your damn ass. Caligari won't let us in if we're a minute late."

Again the feral smile was instant, then gone. "Okay, Ma. I'm coming," she answered. Quickly she checked her things, squeezed a copy of *Movie* magazine, with its cover of Francesca Adair, into her canvas ballet bag and breathed deeply to relax. If the omen was right, today would be important. The great Caligari would notice her, would choose her. Eventually he'd create several roles on her, make her prima ballerina *assoluta*. Only then could she possibly do what she'd always dreamed of doing. Only then could she leave behind the poverty, the mean streets and, finally, most important of all, the voice of her nagging, demanding mother.

The small ladies' room near the audition hall overflowed with highly strung bodies. Like spirited young thoroughbreds before a great race, the dancers were in perpetual motion, bending, twisting, stretching, warming their limbs. The seasoned performers stood calmly near a window sucking air, doing sensible grand pliés while the younger, less experienced hopefuls fixed their hair and makeup, taking turns throwing up in the tiny toilets.

Their conversations were shrill, regularly punctuated with explosions of nervous laughter, a kind of trembling, restless chatter charged with energy. And the subjects were varied yet related: about dieting, chiropractors, vitamins and good nutrition, ballet shoes and, of course, the magical Caligari.

"Why does he always marry his ballerinas?" one inquired.

"You have nothing to worry about," her friend answered, heading for the toilet once again. "He only marries the important ones."

"I've heard that he's bi."

"Oh, don't be ridiculous. He's had three wives."

"Well, at least everyone agrees he's come a long way since his dancing days at the old City Center with Mr. B. Have you seen his latest choreography? It's positively weird. Classical yet kinda funky."

"How on earth can it possibly be both?" her wide-eyed companion asked as she fastened a spray of lavender violets to her friend's French twist.

"Dunno, but it is. My mother and I saw his latest stuff in San Francisco, and we were totally freaked out. You needed a computer to follow the count. Ouch! Not so tight."

"*My mother* thinks he's the greatest," another said. "The

very future of ballet—like Balanchine was forty years ago."

"Oh, God!" one exploded. "Where'd you get your pointe shoes? They're so unusual."

"In Austria," the girl replied with a faint tinge of Katharine Hepburn to her voice. "I was in Europe with the Stuttgart Ballet in 'eighty and my mother just happened to find this quaint little family of shoemakers." She pointed her foot to show off the pretty pink arch.

"Well, just don't wear that silly skirt at the audition," a girl in pale blue said sarcastically. "It may have been okay for the Stuttgart, but Caligari's a perfect nut about raised hips. He'll think you're hiding something underneath it and make you take it off."

"And how do you know that?" the girl asked, nervously unfurling the wisp of black silk that encircled her tiny waist.

"His master class. I took one last year in Los Angeles. He's into very clean lines."

"How very Cecchetti of him," the girl said snidely, shoving her skirt back into her ballet bag.

"Not to mention how very old-fashioned," another teased.

"There's nothing old-fashioned about the dear departed Mr. Cecchetti," an older girl remarked as she came up from a grand plié. "His methods were good enough for the great Anna Pavlova. They should certainly be good enough for you."

Suddenly the door burst open. "Everyone, c'mon. He's about to begin."

"Oh, *merde,*" someone cried.

"*Merde,*" her friend repeated, for good luck.

Then with the sounds of nervous laughter hiding a hundred hopeful dreams, the small bathroom quickly emptied. All that remained was a clutter of hairpins on the floor, long hair strands coiled on dirty sink basins, a snowfall of lipstick-stained toilet paper and a heady mixture of cologne masking the faint odor of vomit.

Chapter 2

All conversation stopped as Richard Caligari, holding a long wooden pointer in his hand, strode into the large and airy rehearsal hall. In black T-shirt and tights, his formidable, muscular build looked magnificently menacing, and his penetrating black eyes as they scanned the room were intense enough to scrape paint off walls or varnish off floors.

"Good morning, ladies and gentlemen," he said, tossing a full head of shiny black hair. "Thank you all for coming." He noted the time on his Cartier polo watch as he removed it and placed it on top of the piano.

"Good morning, Joshua," he said quietly to the pianist. He paused, then glanced about the room in inquiry. Suddenly his eyes narrowed. "Where the devil's Paige?"

"Here," the dimunitive prima ballerina called.

Tiny exclamatory sighs and whispers fluttered through the hall as the elegant ballerina with the huge brown eyes burst into the room. She had once been Caligari's mistress, later his prima ballerina, then his wife. Now she was only his prima ballerina and business associate, a testament to the endurance of art only.

Abruptly, Caligari turned away from her and pointed toward a pair of wooden boxes flush against the mirror-lined wall where he wanted her to be seated.

She had come late deliberately, he thought, and he was angry at her. Yet he also understood. The beautiful dancer had turned thirty-five last year, an age when most ballerinas begin to consider hanging it all up. Nothing could make her more aware of that fact than a room full of eager young dancers.

He sat down beside her, watching as the dancers stretched their bodies against the barre, on the floor and along the walls of the room. At one glance he could spot the really good ones, ones that had been classically taught. He was a snob on that point, but he had to be. The rest of his life depended on it. Especially now—now that his touring plans had changed, now that he intended to make his final bid for recognition. No, not recognition. He already had that. This would be his final bid for success.

Success. He let that elusive word roll around in his mind. In the world of the serious artist, success was a dirty word. It meant profit, mass appeal, commerciality, compromise and condescension. Well, to hell with those outdated notions. He was going to be successful. He was going to master what others before him had tried and couldn't accomplish. He was going to build a new ballet company in New York City, a permanent home with funding, with a private school and an excellent troupe of trained dancers. And it would be both artistically important and financially successful.

When it was time to begin, he gripped the pointer tightly and stood. "Attention, boys and girls," he called, loudly striking the pointer against the floor. "Please take a place at the barre for a short warm-up."

The dancers were stunned. He was actually going to conduct the warm-up class, and that was unusual. Highly unusual for an important choreographer such as Caligari to preside. But then, he was unusual and different in so many ways. Unconventional, innovative, trying to find and put his finger on not only his own place in the future, but the very future of dance itself.

"As you have all obviously read in this month's issue of

Performing World," he said, "the Caligari Ballet Company is conducting auditions to supplement its corps. Also, we will fill several vacant solo positions. Our main goal is to find a permanent home here in New York City. Most of you already know we have a special image to project. Therefore, it should come as no surprise that we cannot take those of you with the wrong body configurations for that image."

Several dancers groaned. Small ones stretched their bodies higher, tall ones tried to shrink into the ground. Alexandra turned her bosom toward the barre.

"Please don't allow this to discourage you from going elsewhere," he continued. "There are many other ballet companies where I'm sure most of you will find acceptance." The room hung on a jagged edge as the dancers nervously awaited the sentence of life or death with his next words.

"Ladies over five feet seven inches would do better to audition for the New York City Ballet. Gentlemen under five feet seven are also dismissed. Thank you very much for coming, but I'm sorry." Caligari hated doing this, but he had no choice. Like most great artists, he had established a particular look for his ballet company and he had worked hard doing it—long, arduous years building a classical image. He just couldn't compromise on that—not ever!

Several disappointed young ladies burst immediately into tears and with quickening steps fled the room. The more vocal gentlemen sailed softly spoken vulgarities across the room like sullied Frisbees.

"Positions!" Caligari called as the door shut behind the last dancer. "In first, second, third and fifth—four grand pliés, front side and back, then reverse." He gestured toward the piano player and a chord was struck.

Shane, clutching the barre with a sweaty hand, took a place behind a young man in green tights and leotards. In first position she breathed deeply and began her grand pliés to the tap of Caligari's pointer, bending her knees slowly to make the movement flow gracefully, smoothly to the floor, then up again. Her green eyes followed the pretty outward arc of her arm, then back again to her center.

Soon the beautiful strains of Chopin filled the skylit rehearsal hall and angular young bodies strained long necks, willowy, engaging arms and sturdy shoulders, some hiding extreme muscular tension, hiding anxiety, even hiding intense pain, showing only their grace and beauty. Within five minutes, warm sweaters came flying off and were slung across the ballet barre, and leg warmers drooped down from tense thighs and rested at tight knees and straining ankles.

Caligari paced the line like a reluctant sergeant inspecting a brand-new troop of incompetent recruits, some of whom he would soon fashion into soldiers of fortune. Tapping out the rhythms with his pointer, he stopped occasionally to correct, to poke at a knee, to push at a bad turnout, an ankle that sickled and wobbled, arms that showed little grace and shoulders that were raised and tight.

Tap, tap, tap. "Straighten your turnout, for heaven's sake. You're a trained dancer, not a cow. Yes. Better, much better."

Tap, tap, tap. "What the devil's wrong with your hands, young lady? They look like lobster claws."

Tap, tap, tap. "Pretty, very pretty. Far too pretty for a boy."

It wasn't his intention to ridicule the young dancers, nor even to make them nervous. But the world of ballet was very tough and he needed the very toughest dancers he could find. It wasn't enough that they be graceful and strong; he needed quick minds and resiliant bodies open to new and exciting endeavors, dancers that could handle hours of grueling rehearsals and travel under the most trying conditions. He needed dancers who were totally dedicated, as avidly devoted as nuns, thick skinned, with a combination of stamina, pluck and courage. With this audition, his own personal baptism by fire, he could easily separate the strong, nourishing wheat from the useless chaff.

"One, two, three, four, développé, hold, hold, hold." Caligari paused, inspecting the line as the dancers balanced their bodies high up on one foot. "Now stretch up to the ceiling and reverse."

Standing with great difficulty, Simone peeked through a small door window and watched the class. Her own muscles tightened with each of Shane's movements. No, dammit, she thought. Not good enough. Push, Shane, push. Harder. Now raise your leg. Higher, higher! No, goddammit, flare your foot and relax those shoulders. Good. That's better. Tilt the head a little more, and for God's sake use your goddamn eyes. Oh, shit! Caligari was at her side and Shane looked like hell.

Where had all that money gone? All the sacrificing, all the scrimping and saving, the doing without, the damned hard work sewing other people's clothes to keep Shane in tights, in toeshoes and lessons, not to mention all their fights about proper nutrition.

She watched the others, carefully noting in her mind the competition, who would or wouldn't make it. That one's too busty, she thought, and the blonde's far too thin; looks like a survivor of some concentration camp. Then her eyes shot back to Shane, grazing the young woman's slender body. Lovely, Simone thought, but not half as beautiful as she herself had been so long ago, before her terrible ordeal.

"Other side, please," Caligari called.

Collectively, the dancers groaned, heaved their bodies and, simultaneously turning around, gripped the ballet barre with their right hands. Colorful leotards clung tenaciously to wet and glistening bodies, and the smell of perfume and sweat mingled in the air. Then at a wave of Caligari's hand, the Chopin chord was struck again, and in unison they began frappés.

Chapter 3

Halfway through the intricate floor combinations, Alexandra studied her body in the mirror, tucking her buttocks firmly up and under, carefully arranging her arms and head in a Madonna pattern.

She should have felt exhilarated. After all, she hadn't missed a single beat, not a count, not a nuance of Caligari's odd rhythms or complicated directions. So why hadn't he noticed her? Why hadn't he corrected her? Why hadn't he so much as cast a glance in her direction or even smiled? Usually a dance master would single out faults and frailties, administering important corrections, but he had said nothing to her, nothing at all. A bad sign.

Wiping the sweat from her hands across the sides of her leotard, she gripped her partner's finger and began spinning. One, two, three perfect turns, gradually bringing her arms in close to her body. Beautiful! Hell, what was wrong with Caligari? What was wrong with her? She had a good strong partner, who was lending firm support for her center, complementing her line in the arabesque with his own masculine grace, and she was giving it everything she had. Still nothing. How she longed for Caligari's attention, longed to hear a correction, prayed he'd poke her just once with his lousy pointer. Anything, even insult her if he had to, but not just simply ignore her. Well, fine, fine. Okay, she thought. She'd just have to try a little harder.

Alexandra fully extended her long leg in the arabesque penché, arched her instep and flared her foot up and out toward the ceiling. Then with the tips of her fingers, she lightly brushed the floor, pertly tilting her head and peering into the mirror to check her position.

"You look great," her partner encouraged, as though he had been reading her mind. "Best penché in the whole damned room."

"Thanks," she answered, slowly coming up. "Tell that to Caligari."

"Ladies," Caligari said, demonstrating as he spoke. "Bourrée front, preparation, snatch the knee up and triple turn if you can. Then attitude front, demi plié up and onto your partner's shoulder, pose and down into a fish. This way," he added, crossing his arms in a graceful position. "And ladies, please, for God's sake keep your hips down in the attitude. Spare me the sight of a dozen pink crotches glaring down at me."

It sounded funny, but he was deadly serious and nobody dared to laugh.

Shane leaned her sweaty body against the ballet barre, carefully watching, listening attentively as Caligari rattled off the combination. She used her fingers to mark the choreography, conserving her energy for the actual execution of the steps.

Whe he had finally finished and the Chopin chord was struck on the piano, she began the combination easily. Then, somewhere in the middle, spinning full out on pointe, she suddenly lost her balance, landing firmly on her tiny butt. So much for omens, she thought, picking herself off the floor.

Miserable, feeling herself on the brink of humiliation, she brushed off her backside and clumped her way toward the rosin box. With tears in her eyes, she dug her toeshoes into the crystals, loudly crunching the hell out of the stuff.

She had been doing so well, she thought, until now, anyway. Caligari must think she's an idiot. And how could she disappoint Simone this way after all her sacrifices?

She wiped her tired, wet arms and the back of her aching neck with a soggy towel, wanting like hell to blame the fall on her partner, but she couldn't. He had been splendid. Then with a deep sigh of resignation, she sauntered back for more punishment.

"Are you okay?" her partner, Seth Pollace, asked, taking her hand. "I'm really sorry."

"It's not your fault," Shane reassured him. "I'm lousy. Can't seem to get it together today."

"I know how you feel. I get that way at auditions too. C'mon, let's try it again."

The perspiration trickled down Dorsey's pale face and neck, joining the larger drops on her back and chest, creating a tiny network of waterways across her entire body.

Like the rest of the dancers, she always observed herself in the mirror as she moved—brisé, chassé, preparation, turn. Watch that ankle. Now smile. Smile, goddammit!

Once again, spotting, turning her head a beat before the rest of her body in a clean triple turn, she came to rest in a beautiful fourth position. Not too shabby. Slim, she thought, praising herself. Just keep it up.

She clutched at her handsome partner's strong right hand, then suddenly, without warning, her legs felt drained of blood, heavy, like dead weights dragging her down to the floor. Her chest closed up tight as a drum. Goddamn cigarettes, she thought, stopping at the barre and jackknifing her body over to catch her breath; must give them up immediately. She ignored the possibility that the uppers and downers she had been regularly consuming could in any way be affecting her performance.

* * *

Caligari watched them with excitement. To a choreographer, there is no more exquisite sight then a room full of young dancers. To him they are beautiful, irresistible, a pulsating form of energy just waiting to be harnessed, rearranged, then set free again. Like a rainbow array of colors to an artist or a lump of wet clay to a sculptor, they are the very tools of his trade.

And to Richard Caligari dancers were so much more than colors, much more than clay waiting to be shaped to perfection. They were his life's passion, and the sight of them sweating, twisting, spinning, jumping, leaping in the air stirred his blood, made his heart beat faster, quickened his pulse and stimulated his brain.

But when they didn't live up to their God-given potential, when their colors ran muddy, when they refused to shine, to blend well, to soar and crackle with life, it always killed him.

"Port de bras," he said to the girl in pale blue, "means the gradual unfolding of your arms, not the savage thrusting of paws. You must learn to phrase smoothly, anticipate the movement in your mind, then let your arms automatically follow.

"And you, young man in green," he continued. "Entrechats are beats of quickness. Your feet should look like the wings of a hummingbird." He demonstrated. "Not pancakes stuck to a griddle."

Someone giggled.

Caligari's menacing eyes searched the row of dancers. "Don't you dare laugh at him," he snarled. "Don't anyone in my presence ever dare laugh at someone who is trying as hard as this young man is. The images I choose are designed to help stimulate, not amuse you."

He wondered for an instant if he was getting just a little too rough, then decided to hell with it. This was, after all, what he and his world were about. If someone in this room couldn't cope, much better that he find out now than later.

Breathing hard, he nodded at the pianist. When the chord was struck again, he reached for a towel, wiped his neck and arms, then strolled toward Paige. Together they carefully observed the full line of dancers leaping, spinning, straining to look beautiful for him.

"Well, pet, what do you think? Have we another Pavlova here? A Kirkland? A Gregory? A Baryshnikov, perhaps?"

Paige responded without a moment's hesitation. "Only two girls and three young men who have possibilities," she answered. And she wrote down their names.

Chapter 4

Richard Caligari studied the names printed on the slip of yellow, perfumed paper Paige had handed him and smiled. As usual, he thought, she had chosen wisely. He leaned over and in sincere gratitude lightly brushed his mouth against her pale and delicate cheek, a gesture meant to express his thanks and appreciation, nothing more. He tried never to encourage her subtle invitations to resume their old relationship. *That* had been over between them for years. Yet it was obvious to anyone with eyes and ears that a long time ago they had been lovers and she still cared deeply for him.

When dealing with her these days, he was strictly professional, yet sometimes also brotherly, particularly when she had gone out of her way to help, as she had today. But he was always on guard, careful not to convey a message she could easily misconstrue. He wanted her help. He needed her sensible approach to business matters, relied on her intelligent resources, her sound judgments and always thought of her as an essential part of what had become his professional success. As a result of their relationship, he was free to do nothing but create and *that* was the most important thing in his life.

In return for her help, he originated and produced the dramatic roles she desired and coveted, always treating her

with the reverence and respect her position as prima ballerina demanded. Yet their past stayed an integral part of their
present, and he kept that in perspective whenever they
were together.

Satisfied, concurring with the choices Paige had made,
he tucked the paper she had given him inside the pocket of
his black cowl-necked sweater. Then he faced the exhausted complement of dancers whose hearts and souls lay
vulnerable and exposed to his decision. Now came the hard
part: announcing selections.

It was like sentencing innocent children to the gallows.
He knew their hopes and dreams, had lived in the heart of
desire for as long as he could remember, but it was necessary to choose, and in choosing came also rejection. As a
defense mechanism, he had devised a way of letting the
losers down easily, in private. So he paused first in artificial contemplation, then took a deep breath and flashed the
enigmatic smile he had become so famous for. Then with a
lump in his throat, he began what had become for him a
tired and cliché-ridden speech filled with sincere praise and
amplified encouragement.

"Ladies and gentlemen . . ."

Sitting on the tattered edge of a Jacobean couch in the
gloomy alcove waiting room, Simone nervously flipped
through the last three pages of a mauled but recent copy of
Dance magazine. Uncomfortable, tired of waiting for Shane
to finish, she tossed the dog-eared issue onto the wrought-
iron coffee table and watched it bounce to the floor.

What the devil was taking so damn long? she thought,
retrieving the magazine and placing it back on the table.
How much time did anyone, including the great Caligari,
need to see how talented Shane really was? Surely he knew
by now. And surely Shane would be among those chosen.

She settled back again, listening as the strains of Chopin
drifted out from a nearby studio. It was a lovely melody,
one she had danced to some twenty-one years ago as a
pretty young girl. She flashed quickly on an image of her-

self dressed in pink tights, romantic tutu, long hair like Shane's all tied up in gossamer, lace and shiny pink ribbons. She had been happy then, as fragile and delicate as the heroine Giselle.

Then powerful outside forces had snatched the wind out of her sails. Recalling those moments made her sick all over. There were things in her past she would rather forget. Along with the pretty pink images came black ones—slashed satin, torn tulle, lace and blood mingling horribly around her ankles. Shuddering, she forced her attention back to the audition and Shane.

Glancing at her shabby Timex wristwatch, she saw that two full hours had gone by. Time. It was a dancer's mortal enemy. Hard enough to defy gravity, fight exhaustion, sustain illness and injury. Yet to keep up with the endless flow of younger, stronger competition, a dancer also had to fight time, and any dancer worth his salt knew the battle could be waged but the war would never be won.

Damn Caligari! What the hell was going on in there? And why hadn't they already finished? There were things she had to do. Frustrated, she dug the rubber tip of her wooden cane onto the dirty parquet floor and pulled herself to a standing position. Slowly, she hobbled toward the twin rehearsal hall doors, which she parted a sliver and with great curiosity peered through. The handsome Caligari stood in the center of the room surrounded by the dancers, and Simone strained to hear what he was saying. But it was far too difficult to stand, and she soon let the doors slip closed.

She moved to the bulletin board, where a gallery of theater announcements, class schedules and daily rehearsal calls hung sandwiched together near a wall telephone. She studied them without interest until a single slip of yellow paper caught her eye. It smelled of perfume and the neatly typed message brought a smile to her lips. She glanced behind to be sure no one was watching, then snatched the sheet and shoved it deep into her pocket. Then like a bird who has just found a juicy worm, she leaned against the wall with a grin.

Applause burst suddenly from Caligari's studio and the twin doors sprang open. Soon the sweaty contingent came rushing out. Some dancers dropped to the floor in a state of near exhaustion while others draped their sweat-drenched limp bodies across the comfortable old couch like rag dolls. Breathless, their scattered comments were a vigorous denial of their real hopes and fears.

"Oh, God, I'm glad that's over with. I wouldn't join his company if he begged me to."

"You have nothing to worry about," her friend commented, fending off some imaginary blow she thought forthcoming.

"Are you kidding me? I'd pay *him* to let me dance in his company."

"So who do you think made it?"

"Well, not me, for God's sake. I was down on my ass ten times."

"Eleven, but who's counting?"

"Am I nuts or is he gorgeous? Did you see those eyes? Like black marbles in clean snow."

"Will you please knock that stuff off? The man is old enough to be your father."

"Uh-huh. So how come your tongue was on the floor when he touched your leg?"

"Her tongue's always on the floor," a friend said. "Runs in her family."

Shane finally shuffled out and hugged Simone's shoulders. "So? When do we start?" Simone asked. "When's the first day of rehearsal?" But Shane didn't answer. A sinking feeling seized Simone's gut. She felt the girl's body close to hers and realized for the first time that Shane was shaking. "What happened in there?" Simone whispered. "What the hell did he say?"

Shane sighed and pulled away. "He didn't say anything. I'm just exhausted, that's all."

"You mean he didn't tell who got in?"

"No, he'll telephone when he decides."

"When he decides?" Simone barked. "Decides what?" Simone grumbled the rest of her words quietly, through tightly clenched teeth. "So what the hell does that mean? Are we in or not?" Silence. She slammed her cane against the floor. "Two wasted hours and he doesn't tell? Who the hell does he think he is?"

"Shh, Mama! Please don't shout," Shane pleaded. "Everyone has to wait. He'll evaluate us and call the ones who fit. It makes perfect sense to me."

"Sense?" Simone hissed. "What the hell do you know about sense? You're a baby." Aware that others were listening, Simone lowered her voice. "Well, Caligari's not God!" she growled. "He can't dangle us on strings like a couple of puppets. We'll soon see about 'sense.'"

As she started for the studio doors, Shane gripped her coat sleeve. "Please, Ma, don't!" Shane begged. There were tears in her daughter's eyes. "Don't do it! Don't chase after him like he's a peddler on Orchard Street. You'll ruin it. Please wait and find out like everyone else."

Simone listened to Shane's pleas but kept the corner of her eye on the dance master as he moved toward the back office. She needed to know the answer *now*, this second, and *he* could tell her. They shouldn't have to wait like dogs for a bone. But when she glanced at Shane, at the fear fluttering in the girl's green eyes, a smile softened her hard features. "Okay, all right already. So maybe you're right this time." She tapped Shane's butt in affection. "So get a move on and change your yucky clothes." Instantly, the dark veil lifted from Shane's eyes. "And hurry it up," Simone added. "I've got tickets to the Bolshoi tonight. Ilya Kremorkin's dancing 'Le Corsaire.'"

With her makeup artfully applied, Dorsey Childs rolled her wet leotards and tights into a large white towel, stuffing them into a plastic sack, then into her ballet bag. She dried her long blond hair with a hair dryer and wove it into a loose fat braid that fell to her buttocks in wispy blond ends. She pulled on a red cable-stitch sweater, tight gray corduroy jeans and white snakeskin boots. On her head went a white Angora beret. Now she was ready to meet her father for lunch.

In the alcove waiting room, she glanced casually at her gold Rolex wristwatch and felt her heart skip a beat. Jeez! It was a quarter past twelve. Hell! Her father should understand *this* time, she thought. It had not been deliberate. She'd had no idea Caligari's audition was going to take this long. She walked quickly to the telephone to call him and explain. If there was one thing Senator Childs always demanded, it was punctuality, and she was already fifteen minutes late.

At the telephone she stuck a quarter into the coin box and dialed. On the first ring, a feminine voice answered sweetly.

"Senator Childs' office. May I help you?"

"Yes," Dorsey replied. "Is the esteemed Senator in?" She smiled at her choice of words. If the Senator was anything at all in the eyes of the public, it was definitely esteemed. Little did they know. . . .

"And who may I say is calling?"

Dorsey bristled. She'd spoken to her father's secretary for years. How long would it take for the stupid woman to recognize her voice? "Tell him it's Dorsey."

The saccharine voice became lightly beneficent. "Oh, I'm so sorry, dear, but he's gone. Meeting Mrs. Childs for lunch and shopping. Left about ten minutes ago, as a matter of fact." The voice paused. "Will there be any message, dear?"

As usual, Dorsey tried to think of something witty to say, something amusing and frivolous to cover up her real feelings. But her mind drew a weary blank and her throat clenched as tight as a fist. The new Mrs. Childs was not one of her favorite people. "He had a date with *me* this afternoon," she said, keeping her disappointment and jealousy in check. "Would you remind him of that?"

"Oh, goodness," the secretary sighed. "Hold on a second, please." There was a sickening pause again and though she fought it valiantly, Dorsey's blood went from simmer to boil. "Well, it's not on his master calendar, dear," the secretary said when she returned. "I'm really sorry. Anything special I can tell him when he comes back?"

Before she could think, before she could stop herself, she shouted, "Yeah! Tell him to go fuck himself!" And livid with anger, she slammed the phone on its hook.

She held her breath until the violent feelings subsided. She felt sick to her stomach and had a strong urge to cry, but she composed herself quickly, thinking she could never allow anyone, especially strangers, to see her so vulnerable, so capable of disintegration, especially because of *him*. Over the years, she'd become such a master at hiding, at manipulating her emotions she sometimes couldn't feel them; that is, until they'd overwhelm her.

So why hadn't she learned by now? Surely she should never expect any more than a foolish rejection from him. He'd been that way for a long time—harsh and heartless, callous and unfeeling, especially with her mother before her death five years ago. Yet she knew he was not being deliberately cruel, dammit. These were just facets of his complex personality, like having blond hair and blue eyes. Simply in his genes.

To soothe her trembling, she opened a vial of white pills and swallowed one without water. It went down smoothly and she soon began to relax. Well, one day he'd be sorry, she thought, snatching her ballet bag from the floor and striding toward the exit. A time would come when she'd force him to face some truths about himself and their relationship. She'd have to confront him eventually, just to keep her sanity. And when that time came—and it would —all scores between them would be settled, evened down to the last hurt and disappointment.

* * *

Alexandra stood on the bustling street corner, oblivious to the life around her. The bright afternoon sun snatched the chill from the day, promising springtime. Above, the sky shone the merest blue, pierced by the tips of tall black towers. And though the noisy city offered a smorgasbord —Irish stew, Puerto Rican rum, French pastry—she was blind to the beauty, deaf to the din, starving, while the city sang its sweet and sour songs.

Lost in her thoughts, she wondered if Caligari had even noticed her. Dream on, Alexandra, dream on. There were at least ten girls better than she and just a few openings to fill. Yet, deep in her heart, she knew she had danced well, had "delivered" as they say, each and every time. Hell, why shouldn't she be chosen? She'd spent twelve years studying, learning, training in schools all over the world, browbeating her body into total submission. She must have done something to please him!

Anticipating rejection, she tilted her head reverently toward a patch of blue sky and began to pray, to barter with God for her heart's desire. She'd gotten no farther than "Dear Lord" when an ebullient voice sang a cheerful greeting in her ear.

"Hi! Didn't I see you in audition?"

"Why, yes," Alexandra said. She recognized the girl instantly, recalled with a smattering of jealousy the lean body, the neat, rounded pinhead perched perfectly on the long neck, the raw power and simple beauty the girl had projected in her every move. She shook the outstretched hand. It was cold to the touch and as delicate as spun glass. "I'm Alexandra Romanov—Alex to my friends."

"Dorsey, Dorsey Childs. Nice to meet you." She dropped her ballet bag on the sidewalk and opened a fresh pack of cigarettes. Tossing the cellophane wrapper into the gutter, she offered a cigarette to Alexandra, who declined. "So? What did you think?"

"Well, I don't think I made it, if that's what you mean."

"What are you talking about? I saw your stuff and

you've got some good moves. I mean your arabesque penché was *the* best!"

"Sure," Alexandra said, crestfallen. "I was just great. Didn't fall, didn't forget a combination. Didn't get a *single* correction either."

Her remark hung in the air like dirty laundry. Each girl knew what it really implied. Not to be corrected by the dance master was the mark of Cain.

"Well, excuse my French, kid, but it don't mean shit." Dorsey lit her cigarette, drawing the smoke deep inside her lungs and releasing it in twin streams from her pert little nose. "He also didn't correct the girl in front of you either —you know, the one with the pushy mother—and I'll bet you ten bucks right now *she* makes it."

"Thanks for the encouragement," Alexandra said. "It's sweet of you to say."

Dorsey made a face at the stale taste of her cigarette, then flipped it in a wide arc out into the street. It hit the fender of a passing taxi, and an angry driver screamed obscenities at her. She gave him the finger and Alexandra giggled. "Hey, there's a great deli around the corner from here," Dorsey said. "Wanna have a bite?" Her eyes came alive with mischief. "Think of the fun we can have picking everyone apart—Paige McDowell, Caligari."

"Yeah," Alexandra said, lifting her things from the sidewalk. "I can't think of anything more nourishing than revenge on rye."

Chapter 5

The naked young man was a stranger, a Broadway dancer she'd met last night at a disco. Francesca Adair smiled as she watched him sleep, his broad head against her bare, ample breasts, nutmeg ringlets curling like baby fingers around her silky pink nipples.

He'd been fair in the sack, she thought, able to go the distance. But not far enough to satisfy all her lusty needs. Just an hors d'oeuvre, a juicy morsel, and now it was over. Now it was 5 P.M., time to rise, time to dismiss him. Time to dress, to comb her platinum hair, to put on her jewels, her furs, her famous persona. Time to relax in her seat at the New York State Theater, to gaze at the sexiest Russian dancer of all time, Ilya Kremorkin, superstar of the Bolshoi Ballet.

She shook the sleeping body beside her, then kicked it out of bed.

"Hey! What's the big idea?!" the young man cried from the floor.

"I wouldn't say that if I were you," Francesca goaded him. "You didn't have a big idea all evening."

On the bustling steps of Lincoln Center, the evening turnout was splendid. In the cold April air, lush furs hugged gowns of silk; jewels sparkled like brilliant stars against the Palm Beach throats of New York City's most glamorous, affluent patrons. And they were all there to see *him*, to watch Ilya Kremorkin's final American performance, to drink in his masculinity, witness his ballon, breathe in and admire his sexual power, his charismatic strength and artistry. Not since Rudolf Nureyev had a dancer so electrified the world.

Inside the theater Francesca Adair sat in her comfortable mezzanine seat, hoping no one would ask for her autograph. *He* was all she wanted to think about. One week ago they'd met at a private cocktail party. He'd simply kissed her hand. Since then she hadn't been able to scrape his scent from her skin. Two Russian guards had hovered close by to be sure the charismatic *premier danseur* would behave. But she'd take odds against their ultimate success.

She could smell his restlessness, his extreme dissatisfaction. One of these days he'd defect, she knew. Six months, a year, maybe two. It was only a matter of time. And when he did, she'd be waiting, eager to satisfy her curiosity about all the wild rumors about him, hungry to experience him every way she could.

Until then, she'd follow him everywhere: Rio, Japan, Rome, London, Paris. Everywhere. She'd sit in the audience and soak him up like a sponge. And when the right opportunity presented itself—and it would—she'd fuck his gorgeous Russian brains out.

Alexandra followed her mother down the plush aisle of the theater to their orchestra seats. It felt strange to be out with Julia, but tonight they were together for special reasons.

Ballet star Ilya Kremorkin was a distant cousin, and because tonight was his last American performance, Julia had hoped they'd be permitted backstage for a short visit. But no such luck. There had been no answers to any of her messages from either Ilya, whom she had met briefly in

Paris, or from the Russian government. So they'd taken their seats to watch his performance.

"Didn't he even acknowledge the flowers you sent?" Alexandra asked.

"No. Not a word. Not a single solitary word."

"Maybe he can't answer," Alexandra said, opening her program. "Maybe they won't let him."

"It's possible," Julia agreed. "Anything's possible."

"Are you still upset about not being invited to that cocktail party?"

Julia's eyes narrowed. "Livid's a better word. But I had nothing to say about it. The Russian authorities screened the guest list and I became a casualty."

Alexandra thought about it. "Maybe they're afraid for you to see him," she theorized.

"Could be. Though God knows what sort of threat I pose to the Russian government. I mean, Ilya and I are just distant cousins. I only wanted to say hello, not kidnap him."

"There was silence for a moment, then Julia changed the subject. "By the way, have you heard from Caligari?"

"No," Alexandra replied. The sound of her voice was sad, dejected, as she answered.

"Want me to call some people, pull some strings?"

Alexandra felt her blood suddenly boil. "No. Please don't," she said, keeping the anger from her voice. "There's still time for him to contact me."

"Yes," Julia reassured her. "He's probably still deciding." She paused. "But what will you do if he doesn't accept you?"

That's when Alexandra dropped her little bombshell. "Who knows?" she answered. "Maybe go with you and Vidal to Monte Carlo."

Five minutes before curtain, an uneasy Simone handed Shane the rented binoculars. They were high up in the balcony of the theater. Cheap seats, but what the hell, it was better than nothing. Besides, it was all they could afford.

"Oh, my God," Shane said excitedly. "There's Francesca Adair down there in the first ring." She passed the glasses to her mother, who refused them with a sneer.

"Who cares!" Simone said. "I see tramps all day where I work. I don't have to look at them here."

Shane drew the glasses hungrily to her eyes and focused. She was a movie fan, and Francesca Adair was her favorite. "She's not a tramp," the girl said, continuing to stare at the magnified image of the actress. "She's a fabulous movie star."

A young couple squeezed by their feet to the next seats. Simone drew her legs in to let them pass, but the man accidentally kicked her shin. The pain made her wince but she said nothing. Another time she'd have read them the riot act, but right now she was preoccupied.

Ever since that telephone call tonight, she'd been a nervous wreck, waiting for something terrible to happen. Before then, she had been so sure they were safe and could not be found. Then, five minutes before leaving for the theater, that call had come. It was a coincidence perhaps. Just a common garden-variety New York sex maniac. Nevertheless, the silence on the other end frightened her, made her recall what she'd been trying to forget for the last eighteen years.

Now she was fearful, afraid to speculate on what would happen if she and Shane were located. Afraid to find out what her daughter would do if the whole messy truth were revealed. How could she tell such a sensitive young girl that both their lives had been based on a lie?

"Look, Ma, there's Caligari," the girl squealed.

This time Simone grabbed the glasses and searched the sea of coiffed heads. "Where? Where?"

"Over there," Shane pointed. "Two rows behind Francesca Adair."

Simone easily spotted Francesca's bright platinum hair,

then drew the glasses sharply back two rows. Yes, she thought, focusing on his head of black hair, there he was. The dance master. The star maker. The bastard. More handsome than ever. At least *he'd* get some sleep tonight, she thought, handing the glasses back to her daughter as the curtain rose. What the hell did he have to worry about?

Chapter 6

It was three in the morning, hours after the fine Bolshoi performance, and Richard Caligari lay awake in his bed staring at the ceiling of his SoHo loft. A lifelong insomniac, he was mulling things over. He had been in New York City for almost two months now, and the money he had put aside for his last hurrah was being put to the test. A strong man, he was not easily given to states of panic, but there was something close to that stirring inside him.

To ease the tension, he donned his black velour robe and walked into the living room where his Spanish guitar lay. Burying his cheek deep in the curves of the instrument, he sat on the white couch and plucked the strings. The chords he strummed were sad ones, old Spanish melodies taught to him by his mother, Maria, a Sacro Monte Gypsy from a small Andalusian village in southern Spain. But after ten minutes of closed eyes and feigned attention, he realized his efforts were useless and he set the guitar aside to stare at the fireplace where several logs crackled, sending flickering shades of soft orange light across the darkened room.

He poured a glass of red wine and stroked the neck of his beloved Rodriguez instrument. Sometimes even old, trusted friends could let a man down. But that didn't surprise him anymore. He had learned that lesson a long time ago, the hard way.

He leaned back on the white couch and crossed his muscular legs over the black Lucite coffee table where a white porcelain vase embraced fresh yellow tulips. He wondered where it was going to come from—the money, the support system every ballet company needed to survive. Where was his Lincoln Kirstein, his Rebekah Harkness, his Lucia Chase? More important, what would happen to him and all his dreams?

Even though he was well-known in serious ballet circles, and had toured the world to standing-room-only crowds and rave reviews, he had never been granted the attention resident ballet companies usually enjoyed. Those who supported such companies liked to see the seeds they planted bloom in their own back yards, not in some small and distant city. So he'd come to the Big Apple for just that reason. If he put down roots, sat at their tables, discussed his projects with them—an idea he positively abhorred— if he played footsy with the rich ones, the right ones, let them get close enough to smell and fondle his genius, which was what they'd demand in return, he might get what he desired: a decent school in the city and a permanent company theater where he could mount his newest works.

Though his old way of life had been satisfying in past years, it had now become intolerable. He was exhausted, tired of touring, tired of living from suitcases, of not knowing what the next season held in store. Almost forty, his only family had become his small company of dancers, and even their faces kept changing at an alarming rate. And the sad scenario was always the same. He'd discover some dancer with a lovely quality and bring her along, coach her, train her, shape her raw talent into sheer magnificence. Then she'd leave him for a more prestigious company.

He understood when that happened. But in the last years he'd begun to feel like a way station for talent, feeding the commercial companies the warm and nourishing wheat he had broken his neck to plant and harvest. With a company of his own, he could enjoy their beauty to the fullest, keep then in the fold.

To hold his most important ballerinas under his thumb, he had even romanced and married some. Three times he'd done that, and except for Paige McDowell, faithful Paige, they had all left anyway, and several years ago he'd given up that little tactic for good.

But stability wasn't all that he needed. He wanted more, much, much more. He wanted some of what he'd seen tonight at the Bolshoi. Tired of canned music, he longed for the downbeat of a live orchestra, wanted real silk chiffon for his dancers to wear and not polyester. He craved original scores and a scenic designer who would build lovely backdrops against which he could stage his newest ballets. He wanted a company physician and enough money in the bank to pay his dancers a decent wage. They deserved all these things for their dedication and hard work, and so did he.

The room felt suddenly chilly. Draining his glass, he poured himself more wine. He kneeled at the fireplace and placed a new log on the hearth. When it was glowing and warm again, he sat down on the couch and rested, letting the spirits draw him back to the first ballet he had ever seen. Even now, Kurt Jooss' "The Green Table" brought a lump to his throat.

He had been thirteen then, sweeping out an old theater near his home on Royal Street in New Orleans' French Quarter, a job his demented father had demanded he take after school. He had gone there at 3 P.M. to clean the aisles, to turn up the seats, for which job the management paid him the princely sum of three dollars a week. On that particular day, he had finished late.

The dance company was on stage in dress rehearsal, and as the lights dimmed, as the red velvet curtains slowly parted, he stood with his broom in the back of the darkened theater, mildly amused. Soon a bright spotlight illuminated

the black stage and a group of dancers dressed in mock
tuxedos, colorful wigs, white gloves and masks postured
around a green table. It all reminded him of Carnival and
Mardi Gras, so he stayed to watch a little longer. Soon the
music drew him closer, and the dancers' striking moves
intrigued him. Before he knew what had hit him, he fell
mesmerized into a seat. He fixed his elbows on a chair in
front as an instant spark of recognition, a kinship to the
Spanish rhythms his mother often sang, carried him away.
The intense dancing, the driving music and the intriguing
story held him riveted and transfixed, frozen like a wax
dummy. But the feelings that stirred inside him were made
of anything but wax.

He felt as though lightning had struck, pierced the bones
of his skull and ignited a fire in his brain. It wasn't an
ordinary fire but a blazing conflagration. For days, for
weeks after he could hardly speak. Haunted, he walked the
streets of the Quarter in a daze, sat for hours near Lake
Pontchartrain, staring at its vastness, at its surface calm,
aware of the turbulence lurking deep beneath its murky
waters. From that moment on, there had been no question
about his future. From that moment on, nothing but the
dance would ever really matter.

Now it was almost five in the morning, and he stood
shivering at his loft window, staring down at the darkened
streets below where a sanitation truck ground its gears to a
halt, then swallowed whole the contents of six regulation
garbage cans and four plastic ones.

Inside the living room the brilliant fire which had
warmed him throughout the night had died, leaving a pyra-
mid of gray dust lying in the grate. He wondered if his life
would come to nothing more than that—once a brilliant
blaze, now just an ash heap.

Dorsey's fight with her father had been one hell of a
scene, with the two of them screaming at the top of their
lungs like a couple of animals. She had gone to his plush

office at the United Nations Building after her lunch with Alexandra and behind closed doors he had read her the riot act.

"You've no cause to use such ugly language, young lady," he had shouted. "Not to me or my secretary." His every word reeked of alcohol and his lips quivered with rage.

"And you've no cause to treat me like dirt," she had countered.

Back and forth they had quarreled for one solid hour, never hitting on the real issue between them. Then Dorsey fled from his office in despair and tears.

She took a cab to her hotel suite at the Plaza, where she had elected to stay after her father's sudden marriage to Deandra Pope seven months ago. There she telephoned the young man she had spent the previous night with, but reached his answering machine instead. Alone, she cried for two solid hours on her rumpled bed, then summoned the one blessed friend she could always count on.

To relieve her anguish, she had snorted four lines of Colombian flake, scored from her friendly dope dealer, and a half quart of Grand Marnier purchased at a busy liquor store on Third Avenue. The effects last night had been dazzling, but this morning she was hung over, with a thick coat of mung growing inside her mouth and a headache the size of a football field.

And when the telephone rang at precisely eight-thirty, the sound seemed to bore right through her skull. She could hardly think, let alone speak. She picked up the receiver on the third ring, fearing another confrontation with Daddy, but a feminine voice caught her totally off guard.

"This is Paige McDowell calling. May I speak to Miss Dorsey Childs?"

Dorsey's heart thumped wildly in her chest. "Hello, Miss McDowell. This is Dorsey speaking."

"Hello, Dorsey. How are you?"

"I'm fine, thank you." She swallowed a mass of bloody

phlegm, which slid from her nose down into her throat, testament to last night's excesses.

"I'm calling for Mr. Caligari," Paige continued. "We'd like to welcome you into the company. Can you be here Monday at noon?"

"Yes, of course," Dorsey replied. She hoped her voice would sound normal, enthusiastic, with no trace of last night's escapade.

"Well, that's fine," Paige said. "We'll look forward to seeing you then."

As Dorsey placed the telephone back on the hook, she let out a scream and jumped on her bed for joy. She threw the covers and all the pillows high in the air and watched them tumble in a heap to the floor. Then she dove on top and rolled around like a kitten. She could not remember the last time she had been this excited and happy.

Imagine! Dancing for the great Richard Caligari—the man who had discovered Caroline Forbes and Genevieve Millay. The great and distinguished choreographer who had written ballet classics, a man who had shaped the careers of some of ballet's most magnificent dancers. And now he was asking for *her!* Little Dorsey Childs.

Her headache miraculously faded, the hangover mysteriously disappeared, and it was then she made some serious promises to herself. No more coke! she swore. And no more liquor, either. No more fights with Daddy, or even Deandra, for that matter. Right now Dorsey Childs loved the world.

She was finally going to be somebody, to belong somewhere, a member of a real ballet company. And not just any company, but a critically important one. Caligari was respected everywhere in the world. Who knew what could happen to her life now? Caligari could take an interest in her—decide to make her a star. Then perhaps the esteemed Senator Childs would sit up and take notice. He might even be proud.

To celebrate she reached for the telephone and dialed room service. She ordered eggs Benedict with double hollandaise sauce and extra-thick ham. She asked for a chilled bottle of Dom Pérignon and a quart of cold orange juice with a tray of assorted jellies and jams. She ordered a full pot of fresh coffee, whole cream and lots of sugar, with four thick slices of her favorite chocolate cake.

She would eat everything, every single drop of food on her tray. Then when the binge was over, she'd go the usual route: stick two fingers down her throat and throw it all up. After that, she'd take an enema to purge anything left in her system and attend class at two. She laughed. Such an easy way to stay slim, she thought. And that *was* the name of the game. She was only twenty and already knew how to have her cake and eat it too, without gaining weight in the process.

In their run-down Brooklyn apartment, Simone shuffled her slippered feet across the dingy kitchen floor, preparing Shane's breakfast: one poached egg for protein, one slice of wheat toast, no butter, and freshly squeezed orange juice with all the pulp. She watched her daughter's diet like a hawk and weighed her every single morning on a computerized scale. If Shane gained even one ounce, her food portions were cut until the weight disappeared. A ballet dancer had to stay reed-thin to look beautiful on stage, and Simone always made sure that Shane ate correctly. She took care of things like that because Shane's future depended on it. And whatever Shane's future depended on, hers did too.

A single-minded woman, she knew the pitfalls of the ballet world and was determined that Shane would know none of them. If only her mother, Sheindel, an ignorant Polish immigrant, had cared as much, had not sent her out *that* day, things would have turned out differently.

So what's the use? she thought, turning on the water and scrubbing scum from inside her chipped porcelain sink. We live and we learn and life goes on. Of course, she sighed, it'd go on a lot better if certain plans were made and stuck to like glue.

She placed the damp sponge on top of the sink and called Shane to breakfast. She was about to call again, but the telephone rang. Stumbling along, she made her way into the living room where, braced against the dirty gray wall near an easy chair, she lifted the receiver and answered.

The caller's voice was sweet, pleasant, unrecognizable. "Shane Laser, please."

"This is her mother speaking."

"Good morning, Mrs. Laser. This is Paige McDowell. I'm calling for Richard Caligari and we'd like to welcome Shane into the company."

For a moment Simone thought she would faint. She placed a hand over her wildly beating heart and clutched her blue chenille robe to her chest. Then like a dead weight, she fell into the chair beside her. "Isn't that nice," was all she could say.

"Can Shane be here Monday at noon," Page continued, "so we can discuss the situation?"

Every bone in Simone's body screamed 'yes'. It was a moment she'd been praying for. But she didn't want to sound too eager. "One moment please," she said. "I'll check."

She placed the telephone on the table beside her chair and rattled some nearby papers for effect. Then she grabbed the receiver again and cleared her throat. "Why, yes," she said a trifle theatrically. "Shane will be there."

As their conversation concluded, Shane stumbled into the living room half asleep. She flopped onto the couch with her long, bare legs splayed across the coffee table like the wishbone of a chicken. She rubbed sleep from her eyes and hugged an old pillow. Then yawning wide, she asked who had called.

Simone smiled as she rose from the chair and headed back toward the kitchen. "Oh, no one," she said before disappearing inside. "Just Paige McDowell." She stood waiting for the remark to sink in.

"Who?" Shane asked again, yawning.

"You remember," Simone called out from behind the kitchen door. "That pretty ballerina from Caligari."

There was the sound of silence, the kind that accompanies a moment of puzzlement and shock. Then came the acknowledging whoop, an ear-shattering scream. Simone covered her ears as Shane dashed into the kitchen, dancing around her mother as if Simone were a maypole.

"I made it, Mama? I really made it? Are you sure? Are you absolutely sure?"

Simone nodded and smiled. "Sure I'm sure. What do you mean? You were the best one there."

"But, Mama, I actually made it. Do you know what that means? I'm really in. Aren't you pleased? Aren't you happy for me?"

Simone patted Shane's cheek, then quickly drew away. She was not a woman who felt comfortable with affection either in the giving or receiving. "Of course I'm happy," she said. "It's just that I'm not so surprised as you."

Shane clasped her hands to her bosom. "Oh, God! Me and Richard Caligari. I can't believe it."

"What's to believe?" Simone asked, lighting a fire under the coffee. "You deserve it. You were ten times better than all the others put together. I saw them. I knew in five minutes he would pick you."

"Oh, God! I've got a million things to do," Shane announced. She ran wildly from the kitchen to the living room to the bathroom, then into her messy bedroom where she scrambled through her dresser one drawer at a time. "I have to get organized," she said, tossing her clothes in the air. "Have you seen my new leg warmers?" she called to Simone. "And my tortoiseshell combs?" She found some old tights but threw them into a wastebasket with a contemptuous look on her face. "And these will have to be burned, of course," she said to herself. "I need new ones, beautiful ones, more fitting for my new station." She was about to call her mother again when Simone's demanding voice suddenly filled the hallway.

"Come back in this kitchen, Shane, and finish your breakfast."

Doing piqué turns, Shane entered obediently, then paused to mime a curtsy usually reserved for respected ballet masters. She sat at the chipped red Formica table, where she swallowed whole her cold poached egg, stuffing chunks of unbuttered toast inside her cheeks like a chipmunk. When she rose to leave, Simone's hand fell like lead across her shoulder.

"You'll swallow first, of course," Simone said with a wicked grin on her face. She was wise to that old trick. As a young girl, she had saved hers for the dog or the toilet. "Then you can get your things ready."

When Shane had finished, Simone sat alone at the table, drinking another cup of hot coffee. Although she had not been demonstrative, Simone was happy for Shane. Well, maybe she felt just a touch of sadness, even jealousy for what might have been for herself. She sighed and wiped away a tear. Beyond that, she refused to acknowledge any negative feelings, including those about the phone call from the previous night. No! Today was more important than some old, miserable memories. Today she would enjoy, revel in what they had both struggled for and finally accomplished. And of course it was only the beginning.

She remembered all the scrimping and saving, working like a dog to give Shane the things she herself had always wanted but could never have. For a long time they had been a team, but now she wondered what would happen to their relationship. How would she fit into Shane's life with a strong man like Caligari in the picture?

She finished her coffee on that note and recalled the perfumed slip of paper she had snatched from Caligari's bulletin board. Instantly her face brightened. It was almost time now to make that call. If things went well, she wouldn't have to disappear from Shane's life at all. She wouldn't have to relinquish anything.

Feeling a ray of new hope, she moved with vigor to the front hall closet, opened it and removed the crumpled paper from inside her coat pocket. She felt excited, flushed as she made the decision. She sat down in the easy chair near the telephone. She was about to make her call when the phone rang. She lifted it instantly, thinking it would be more good news, but when the voice on the other end called her name, then the color drained from her face.

She sat bolt upright in the chair, as white as a ghost. Her heart pounded as she listened. All her fears had come true. She clenched her teeth tightly to keep from screaming out loud. And when she finally found the courage to speak, her voice was filled with burning hatred and contempt.

"I told you not to look for us," she snarled. "I told you to forget we're alive." Then she slammed the phone down and shut her eyes. Oh, God, no! She was right. They had been found. Once again they would have to move.

When Shane entered the living room, she had an armful of ragged clothing. "Who was it, Mom? More good news, I hope."

Simone answered quickly. "Nobody, honey. Just another kook with a wrong number." She stood up, ignoring the pain creeping up the side of her leg. Then she eyed the clothing in Shane's arms and knew she had to make some decisions. "Okay! Let's go," she said. "Let's throw that crap out now. Starting Monday it's a brand-new beginning. We're even going to find a better place to live."

"Again?"

"Again."

Chapter 7

She'd been thinking about solutions ever since she and Alexandra had gone to the ballet to see Ilya. But without success. She was in a hell of a quandary. New York City's most glamorous woman had hit a snag in her well-ordered life, and she couldn't seem to deal with it. Yet she had to make some decisions. There were important things at stake: her tenuous relationship with her highly independent daughter, Alexandra, and the satisfaction of her own selfish but nevertheless deep needs. Both were important. Very important.

They called her a sorceress, one of the city's most bewitching women. Written about by society columnists on both coasts, sought after for interviews by foreign journalists and wicked paparazzi in Rome, London, Paris, anywhere the lovely Julia Ilana Romanov traveled. And why? Because she was rich and beautiful, could walk into any room anywhere in the world and possess it in an instant, hold it in the palm of her hand and shape it to her heart's content.

Men were drawn first to her beauty, to her heart-shaped face and high cheekbones, to her perfect chin which curved to a point, dented delicately by a tiny cleft. They stared mesmerized into her electric-blue eyes, a color so startling it impaled with its intensity whomever she gazed upon. And they adored her sensuous mouth blooming magnificently in this, her thirty-ninth year, and reached without inhibition for her honey-brown hair, which hung like a satin curtain just above her shoulders. Women, on the other hand, envied her; envied her courage, her mysterious and private airs, her feminine elegance and grace. But it was her money that kept them all hopping, kept those around her so totally involved in whatever it was she had to say.

Now it was early afternoon and she settled inside her chauffeur-driven Rolls-Royce, disposing of New York City's shrill and driving noise with a single flick of her long red fingernails on a simple eighteen-karat gold switch. It quietly rolled closed the soundproofed, gray-tinted window which permitted her to see clearly out but allowed no one to see in. She preferred it that way. She had always cultivated anonymity in her life. Privacy was paramount, vital and important to her sense of well-being. She had made that discovery twenty years ago and until recently had seldom deviated from its protective armor.

Heading home, she relaxed into the contours of the pearl-gray leather interior of her luxurious car and after a cursory examination of the *Wall Street Journal,* lifted the telephone and dialed her Park Avenue attorney, Gregory Kingston.

"Sell all the Scottsdale land on Old Scottsdale Road," she told him when he answered. "And notify my broker to dispose of the Al-Cal Stock. All of it!" She crossed her legs and smiled; she could almost see the sweat rolling down Kingston's upper lip. The ultraconservative attorney responded that way whenever large sums of money were at stake, and they were now discussing several million dollars.

"Not a wise move at this time, Julia," the very senior partner of New York City's most prestigious law firm, Kingston, Green and Stine, cautioned.

"But one I nevertheless wish to make," Julia assured him.

She issued instructions regarding the storage and disposition of some Degas art treasures she had recently purchased at Sotheby auction, then simply hung up. The call had, she estimated, added a profit of almost ten million dollars to her monetary worth, which was estimated by *Fortune* magazine and most Wall Street money movers at an easy six hundred million, most of which lay in worldwide undeveloped land parcels and primary Midtown Manhattan real estate.

One-third of her enormous fortune had been inherited outright from the estate of her late father, Dimitri Romanov, an immigrant from Russia who had come to America with nothing more than the clothes on his back and a strong belief in the American dream. Julia had tripled his fortune by virtue of her own fierce purpose and resolve, a restless and unrelenting determination to become a force to be reckoned with.

An independent and enterprising woman, she knew first how to earn money, then make it work for her. She had learned well how to attract it, to multiply it over and over, and by so doing create what she had long ago decided was the single most important thing to cultivate in life—*power*.

She had been dedicated to that goal since the tender age of nineteen, the weekend she had fled her honeymoon manor house in the Cotswold Hills of England, terrified, alone, already pregnant with her daughter, Alexandra. After that experience, she had deliberately set out to build an empire, a task she had taken on with a passionate fervor no one, including the closest members of her family, could fathom. And for the last twenty years of her life, she had devoted herself to balance sheets and stock reports and twenty-four-hour-a-day work schedules.

Now as the Rolls approached the busy intersection of Fifth Avenue and Sixty-second Street, Julia pulled the Russian sable blanket close to her long, shapely legs. Even inside the comfortable limousine, whose temperatures she steadily maintained for the well-being of her baby-white orchids, which lay perched in delicate Lalique crystal vases near her window, she felt a slight chill.

These last days of April were far too cool to suit her taste, and she was afraid of catching one of her debilitating colds. The last one had laid her out for two whole weeks, and she couldn't afford to spare the time or energy on another. Certainly not now. There were too many things to do: take inventory on her art treasures, for example, and prepare notes for the coming fiscal year. After that, she had planned to fly to Paris for an important real estate deal she was in the midst of concluding on the Avenue du Maine near the Tour Montparnasse.

To sweeten the trip, she had asked her dashing new lover, Vidal Genero, to accompany her. She wanted him with her at her magnificent apartment on Avenue Foch for a few days of mad Paris shopping, and he had agreed. Later they would motor south to Monte Carlo for a bit of Grand Prix and some gambling at the *salon privé*. She had chartered a yacht there instead of engaging a hotel suite, and if things went smoothly they could attend the Cannes Film Festival, then fly to London for the Royal Races at Ascot. Most of all, she wanted to forget about business for a while, throw caution to the wind and have some fun for a change. She would dine and dance, gamble and indulge herself like a spoiled little child, something she had never done before.

A smile curled the corners of her pretty red lips; mischief danced in her neon-blue eyes. But that always happened when she thought of Vidal. Eleven years younger than she, he was a born master at sexual technique. An easy young man with a rock-hard body hewn from his disciplined years as a premier danseur in London, he gave her new confidence, made her feel not only sexually desirable but also comfortable with her unclothed body. When they were together in bed, he expressed himself without inhibition, and Julia appreciated and envied those qualities in a man. She loved them especially in Vidal, particularly in

the bedroom where she needed to be captured and wooed
with extreme patience and skill.

Her own inhibitions left her feeling unfulfilled, unable to
express or enjoy the true pleasures of the sexual act. Although she loved the closeness and warmth that it brought,
she had never tasted a sense of real abandon, had never
been able to coax from her own body the secret and delicious pleasures her mother, Tatiana, had always teased
about. And even if she was not in love with him, had never
really been in love with anyone, including Alexandra's father, Vidal had brought her as close to passion as she had
ever come.

Confused and unsure about what to do, she tugged nervously at her diamond earrings, fluffed her hair, then
reached for the telephone again. But she drew away, wondering if this was the right thing. Was it all so important?
Was it all so damned important? That's when she thought
of Vidal again, of last evening in her bedroom, of that
moment she had been waiting for so long. But the moment
was lost in an instant because of Alexandra's needs which
she did not know how to satisfy.

Nothing on the face of this earth had ever been more
beautifully designed, more conducive to romantic and sexual pleasure than Julia's bedroom. The upper mezzanine of
a trilevel penthouse apartment overlooking Central Park, it
was called by the few men who had been privileged to
sleep there, a bowl of peaches and cream. The room itself
was enormous, but when the peach brocade curtains were
closed, when a dazzling fire crackled in the carved white
marble fireplace, it became cozy, warm and intimate. From
the thick white cashmere carpeting to the handmade peach
lace canopy and four-poster bed strewn with peach silken
sheets and a blanket of brown sable, it was very erotic.

"Until you've made love on silk and sable, *maya daragaya*," her mother, Tatiana, had once told her, "you've
never made love at all." And as usual, the wily old White
Russian had been right. Julia had quoted Tatiana's words to

Vidal as they lay naked in her bed together yesterday, and he had heartily agreed.

"Lying beside you makes me feel like a king," he had whispered. The vibration of his words resonating against her throat, that beautiful English lilt to his voice, made every nerve, every fiber in her body come alive with desire. She found herself responding so easily, reaching out and curving her long fingers around his head, smoothing and twisting the thick brown waves that clung to the nape of his broad neck. Their eyes met for a fiery instant and she felt herself suddenly spinning, feeling weightless yet dangerously trapped in the tangle of his arms. Yet this time she wasn't afraid.

She dove into his liquid gray eyes confidently, and for the first time in her life simply swam free. Limp and adrift, she felt his mouth crush hers in a kiss so consuming and passionate she thought he had stolen the breath from her throat. Then just as quickly he released her, smiling, scattering tiny kisses across her eyes, her nose, her chin, burying his handsome face in the silk of her honey-colored hair, which lay strewn like fringe across a pillow.

She cradled his head as the fullness of his mouth came to rest at her breasts. Then dizzy, transported on a fragrant and fleecy cloud, she bent to kiss his forehead.

These glimpses of surrender were new to her. Before now she'd been the consummate actress, a performer who could feign her movements, including the sound of her voice. But Vidal was changing all that. Before him, no one had ever listened to the real melody playing inside her, the strident one, the fearful one which began with a white silk charmeuse wedding dress and ended in colors of fear, brutality and despair. But that was long ago, so far away, and now she was here, safe and happy in *his* arms. Making love to the others had been like treading water; making love to Vidal made her feel she was being carried on a wave.

With his head against her heart, she inhaled him deeply: musk, vanilla, leather, the scent of a man. An exhilarating tension seized her throat as his moist lips surrounded her hard nipples. She felt him suck, felt his tongue relish the pink buds, his teeth rake lightly across her delicate skin. Responding, her knee raised to cover his thigh as over and over she kissed his ear.

She felt his fingers trace the length of her body, brushing like feathers along her hips, quivering at her navel, vibrating like bird's wings where her thighs parted to receive him. He looked up and smiled appreciation at her through the lashes of his warm gray eyes.

"C'mon," he cooed as his fingers probed her milky insides. "Papa's going to make you come." Against her skin, his hot and cold whispers sent shock waves down her spine. His wavy brown hair as it drifted along her inner thighs felt like damp silk.

She arched her back as his mouth found the bud, and she moaned with delight at the friction. She shivered, waiting, anticipating what was about to happen. Frenzied, her arms flew to tangle his hair as she pushed him into the burning between her legs. She wanted him to put out the fire, to quench all her desperate needs.

"Beg me," Vidal murmured, running his tongue along her inner thighs. "Beg me for what you really want."

His arrogance increased her ardor, and she found herself obeying, begging him like a slave to take her. Then his weight suddenly shifted and she trembled at his strength.

In a flash he had pinned her wrists, was kneeling over her, kissing her face, her breasts, separating her thighs with his knee and teasing the vaginal folds with the tip of his cock. The heat of his body was so intense that a thousand colors flooded her brain, flashed beneath her eyelids like blazing firelight—scorching reds, dazzling oranges, searing whites—and she dug her fingernails into his skin as her whole body arched beneath him in anticipation of her first climax. And when he was deep inside her, pushed so high she could feel him throb, she thought her pelvis would split in two. And just as she began to move in rhythm with his battering, just as she was about to come, the intercom blared and Alexandra's voice flooded the room.

"Mom? You up there? Hey! Anybody home?"

The mother in Julia instinctively responded. All her lusty feelings instantly vanished. She pushed Vidal away, sat up and pulled the sable blanket close to her naked body, desperate to keep the breathlessness from her voice. "Yes, Alex. I'm here."

"I hope I'm not interrupting anything."

"No, of course not. What is it?" Julia half smiled at Vidal, who was sitting at the bedside already buttoning his trousers.

"Well, I still haven't heard from that rat Caligari," Alexandra said, "so I thought I'd console myself, maybe join you on that trip to Paris, if it's okay with you."

In the twinkling of an eye Julia's mood changed. All her grand plans to be alone with Vidal flew out the window. She didn't want to hurt Alexandra's feelings by not welcoming her along but she desperately needed this trip for herself. Instead, she offered her daughter the only thing that came to mind. "I can still call Caligari, you know," Julia said. "Persuade him to take you on."

"No way!" Alexandra protested. "Don't you dare. I'd never speak to you again if you did. And I mean it."

"But I'm in a position to help you, Alex," Julia continued. "After all, I do know a few people in this town."

"I know you mean well, Mother," Alexandra said, "but there are some things even your money can't buy."

So you think, Julia mused as the memory of Vidal faded and the Rolls-Royce stopped for a light near Sixty-eighth Street and Park Avenue. So you think. Then with her mind finally made up, she reached for the telephone and called her attorney again, asking him to collect and send a file on Richard Caligari. If she could find something the dance master wanted, she'd oblige. Then she could continue with her own plans with a clear conscience. She and Alex could both have their heart's desire. And what could be wrong with that?

Chapter 8

It was early morning, days after Ilya Kremorkin's last performance at Lincoln Center, and Francesca Adair still hungered for him. He had become an obsession she could not remove from her mind. Since that night, she'd dreamed of him constantly, conjured visions of him probing her with his tongue, touching her thighs, raking his nails along her body, fulfilling all her wicked wishes. She would have him, she knew. It was just a matter of time. But waiting was not one of Francesca's virtues.

Lying naked in her big brass bed, with its free-form headboard, she let her eyes close. In the blackness beneath her eyelids she could still see Ilya's long, lean torso prancing boldly on stage, see the corded muscles of his chest, the strong arms, the wild blond hair that whipped about his face and neck like the mane of a stallion.

She squeezed her thighs together to quiet the ache.

Ilya.

She had to have him.

But what to do until then?

Follow him.

Finding the Bolshoi itinerary, she reached for the telephone and buzzed her secretary. "Charter a jet," she told the young woman. "With accommodations in Toronto, Tokyo, Rio, London and Paris. I'll give you the dates."

She paused a moment to listen.

"No, Sandy," she replied, answering the question. "It's not a new film. Just a project I'm researching."

Then, after breaking the connection, she pushed the receiver between her thighs and, laughing lasciviously, slowly stroked her skin.

Paige glanced at her wristwatch. "Hurry, Richard," she called. "Hurry or we'll be late."

Richard Caligari stepped from his SoHo apartment into the cold and windy air, sprang the latch on the rear door of a yellow taxi and held it open for Paige. She slid in, smoothing the folds of her brown mink coat against the tan leather seat. Caligari followed behind her, shutting the door.

"La Caravelle, West Fifty-fifth Street," he said to the driver. Then he settled back beside her.

Paige observed him for a few moments, watching as he stared out the smudged window of the car. Nervously, he was either invading the pockets of his dove-gray trench coat or placing his narrow black tie in alignment with the buttons of his dark gray shirt. She knew he was uneasy and she decided to break the ice. "You look pretty snappy," she said as the taxi lurched left, then out into city traffic.

"And so do you," he answered without turning his head.

She tried to suppress a giggle but was unsuccessful. "Thank you very much," she said.

At the sound of her laughter, he turned, and his raised black eyebrows and dark eyes caught and held her. "And what's so damned funny, Paige?"

"You are!" she said. "You've been too busy being nervous to notice what I'm wearing. What's the matter with you? I've never seen you like this before."

His fleeting grin eased the tension. "Frankly, I am nervous," he admitted. "Then again I've never had to beg for money before."

She was surprised he had put it that way. It wasn't at all the truth. Yet she understood. His anxiety about money came from a time long ago. "Is that what you think we're doing?"

"Well, isn't it?"

She placed her hand across his to both dispute and comfort, but his already cold fingers grew stiff and rigid beneath hers. "Definitely not," she said, drawing her hand away. "We're entitled to share in public monies like any other important dance company having temporary financial difficulties." She emphasized the word *temporary*.

"Personally, I think it's more than that making you so nervous, Richard. Something a lot deeper."

His response to her comment was a dark and stony silence. It served to emphasize the wall between them—a wall he had built, and upon which he'd erect towers when he didn't care to discuss something. And he was doing that now. She didn't like it but held her tongue out of love and respect for him. Richard Caligari, despite his strength, was a sensitive and private man. One never intruded where not invited and still remain a confidante for long.

She turned her attention to the window and watched the busy midday traffic become a blur, watched the people bunch at the traffic signs as they waited for the lights to change. But it wasn't long before she was distracted back in his direction, and from the corner of her eye she drank in his unique good looks.

He was so handsome, she thought, feeling her heart beat a little faster. But then he always had that effect on her. Always.

His thick black hair, which usually fell across his black eyes whenever he danced, was now brushed high above his forehead in a natural rise, revealing a noble brow and emphasizing his aquiline profile. His dark eyes smoldered with such intensity. She hated to admit it, but all the old feelings were still there, buried beneath a layer of scar tissue so thin that half the time she feared it would split and her soul would come spilling out.

He startled her as he suddenly spoke. "So, what did you find out about our Senator Childs?"

Paige was glad for the interruption, glad to have her thoughts diverted. "Well, he's controversial," she replied. "A rather flamboyant man involved with the Senate Foreign Relations Committee, NATO and all that international intrigue." She thought for a few moments, trying to recall the information she had gleaned about the Senator from newspaper reports and telephone calls to personal friends. "His first wife died very tragically. A suicide."

Caligari winced.

"Well, everyone knows, Richard. It was in all the newspapers." She paused. "He also married again—just recently, as a matter of fact."

"Poor Dorsey," Caligari murmured.

"Yes, indeed. But the child seems to have weathered the storm, or so it seems. She's magnificent, moves like a dream."

"She's talented, Paige. And though I sympathize with her personal problems, her dancing still needs work."

Paige smiled at his remark. It was the sort she should have expected. No one had ever totally pleased him, herself included. There was always something—some tiny flaw or shortcoming he'd focus on in his constant quest for perfection. It was a quest she knew he'd continue all his life but never fulfill because perfection in dance just didn't exist. Each dancer had some special quality—an excellence all his own, a line, a carriage, grace—a unique and indefinable air that sometimes defied description. But no dancer had it all.

Caligari cleared his throat abruptly, and she turned instinctively at the sound of his voice. "Tell me more," he said. "About the Senator, I mean."

She searched her memory for more details.

"Well, I feel he's receptive to helping us. At least he said he'd try. He thinks it would boost his standing with Dorsey a little. Apparently there's some sort of rift between them. He claims it's his work, but I'm told it's his new wife, Deandra, who, by the way, is only seven years older than Dorsey."

Caligari stared at her. "Where did you learn all that?"

Her pretty face lit up with an impish grin. "Oh, here and there."

Caligari patted her hand. She noticed it had grown a little warmer since the last time their fingers had touched. "You're a constant surprise to me, Paige," he said as the taxi drew up in front of La Caravelle.

Inside, they followed the headwaiter past the mirrors and pretty wall murals to Senator and Mrs. Childs' table. After the usual greetings and introductions were made, they settled down to a bottle of Perrier-Jouët champagne, which sat chilling in a baroque silver ice bucket near a huge mound of beluga caviar.

"I took the liberty of ordering some refreshments," the white-haired Senator said, settling back in his red velvet chair and placing his napkin back across his lap. "I hope you don't mind." His engaging, broad smile revealed even white teeth which complemented a lush caramel-colored tan that framed twinkling but slightly bloodshot green eyes.

"Not at all," Richard Caligari answered. "It's very thoughtful."

The waiter appeared, offering menus. The Senator's strong voice boomed loudly as he refused them, requesting permission to select lunch for everyone.

Paige wondered what was going on in Caligari's mind as he nodded confirmation to the Senator's request. The fiery dance master was not used to having another male strut or dominate in his presence.

"We'll have the fresh turbot, please," Senator Childs said to the waiter. He spooned another mound of caviar into his mouth, following that with a huge swig of champagne.

Paige turned her attention to the young Mrs. Childs, who gazed lovingly at her husband as he poured champagne. A quiet California blonde with a yard-wide smile, she kept her baby-blue gaze on her husband's face in obvious admiration.

When their crystal glasses were filled, Senator Childs proposed a toast. "*À votre santé,* as the French say," he said, raising his glass. Everyone joined him, repeating the phrase.

"Now," Senator Childs said, pressing his napkin to his lips. "What can I do for you?"

Paige waited a moment to see if Richard would say something, but he remained silent, leaving the task of talking money to her.

"Well, Senator," she said, "it's no secret we've come to New York City to establish a permanent home for the Caligari Ballet Company, but we've been having some problems."

As she continued to explain, the Senator drank another glass of champagne, and it was then that Paige suddenly became aware he was several glasses ahead of everyone else. She hoped the alcohol would not interfere with his ability to comprehend the importance of their mission.

"What is it exactly you want me to do?" the Senator asked bluntly when she'd finished speaking.

"Well," Paige continued, "the Caligari Ballet Company has never asked for special favors before. We've always been self-supporting." She sipped some champagne for fortification. "But ever since we stopped touring, money's been difficult to come by. And after going through all the regular channels—applications for grants-in-aid from the National Endowment—we just couldn't seem to get any response.".

"I see," the Senator said. "So you thought perhaps I could speed the paperwork up for you, is that it?"

Caligari jumped in instantly. "If this conversation is out of order, Senator, we can stop right now."

"Nonsense!" the Senator said, pouring more champagne for everyone. "I'd be delighted to help. I'm just not sure I can do anything, that's all. Naturally, I can check your applications, even knock down a few doors. But I doubt it would help. There's not enough endowment money to go around. And it's going to get rougher in the months to come, so be prepared."

Paige began to worry for the first time in her career. It just wasn't possible that help would not be available. What would happen to their company? To her? To Caligari?

The waiter arrived with their fresh turbot, served elegantly and accompanied by a bottle a bottle of Bâtard-Montrachet 1978, which the Senator tasted and heartily approved. All conversation ceased until the waiter finished pouring wine, then the Senator continued. "I'll tell you what," he said, lifting his crystal wineglass to his lips. "I'll make a few calls to some good friends here in New York City and also D.C. Let's see if I can move your paperwork a little faster. Then, as soon as I'm able, I'll throw you a party, an introduction to the city's upper crust. I have lots of rich, influential friends, people who don't seem to know what to do with their money. Maybe we can find you an angel."

The corners of Paige's mouth lifted. She finally began to relax, to experience the exquisite taste of her food, which until this moment might just as well have been cardboard.

The Senator wiped his lips with his napkin, then placed it on his lap with a shy flourish and an embarrassed smile. "Now, let's hear a little about my Dorsey," he said.

"She's lovely," Paige said.

"Yes," Caligari agreed. "She shows a great deal of promise. In fact, I'm thinking of using her in a new ballet —something I've just begun to create."

Paige felt her stomach sink. He hadn't shared *that* with her, and because he hadn't spoken of it to her first, all the old rivalries stirred her emotions. She had kept herself in magnificent shape, and though she knew in her heart that at thirty-five she had to make way for the younger ones, it still hurt to hear him plan a ballet for someone else.

"I'm delighted you feel that way," the Senator responded with warmth. "Dorsey's had a rough time of it these last years, particularly since her mother's death. It's time she experienced a little happiness. Time she had something of her own. I'd like to contribute to that, if I can."

"We'll do what we can to give her support," Caligari said.

Paige watched the new Mrs. Childs' smile flicker into something like a sneer.

"Of course, Dorsey's doing much better now," Senator Childs continued. He toyed with the food on his plate. "But her mother's death was a horrible shock—for both of us."

He reached for the wine bottle again and poured, gazing into space as if there was more he wanted to say but didn't know how to say it—or perhaps didn't want to. "Well," he continued, returning with a new and jaunty note to his voice, "I hope I've helped you. Now let's have some coffee and dessert." Then he added, "And maybe just a wee nip of brandy."

In the taxi going home Richard Caligari loosened his tie around his collar. He felt uneasy, uncomfortable. The meeting with the Senator had gone well, at least on the surface, and he should have been happy. Yet something scratched the insides of his brain. He watched the traffic as they inched along, trying to figure it out.

"Lunch was delicious!" Paige exclaimed, breaking the silence. "And Senator Childs is a very nice man."

He pushed back his hair and gazed into her large brown eyes. "Yes, I enjoyed lunch. But I'm not so sure about the Senator."

"I don't understand," Paige said. "He offered to do whatever he could to help."

"He did," Richard said. "But most of it sounded like political hogwash to me."

"Sometimes you confound me, Richard. The man couldn't have been more delightful. He obviously adores his daughter, and for that reason alone I think he'll keep his word."

She began defending the Senator, enumerating his prom-

ises. "And I bet he'll make a healthy financial contribution
of his own. What else does a person have to do to make
you believe him?"

"I don't know. I don't know!" he told her. "Sure, he said
some encouraging things, but nothing that makes me feel
secure. We need financial help *now*, not a month from
now."

Paige turned away before responding. "It's his drinking,
isn't it?" When he didn't answer, she repeated, "Well, isn't
it?"

Caligari didn't respond. She had touched a nerve deep
inside him. As usual she was making sense, but he
couldn't acknowledge that. The subject was still sensitive.
Too sensitive to talk about even now. So he rationalized.

"Paige, please. I'm just trying to make a clear evalua-
tion, that's all."

"Well, it's impossible to make sense of things when you
keep living in the past," she said. "And since I'm the one
who's kept the finances of this company intact, I say we
have nothing to worry about. Senator Childs has pledged to
help us. And I believe he'll follow through."

He wished he felt the same. But he had ceased lying to
himself a long time ago. "And what makes you so sure?"

"A matter of survival, Richard. Yours as well as mine. If
you go under, so do I. And frankly, I'm not ready. Senator
Childs will do what he says because he said so, and because he loves his daughter. And the past be damned,
Richard."

He glanced at the floor of the taxi, feeling his heart
pound at her words. He knew she hadn't meant to be mali-
cious. He knew she loved him and was only reminding him
of things that could interfere with his growth, with the
company's progress. But there were things he'd rather forget. Well, maybe she was right about the Senator. Maybe
there *was* nothing to worry about. Maybe the Senator
would come through for them. Maybe his life's work
wouldn't come crashing down around his ears like a house
of cards. Maybe. And maybe not.

* * *

Even as a child in New Orleans he had a passion to create things: small toys for the neighbor children, baskets of flowers to sell at Mardi Gras or at Spring Fiesta on the sidewalks of Pirate's Alley, where local street artists hung their magical paintings for sale.

"You trying to *gyp* me, kid?"

The word always stung his young ears like an angry scorpion. Gyp. It was short for Gypsy and a direct insult to his beautiful mother.

A full-blooded *gitana,* she had been born in the region of Andalusia, in the olive- and basil-scented village of Arriate, Spain. Soon after World War II, at the age of sixteen, she had been brought to America by his soldier father.

Like her parents and their parents and generations before even that, she had been raised to dance and sing the flamenco in the Sacro Monte caves of Andalusia. For that, she had earned the nickname "Golden Gypsy" because her skin had the color of dark honey and her voice was like golden magic.

In those early years she had been trained by her family to sing *cante grande,* or "deep song," and it was a thrill just to listen to her. Whenever she performed, the audiences cheered and begged for more. No one in all of Arriate could move people to tears as she had.

But at sixteen she had gone against a long Gypsy tradition and had fallen in love with an outsider, Robert Anthony Caligari, publicly naming him her *novio.* For that sin she was brought before a Gypsy tribunal, tried and judged by her elders.

"If you marry the *gadjo,* you and all your offspring will become outcasts, exiles forever, and you may never again return to us." But their harsh words fell on deaf ears.

As they banished her, the beautiful and brooding Maria Isabela Manuela Rosario prepared for her trip across the ocean. Long before the Gypsy trial, she had made up her mind. She would go to America because she loved the *gadjo* and believed he would make a *new* home for her.

She would go because she believed him when he told her New Orleans was so much like her beloved Andalusia, with fountains and cypress trees covered with Spanish moss. But most importantly, she would go because she knew without question that she was pregnant.

Carlos Ramon Ricardo Caligari, called Ricardo by his mother, was born in 1945 on Royal Street in the dreary basement of an old brick house in the French Quarter of New Orleans. Outside lay a huge sunny courtyard of rectangular flagstones shaded by a huge old cypress tree. In one corner was a lopsided swing, and bright red geraniums bloomed along the decorative cast-iron fencing and white lattice doors. But inside the basement where he and his parents lived lay a thick and smothering alcoholic darkness —three tiny rooms illuminated by artificial light and two small window vents located near the dirty ceiling.

An old abandoned slave quarters, the building had once been a "sporting" house, then later a fencing academy, and though Ricardo loved New Orleans with a passion, he hated that basement apartment with all his heart and left its bleakness, its blackness every chance he could.

His father, a timberman when he could find work, was a drunkard who lived off Maria's *dukker*. She had turned to the old way of fortunetelling because her husband had forbidden her to ever sing and dance again.

She was a beautiful woman, warm and passionate, with long black hair and dark Gypsy eyes, and when he was very young, Ricardo loved her deeply. But as he grew older, all of that changed. He saw in her his own potential weakness, saw in her a blind obedience which he hated and ran from.

As a boy, Ricardo roamed the streets of the Quarter until the darkness outside drove him back to the apartment where his father waited to beat him and his mother comforted him when she could, with a passionate and smothering love. Sometimes he thought he would suffocate between her huge breasts and, terrified, he would push her away, crying, "Why do you hug me so tightly, Mama?"

"Because I love you, my son," she would whisper against his thick black hair. "Because you are my flesh and blood and I love you."

In a drunken stupor his father would sulk at their shared affection, then suddenly lash out. He'd smack the boy's face, then demand his wife come to his bed as if to prove his manhood. An obedient Gypsy wife, she would always submit. The boy would cover his ears to keep out the filthy noises they made. And the fact that in spite of his drunkenness, his inability to take care of his family, Papa Caligari still ruled the roost, drove Ricardo insane with anger and frustration.

As Ricardo grew, his father's envy grew and he pounced on the boy's every word and deed with such violent beatings and criticism that Ricardo kept to himself. And while his mind claimed the truth, his lips still uttered the lies Papa wanted to hear.

"Yes, Papa, I have a job after school." This, at only ten years old.

"Yes, Papa, I won't waste food anymore." This, because he had left a small portion of peas on his plate.

"Yes, Papa, I hit the other kid harder." This, because he had come home with a black eye and a bleeding wound on his upper lip which had to be sutured closed in a hospital.

But there were lovely memories too. When his father was away, his mother would play the guitar for him, one she had brought with her from Spain. Handmade, with deep, resonating tones, it was beautifully molded from Spanish cypress wood adorned with a Cuban cedar stem. On that seasoned guitar she played and sang songs from her homeland, songs with mythical Gypsy themes of love and romance, of death and despair, of loneliness and longing.

She sang sad *soleares*, improvised fast *bulerias* or deep *cante grandes*—those profound and ancient songs of Andalusia for which she had been specially trained. Ricardo loved them all and would sit for hours at her feet as she entertained only him. Sometimes she would close her eyes and cry, clapping her hands over the guitar strings in *jaleo*, letting them vibrate to the demanding and complicated Spanish rhythms. But it would all stop when Papa came home and Ricardo would run to the bathroom and hide.

And his mother showed her love in so many ways. In the summertime when it was warm and her skin smelled of almonds, she would bake him tiny cookies called Maria's kisses. In the winter when it was cold, she would hold him close to her body and fix him *café con leche*—sweet coffee laced with milk. During Semana Santa—a holy week commemorating Jesus and the Virgin Mary, celebrated in Spain, much like Mardi Gras—she would cook *torta de chicharrones,* thick slices of bread smothered with fresh roasted pork and hot fat. And because of her sweetness and her generosity, it always puzzled him why he both loved and hated her at the same time.

When they were alone, she would dance the flamenco for him too; wildly, with her feet stomping, her black hair flying and her skirts whirling just above her knees. It was here, in this dreary apartment, that his love of music and dancing was born. It was she who had been his inspiration from the very beginning, even before he had seen "The Green Table" and began his dance lessons. It was she who had taught him to love beauty and to seek its pleasure.

With a hunger he was compelled to explore, he found a small dance studio on Bourbon Street. The old teacher who ran it claimed she had been taught by the great Cecchetti himself. He attended her classes faithfully. There, in that seedy little room surrounded by broken mirrors, he listened to the scratchy record player and strove for the perfect leap, for that pure and classical line, struggled to free his body from the limitations of space and gravity. Consumed by the power of work, he was enthralled with the things his body could do and angered by its miserable limitations. Testing his prowess, those broken mirrors became his constant companions, and in time he dazzled everyone with his energy and desire, with his drive, concentration and total dedication.

Then at the age of sixteen, his schoolmates discovered his secret and teased him mercilessly. They called him a sissy, a faggot, but Richard, as he now called himself, didn't care. Nothing mattered more than dancing. Recreating "The Green Table," the first ballet he had ever seen, was more important than anything else in his life.

Then his father discovered the boy's passion and began hammering away in his thick southern drawl, drunk as usual.

"Goddamn fairy! That's what you are," he said, staggering, chasing him around the chairs and table. "A sissy boy —dancin' and prancin' on your tippy toes like a pansy." Standing there in a dirty T-shirt with his beer belly fully distended over his urine-soiled trousers, his father removed his belt and beat Richard to a pulp. "I'm ashamed of you, boy," he hollered. "Ashamed! You hear?" While his father beat him, his mother hid behind a door and Richard felt unbearably humiliated. He could understand his father's anger, but his mother's silence confounded him.

When he finally packed and left, she stood silently on the doorstep without uttering a word. But it wouldn't have mattered if she'd begged him not to go. Nothing she could have said or done would have kept him from leaving. Richard Caligari was on his own.

He arrived in New York City in the summertime of 1962, working day and night to pay for dance lessons which had now become a daily habit. Like a drug, dancing calmed him, filled him with ecstasy, satisfied his each and every need. He could go without a meal but not without dancing. When he didn't take class, he experienced withdrawal; with cramps in his belly, even nausea and insomnia.

By the age of twenty-four he had already danced for the greatest choreographers in America—Balanchine, Robbins, De Mille and Loring. By the age of twenty-seven he had partnered the greatest ballerinas of all time. And by the age of twenty-nine, when he had learned all the rules, he began to break them, to create works of his own. Dancing satisfied him, but the act of creation held promises of immortality.

Creation. New dance forms bubbled from his mind and body with the force of a Niagara Falls. He couldn't have stopped the outpouring if he'd tried. And he had continued creating until today, when the only thing that threatened his existence was finding enough money to continue his work. Richard Caligari needed work the way other people needed air or water. And he hoped and prayed that Senator Childs was not just another drunk who would hurt and disappoint him.

Chapter 9

In the waning sunset Julia Romanov's long, sexy legs slithered from her custom Rolls-Royce. Walking briskly under the forest-green awning toward the lobby of her Fifth Avenue penthouse, she carried the file her attorney, Gregory Kingston, had given her, tucked inside her leather Gucci briefcase. The elegant container matched her Gucci boots, tan Claude Montana cape and trousers, and a twenty-four-karat gold snake necklace studded with pavé diamonds.

At the building's entrance the uniformed doorman greeted her with a warm smile and a tip of his visored cap.

"Good afternoon," he said, opening the door.

"Good afternoon, Martin," she replied, whisking by him.

Inside the pristine lobby, with its sparkling crystal chandelier and red silk Louis XV couch, she clicked her heels along the highly polished black and white marble floor toward the bank of elevators. At the white marble wall, she pushed her gold key into the lock, summoning her private lift. Then with a raised eyebrow, she motioned to one of three security guards, who came quickly to her side.

"Call Mr. Norton immediately!" she said quietly to him. "I want the floor by that ficus tree shining like glass. If he can't keep this lobby in apple-pie order, tell him I'll find someone who will."

When her elevator arrived, she stepped inside and touched the penthouse button, leaning her body against the antique mirrored wall. In an instant she was thrust upward like a breeze. She was anxious to be home, longing to throw off her clothes and take a hot Jacuzzi. She wanted to relax, to enjoy some of Birdie's special vichyssoise sprinkled with freshly cut chives. Then, rested and satisfied, she could settle down in bed and peruse the file Kingston had prepared.

She had been thinking about her dilemma nonstop ever since Alexandra had intruded on her romantic interlude with Vidal the other evening. And she had come to the following conclusions. Her daughter wanted to dance for Richard Caligari. She wanted to go to Paris alone, with Vidal. If she could zero in on what the choreographer wanted, she could give it to him and everyone would be satisfied. How simple!

And she had no doubt that Caligari would accept. In all her travels, in all her business dealings around the world, and contrary to Alexandra's innocent notions, Julia knew without question that anything could be secured with the right incentives.

The elevator stopped gently at the top floor, opening onto the white and apricot colored foyer of her luxurious apartment, where a uniformed maid greeted her and took her cape. Julia breathed a sigh of relief the moment she entered the living room. Home at last!

She loved this place with a passion, enjoyed returning daily to its many art treasures and antique furnishings, relished the breathtaking ten-foot-long crystal chandelier she had purchased in London three years ago, one the interior designer had assured her could never be anchored or supported by the corbeled ceiling vaults. Yet there it hung in all its sparkling beauty, like a crystal waterfall.

Naturally, Julia's will had prevailed. But it had taken many such contrary decisions to design and furnish the place exactly as she had desired. And each time the builder, the designer, the architects scoffed and told her she was crazy, that what she had planned in her wild imagination just couldn't be done, she'd laughed and not only demonstrated the impossible, but accomplished it with a dash of drama. The result was this magnificent apartment, two and one-half floors of French antique beauty all currying the unmistakable imprint of her cultivated taste and unique flair.

Moving down the wide hallway past a gallery of family portraits, she entered the warmth of the French country kitchen where Birdie was stretching to hang a large copper kettle on the ceiling rack above the rectangular cooking island. A lit cigarette trailed smoke from the cook's thin red mouth into her pinched nostrils, past her watery hazel eyes and into her pure white hair, which sat on her head like a white meringue crown.

Julia said hello, closed her eyes and inhaled deeply. "Mmmm! What smells so delicious?" she asked.

"Double chocolate mousse," Birdie replied, reaching for some stalks of celery. "I made it for Alex. Kid's been in a funk lately, and I thought it would cheer her up."

"Honestly, Birdie," Julia scolded. "You shouldn't encourage her passion for food. She's been gaining too much weight lately."

Birdie glared at her mistress. "Are you kidding? Have you seen her in a bikini recently?"

The remark struck Julia as peculiar. She reached for a stalk of celery and placed it in her mouth. "As a matter of fact, I haven't. Have you?"

"This morning," Birdie answered. "She tried on some brand-new ones, for when she goes to Paris with you and Mr. Genero."

Julia's white teeth snapped the celery stalk in two. "I see. And where is she, by the way?"

"Taking class with Mr. Genero."

Julia nearly choked. She swallowed the mouthful of celery with difficulty, tossed the rest in a wastebasket and stormed from the kitchen. There was precious little time to study the file and do what needed doing.

It was an obvious fact: Alexandra had not only inherited her mother's beauty but her stubbornness as well. Despite not having heard from Caligari, she was taking an advanced class today and working as hard as she could to execute the difficult combinations. Someday she would make it in ballet despite the odds, she thought, despite the stumbling blocks—if only she could find someone to believe in her.

As she passed the mirror, she flinched at the sight of her body. Curves! Too damn many curves. If only she could lose ten pounds, go on a diet. Well, maybe. Perhaps. Perhaps when she returned from Paris. It was at that exact moment she realized she had given up ever hearing from Caligari and her heart sank. But the feeling didn't last long. When the piano chord was played, she took her position with the others, stood straight as an arrow and prepared for the next combination.

"Fourth position, piqué turns to fifth," the teacher demonstrated. "Then turn—women do doubles, men, triples—then attitude front, plié, nice port de bras, then reach out and hold."

As soon as she began dancing, as soon as her muscles were engaged, her spirits soared. She was transported—alternately a wisp of chiffon floating on a warm summer breeze, a leaf flung from a tall tree. Heaven help her! Nothing compared with this feeling. Nothing in the world left her so limp and so satisfied. Dancing was love, a total embrace by God. It was everything in the world to her and more.

Soon the familiar taste of salt filled her mouth and she swallowed hard. Over the years she had become accustomed to that taste, accustomed to the brine of her sweating body. But what she tasted now, she soon realized, was not the salt of perspiration but a trail of very bitter tears.

* * *

Snuggling inside a peach satin robe, Julia opened the file and spread the pages of Richard Caligari's public life across her bed. With small reading glasses perched on the end of her nose, she leaned against the goosedown pillows, searching the papers for clues.

Immediately certain phrases caught her eye as she scattered his reviews across her lap.

". . . a true romantic . . . an artist of subjective and objective vision . . . innovative . . . aloof and ambitious." *Ambitious*. Yes. A word she understood. ". . . married three times." She smiled and continued reading.

Toward the end of the file, she leaned back and devoured one red-lined article in its entirety.

PERFORMING WORLD

January 23, 1985

This New York City dance season jetés into spring with the arrival of Richard Caligari, director of the Caligari Ballet Company. Tired of touring, the choreographer wants to put down roots and is seeking blue ribbon funding to insure the survival of his small but nevertheless artistically important company in, of all places, New York City. Yes, balletomanes, just what this city needs —another ballet company, even Caligari's!

Like the rest, he's been surviving on fellowships and grants-in-aid. But we also know (from private sources) that, like everyone else, he's really feeling the pinch. Some insiders say he's in desperate trouble, but you'd never know it by listening to him. "We're planning a new school," he told us while nibbling on his favorite lunch of iced tea and salade niçoise. "And looking for a theater to present three new world premieres."

Hardy ambition in such *hard* fiscal times, we think. But the dance master—called a genius by some and a madman by others—didn't agree. Nevertheless, we do wish the unique, internationally acclaimed Caligari the very best of luck. We think he's going to need it!

. Sitting upright in bed, Julia finished the last article, then shoved the others in a heap beside her. Now it was time to think. Plumping the pillows behind her, she leaned back and made a mental summary of Caligari's life and times.

He was a man without a family. No parents, no wife, no kids. Nothing but his work. Good! That narrowed things down. He was also ambitious, thank God. The article said so. And he was just shy of forty. Last chance to make his mark in the world. And that's how she would appeal to him.

She would offer him the one thing he needed to keep working—and that was money. Without money, he couldn't exist. He was a choreographer, not a painter. It wasn't as if he could run out and buy new paints when the old ones ran dry. The dancing arts were expensive. A choreographer needed warm, living bodies to work with. And those warm, living bodies had to be paid.

So she would offer him all the money he could ever need. But with one small string attached. Namely, Alexandra. And that was the problem. He was depicted by Kingston as a principled man. Not one to be pushed around. Taking Alexandra would be like swallowing a bitter pill. But if she stuck the pill inside a sweet cake, the way she had with her sick puppy when she was a child, the ploy would work.

Like most artists, Caligari had a huge ego. It was the key to his nature. And it would not be the money alone that would tempt a luminary like him, she knew, but his chance at immortality. And that's how she would really nail him.

But it still left just one problem. A lulu. Alexandra.

If Alexandra were to find out the dance master had been manipulated, that Julia had paid him to take her, she'd be humiliated beyond belief and their already tenuous relationship would be destroyed forever. That was a price Julia was not prepared to pay.

With that in mind, she reached for the telephone to dial the number Kingston had written on a separate piece of paper. Several rings later, the masculine voice responded with a gruff hello, and Julia's voice dripped with honey as she began the conversation.

Chapter 10

Richard Caligari had spent his professional life scratching for company wages, kissing society's ass, begging permission for rehearsal space and theater space. He had frequently gone hat in hand to feed at the public trough, but lately he had avoided all that, leaving the fund raising to Paige.

So when the strange and feminine voice on the telephone had told him he could have it all, he was totally taken aback, struck not only by extreme curiosity but also by his usual dollop of cynicism. Discussing even small amounts of money always left his stomach queasy. The thought of talking great sums—"enough for you and your company to have everything you need"—had him totally crazed.

He suspected the origin of his uneasy feelings. *"Hey, kid, know how to make a Gypsy omelet? First steal two eggs."* But even realizing the insecurities he felt over his background didn't help. Besides, nobody simply gave it all. *Nobody!* There had to be strings attached. Short strings, long strings, pretty strings, all packaged to look supportive and beneficial, but they'd be strings nevertheless. And Richard Caligari was nobody's puppet.

At first the call had thrilled him as he thought perhaps Senator Childs had made good on that promise of his to find the company an 'angel.' But the feminine voice never mentioned the Senator in conversation, stating only the recent interview the choreographer had given *Performing World* as her primary source of information.

He had been caught off guard, interrupted and breathless in the middle of a hard barre. He must have sounded gruff, he reflected later.

"Hello!" he had answered.

"Richard Caligari, please."

"Speaking!"

"Have I caught you at a bad time?"

When he was working, every time was bad, but he would not be rude. So he ignored her question and posed his own. "What can I do for you?"

"It's difficult to explain on the telephone, Mr. Caligari," the voice said, pausing.

Her cagey answer infuriated him. "I'm sorry but I'm unavailable for interview right now, so if you'd call my office and make an appointment I'd be happy to answer your questions at that time."

He was about to hang up when her charming laughter rippled in his ears. "You misunderstand, Mr. Caligari. I don't have any questions, just answers. Answers to *all* your financial needs. How does that sound?"

He took the bait. Flopping onto a nearby canvas chair as he wiped sweat from his head, face and neck with a yellow terry towel, he answered, "Sounds interesting. Tell me more."

"As I said before, Mr. Caligari," she continued, "it's rather difficult to discuss on the telephone. So I'd like to propose lunch; someplace where we can quietly discuss the matter of my completely funding your company."

The word "completely" sent shivers down his spine. A new enthusiasm swelled inside him, and as his breathing stabilized, his voice softened. "I'm sorry, I didn't catch your name."

"How could you?" she answered playfully. "I didn't throw it."

Her response didn't amuse him. "May I ask the reason for the subterfuge?"

"You may," she said. "Anonymity, of course. The offer I intend to make must be held in the strictest confidence. Let me assure you, Mr. Caligari, this is not a joke. What I'm speaking of is a total commitment to you and your company."

Damn! She had uttered that word again. And her voice had a rich and extravagant ring, with clever and arrogant undertones. How could he ignore such an intriguing proposal? Then he thought of Paige. Paige would be furious at being left out of a business meeting.

"How far does your need for anonymity go?" he asked. "I have a trusted artistic director who handles all company finances. Am I to exclude her from this lunch you're proposing?"

Her response was crisp, unwavering. "You are. I'm prepared to deal only with you. Alone. Just the two of us. That's how it has to be. If there's any publicity, even a hint of our association, consider the offer rescinded and the matter closed."

It wasn't difficult to believe her. Wealthy people were like that. Eccentric, bizarre, used to getting their own way.

"Well, what do you think?" she asked. "Shall we make a date?"

Caligari moved to his desk, where his calendar lay open. "Okay," he said. "Tuesday noon?" He began to ink it in.

"Tomorrow," she said confidently, correcting him. "Sunday, promptly at noon. I have your address and I'll send a car."

Before he could accept or refuse, she was off the line, and he stood, listening to the dial tone hum its grating tune in his ear.

When Julia hung up, she was wearing a satisfied smile. She had called him, engaged his interest and it had been so easy. But then, she always knew he would come. Money had a special way of communicating and getting results. It had never failed her yet.

She spent the rest of the morning at Elizabeth Arden's having a facial and a manicure and getting her hair trimmed and conditioned. Then she shopped for the things she needed to make salade niçoise: imported tuna, anchovies, shallots, potatoes, hothouse tomatoes, green beans, sweet Boston lettuce and those delicious Mediterranean black olives she enjoyed so much.

That same evening Birdie prepared her famous French potato salad, drenched in shallots and wine, all mixed while the spuds were still warm. Then everything was placed in the refrigerator to marinate overnight.

She slept fitfully, dreaming of a strange knight who carried her off to some foreign kingdom where a young princess had her beheaded for wearing the color red. She wakened from the dream with a rapid, pounding heartbeat and a collar of sweat. If only her mother, Tatiana, were alive, she would have told her the dream's significance.

Chapter 11

Saturday night had fallen upon Caligari like the lid of a coffin, and he endured its smothering blackness in a redemptive sanctuary of loud music and vigorous dance. With his arms in a rounded second position, his stomach sucked tightly in and his head pulled to the ceiling by an invisible silver thread, he stood center floor listening to the allegretto movement of Shostakovitch's Fifth Symphony, pushing his grande battements to the limit.

He followed the heavy drum beat, fully extending the muscles of his thighs and calves, tensing his buttocks, arching his toes and feet till his body screamed in defiance. Not satisfied, he played the faster fourth movement allegro, doing grands jetés, barrel turns, tours jetés, spinning and leaping across the room with a *ballon* even Baryshnikov would have envied.

Drenched in sweat, unable to move another inch, he turned up the volume, slumped breathlessly in a heap on the floor of his SoHo flat and let the Brahms Double Concerto invade his brain and repair his worn-out body. It was like a transfusion. Within minutes the soft violins calmed him, and the cello, with its counter harmonies, stilled his spiraling senses. By the end of the last movement he had forgotten his problems and had fallen into a deep and satisfying sleep, awakening Sunday morning in time to shower, shave and dress for his mystery luncheon.

Julia wakened early Sunday morning, breakfasted on imported English tea and dry Carr's biscuits, then jogged around her circular penthouse terrace for twenty minutes. Finished, she sat peacefully in the steam of her black marble Jacuzzi, staring up at the morning sky through the overhead sun roof.

Of course Caligari would accept. Only a madman would refuse the kind of help she was prepared to give him. *Madman.* It was a word she remembered the interviewer had used in Calgari's last interview.

Finished bathing, Julia put on a peach maribou-trimmed robe with matching slippers, and from a temperature-controlled wardrobe room she chose an elegant Halston suit to wear: two-piece ivory wool with a short jacket and matching white Botega Veneta kidskin boots and purse. To complement the suit, she chose a single strand of nine-millimeter black pearls and matching earrings, all set in woven platinum braid.

When she had finished dressing, she sat at her antique mirrored table with its ornate Georgian silver frame, brushing her satin hair to a high gloss. With an old silver comb, she parted the silken strands on the left side of her head and let the straight shiny curtain fall naturally across her right eye. She kept her makeup simple. With her skin moist and dewy from yesterday's facial, she barely touched her eyelids with navy eye shadow, applying lots of black mascara to frame her startling blue eyes. Then, with a light layer of frosted pink lip gloss on her pretty mouth, some blush, and a spray of Opium cologne, she was ready to leave.

Calling down to Birdie at precisely 11 A.M., she was informed that the Rolls-Royce had just arrived downstairs. And with a last satisfied glance in the mirror, Julia slipped on her full-length Fendi chinchilla coat and matching beret and left her apartment feeling cautiously optimistic.

After a short ride through the city streets with a stop-off at Berwil's for a bouquet of Cattelya Hawaiian orchids, the Rolls-Royce deposited her at the front of Trump Tower.

Julia quickly entered the uncluttered and immaculate lobby, making sure she had not been seen by anyone except the doorman. That was important. Hounded by paparazzi who coveted her photographs for the covers of their cheap tabloids, she had chosen to meet Caligari here rather than at some fashionable restaurant where a greedy "stringer" might report their meeting to the society columnists. If Alexandra discovered what it was she was up to, everything would be over. As things were now, she could hardly buy her independent daughter a decent lunch, let alone a career. She laughed at *that* observation. Like mother, like daughter. It hardly surprised her.

The elevator ride was swift and silent, and in a matter of moments she was high up inside the magnificent apartment, placing the orchids in water and scrutinizing every detail for Caligari's arrival.

Designed and decorated by her own hand, the ten-million-dollar suite, surrounded by floor-to-ceiling windows, was papered in ice-green silk with ivory wood trim and bright coral touches and she loved every inch of it. Besides being a sound investment and a place where she occasionally conducted private business, the lofty apartment made a dramatic backdrop for the vast array of Oriental art treasures she had collected over the years.

She set the spray of orchids on the round coffee table in front of the curved green velvet Cantwell couch, which cradled a multitude of cream silk pillows—all hand embroidered in coral with Chinese symbols for luck, health and happiness—then lit a crackling fire in the green marble fireplace. And when everything, including lunch, had had a last-minute going over, she opened the balcony windows for air, listening to the faint and pleasant sounds of Sunday morning church bells pealing below.

* * *

The church bells rang out boldly as Richard Caligari paced the length and breadth of his SoHo apartment, waiting for the lady's car to arrive. He was nervous, already struggling with the questions and answers he hadn't even heard yet. When the doorbell rang, his stomach responded with a flip-flop. He glanced out the stained-glass window of his apartment and saw the shiny black Rolls waiting, double-parked below. He called down for the chauffeur to wait, then made a last-minute check in the hall mirror before departing.

Dressed smartly in tailored black wool Savile Row trousers, black cashmere turtleneck sweater and Harris tweed jacket, he wondered if perhaps he was too casually attired. But it was too late to change. And with a last desperate run of his fingers through his silky black hair, he grabbed his trench coat, shoved his keys inside a pocket and ambled downstairs.

Inside the car he continued to fret. What was it the lady *really* wanted? And how much crow would he have to choke on to give it to her? Most of all, would he be strong enough to refuse her money if the price she asked was too high? He knew what he would have done at twenty. But he wasn't twenty any longer. Could he say no now, even if she offered him the moon?

Before he could answer his own questions, the limousine had arrived and he was soon in an elevator ascending to the top of Trump Tower. When the doors finally opened, she was waiting for him with a warmly extended hand. The moment he laid eyes on her he could feel her heat.

She hung his coat in the hall closet and invited him into the living room, where she joined him on the couch.

"I'm glad you're here, Mr. Caligari. I'm a ballet fanatic and I've always admired your work," she said. "My name is Julia Romanov."

He leaned back against the pillow and drank in her

beauty. "Thanks, but I had to come. It's not every day I get such intriguing phone calls."

"Really?" she said. "I would think a handsome man like you would be inundated with such calls."

He was embarrassed and fixed his focus on the surroundings so she couldn't read him.

"Won't you please have something?" She extended her long, graceful hand over the table.

He smiled at the array—pâté, malossal caviar and assorted exotic cheeses. She was a mind reader, he thought. They were *all* his favorites.

She spread some pâté on a cracker, offered him a plate, then poured him a glass of iced tea.

"I must admit you have me at a disadvantage," Caligari said, tasting the triangle of caviar. "You not only know what I like to eat but what I enjoy drinking, as well."

"I make it my business to please, Mr. Caligari. Whenever I can."

"And you do it so well." He instantly regretted making such a pointed remark and apologized.

"Oh, don't apologize. As a matter of fact, I appreciate candor—especially from the men in my life."

"But I'm hardly in your life yet, Miss Romanov."

Her blue eyes sparkled. "As the saying goes, sir, 'All's fair in love and war.'"

In spite of himself, Caligari's enigmatic smile broke through. "I didn't realize the stakes were so high."

"I'll let you be the judge of that." She touched a delicate Belgian lace napkin to her pretty mouth, then placed the cloth on the coffee table. "Ready for lunch now?"

He raised his dark eyebrows. "I'm not sure. Lunch with you sounds dangerous," he quipped. "My mother used to say the way to a man's heart was through his stomach. And with this fabulous caviar, you're halfway there."

"We have a lot in common, Mr. Caligari," Julia said, laughing. "Because my mother always said that too."

Her sense of humor appealed to him. She was playful and beautiful, and his changing feelings about her were beginning to make him uncomfortable. What exactly was she selling? "Are you, by any chance, related to *the* Romanovs?" he asked.

"You're referring to the Czar, of course."

He nodded.

"Who knows? I suppose if you had asked my dear, departed mother, she'd have said yes. But then, Tatiana would have said anything." She giggled and her face was fresh and beautiful in the bright light. "Mother claimed we were distant cousins to Dowager Empress Marie, the Czar's mother. But I never knew when to take her seriously. Of course, I do have some relatives in Russia." She smiled demurely. "You've heard of Ilya Kremorkin?"

"Of course! I enjoyed his last performance at Lincoln Center the other evening."

"I know," she said. "I saw you there." She smiled. "However, the Romanov name *is* real. It belonged to my father."

"So there *is* a royal Romanov in your background."

Her head fell back in joyous laughter. "Papa would have loved to hear that. He was a Jew and Czar Nicholas was phobic about them. Poor Nicholas would have killed himself if he thought even a drop of Jewish blood ran through him."

Caligari was still confused. "Then where *did* the name come from?"

"From America, of course. When Papa landed at Ellis Island, the commissioner sliced the end off Romanovitsky and announced the new name as 'Romanov.' At first Papa waited for a Cossack to chop his head off for his effrontery, but it never happened. In America he could have any name he wanted. Then it became a matter of justice. The Czar had stolen all his belongings, kicked him out of Russia like a dog—so he felt it only fair to steal something from the Czar. And he kept the Romanov name for spite."

Caligari laughed. "Sounds like quite a fellow."

"He was. And I miss him."

"Then you've never married."

Her face flushed a pale crimson and she stared into the distance. "Yes, for a few months, a long time ago."

There was a moment of awkward silence as their private thoughts collided, as if each was aware they had stumbled onto forbidden territory and the only solution was a quiet retreat. Then Julia invited him to join her in the dining room.

Caligari placed his half-empty glass on the cocktail table and followed her up the green-carpeted steps into an informal mezzanine which overlooked the city. While she busied herself in the kitchen, he peered through a telescope at the antlike figures crawling around in the busy streets below.

He wondered what the beautiful creature had up her sleeve. Nothing, perhaps. Maybe everything. She wasn't cold or mechanical as he had anticipated but rather warm and very real. And he was attracted to her in a way that surprised him.

She soon entered the dining room wheeling an antique tea cart laden with gold-rimmed Haviland china which formed a rich backdrop for a magnificently arranged salade niçoise. Complementing that was solid-gold flatware, Baccarat crystal glasses and a chilled bottle of 1978 Meursault. If her intention was to impress him, she certainly succeeded.

He reached for the plate she carried, to help her, and in that small exchange their fingertips brushed. He felt a rush of electricity run through him, setting off romantic memories of Paris, Rome and the lush green of Clonsilla County, Ireland, where he had once vacationed many years ago. She was dredging up a host of memories he had long ago buried, and there was something inside him that wanted to rebel.

He pulled a chair from the table to seat her and an exotic scent drifted from the nape of her neck into his nostrils. She was, without question, an enchanting and delicious creature.

But she still had not exposed anything of significance. She still held each and every card in her hand. For a split second he felt like bolting from the room. "You have a beautiful art collection," he said instead. "I've never seen finer pieces except in museums."

"Now you've discovered another of my passions," she said, lowering her eyelashes. "But then, I've always been attracted to beautiful things."

He tensed and swallowed his food deliberately as she watched him. The remark, couched in a most seductive manner, was not lost on him.

"I really mean that," she said, flicking her pretty pink tongue around a ripe black olive. "I have a remarkable collection of paintings and sculpture. Degas, Brancusi, Picasso, Rodin. You must come and see them sometime."

He watched as she placed her gold fork across the plate and slowly wiped her mouth. For an instant her blue eyes flashed to clear turquoise, then back again to electric blue. In his whole life he had never seen a color like it before.

"As a matter of fact," she continued, "I do a little sculpting myself."

"Are you working on something special?"

"Not really. And I don't consider it work. It's more like a hobby."

She seemed to dismiss his question, so he persisted.

"Tell me a little more," Caligari said.

She cocked her head to the side, considering his question. "I suppose I see the subject in my mind first. Then when I decide what kind of figure to make, I construct an armature."

"So you only sculpt bodies, then," he said, interrupting.

"Why, yes." Her pause, and the startled look on her face, suggested she had never given it much thought before. "I suppose I do."

"And do you only work with clay?"

"Well, clay is easy—sensuous too, and certainly the oldest of the art forms. God only knows when some caveman picked up a handful of clay and squished it into a thing of beauty. Of course, people do it all the time. Snowmen in winter, sand castles at the beach. It's a primitive urge, I suppose." She sipped her wine. "When I do something I really like," she went on, "I'll turn it over to a stonecutter."

"A little like cheating, isn't it?"

"Not any more than a choreographer's reproduction of Petipa's works," she countered.

"Touché!" Caligari said, realizing she'd finally opened the door to his main concern. "And speaking of ballet, isn't it time you told me why I'm here?"

"Yes, of course," she told him. "You've been very patient. Now let's go back to the living room and share a brandy."

He pulled her chair from the table and escorted her into the living room, where together they sat on the couch near the fireplace. She poured vintage Napoleon brandy into twin crystal snifters and offered him some, but he politely refused.

"I'm a patron of the arts, Mr. Caligari," she told him. "I always have been. And I contribute regularly to many creative endeavors. But ballet is very special to me. For many reasons."

He wondered at her momentary, wicked smile and felt her eyes stray from connecting with his to delve instead into her twirling brandy glass. "I have a daughter, Mr. Caligari, who also happens to be a ballet dancer."

A faint bell sounded inside his head. His stomach knotted. He was beginning to understand. It was like a scene from the movie *The Red Shoes,* where the rich patroness invites the impresario Lermontov to a lavish party so her daughter can perform for him.

"As a matter of fact, she auditioned for you just last week," Julia continued.

He tried to remember the girl, tried connecting some face and body with the name Romanov, but nothing came to him. "I'm sorry, I don't recall."

"Well, unfortunately, she does. And all too well." She looked directly at him now, eyes boring into his. "You rejected her."

The bell which had sounded before grew to an alarm.

"She's been walking around the house like a zombie for the last few days," Julia went on. "She stares at the telephone all day and night as if it held magical powers. And in a way, it does." She leaned her body toward him and touched his arm. "I'd like that phone to ring for her, Mr. Caligari. I'd like *you* on the other end."

The alarm in his head ceased, and a siren sounded. He started to rise, but her arm gripped his sleeve with a hardy strength.

"Please, Mr. Caligari," she begged, "don't go! At least hear what I have to say."

He was reeling as she released him. He more than wanted the help she claimed she could give him, but he would never take her daughter. Never!

"I'm a rich woman," Julia continued. "Very rich."

"Unfortunately, however, I'm not for sale."

"But it's not *you* I want to buy."

"Oh, yes, it is."

"It seems that way at this moment, perhaps." She stopped as though she had tired of parrying. Then, setting her snifter on the table, she took a deep breath. "I'm in a position to underwrite your whole company, Mr. Caligari. *All* of it. In any amount you say. With one phone call you can have a theater, a school, a year-end Christmas gala with a summer residence in the Hamptons to prepare for a European tour which I'll personally underwrite.

"Think of it, Mr. Caligari. No more committees to answer to. No one peering over your creative shoulder, telling you what you can and cannot do. No more begging for financial handouts. You'll have new sets, new costumes, an orchestra, and with the wages you'll be able to pay, you'll never have to lose a single dancer again."

It was uncanny! She was reading him the way a blind man reads Braille.

"Think of what you'll accomplish, Mr. Caligari," she went on. "The new works you can mount. Scholarships that will make your name live on. But most of all you'll be creatively free, free to do whatever pleases you. Are you really prepared to throw that away?"

His heart was pounding, his palms sweating. "Tell me exactly what you want!" he demanded.

"I'm hardly a philosopher, Mr. Caligari. But to me, life has always been a little give, a little take."

His patience was wearing thin. "Stop beating around the bush and be specific!"

Now her eyes sought his without shame—straight as an arrow. This time she didn't waver. *"You* take my daughter, Mr. Caligari, and *I* give you total backing. You take my money and, in return, give Alexandra a dream."

"Sounds sweet. And don't misunderstand. I admire your devotion to your daughter. But unlike you, my art is not a hobby. I have integrity—standards to maintain."

"But you have dreams too, Mr. Caligari, and some dreams unfortunately have price tags. Think about it. Imagine what a winter gala in New York City could do for you and your company. After that, you'll generate your own finances. Then, if you decide it's best, you can let Alexandra go! One year," she pleaded. "All I'm asking for is one year."

Before he could respond, the telephone interrupted and Julia gave him a pleading look. She reached for the intruding instrument and, after delivering a brusque hello, asked Caligari to wait while she took the call in the next room.

Alone in the living room, he thought about her arguments. She was talking about his life's work, his soul. She was offering him not only the moon but the stars as well, and how could he say no to that? Imagine, he thought. Just imagine having it all. Everything he could ever wish for. But what a price to pay. Just how much was a man's integrity worth these days—because that's what it would cost if he accepted her offer. And that's when he thought about having to tell Paige, about living with this decision for the rest of his life. And when Julia returned, he had his answer.

She sat beside him on the couch again, clutching her brandy snifter. She paused a moment as if waiting for him to begin, and when he didn't, she leaned over conspiratorially toward him. "Well, Mr. Caligari, what do you think?" she said.

He said nothing, just rose and politely asked for his coat. "Thanks for lunch," he said, leading the way to the door. "And for such a terrific offer. But I couldn't sleep nights if I accepted it." He waited for her to explode, to shout, but she merely held the door.

"Before you say a final no, would you at least take a little time to think about it?" she asked.

The question brought a smile to his lips. "I probably won't be able to think of anything else," he told her. "Sure, I'll give it a few days."

She stared at him coldly. "I don't have that much time, Mr. Caligari," she said. "If you don't call by midnight tonight, the offer *is* dead!"

The moment she slammed the door, she kicked the nearest chair. Impudent bastard! Who did he think he was? Well, she'd fix him. She'd show him a thing or two. Two could play his imperious game, and at games she had always been a winner.

Nothing on the face of the earth would stop her now. She'd get him. She'd fix the dance master's holier-than-thou attitude. And when she was through, he wouldn't know what had hit him, or who, for that matter. He'd take Alexandra into the company before the weekend was over. Of that there was no doubt!

Chapter 12

He wakened Monday morning in a state of pain. That was not unusual; he always wakened in pain. Pain was a dancer's constant companion, the agonizing remnant of so many years spent flexing and extending muscles, of bending and stretching the spine, of twisting the hip sockets, the kneecaps and ankles into highly unnatural positions. And like other dancers, he had learned to make friends with pain. But this was a different agony. It was born of extreme guilt, of a terrible shame at what he had done. God! He could hardly believe it.

At eleven he showered, breakfasted lightly on wheat toast, cottage cheese and iced tea, then changed into T-shirt and black leotards. At eleven-fifteen he took two buffered aspirins for a screaming headache behind his eyes, and when the phone repeatedly rang, he didn't answer. He knew it was Paige and he was in no mood to go over it again. Everything about Alexandra Romanov had been settled yesterday. Everything! So at noon, with his head held high and his carriage erect, he strode into the rehearsal hall, where the full company of dancers waited for him to deliver an orientation speech.

They were all there in brand-new pink tights and black leotards—bright-eyed and bushy-tailed, beautiful, eager, waiting for the dance master to impose his will upon their minds, bodies and souls. He saw them searching his face for answers, for signals, aching for his attention, lined up at the barre like lilies of the field to be fertilized, pruned, staked, even rained upon. And if the sun shone in the form of Caligari's approving smile, they would bloom for all the world to see.

The pecking order established itself instantly. Those who had been with the Caligari Ballet Company longest stood at the coveted front of the line. Those who had just joined took their places in the rear. It had been that way since the beginning, ever since they were children attending their first classes. "Step to the front," teacher would say to the best ones, and the others would grow green with envy. Everyone wanted to be there. Front was where the action was.

But being up front was also a doubled-edged sword. Up front they were spotlighted, seen and corrected by the dance master, singled out and praised for the beauty they displayed. And they were expected to display their best, to lead and inspire those behind. But heaven help them if they led the others wrong.

"Good afternoon, everyone!"

Caligari's voice boomed loudly as he took his place at the front of the rehearsal hall and gripped his pointer. His dark, magnificent eyes scoured the length and breadth of the room in a prideful check of his charges. "I'd like to welcome our newest company members, and tell each of you I expect this season to be our most exciting one."

He paused for a second, unconsciously digging his pointer into the floor. "I'm also glad to report that in a short while we'll be moving to larger quarters—acquiring a new theater and school—and if everything goes well, we'll be in Europe this fall, touring, then home again to prepare for our first Christmas Gala." There! He had said it.

Wild applause and rousing shouts of glee vaulted from every corner of the room. Only Paige remained silent.

Dorsey Childs beamed a warm, engaging smile.

Shane Laser's knees quivered beneath her.

Alexandra Romanov, the newest company member, tightly clutched the barre.

Caligari took a deep breath as he moved aggressively toward the line of dancers. When he spoke his voice was deep and compelling, territorial and firm but always clear in its meaning.

"You'll find my company classes demanding," he announced. "And I expect each of you to attend without question. I don't give a damn if you're sick or dying!" He rapped his pointer on the floor for emphasis. "I expect you here. This profession is about pain. Make friends with it and your battles are over. Allow it to become your enemy and the war is lost."

He continued down the line, staring pointedly at each individual as he passed. "If you're ill or injured, sit in the back and mark the steps with your fingers, *but be here!* You chose to dance and you marry my company as if you were brides of Christ. If you can't give me total commitment, you don't belong here."

When he reached the end of the line, he realized how still the room had become and knew his words sounded harsh. But he had to establish a beachhead. That was vital to the company's future. He was the artist; they were his colors. How brilliant they would become, depended upon the strength of his brush stroke. And that depended further, on their pliability.

"Our days will begin at eight-thirty sharp with company class," he continued. "Then center floor and variations at nine-thirty. Women will do pointe work while you men concentrate on turns and jumps. After that we'll come together for pas de deux, then break for lunch." He scanned the line again for emphasis. "And please, people, eat intelligently," he said as he turned and strode toward the mirrors. "If you come to class filled with nicotine, candy bars and coffee, you stand a good chance of injury, and that's a luxury I cannot afford."

He felt their scrutinizing stares warming his back, and for a moment he flushed. It was unusual, a feeling he was unaccustomed to. Could they see through him? he wondered. And if they did, would their judgment of what he had done be harsh?

"After lunch we'll start rehearsing," he said, turning around. "And as we work together please remember this. The Caligari Ballet Company is a monarchy and I am its king. We project one image here. *Mine!* All artistic decisions ultimately rest with me. The only word I will never tolerate from anyone is 'why,' so please—when you come to class, remove it from your vocabulary."

He said that especially for Paige, who sat stoically near the mirrors with her arms folded rigidly across her chest. Explaining Alexandra's acceptance to her last night had been tough, and it was going to get even tougher, he knew. If Paige McDowell was anything at all, it was tenacious. She would keep digging until she'd unearthed the truth.

"You must trust me," he continued. "Believe that I'll do what's best for you, and what's best for you will always be what's best for this company. We are one unit here, just a family of dancers with no room for prima donnas. My job will be to train your minds and bodies. Yours will be to pay attention and give me everything you've got."

As he uttered those words, he tasted his meager breakfast. It floated up from his stomach in short, bitter waves, coating his tongue and palate like sour vinegar. At first he tried ignoring it. "You're all talented or you wouldn't be here," he continued. Then his gaze fell on Alexandra, and he nearly gagged. Instantly his queasy stomach rebelled even further, and he knew he would have to leave the room.

"That's all I have to say for now," he said with his head shyly bowed. "Except, thank you." And with that he wished them good luck, then turned the class over to a scowling Paige.

He walked rapidly from the room, hearing the familiar sound of applause ring in his ears. The tribute was expected; it had always been that way. It was tradition, a sign of respect. Usually he stayed to enjoy it, but this time he couldn't. He was feeling far too ill. And with the applause still trailing behind, he shut the rehearsal hall door and made his way to the inner office, where he fell wearily across the old couch. As he stared up at the cracked ceiling, his thoughts drifted back to Julia and the moment he'd left her apartment yesterday.

He'd felt so confident then, so proud of himself for refusing her offer, for sticking to all the principles he'd always believed in. Then how quickly everything had changed.

Arriving home, believing the incident behind him, he'd found Paige on his doorstep in a state of panic.

His mother would have called what had unfolded next God's will, fate, something for him to accept, as she had accepted the Gypsy tribunal's judgment of her.

He remembered leaping from the limousine and moving to Paige's side, placing an arm on her shoulder to comfort her while he searched for the keys to his apartment. Confused and concerned, he hadn't known what to make of her behavior. The unflappable Paige was shaking through a warm mink coat.

He remembered unlocking the door, escorting her upstairs into the living room, then sitting beside her on the couch, stroking her cheek, her hair, trying to soothe, to calm her so she could explain.

She'd looked everywhere except at his eyes, fumbling over and over with a rumpled tissue clutched tightly in her hand. "We've got problems, Richard," she'd said. "Real problems."

He'd held her shoulders to comfort her, to make her eyes connect with his. "What kind of problems?"

Her lips quivered as half a dozen times she'd started, stopped, then begun again. "We have to vacate the rehearsal hall, the theater, our offices, everything. The building's been sold and we've been ordered to leave immediately."

"But I don't understand," he'd said. "We have a lease."

"It's no good," she'd told him. "Not anymore. There was a clause—something about the right of the landlord to sell if a buyer with the right price came along. And one apparently did."

He'd felt then as if he'd been kicked in the gut by a mule. "Jesus!"

He'd stood abruptly, paced, wondering what could possibly happen next? He'd searched high and low for this rehearsal hall, and now he'd be forced to find a new one. But there wouldn't be time. What would happen to their crowded schedule? he'd thought. To the fall season they were counting on and preparing for? The money he'd been saving for their New York appearance was supposed to garner rave reviews, stimulate financial interest, keep them going until an angel could be found. Now he'd have to spend it on moving to new quarters—*if* they could be located on such short notice.

"How much time do we have?" he'd asked her next.

"Two weeks—that's it."

He recalled violently kicking the couch, screaming, "Who the hell are they kidding? I couldn't wipe my nose in two weeks."

He'd grabbed the phone, made a few frantic calls to some legal contacts to check on his rights. But within half an hour he'd soon realized he had no legal leg to stand on. Then thoughts of Julia's offer surfaced and he'd realized the decision had been taken from his hands.

Alone, he'd telephoned Julia and within half an hour he was with her again, this time drawing up a deal memo.

Sitting in her apartment, he'd agreed to her demands. Then he'd made some of his own. If he was going to let her buy him, the price would be as high as the market could bear. And so the game between them had begun.

To his demands for enormous sums of cash, Julia

had merely nodded. Then is was *her* turn again, and the vibrant lady with the hard-boiled edge said it all without a single qualm.

"Remember this, Mr. Caligari," she'd told him, searing his skin with those electric-blue eyes. "Should Alexandra find out about our agreement, it becomes null and void, and I'll not only be entitled to full refund, but damages as well."

He remembered initialing the fine print in a few places, wishing it were over so he could go home. No victory like defeat, he recalled thinking as she'd handed him the pen. That's when he'd signed his name. Ten minutes later he'd telephoned Alexandra, inviting her to join.

At eight that same evening he'd dined with Paige, exposing what he could about his new "good" fortune.

"I had no choice but to keep the meeting from you," he'd told her. "It was one of the conditions of the deal."

Paige seemed on the brink of tears.

"I don't understand, Richard," Paige had said. "You've never gone to a meeting without me before. You've never made a business deal without asking my opinion."

He'd felt terrible. Things in his life had been bad enough, and now he had lied to the one person in the world who'd always believed in him.

He'd tried to comfort her. "Please understand, Paige. Those were the terms of the agreement," he explained. "The person's total support in exchange for anonymity. Think of what we'll have in return."

Over and over he'd continued, feeling with each word as if he were digging his own grave. "I didn't tell you about the offer because I didn't think I'd ever take it. Then you dropped that bombshell about vacating the building and that left me no choice."

He'd turned away from her, then looked back, shouting, "Hell, Paige, what the hell am I supposed to do? It's the opportunity of a lifetime. We'll finally be financially free. Please, Paige. Look at the bright side."

When he had finished speaking, waiting for her approval, she'd offered him nothing.

And then finally she spoke.

"Nobody hands you that kind of deal without a sacrifice," she'd told him. "What did you promise in return?"

"Nothing!" he'd shouted.

He'd felt like a spectator at his own funeral as the lie he'd told settled over his head like a shroud.

Now, inside the office as he lay on the old tattered couch still staring up at the cracked ceiling, it was all too much. In the background he heard Joshua's concluding chord strike the piano. Within moments class would be over and Paige would come storming into his office with more of her damned questions.

Predictably, the office door opened and her perfume preceded her. In a few seconds she was standing over him, tapping her foot while he feigned sleep. He wouldn't permit himself to react. He was far too exhausted to go another round.

Sure, he had noticed the look on her face when she'd entered the orientation class this morning and found Alexandra, Mark and Rory—three new pupils at the barre. And since she'd never approved any of them, he knew eventually he would have to explain their presence. But now he had no reasonable answers to give her.

How could he tell her that one, Alexandra Romanov, was the daughter of their benefactor, the others, Mark and Rory, simply there to cover his tracks. Paige was clever. She would easily have put two and two together and realized the money connection. So he'd cooked up that little ploy on his own. Oh, he'd account for it later somehow. But now he knew that in order to have what he needed it was necessary to overlook and avoid.

Yes. He knew all that and much, much more. But what he didn't know was that it wasn't fate that had decided his hand, but Julia Romanov, who, with a single phone call, had bought his building and forced it.

Chapter 13

It was natural for new company members to cluster together for self-preservation and security, to fortify themselves against the already established old guard. So it was no surprise that Shane, Dorsey and Alexandra huddled together whenever they could, and in less than a week's time had begun to share their hopes, feelings and dreams about the dance master.

"Isn't he wonderful?" Alexandra sang one afternoon as they lunched in the noisy pizza parlor around the corner from the old rehearsal hall. "When he called me on Sunday to say I was in, I nearly freaked."

"*He* called *you?*" Dorsey asked in surprise.

"Yes," Alexandra replied. "Who called you?"

"McDowell," Dorsey replied sourly.

They both looked at Shane, but the girl only yawned.

"EXCUUUUUSE me!" Dorsey complained. She lit a brown Sherman cigarette. "I hope we're not keeping you awake!"

Shane's normally pale skin flushed crimson as she strained to open her green eyes. "Sorry, but that long subway ride from Brooklyn every morning and night . . ."

The smoke from Dorsey's mouth burst forth with her raucous laughter. "Brooklyn! Are you kidding? I wouldn't live there if you paid me. Jeez! I'd be too damn scared to ride the subways."

"It's not that bad," Shane said.

"Sure, sure," Dorsey reiterated. "With a Guardian Angel by your side."

"Well, I don't have any choice," Shane said, biting into her double-cheese pizza slice. "My mom's a seamstress. All her clients are there. Besides, we just moved."

"Big deal!" Dorsey leaned forward on both elbows and playfully wagged a finger. "Now don't tell me a big girl like you is still living with Mama."

Shane wiped her mouth with a paper napkin and shrugged her shoulders. "Got any better ideas?"

"Well," Dorsey said, "you could share my hotel room, but they're kicking me out this weekend, so I have to find a new place myself."

There was a moment of quiet assessment, then Dorsey slapped the table so hard the silverware jangled. "Jeez! Come to think of it, I do have a better idea. Why don't you and I share a place—together."

Shane wrinkled her nose. "No," she mumbled. "I don't think so."

"What do you mean you don't think so? You're earning a salary," Dorsey reminded her. "We'll find something *fab*, with two bedrooms, close to the new rehearsal hall. Then you won't have to ride the trains and be so fagged out every day. Besides, we'll be going to the Hamptons in July and August to prepare for the European tour. So if things don't work out between us, you can always split."

Outside, the sun moved from behind a cloud. It sent a dazzling ray through the plate-glass window and Alexandra shielded her eyes from the glare.

"How about you, Alex?" Dorsey asked.

"I've already told you," Alexandra answered, spearing a tomato. "I live at home too."

"My luck," Dorsey exclaimed. "Two big babies in one day. Well, it's not gonna last. You better move in with Shane and me." She ignored Alex's attempted protest and continued excitedly, "Jeez! Why didn't we think of it before? The three of us. Sharing one big jazzy apartment." She howled with joy. "C'mon, you two, we'd have a blast!"

"Hey! I like that idea," Alexandra said. "What do you say, Shane?"

The two girls stared as Shane considered the possibility. "Gosh, I really don't know."

"It's your mom, isn't it?" Dorsey said. It was more a statement than a question, and the boldness of Dorsey's words brought Alexandra to Shane's defense. She pinched Dorsey's thigh under the table to make her drop the subject.

"Well, what else could it be?" Dorsey persisted. "So why lie about it?"

Shane's body drooped with the admission. "You're right. But what am I supposed to do? My mom's waited for me to get into a real company for years. She's worked like a dog. Now that I'm in, how do I just dump her? Besides, we just moved."

"Give me a break!" Dorsey complained. "It's a parent's duty to make you feel guilty. But sooner or later you'll have to leave. It might as well be now."

On her way home after class, Alexandra stopped at Bloomingdale's and bought a new diary: marbled white leather with blue lined pages and a strong lock to guard her secrets. Like most ballet dancers, she had kept journals all her life, committing to their pages her feelings and dreams, her hopes and desires for the future.

Each one had been dedicated to someone she loved and respected, but the dedication for this one made her shiver.

After hugging Birdie hello in the kitchen, she hurried upstairs to her whisper-pink bedroom, flung herself across her white chenille canopied bed and tore off the wrappings. Then with a flourish of a gold Gucci pen, she wrote the following passage, dotting all her i's with tiny circles.

*I dedicate this diary to Richard Caligari. I'll
always remember the way his voice sounded on
the telephone the night he asked me to join his
company, so warm and masculine. And on the
pages of this diary I swear to never let him down.
I love you Mr. C and I commit my whole life and
all my being to pleasing you.*

She signed her initial *A* at the bottom and below that
wrote, *"Friends forever—Dorsey Childs and Shane
Laser."*

Pleased with herself, she placed the diary under her pillow and lay back to daydream.

She saw herself poised on a white cloud, dancing a pas
de deux in a romantic tutu with the handsome dance master. He was strong, holding her by the waist, lifting her
above his head as though she were a delicate white bird, as
light as a feather in his strong arms.

There were soft lights surrounding them, heavenly
music, and when they had finished dancing, wild applause
with bouquets of bright red roses which she shared with
him.

A soft knock at the bedroom door delayed the daydream's end. She called, "Come in," and Julia entered.

She became self-conscious about her bedroom's slight
disorder and waited for Julia to chastise her for it. But her
mother made no verbal pronouncements this time.

"Well," Julia said as she joined Alexandra on the bed.
"You've been a busy little bee, haven't you? What's going
on in your life these days?"

Alexandra sat up and crossed her legs in a yoga position.
"It's very exciting," she replied. "But strange. I still don't
understand why Caligari chose me."

Julia's hand rested on Alexandra's shoulder in an unusual display of affection. It felt odd sitting on her warm
body, like a cold and impersonal lump.

"I don't think it's strange at all," Julia said, glancing
away. "You're a good dancer, certainly a dedicated one."

"But I'm too heavy for his 'look.' And I keep wondering what he really saw in me."

"Let *him* worry about that," Julia told her. She paused, using the softer version of her voice. "Birdie tells me you've started a new diet."

Alexandra gave a silly giggle. "Sort of. He's going to start weighing us every Monday morning. I really dread it."

"You'll be fine," Julia said. "In fact, I found this wonderful new diet. You can actually lose five pounds in a week. Shall I have my secretary send you a copy?"

Alexandra felt the hackles rise on her neck. She hated when Julia offered advice. It never seemed to stem from any real desire to help, but was more from a need to show how together she was.

"No thanks. I think I've got it under control," Alexandra lied.

Julia seemed to sense the rejection. "Well, it's getting late and there's some real estate near the library I'll be looking at. Care to join me?"

"No. But speaking of real estate," Alexandra said, suddenly remembering her conversation with Shane and Dorsey, "what would you think of my sharing an apartment with two other girls?"

Julia's eyebrows raised. "I hadn't thought about it, but I suppose it could be fun for you."

The ease with which Julia responded surprised Alexandra. It wasn't every day her mother agreed with her. "Really?!"

"Why not? I can even help you find the perfect apartment." Without waiting for an answer, Julia reached for the pink Princess telephone, but Alexandra stopped her.

"Thanks. But we'll probably start looking for a place over the weekend—together."

Julia's exasperation finally surfaced. "For heaven's sake, Alex, aren't you carrying this independence thing a bit too far? I *am* in the business and I am your mother. Won't you at least let me help?"

She hadn't expected such attention and almost surrendered. Raised in the beginning by nannies and private nurses, Alexandra was unaccustomed to even sharing Julia's company. Later it became a battle where emotional independence was the issue. *You don't need me and I don't need you.* "Thanks, but there are three of us in on this, and I wouldn't feel right making the decisions for them. Besides, half the fun is in the looking."

"Okay," Julia said rising. "Have it your own way, but my offer still holds."

When Julia closed the door, Alexandra reached for her diary. She opened to a clean page and after scribbling the date, wrote the following:

> *Julia's been acting weird lately and I don't know what to make of it. Strange! She's never been nicer, yet at the same time I feel her anger more than ever.*

Without concluding anything from what she had written, she washed her face and hands and took the elevator downstairs.

In the warm kitchen she found Birdie dotted with flour, stacking a batch of newly baked chocolate chip cookies in a jar. Without thinking, Alexandra reached for one but a sudden rap on the knuckles startled her. She felt ashamed.

"You told me not to let you eat those anymore, remember?" Birdie said.

Alexandra permitted herself a smiling pout, the kind that usually played on Birdie's emotions and made her give Alexandra anything she'd asked for. But Birdie held fast. "I only wanted one," she said in a baby voice.

"One is all you need. Then you'll have to have another and another and another." Alexandra followed Birdie's lead to a nearby barstool and sat beside her. "Come on, baby," Birdie said, hugging her. "We talked about this yesterday and the day before that, didn't we? And didn't you tell me,

'This is it, Birdie; I'm really gonna lose weight for Caligari.' Didn't you say that to me?"

Alexandra's pout changed to a frown, then to the merest smile of resignation. She kissed Birdie on the cheek. "Thanks," she said to the cook. "Thanks for caring." She felt the tears fill her eyes as Birdie hugged her.

"Hey! Quit sniffling. Ain't you my baby? Haven't you always been?"

Dorsey met her father for dinner at her favorite restaurant, Lutèce. This time she was carefully prompt, putting Senator Childs in a good frame of mind. They met on the candelit second floor at a beautiful table near the window, where a waiter in a black tuxedo greeted them and presented the menu.

With a jaundiced eye, Dorsey watched her famous father operate, nodding to Jackie Onassis, who sat at a nearby table with a female companion, then at a political crony who stopped by to say hello.

Her father was handsome, she thought—white hair, perpetual tan, lively green eyes, all the ingredients of a roué. After that night, after all that had happened, she'd hoped they could be friends. But his sudden marriage to Deandra had fixed that little notion. Once again, Dorsey had been betrayed. Now she felt more isolated, more lonely, more detached from him than ever. And she blamed him and his weakness as much as she blamed herself.

"We'll have a bottle of Clicquot 1976," Senator Childs said to the waiter when the political crony had left. "And some of your finest caviar."

The waiter listened as the Senator went on.

"For dinner we'll have *le mignon de boeuf en croûte, s'il vous plâit, et vôtre soufflé glacé aux framboises.*" Finished ordering, he looked at Dorsey and smiled. "All your favorites, baby. See? I remembered."

She smiled back at him. Big deal. Long ago she had been impressed with his flawless French, with his knowledge of foods and wines, but the glamour had faded with time and circumstances. Now she thought all politicians were the lowest form of life, and he, in particular, as phony as a three-dollar bill.

"What's Deandra doing these days?" Dorsey asked.

The Senator flourished his pink linen napkin into his lap. "She's with her mother in California."

Good place for her to be, Dorsey thought. She should stay there. Better than that, her plane should crash.

"How's the dancing coming?" the Senator inquired.

"Great!" Dorsey answered. Small talk always made her fidget. It took time to get reacquainted with him. "I did want to apologize for our last fight," she confessed. "I didn't mean to upset your secretary like that. I just got annoyed at—"

"Forget it," he interrupted. "She'll get over it. I'm more concerned about you. Getting thrown out of another fine hotel."

He'd done it again—taken the spotlight off her need to explain and brought it around to what he wanted to say.

"Oh, Dad, it's no big deal," she said. "They all have such goofy rules. Besides, I'm going to start sharing an apartment with some other girls in a few days."

"How nice. Do I know then?"

"No, I don't think so."

"Well, as long as they're respectable."

No, she thought, they're grody dimwits. "Sure. Both come from terrific families. You'll see for yourself when we have an open house."

The waiter appeared with their champagne and caviar and Dorsey dug in, knowing full well her father was scrutinizing her every bite. She didn't mind. It seemed the only time, the only real time she could ever hold his full attention.

"How's your money situation?" Senator Childs asked as he drank champagne.

Another stupid question, she thought. "Fine. You know Mom left me a hefty trust, so I have everything I need."

Except you! she thought. You're too damned busy fucking Deandra to really give a shit.

They continued their small talk, eating caviar, drinking champagne, never discussing or touching on their real feelings. Then dinner came. Lovely fillets of beef with goose-liver pâté and mushrooms stuffed in a light pastry shell and baked to perfection.

Dorsey gobbled her meal with gusto, rarely speaking. Then she attacked the frozen raspberry soufflé dessert while the Senator watched in amazement.

"Where do you put it all?" he finally asked. "You eat like a horse and stay as lean as a toothpick." He patted his own tummy. "What's your secret? I'd like to patent it."

"Just dancing," Dorsey said quickly. "It's a very strenuous business."

But five minutes after she'd finished the last delectable morsel, she began to twitch, wriggling in her seat like a worm on a hot sidewalk.

She could feel all that nice rich food winding its way down through her stomach, fastening on to her hips and legs, clinging to her buttocks and chest, building a host of fatty tissue all over her body. Ugh! How disgusting. She loved tasting and eating the food—she just hated what it did to her fabulous body.

She excused herself on the pretext of fixing her makeup, then locked herself in the ladies' room. A few seconds later she was over the toilet bowl, sliding two fingers down her throat, gagging and throwing it all up.

She couldn't wait to get rid of it. All of it! A dancer's duty was to stay lean, but her father would never understand that. What the hell did he care or know about ballet, about grace and line. And how many times had she told him that the stage, the lights put ten pounds on a dancer's body, and if she wasn't careful her career could be over before it began. No. He'd never understand, even if she explained it to him in detail again and again.

Finished, she flushed the john and washed her face and hands, then reapplied her makeup. She sprayed cologne on her neck and hair and breath freshener in her mouth to disguise any lingering odor. Skinny? she thought, looking at herself in the mirror. What a jerk. Didn't her father have eyes? Couldn't he see? She was five pounds overweight, dammit, and would go on a diet tomorrow morning.

When she returned to the table, her father had already paid the bill and was waiting for her.

"I've got an early schedule," he said, taking her elbow. "I'll have my chauffeur drive you to the hotel."

Outside, as the limousine pulled up, she asked her inevitable question. "Can I spend the night with you tonight, Daddy? I mean Deandra's not home."

The Senator opened the car door for her. "No," he said. "I don't think it's a good idea, princess."

His answer hurt her deeply.

Inside the car Dorsey tried to hug him, but he unlaced her fingers from behind his neck and gently patted her knee instead.

"It's time to go home now," he told her.

She turned away from him and peered out the tinted window into the night. She didn't want him to see her tears. Outside it had already begun to rain.

When Shane exited the bowels of the BMT subway, it was dark and raining. Just what she needed! One more stupid thing to contend with. She hoisted her ballet bag over her head and made a run through the downpour—four straight blocks.

She thought about what had happened today at the pizza parlor, about the plan Dorsey and Alexandra had cooked up for her, and she was nervous. At lunchtime it had sounded good, almost comical and so easy to pull off. Alone now and with no moral support, it seemed wrong and cruel.

She didn't like the thought of having to scare Simone, or of lying to her so blatantly. But what else was she supposed to do? She desperately needed to break away from her mother's influence, to grow up, to be her own person. It was touchy any way she looked at it. She knew it would be hard making Simone face the reality of their ultimate separation, harder still to face it herself.

Inside the hallway of the musty-smelling apartment building, she poked the downstairs doorbell with a cold, wet finger and waited.

"Shane? Is that you?"

"Hurry, Mom. Open up. It's freezing down here."

The buzzer rang back, releasing the lock, and Shane passed through. She rode the rickety black elevator, with its dirty oval window, to their third-floor apartment, rehearsing her lines. When the elevator opened, she was ready.

"Why the hell are you so late?" Simone demanded, following after her. "I was crazy with worry."

Shane tossed her wet things on the hallway floor, then, as previously planned, she lunged for Simone and began to cry. "Something terrible happened on the subway," she sobbed. "It was awful. Thank God some men stopped him before he could . . ."

Simone gasped. Both her hands grasped Shane's shoulders. "Stopped who? What? Tell me what happened."

It was cruel, Shane thought as she continued. But there was too much at stake. "I fell asleep on the subway and when I opened my eyes this filthy degenerate had his hand up my dress. I tried to get away but he chased me." She paused for a breath she really didn't need and continued, "It was horrible, God!"

She didn't dare look at her mother's face. Simone always seemed to know when she was lying.

"Let me look at you," Simone said, leading her into the lighted living room. "Are you okay? Are you hurt? Where did he touch you?"

Shane fell into the old chair near the telephone. "Over here. On my thigh," she said, averting her eyes.

Simone picked up the telephone and began to dial.

"What are you doing?"

"I'm calling the police," Simone announced.

Shane panicked. "No, Ma. Don't! I'm fine. Really. Besides, I couldn't talk to them about it. Too embarrassed. I only want a little dinner, that's all, and time to wind down. You understand, don't you?"

In half an hour Simone had calmed down, and after rinsing Shane's leotards and tights in the sink and hanging them in the shower, she served dinner. Boring broccoli for calcium, pukey potatoes for potassium, and a broiled skinless chicken breast for protein.

Shane chewed her food slowly while her mother hovered over her like a brood hen. Maybe she had played the part a little too well. Maybe it would backfire.

"So, what happened in class today?" Simone asked.

"Nothing much."

"You had a bowel movement?"

"Sure."

"What color?" Simone asked.

"Brown, like always."

"Hard or soft?"

"In the middle," Shane replied. She made a face. "I'm eating, Ma. Can we please talk about something else?"

"All right," Simone agreed. "But if *I* don't watch out for you, who will?"

Shane wanted to say "myself" but didn't. She just sat there like a dummy, chewing and swallowing her food.

"So, how are all your new friends?" Simone asked.

Well, Shane thought, here comes the green-eyed monster. "Which ones?"

"You know—the skinny one, and the other, with the big chest. Is she still in the company?"

Shane's mouth fell open. Some of Simone's comments were incredible. "Of course. Why shouldn't she be?"

"I don't know," Simone replied, making a sour face. "She's too fat. He's probably sleeping with her."

Shane threw her fork onto the plate. "Why must you say such terrible things about a girl you don't even know?"

"Because—it's probably true, that's why."

"For your information, Alexandra is a hell of a dancer."

"Alexandra, huh? Maybe. But she's still too fat for his company."

There was silence again as Shane continued eating. Her every move was scrutinized, her every gesture weighed and questioned.

"So, what did you eat for lunch?" Simone asked, breaking the silence.

Shane stumbled. "Fruit salad," she replied. She was afraid to tell her mother the truth. Pizza.

She felt Simone's disapproving glance. "Very bad for you."

"What do you mean, bad?" She couldn't win no matter what she said.

"You work too hard to live on fruit salad," Simone said. "A dancer's body is like any other machine. It needs the right fuel. Proteins and vitamins, not sugar."

"Well, it's not as if I'm living on the stuff," Shane countered. "I just wasn't hungry today." She swallowed the dry chicken lumping in her mouth. "Can we please talk about something else?"

"Like what, for instance?"

The perfect opportunity to tell her mother about the apartment, she thought. But she was still afraid. She needed someone in her corner, cheering her on, someone like her nana, who had died eleven years ago. Anyone who could stand up to Simone's tirades and keep her from sucking the marrow out of Shane's bones. But the time *was* now, and as she stood staring at her mother with that measuring tape hanging around her neck like an albatross, a strange courage grew insider her.

"I need to talk to you, Mom."

"Sounds serious," Simone said. She stood up and clattered the dinner plates into the sink.

"In a way, it is."

Simone didn't look at her. "The only thing you kids have nowadays that's serious is zits." She turned and folded a dish towel in her hands. "So go ahead—talk. I'm listening."

Shane gulped air. "Sit down with me first."

Simone gave Shane her fish-eyed stare. "What on earth could be so serious I have to quit cleaning the dishes?"

Shane tried to speak, but she felt too intimidated.

"I'm waiting," Simone said, reaching for a fork and drying it.

Shane gulped air then finally let it fly. "I never considered it before now, but after tonight, after what happened on the subway, well, it just makes sense."

"What does?"

"Alexandra and Dorsey, the other new girls, they asked me to share an apartment with them and . . ."

Simone dropped the fork she was holding. "Over my dead body," she said emphatically.

Shane pleaded. Her voice was still reasonable but with a touch of whine. "But I'm almost twenty, Mom. Not a baby anymore. And it's practical too. I'm afraid to ride the subway. What if I close my eyes and wake up with some creep's hand up my dress? Besides, there's just no reason not to move in with them."

"You want reasons? I'll give you ten," Simone said.

"I don't need ten. Don't you understand? I was nearly . . . well, raped today." Shane swallowed a lump in her throat the size of a baseball. "I don't want to take that chance anymore. I want to live in the city with my friends."

"You mean tramps, don't you?" Simone said bitterly.

"Why is it every girl I know is a tramp to you? For your information, Dorsey's father is a senator and Alex's mother is a very wealthy socialite."

"Aha! There it is! All politicians have trampy daughters. And now I know why the fat one was picked."

Shane sprang from her chair so hard it clattered to the floor. "That's it!" she said, throwing her napkin on the table. "*I have had it!* I'm going to take that apartment and I don't give a damn what you say." Frustrated and angry, Shane ran toward her room.

"Sure. Go ahead," Simone yelled, dragging after her.

"Go ahead and leave me! What the hell do I care? I've only worked like a goddamn dog for you all my life."

Shane spun around and faced her mother. Her heart beat like a hammer in her chest. "No, dammit, I've worked too," she yelled. "Day and night, with bleeding toes and blisters and backaches. So don't pull that guilt trip on me —ever again!" She stormed from the room with her mother in pursuit. Inside her bedroom, she slammed the door.

As the door slammed in her face, a shocked Simone retreated to a living room chair to collect her thoughts. She had not expected anything like this to happen. God—it hurt! Shane really wanted to leave her.

With tears in her eyes she suddenly realized that things had been changing for a long time. Shane had been growing up, and she would have to learn to talk to her daughter in a grown-up way. Of course she would be lonely without her little girl. After all, they'd been together from the beginning. A team. But staying with her friends could also be a blessing in disguise.

Living away from home for now could be safer—harder for *them* to trace Shane in the city than here in Brooklyn. And it might just prove a few things to Shane too. Maybe on her own she would realize how much Simone loved her and how much Shane really loved and needed Simone. Perhaps she'd come back then on her own, and it would be like old times, when Shane was little.

She dabbed her eyes with a hankie. All right, she thought. Go. Go, already. Test your pretty little wings. Take all the rope you need, but don't strangle yourself. That decided, she dragged herself from the chair and shuffled off to Shane's bedroom to apologize.

A crack of light fell across Shane's face as Simone entered the darkened bedroom.

"Shane? It's all right, baby."

Simone sat sheepishly beside her daughter, stroked her head and whispered in her ear. "It's okay. You can go with the others to the apartment and live there if you want to. I'm sorry I yelled."

Lying in Simone's arms, Shane was shocked. She didn't know whether to laugh or cry. But Simone's words had been real enough. So with happy tears she rolled over and vigorously hugged her mother. Then later, after Simone had gone, she lay mulling over what had happened. She decided something about the incident wasn't right. It had all happened too quickly. She knew her mother well. Simone didn't hug without reason, wasn't the type to give in so easily. She had to have something up her sleeve. But what? It was then, as she lay falling asleep, that she realized Dorsey's silly plan had somehow worked.

Chapter 14

When Shane returned with her good news the following day, the three girls bounced with excitement.

"What fun," Alexandra shouted.

"What a gas!" Dorsey exclaimed.

"What a time I had lying to my mother," Shane said.

"But it worked, didn't it?" Dorsey asked with a sly smile.

"Oh, it worked all right," Shane replied. "But something was weird—like she let me go a little too easy."

"Oh, pooh!" Dorsey said, dismissing her. "You're just scared, that's all. Hell, I was too. The first time I left home I cried like a baby."

"How old were you?" Shane asked.

"About ten or eleven, I think. It happened so long ago, I forget."

Shane dropped Dorsey's hand and looked directly in her eyes. "Are you kidding me?"

"Of course not. Why would I lie?" Dorsey answered.

"But that's too little to be away from home," Alexandra said. "Where did you go? Where did you stay?"

"Switzerland. A private school my mother chose." Dorsey pinched her nostrils together with her fingers. "Very posh. Very strict. Very upper crust," came the nasal whine.

"Who cares about upper crust. That's still too young,"

Shane insisted. She looked as if she could have cried. "Why did you let them do it? Why didn't you say something?"

Dorsey shrugged. "When you're ten years old you don't ask questions. You just go." She paused, eyes cast downward. "Besides, I was glad to be rid of them anyway. My mother liked her gin, and my dad, well, he was out to save the world." The pregnant silence lay stillborn. "Well, enough of that crap. C'mon, let's get crackin'. We've got a lot to do."

On their way to the deli, Dorsey stopped at a newsstand and purchased a paper. "We'll look through the rent ads first," she explained. "Then make some appointments. With the three of us looking, we're sure to find something soon."

At a table inside the deli, the three girls marked the for-rent ads in the six-hundred-dollar price range. Then, whenever time would permit, they hunted.

"A piece of cake," Dorsey had predicted. but after four vigorous days of searching, she recanted, correcting herself. "A piece of stale cake."

On the fifth day, standing at a filthy corner on the outskirts of Greenwich Village, a pall of despair had settled over them. They'd been everywhere, had seen everything and it was all bad news, with roaches, rats and refuse in every apartment. All the fun had gone out of looking as reality settled in. And it was then, with great reluctance, that Alexandra informed them of her mother's offer.

Dorsey tossed her toeshoes at Alexandra, screaming, "You silly twit. We've been out here for five days, busting hump, and you have an inside track. Why the hell didn't you tell us that in the first place?"

Alexandra barely caught the shoes, then hemmed and hawed to avoid answering. But that proved impossible. So the truth slowly unfolded.

"I wanted us to do it on our own. Christ! I hate asking her for favors. She's an operator, and this is right up her alley. I can just see her, picking up the telephone and making that one call, getting everybody to jump through hoops for her."

"What the hell difference does that make?" Dorsey said. She snatched her shoes from Alexandra's hands. "We don't care, do we? Besides, everyone in the world's an operator." She put an arm around Alexandra's shoulder. "Okay. We forgive you. Just swallow your silly pride, get on the horn and call her. Now! Let's get this shit over with. I don't know about you two, but I'm too damned exhausted to look one more day."

Alexandra made a sour face. "Okay," she said finally. "On one condition." She waited as the others nodded agreement. "It has to be something we can afford on our salaries. That's the *only* way I'll do it."

"You got it!" Dorsey shouted.

"Ditto!" Shane agreed.

In the days that followed his signing of Julia Romanov's agreement, Richard Caligari's feelings of shame and guilt began to subside, replaced by a subtle sense of financial freedom and a professional security he had never known in his career. Consequently, his days were spent examining the new quarters Julia had provided for his ballet company, searching out new composers, spending time with musicians, costumers, decorators, set designers and, best of all, since the need to chase after money had been eliminated, he had time to devote to his first love—the creation of new ballets.

He was beginning to like it, to settle in, to think in terms of actually accomplishing what he'd set out to do in the first place: achieve personal and financial success. And it felt marvelous. So it was unsettling at best when Paige McDowell cornered him in the old company offices a few days before they were scheduled to move, hitting him right between the eyes with more of her demands. Ordinarily, he would have told her to take a hike. But Paige was his friend, important to his life. She was also his prima ballerina. As such, he permitted her to question him, to make remarks that under other circumstances he never would have tolerated.

They were packing cartons, emptying the contents of an old gray file cabinet which housed the remnants of their short stay at the old building, when she tossed him the curve, and he did his best to answer her intelligently, trying to stay calm while under fire.

"I think it's time we dismissed the Romanov girl," Paige said.

Caligari studied her face and realized she was dead serious. He tried to appear nonchalant and casual as he responded. He didn't want to arouse her suspicions or make matters worse than they were. "Why?" he asked. "She's doing well."

"It's obvious why," Paige told him. She continued stuffing the papers he'd handed her into a cardboard box. "For as long as I've known you, Richard, it's always been the ladies who have challenged you to create new ballets. I see nothing in this young woman to inspire any of those things."

"I don't agree," he told her, continuing with his work. "Alexandra has very strong legs, excellent lines and—"

"Lines," she interrupted, "that are all distorted by her weight problem, which she seems unable to deal with." She tossed some old papers into the trash can, then continued, "Oh, I've no doubt she'd turn heads on the Riviera dressed in a bikini. But, on stage? She'll look like a cow in one of your beautiful new ballets."

"Give her some time," Caligari responded. He opened another drawer and pulled out some files. "When she loses the weight . . ."

"*If* she loses the weight," Paige corrected.

Caligari glared at her.

"I said *when*," Caligari repeated. "*When* she loses the weight, she'll surprise even you."

"And what do we do until then?" Paige asked. "Watch every bite she takes? We're not her parents, you know."

"Oh, yes, we are, Paige," he quickly answered. "In a curious way these students are *all* our children."

Alexandra's relationship to her mother had always been a strained one. But Alexandra never reasoned why. There was this thing between them, a friendly antagonism, some unexplainable discord, a distance, a breach, a line each respected but neither ever dared to cross. Alexandra saw Julia as a woman on a fierce journey, with herself a simple detour on the way. It was an unpleasant feeling, as if she were a boarder in her own home.

Besides that, there was this thin veil of anger to Julia's tone when they talked, which sometimes blossomed at the oddest moments. And for some reason Alexandra felt responsible for it, as though she'd somehow had a hand in its creation. Consequently, she never confided her feelings to her mother, had never felt really close to her, and in general tried to avoid her. To ask a favor of Julia now, when her own independence was so vitally at stake, was almost more than she could bear.

But there were her friends to consider now, and she would do exactly as she'd promised. And since Alexander was by nature practical in most things and certainly not one to beat about the bush, the phone call to Julia was short, sweet, direct and to the point. "Nothing over six hundred dollars, please. Two bedrooms with two baths, if possible, and also security."

Julia was glad their conversation was being held on the telephone. Had Alexandra seen the amused expression on her face, Julia would never have gotten away with what she was about to do. "Of course," Julia replied, smiling. "I'll telephone Gregory at once. I think it's a splendid idea."

When Julia hung up, she telephoned her attorney, Gregory Kingston, and explained the situation to him. "You know how Alex is, for heaven's sake, so please be careful. Draw up a dummy lease for that marvelous place on Sixty-eighth Street and send it over."

"Are you joking?" Kingston cautioned. "That apartment's going for three grand. Alex is no fool. She'll know in a minute it isn't worth six hundred a month."

Julia laughed. "You know a lot about law, Gregory, but nothing about impressionable young women. She has no real conception of money, none at all. So please. Just do as I ask."

"Okay," he said. "But I hope you know what you're doing." He paused. "Will I see you at the Founders' Charity Bazaar tonight?" he inquired before hanging up.

"Of course," Julia replied. "Vidal and I will be there with bells on."

Chapter 15

Shane squeaked with delight as Alexandra opened their new apartment door. She had never seen anything so beautiful. Two bedrooms and den, an L-shaped kitchen with a rectangular cooking island, two full baths and windows everywhere. Heaven on the fourteenth floor.

"It's gorgeous," Dorsey said. "Where do we sign?"

In less than one week they had packed their belongings and were moved in.

Dorsey begged to have the smaller bedroom to herself, offering to pay an extra fifty dollars per month for that privilege. "I'm told, by very reliable sources, that I snore," she said, trying to convince the others.

Shane and Alexandra quickly agreed.

Then the decorating began.

Julia offered them the use of almost new furniture, confiscated from myriad tenants who had refused, or were unable for various reasons, to pay their rent. And for three hours on a rainy Saturday they walked through a warehouse, making their way through a maze of repossessed couches, chairs, tables and bedroom sets, the sad remnants of other people's dreams gone awry.

In the Wedgwood-blue living room, they settled on white wicker furniture, chintz-covered sofas and chairs and red cloisonné ginger-jar lamps topped with white fan shades. For the small dining room they chose an oval glass table with matching cane-back chairs. Dorsey decided on a king-sized bed with a matching blond dresser for her bedroom, while Shane and Alexandra, sharing the master bedroom, opted for double beds with a large nightstand situated between them and two tallboy dressers for their clothes.

After the furniture was delivered and set in place, they purchased lush green plants, setting and hanging them everywhere as accents, along with beautifully mounted and framed posters and photographs. Finally, at the end of four days of intense decorating, they stood back, scrutinizing and examining their handiwork, deeming it a definite success.

Then came the special touches as each girl marked her corner of the house the way a cat marks his territory. For Dorsey it was a pair of tiny white crocheted ballet slippers strung with delicate white satin ribbons. They had been made long ago by a favorite nanny who loved her, and she hung them on her mirrored dresser, one against the other, over a Baccarat crystal bowl filled to the brim with a colorful assortment of pills.

For Alexandra the personalizing of her space was done with a magnificent array of stuffed animals she'd collected over the years, each one bearing its own special name and taking its own particular hierarchical position against the pillows of her bed.

For Shane, the personal touch was provided by a huge photograph of Francesca Adair and a multitude of handblown crystal figurines, each one so tiny and delicate that a single, unthinking blow to her dresser might have rendered them little more than a fistful of glass.

They scoured the dime stores for the rest, purchasing clear glass dishes, bright red and yellow coffee mugs, pots, pans and stainless-steel flatware. And when they had finished, including a stop at the supermarket, where Shane lectured them on the value of one thousand as opposed to four hundred sheets of toilet paper per roll, they considered themselves house veterans, ready to take on any decorating assignment thrown their way.

The first night they spent together at the new apartment the three pledged devotion and· support for one another, swearing never to participate in the usual competitive backbiting so common among ballet dancers.

They communed on Dorsey's king-sized bed late at night, with a flickering candle casting shadows across the ceiling and walls. Sitting cross-legged in T-shirts and panties, with Clearasil dotted on their pimples and their long hair hanging loose over their shoulders—"resting" from the regulation bun required in daily class—they crunched popcorn and swore that their friendship would always be special.

"We'll be like sisters," Alexandra promised earnestly.

"Yes," Shane added, spitting popcorn as she spoke. "Like the Three Musketeers."

"One for all and all for me," Dorsey laughed.

Alexandra's small teddy bear landed on Dorsey's head. "Quit kidding, you goose. This is serious." She retrieved her furry companion and straightened the ribbon around its neck.

"Okay," Dorsey said. "Then I'll share all my dieting secrets with you and you'll both be as gorgeous as me."

"And you can borrow my leotards and tights," Shane offered, digging her hand deeper into the popcorn bowl.

"But ask permission first," Alexandra added. Her eyes hungered after the popcorn. "Respect each other's space."

"And if one of us finds a good dance partner in class," Shane said, swallowing popcorn, "we won't hoard him."

"Wait a minute," Dorsey said, holding her hand up like a stop sign. "You're in dangerous territory now. A line must be drawn when it comes to men."

Embarrassed, Shane explained, "I didn't mean it *that* way."

They joked a little longer, then Alexandra continued in a

more serious vein. "And we should help each other—in every way," she said. "I mean it."

"Of course," Dorsey added with a straight face. "I, for one, promise never to stand in the wings praying for one of you to break a leg so I can dance your part."

She laughed as fistfuls of popcorn rained on her head. Soon the hour grew late and Shane and Alexandra trotted off to bed with the former blowing out the candle as they left.

An hour later Dorsey wakened to the sounds of someone sobbing in the house. She left the bed and opened her bedroom door to find Shane in the living room, crying, huddled in a wicker chair, with her knees drawn up to her chest, cradling a fistful of Kleenex. Dorsey sat down beside her and covered Shane's shoulders with her own thin arms.

"There, there, Shaney baby," she said, hugging her friend. "Don't cry. The first night away from home's always the hardest."

Shane blubbered something incoherent against Dorsey's rail-thin body, then let her tears fall freely. "I don't understand," she said between gasps. "I always thought I'd be happy to get away from her but I . . . I miss her, dammit, and I don't know why. Most of the time she just carps at me."

Dorsey lifted a tissue from the box and dabbed at Shane's eyes. Then she closed one around Shane's nostrils. "Blow!" she urged. "Come on. Get the snot out. You'll feel better."

Shane took the tissue from Dorsey's hand and blew into the soft paper. "Why is life so damned confusing?" she asked, sniffling back. "Why?"

Dorsey had a hundred answers to Shane's question, and a hundred and one questions of her own. *Why indeed is life so damned confusing?*

"I can't answer that for you, Shane," Dorsey replied. "But you're not going through it alone. We all feel like that sometime or another. Even your mom must have problems."

She wrapped an arm around Shane's shoulder, cradling her head, rocking her gently as her own memory, prodded by Shane's tears, wandered back to a certain summer five years ago, almost one year to the day before her mother had killed herself.

"And mothers aren't angels. They don't always like us, either," she explained. "I remember flying home from Switzerland one summer, happy as a lark. Two days later my parents started arguing about *me*. I'm talking knock-down drag-out stuff that went on for hours. A stupid marathon." She laughed, but her laughter wasn't joyful. "Thank God for my dancing! I could always escape to ballet."

Shane smiled, understanding her remark.

"Well," Dorsey continued, "on the fourth night they stopped, then started up again and I sneaked to the top of the stairs to spy. My dad was acting like an asshole—silent as usual. And that always made my mother angrier." She mocked her mother's high-pitched voice: " *'I don't see you for months, Tom, for months on end.'* My mother was drunk at the time, you understand, but still very sharp." She imitated her mother's voice again. " *'Then you come trotting home from D.C. together with your lousy promises to be with me and I fall for it. Then the brat arrives and you spend all your time entertaining her.'* I sat there like a jerk, listening to the two of them carve each other up and blame me in the process. And I don't have to tell you how bad it hurt. But time marches on, and after she died, well, I missed her—a lot. Sure, I hated her for what she'd said that day. But I also understood. In spite of everything, including her sharp tongue, I loved and needed her. I still do."

Shane kissed Dorsey's cheek. "I'm sorry, Dorsey. I shouldn't complain or act like a baby anymore." She fidgeted for a second, as though she were trying to muster up courage. "Can I ask you a personal question?" she said.

"Shoot!" Dorsey replied. She sensed what was coming and steeled herself.

"Your mom, how did she . . . ?"

Dorsey's body grew cold and rigid. "Don't ask me that, Shane. Never ask me to talk about what happened that day."

She started to leave abruptly, then turned around. "But I will tell you this, if it means anything at all. There's a bottom line to everything in life, Shaney babe, and it's this. You're all you've got in the world and you'd better learn to count only on yourself. Now, c'mon. Let's both get some rest."

In her dream Alexandra climbed a mountain. Thirsty, drained, she was fighting to reach the top, where some clean white snow lay waiting. When she reached her destination, she sucked in a handful only to discover it wasn't snow at all, but sweet whipped cream. Headfirst, she plunged into the drifts, swallowing until the mountaintop was gone and her stomach was satisfied.

She wakened with a start at 4 A.M.

In the blackness of the room she grew aware of how hungry, how ravenous she really was. At first she was afraid to move, afraid if she did she would rush to the kitchen and devour everything in sight. Then she talked silently to herself the way Birdie would have. No, she swore. Not this time. This time she was going to succeed.

She pulled her knees into a fetal position, drew her pillow around her head and prayed. She prayed the pangs of hunger digging holes in her stomach would recede. But they didn't. Instead they held greedily, creating an emptiness, rumbling in the deepest part of her belly. She knew then that the act of dieting, of prohibition had only increased her desire for food.

Food!

She yearned for a bowl of Birdie's rice pudding, for her seven-layer fudge cake, for those chocolate chip cookies hoarded in the cookie jar. That's when she remembered the

Hershey bar stashed inside her leather purse, and she knew then it was all over.

She left the bed, tiptoed through the darkness, her mouth watering, salivating, needing the sweet the way a dog craves water on a blistering day. When she reached her leather purse, she opened it and groped inside for the candy. Finding it, her heart beat wildly. She looked across at the sleeping Shane, then snatched at the candy. Quickly she left the room, unable to wait another second.

Inside the darkened living room, she slumped feverishly in a corner, ripping off the wrapper, smelling the aroma, taking the first bite, letting the rich sweetness dissolve slowly in her mouth. Everything tasted good, wonderful— everything but the guilt.

Chapter 16

The night before the new quarters officially opened, Richard Caligari strolled through the carpeted hallways, the airy rehearsal halls, the multipurpose schoolrooms and the magnificently furnished offices. He felt like a king. Just a few weeks ago he'd had nothing to his name, including hope. Today, he was gazing at everything he could ever wish for and it was turning him on. The beautiful Romanov witch had not only kept her part of the bargain, but she had done it with high style and very expensive taste. The rest was up to him.

Still wearing his dance apparel, he strolled onto the darkened stage of the ground-floor theater, carrying several local newspapers in his arms. New York City's most important critics were already speculating about the dance master's newest works, and he wanted to read every article.

Besides that, he'd been inundated with phone calls, bombarded with nosy questions from a curious press that wanted to know about his secret benefactor. He'd spent a good deal of time throwing them off track, hiding behind jokes. And so the mysteries flourished, a state of affairs that tickled him.

None of their questions really worried him. There was no way anyone could uncover his money source. Julia would keep her silence because of Alexandra. And it would take a shot of sodium pentothal to make him talk.

He strutted through the wings of the empty stage, strolled past the computerized call board, looked down at the open orchestra pit, around at the proscenium with its enclosed gold-leaf arch, up at the spotlights, down at the footlights, out to the mezzanine and balcony and it was heaven.

By the time they returned from their European tour for the gala, it would be finished, complete with that magnificent chandelier hanging from the ceiling's center and the seats smothered in new red velvet. Of course it wouldn't be as large as the old City Center, or as grand as Lincoln Center, but its promise was one of beauty, and best of all it belonged to him.

Down in the orchestra section of the theater, he sat seventh-row center and leaned back, dreaming of the Christmas Gala. From there, his thoughts wandered off to the several new ballets he was creating, all in various stages of mental gestation. One, a story ballet, concerned Dracula, that pathetic and loveless man doomed to wander the earth searching for the one woman willing to die for him so he could rest forever in eternity. Another, "The Lovers," he had drawn from a famous Picasso painting he had always admired.

The juices were flowing inside him again now that he'd given up the miserable guilt, and he was ecstatic. At last he could concentrate on his work and on the several new dancers who were beginning to inspire and touch his imagination.

There was Shane Laser, for example, so lyrical with her perfect balances which made for such dramatic moments on stage—and her hairpin turns, which were breathtaking. And Dorsey Childs, with her amazing and articulate feet and those incredible bourrées, which gave the impression she was floating across the stage, borne on invisible wings.

He closed his eyes in the darkness to visions of the crimson and gold curtains rising, to a conductor's baton raised and poised for a downbeat and he realized he could never go back again to the way things used to be. Now he was free from worry, free to create, able to express himself in any way he desired, and it was exhilarating. It was the opportunity of a lifetime, he thought. And it was all because of her.

Julia.

He'd been thinking about the wicked lady far too often lately, thinking of those incredible blue eyes, thinking of those long legs curling under her thighs and of that pretty pink tongue flicking its point around those ripe black olives.

He wondered how her tongue would feel along his lips or thrust deep into the warmth of his mouth, sliding along the ridges of his teeth. Soon the muscles in his stomach quivered with excitement, wakening with her sexy image, and he twisted in his seat to contain the feelings.

It was a useless maneuver, though. Through his tights, underneath his strong dancer's belt, his cock throbbed and hardened, grew rigid and thick against the muscle of his thigh. He sucked in his breath and pressed a fist against the hard-on for relief, shifting and pulling the cotton fabric away for comfort.

This evidence of his strong attraction to her not only surprised him, it made him uneasy. Julia Romanov was certainly not his type. The females he'd romanced in the past—and there had been many—had all been younger, naïve, more easily molded to his tastes. Julia Romanov was not only mature, she was tough, unaccustomed, he imagined, to softness or surrender. And in any relationship, those things were important to him. But did it matter? He couldn't imagine anything serious happening between them anyway. So there was no reason to dwell on it.

As his sexual feelings subsided, he switched on a small tensor light located near the seat beside him and opened the pages of the newspaper. He bypassed the awful headlines, turning quickly to the theatrical section, where reports about his company's progress lay. There, near an article on

Francesca Adair and her nightly treks to see Ilya Kremorkin's performances in Japan, lay a photograph of Julia.

He studied her face for a while, trying to place the very familiar male companion sitting beside her, but nothing registered. Then a light inside his head switched on. With a touch of fascination which turned to instant recognition, he burst out laughing. Was he seeing things? Was it really him?

Getting hold of himself, he smirked as he read the caption that lay beneath the picture. No. He wasn't seeing things at all. There it was in black and white.

JULIA ROMANOV AT FOUNDERS' CHARITY BAZAAR
WITH CONSTANT ESCORT, FORMER LONDON BALLET'S PREMIER DANSEUR, VIDAL GENERO.

Poor little Julia, he thought, chuckling wickedly. *I wonder if she knows*. And with that thought fixed deliciously in his mind, he folded the newspaper, tucked it under his arm and left the theater laughing. There was more than one way to skin a cat, he knew, and this little kitten was coddling her own weapon.

Chapter 17

Sitting inside Japan's National Theater, Francesca Adair waited for the lights to dim. She had caused a minor stir in the theater's lobby and regretted not having put on a black wig. Thank God for the Japanese sense of decency and decorum. They would do little besides quietly whisper. Now she could relax.

Two weeks ago her jet had touched down at New Tokyo International Airport and she'd had high hopes that the Russian authorities would permit her to visit Ilya Kremorkin backstage. But no such luck. She might just as well have asked for an audience with the Pope.

She recalled her brief conversation earlier with her good friend, Senator Thomas Childs, and bristled.

Sitting at the window of her suite at the Prince Akasaka Hotel, thirty-seven stories above Tokyo's bustling Akasaka District, she heard the phone ring and quickly picked it up. She'd waited hours for the overseas operator to connect her with Washington and it had finally come through.

"Hello? Yes, operator. This is she."

She placed the cup of tea she'd been drinking on the white marble table, covered one ear and waited again.

"Tom? Is that you? Speak louder. I can't hear a word."

"Francesca," Senator Childs called loudly. "How are you? And why the devil are you calling so early?"

"Oh, don't be so lazy, you old goat, and give me some good news for a change."

The Senator laughed. "I wish I could, Frannie. But it's hopeless. They won't budge an inch on this one."

"Fuck them! Why the hell not?" she shouted.

"They say security. Too many problems."

"You mean too many defections, don't you?"

"Probably. But whatever it is, I'd advise you to give it up."

"My God. I just want to meet the man." She paused. "Did you tell them who I was?"

"I did."

"And it didn't matter?"

"Not to the Russians. A Hollywood film star's just a cut above garbage. Now, if you were a chess player I could possibly arrange something."

After some more small talk, they said good-bye. And she was now at Japan's National Theater waiting for the curtain to rise.

The chandelier dimmed finally and as the orchestra began to play, the audience grew silent. There was total darkness on stage, followed by a cone of pale blue light. Then the bold, handsome Ilya leaped on stage dressed in white tights and an open white shirt, with his long blond hair flying about his head like a silken halo.

A delicious heat warmed and invaded Francesca Adair's groin and she twisted her back, shifting her position. She felt heady, faint at his power. Sweat glistened from his arms and chest, and she watched with growing fascination as the muscles of his backside hardened and relaxed. His leaps stole her breath away, his spins raised goose pimples along her arms. And as she watched him move she conjured images of him taking her and making her his slave.

Oh, she would have him all right. It was only a matter of time. In a few weeks the Bolshoi would be in Rio, then Europe, and she would be there, waiting. Waiting for the right moment. And it would come.

Chapter 18

A week before she was scheduled to leave for Paris, Julia came down with a dreadful cold. Miserable, sick with fever, she had to scrap not only her business schedule but her vacation plans as well. In her place she sent Gregory Kingston to barter for the business property she had initially negotiated, postponing the magnificent cruise she and Vidal had planned to take.

At home in her bedroom, dressed in a Dior peach silk nightgown with matching lace jacket draped across her shoulders, she lay in bed on a mountain of satin pillows, pampering herself with a cup of Birdie's homemade chicken soup. Vidal Genero lay at her feet, wrapped in a green velour robe, listening as she barked orders to her secretary on the telephone.

"Have Kingston call me the moment he finishes the Paris deal," she said. "And send over the art-inventory ledger."

While she talked, she scanned the pages of the *Wall Street Journal,* making a mental calculation of the profits she had earned by dumping the Al-Cal stock. Kingston had been wrong this time. Al-Cal had risen ten points the day before she had sold it and had declined a week later, continuing even now on the descent. "And," she continued into the phone, "send my thanks to Mrs. Boothby for her invitation to the Summer Arts Festival. Vidal and I are looking forward to it."

When she hung up, she set down her cup, tossed the papers aside and plumped the pillows behind her. Now it was time to relax.

"I thought you'd never get off that bloody phone," Vidal said, creeping toward her on all fours. "You're supposed to be sick, remember?"

Julia kicked him playfully. "I remember, darling. But there's something about doing business that always makes me feel good."

"Here's something to make you feel good," he said, pouncing on her.

An instant later they were rolling on the bed, giggling like children, with Julia's hands protesting his scattered kisses. "Vidal, please! My bones hurt too much to make love."

"In that case," Vidal said seductively, "allow me to repair your bones."

She smiled, watching in amusement as he crawled to the foot of the bed. Then, with his enchanting gray eyes fixed on her face, he swept his hands beneath the plump satin covers. His slow movements along her legs were all deliberate, willful, designed to excite, to stimulate, to provoke and arouse. She was game, a rosy prey just waiting for capture.

She closed her eyes and felt his articulate fingers explore the tender bottoms of her feet. "Oh! That feels *sooo* nice," she sang as his thumbs pressed against the aching pads of her feet.

"Good," he murmured against her ankle. "Now just relax. Let my fingers do the walking."

She giggled and let her head settle back on the peach satin pillows behind her.

She arched her feet as he separated her toes and sucked each of them into the moist heat of his mouth. In a few moments she was lost to the feelings, melting, clutching the covers. In a few minutes she was ripe, ready to be taken, abandoning herself with pleasure to the warm cream coating her vaginal walls.

She writhed at the hot-and-cold exhalations of his breath as his tongue licked the skin of her calves. She moaned as his strong hands raised the hem of her gown. Soon he was a tangle of hair, all hot breath and snaky fingers undulating like ocean waves toward her burning patch. Each feathery movement was calculated to arouse, perceptively measured to stimulate, each caress molded to the curves of her slender body. Seconds after he had removed her clothes, he teased open his own robe and let it fall.

She stared at his naked body as his robe dropped away. He was gorgeouss, irresistible, all tan and broad shouldered, with a thin line of brown hair that curled down his belly like an arrow toward his cock. She was fascinated with his ease, with his lack of shame.

He came toward her, fell beside her and took her in his arms. Then he crushed her body to his. His prick throbbed against her belly, leaping and pulsating with a life of its own. And as his arms surrounded her, as she surrendered into the warm cocoon, his knee slipped between her thighs.

She spread herself wide to receive him, felt his fingers tickle and stroke her warm insides. Responding, she locked her thighs around his hand and arched her pelvis.

"Make me come," she challenged, tensing and thrusting her groin toward him. "Now. Now!"

He stroked the soft hairs of her mound, letting his thumb vibrate deep inside her. He buried his lips in her hair and sank his teeth in the flesh of her shoulder. She soon realized her bones no longer hurt, that the tension and ache in her body had vanished. But a new fever had taken its place. A burning heat seared her groin as the scent of musk surrounded them.

He kissed her throat and sucked her nipples till the pink buds were sore and burning. When she begged him to stop, he soothed them with his tongue, with puffs of cool breath, and she shivered.

"Oh, Vidal," she whispered. "You're the most exciting man I've ever known."

As his tongue thrust deep into her ear, the ocean roared through her brain. She was high on him, lost on a tropical island of her own design where a hot jungle sun beat down on her limp body.

Then suddenly the bed shifted as he crawled below.

She trembled as he separated the plump cheeks of her behind and let his wet tongue glide along the crack. She moaned with delight as he vibrated at the vaginal opening, fluttering his fingertips along the sensitive folds. Seconds later he kissed her and was on his knees, pushing his cock inside her.

Feeling him enter, she was alive with desire, bathed in fear, in anticipation, holding him, waiting for some unknown salvation.

Her hands gripped his sweating back as his buttocks rose and fell; her nails scratched his arms. And when there was no space between his powerful thrusts, she coaxed and urged him on. Close to climax, she bit his chin, his shoulder, waiting for *it* to happen. And then his body crushed hers, and as he screamed his ecstasy, he came . . . without her.

She wanted to shake him, to slap him, to scream of her need, but she couldn't bring herself to do it. Ashamed, she arched her back instead and, like a hundred times before, began to fake it.

She contracted her vaginal muscles around his spurting organ. She cried out with false pleasure and manufactured sounds of joy. She called his name out loud and let go with make-believe spasms of her own.

"You're beautiful!" Vidal whispered just before he fell limply on her body, into a deep and satisfying sleep. "So . . . incredibly . . . beautiful. . . ."

She forced a smile at his words. She had heard them many times before, and from so many kinds of men—rich, poor, old, young, handsome and profane. They were the words that made her skin crawl because deep inside where she really lived was an ugly duckling who, try as she might, could never reconcile her present beauty with the hidden truths of her past.

Julia Romanov had been born the very ordinary daughter of an extraordinary, vain and sexually promiscuous woman of self-proclaimed Russian nobility. And Tatiana Romanov never let her daughter forget that. For hours on end the young Julia would watch her mother brushing her dark black hair at the mirror and applying makeup to her eyes. For many years Julia believed herself to be just as beautiful, then she accidentally overheard Tatiana's private conversation with Papa Dimitri before retiring to bed. She had gone to their bedroom for her good-night kiss, then stood quietly at the door listening to their conversation.

"I don't know what to do with her, Dimitri. Julia is quite plain. With her funny nose and her weak chin and that tiny forehead, what shall I do?"

"She's a baby, Tati. She'll grow out of it," Dimitri insisted.

The shock waves of that conversation would run through Julia's childish body, reverberating over and over in her mind for years to come. She was actually homely and she had to face that fact. Then, on her sixteenth birthday, Tatiana made some very drastic changes.

She dragged Julia to the finest Fifth Avenue dermatologist to consult on the young girl's mottled complexion. She flew her to the foremost plastic surgeon in Brazil to reconstruct her slightly hooked nose and the just perceptibly receding chin. In Paris, stylist Reña Manon straightened Julia's kinky hair, brightened the mousy color and changed her irregular hairline by painful electrolysis until the tiny forehead was wide and beautiful.

"Thank God for your blue eyes," Tatiana had announced.

At a mountaintop clinic in Switzerland, the finishing touches were made on Julia's overweight body, and by the time Tatiana had finished her recreation and they'd arrived home to New York, Julia Romanov had become every bit as beautiful as Tatiana could ever hope to be. But her mother was still not satisfied. She would continue to interfere and meddle in her life in other ways.

With those physical changes, Julia's social life had become a whirl of romance, with handsome young men courting her, sending her flowers and jewels and extending invitations to the most glamorous places in the world. One of the young men was Giorgio Rivero, the handsome and spoiled son of a rich Milanese businessman whose relatives in America were deeply involved in a dozen business enterprises, only one of which included the shipping of oil. The other was Francis Timothy McIntyre, a handsome and sensitive young Irishman who claimed no wealth but who planned to return to Dublin so he could sculpt. Julia adored him, but Tatiana violently disapproved of their relationship.

They were arguing again, seated in the main salon of their Sutton Place apartment, surrounded by seventeenth-century Florentine tapestries, Venetian chandeliers, tables and settees all gilded and beautifully underscored by priceless, museum-quality silk Oriental rugs.

Tatiana spoke English slowly, with a heavy Russian accent as she crumpled a linen handkerchief in the palm of her hands.

"Do you know what you are refusing, *maya daragaya?*" came the emphatic and imperious pause, the one Julia hated with a passion. "You are forgetting you are cousin—"

"*Distant* cousin," the young and impatient Julia corrected.

"Cousin nevertheless . . ."

Listening to her speak, Julia cringed. She hated when Tatiana dragged out their supposed royal family connections to Czar Nicholas by way of a great-aunt's distant relationship to Dowager Empress Marie, mother to His Royal Highness, who was now living out her life in Copenhagen, an exile from Russia. It might have had meaning in Imperial Russia or even Paris, but here in New York City it was useless nonsense.

"So, when you are knowing this," Tatiana continued, "why you are considering marriage to such a poor man?"

Julia sighed. *"You* married a poor man, Mother, and it didn't hurt you one bit."

"Is true," Tatiana nodded. "Your father was poor when we marry, but he is also ambitious. And I believe always he will give me good life one day." She waved her hand around. "As you see, I am not wrong."

"But Francis is ambitious too, and besides, I have faith in him. More important, I love him with all my heart. He'll make me happy, you'll see."

"Love! Faith! Happy! You don't know what you say. Marry with head, and love will come later."

"Are you telling me you weren't in love with Papa when you married him?" Julia demanded.

"I say nothing except to think carefully before making such decision. Marriage is sacred act, forever, and you are needing more than this thing you are calling love."

"Why are you doing this?" Julia begged. "I've never been happier in my life. I'm in love with Francis and I want to marry him, to bear his children, to take care of him and spend the rest of my life making him happy."

"That I do not doubt, daughter, but will he do same for you if you have no access to Papa's money?"

"I can't believe you're saying this, Mother. It's 1965, not the turn of the century. People in America marry for love. Besides, what do I need with Papa's money? I have plenty of my own."

"Listen to me, Julia," Tatiana said. "In spite of my wrinkles, I am not old. But I have suffered a tragic life."

Julia winced. Here we go again, she thought.

"My mother," Tatiana continued, "your grandmother Juliana, for whom you are named, was beautiful young woman when she died. Before that she lived in Paris, exiled from all she loved, and it was horrible life. They put her in asylum when I am ten years old because she try to kill herself. In Russia she was like princess with everything. After Revolution, inside Paris, she was ugly old woman of thirty watching beautiful ball gowns turn to dust rags."

"Oh, Mother, you've told me all this before," Julia said impatiently. "But what does it have to do with Francis and me?"

"I tell you this because fish cannot live in same home as bird, even if love they share is great. I tell you because it is human nature to stay with own kind. You are rich, young, beautiful girl, cultured and educated too. You have good home and tender affection. Outside, world is cruel and this Francis, he is poor, with no home, no family, no culture and no education. Because of this he has no future. If you are not willing to see, I must see for you. Can you go easily to live in foreign country away from your family?"

"Ireland is hardly foreign," Julia said. "And besides, you and Papa left your homeland and came to America."

"Is different matter, Julia. We are forced to come here. But you will be far from America by choice. Far from your family, away from wealth and affection you have always known. No! Far too many changes for young girl to handle—even you, my pet."

"I appreciate what you're saying, Mother. I just don't agree. If Francis hasn't the money to start a business, I'll give him mine. And we'll grow together, just as you and Papa did."

"Not so," Tatiana corrected. "If you marry before twenty-one, you must wait until thirty for your trust."

Julia gasped.

"Your father do this," Tatiana continued, "how you say, purposely, so fortune hunter could not take it away. So, you will not only live in foreign country, you will have to manage without Papa's money, and I do not think that will be easy."

With Tatiana's continued pressuring, Julia's courage began to falter, finally vanishing completely until the ugly duckling that still lived inside her emerged again and her confidence waned.

Before long, the persistent Tatiana would have her way and a wedding would take place; not between Julia and Francis, but between Julia and Giorgio.

Convinced she now loved her mother's choice, the event of the New York social season happened exactly as the willful Tatiana had wished, with a magnificent church wedding at St. Sophia's, and a reception at the Hotel Pierre with five hundred guests in attendance.

Julia Romanov made a beautiful bride, dressed in a hand-beaded Paris gown with a twenty-foot train that took four months to fashion by seven tailors who worked around the clock. And on the day of her wedding she looked radiant and happy standing next to Giorgio, with his dark black hair and brown eyes, dressed in his pearl-gray tuxedo and silk top hat.

At the reception the side rooms for the Russian guests held islands of *zaccousky,* the deepest, darkest beluga caviar set in swan ice sculptures embedded with blood-red roses. At the bar, crystal glasses were filled with olive oil so guests could coat their stomachs before drinking the one-hundred-proof vodka. Mountains of *bliny, baclazhannaya, eekra* and herring with Russian black bread covered the tables, while Russian Gypsies with ribboned tambourines and golden earrings sang and danced to balalaika music.

For the American guests, there were fountains of Dom Pérignon champagne, finger sandwiches and small *galettes au Roquefort, canapés, pâté de foie gras, crèmes frites* and *fondue au Gruyère* flavored with mushrooms and wine.

In the main ballroom was a dinner fit for a king— chicken Kiev stuffed with iced butter, thick, rare roast beef *au jus* with braised artichokes, *timbale d'asperges,* tiny pearl onions and green peas with new potatoes sautéed in double-rich butter and tossed in fresh parsley.

For dessert was *café au lait,* glazed oranges, pear flan, and rum-soaked babas piled high with chocolate whipped cream and slivered almonds.

Then came the honeymoon.

As the inebriated wedding guests danced until dawn, the bride and groom were whisked away in a Bentley limousine to a chartered jet bound for London where a thousand-year-old manor house in the Cotswold Hills of England lay in preparation for the couple's arrival. Obviously tired from their long journey, Giorgio fell into a deep sleep on the plane with Julia cradling him in her arms, caressing his jet-black hair, which lay on her shoulders. She was convinced more than ever that Tatiana had been right, and she was filled with so much joy and happiness, anticipating all the romantic adventures their first night together would bring.

When they finally arrived at the old house, a coterie of servants stood waiting on the broad sweep of green lawn to greet them—three cooks, a butler, four maids, several groundskeepers, stable hands and a liveried chauffeur.

On their first night together, they were to dine alone in a large private wing that lay separate and far away from the servants' quarters. There, Julia dressed hurriedly in a white silk nightgown and matching chiffon peignoir from the House of Dior.

Excited, anticipating her first sexual encounter, she brushed her glossy hair, dusted her body with powder, sprayed custom-made colognes created especially for her by Guerlain. Everything was perfect. Giorgio Rivero was gorgeous, a rich and pampered young man born in Milan, educated in Switzerland, raised and spoiled by a family who adored and had given him everything he could ever ask for. Julia had met him at Christmastime a year ago on the ski slopes of Gstaad, and though she had not felt as she had with Francis, there had been a strange attraction she could not deny.

His dark eyes and coal-black hair made her knees quiver, her heart flutter, and that had to be some measure of love, she thought. But who could tell?

Now she reclined on a settee in the bedroom, a fire blazing in the black marble fireplace, filling the pale blue room with a soft orange glow. Near their four-poster wedding bed was a silver ice bucket with vintage champagne and two crystal glasses borne on the frosted wings of swans. As Julia waited for Giorgio to join her in a toast to their marriage, she sipped some of the bubbly to relax. She had waited such a long time for this special moment and it was hard to contain her excitement.

Then Giorgio arrived and she shivered in anticipation as he pushed open the door to their bedroom, leaned against it and slowly unbuttoned his silk shirt.

Tossing it to the floor, he stood with his hands on his hips, legs apart, wearing only his riding jodhpurs and long black boots. He looked handsome, like the hero in a very romantic novel. Earlier, he'd excused himself and had ridden across the lush green meadow after their long journey, "to relax," he'd told her, and she could still smell the horse's sweat mingling with his own. She felt incredible anticipation at his nearness and as his dark eyes swept the planes of her body. As he said her name, a strange and passionate heat brewed inside her.

Her breasts rose and fell with his every gesture, and her legs felt like sand as he approached her side. And when he reached a hand to undo the ribbons of her gown, she held her breath and nearly swooned.

The eyes of the innocent young bride followed Giorgio's stride to the champagne bucket, where she watched him draw his head back and drink from the bottle. She joked about his hearty thirst, but he didn't join her in the laughter. Half a bottle later a chill swept through her as he ran the back of his hairy arm across his lips and, without a word, came behind her.

He lifted her in his strong arms and threw her onto the bed as if she were a rag doll. He ran his fingers along the contours of her breast and she shook with terror. She smiled to placate him, but deep inside her a burgeoning fear plowed through her body like a freight train. Then he stood over her trembling body, leering as he opened his fly to expose himself.

She tried not to look, but she could see that he was hard and as huge as a bull, and the sight of his naked body terrified her even more. Beads of sweat broke out on her face and neck as his cold eyes focused on her intently. She quickly scrambled from his reach and drew the covers over her bosom. With a sinister laugh he snatched the quilt from her fingers and threw it to the floor. Then he ripped the beautiful gown from her body.

Her mouth went dry with fear, her heart leaped to her throat. "No!" she screamed as he dropped down beside her. "Don't touch me! You're drunk. You don't know what you're doing."

His response to her outcry was an angry fist across her jaw, and she lay shocked, stunned, unable to move. He held her arm and wedged her legs apart. He pushed his way through her dry folds, thrusting himself deep inside while she screamed in agony.

The pain was unbearable and though she fought him valiantly, her frightened protests only spurred him on. Again and again he slammed her, pinning her against the bed sheets, grinding his boots onto her legs.

"You're my wife!" he shouted as he kneeled across her and slapped her face. "Open your legs and enjoy it!"

Throughout the night he raped her, humiliated her, beat her into a state of total submission. And when she wakened the following morning, she was numb, still in a daze, both she and the sheets a mass of clotted blood. For a few days she couldn't move, could hardly remember who or where she was. Then a kind servant took pity on her and helped her to escape.

Safely in New York City, she set in motion a quick annulment and recovered her maiden name. She tried desperately to put the terrible experience behind her, to look forward to a new future, but that soon became impossible. Nine months later she gave birth to Alexandra, a living, breathing legacy to a time in her life she would rather have forgotten.

Faced with that reality, she resigned herself to two

things. First, she would spend the rest of her days doing the one thing she could always depend upon, and that was making money. In matters of business, one and one could always be counted on to make two, but in matters of love those numbers proved unreliable. One and one sometimes made three. And second, she would never again give in to anyone. Though the danger, the fear of Giorgio had long since passed, Julia remained to this day sexually inhibited, still wanting release but unable to function. And because of this she had never felt like a complete woman.

Chapter 19

On Saturday, the eve of their open-house party, Shane, Dorsey and Alexandra began the day with a strenuous barre, followed by an hour of pointe work, then a short class in pas de deux and by two in the afternoon they were free to clean house, shop and prepare food.

Invitations had been sent to everyone—Richard Caligari, Paige McDowell, Joshua, all the company members, and to each of the girls' parents. Everyone had agreed to attend, including Senator Childs, who would be flying in from London that same day.

Five days before the affair, Alexandra had begun limiting herself to eight hundred calories a day, and she was in a state of euphoria at her successful accomplishment. Although she hadn't lost more than a few ounces, she believed her weight problem was now firmly under control, and *that* was the most important thing to consider.

The night before the party, she had written in her diary of her private feelings and had closed and placed the book under her pillow. But sometime before the guests were scheduled to arrive she had retrieved it and sat cross-legged on her bed, reading what she had written.

*He's magnificent! Strong and handsome, and
he seems to know what everyone is thinking before
they even think it. Yesterday he came to my side
for the first time since I joined the company and
when he touched the inside of my knee for correction I almost jumped out of my skin. What
strength! What presence! And his voice—God! It
sounds like velvet, all soft and dark and deep.
Shane and Dorsey say I have a crush on him and I
suppose they're right. I don't know. All I know is I
want to dance for him, to jump and shine, to glide
across the stage like Makarova. But I can't deny
what they say, either. I do get these strange and
gooey feelings when he's around. Oh, well, who
knows!?*

Love,
A.

When Shane arrived home, she set a bouquet of spring
flowers in an old crystal vase, arranging them around some
delicate maidenhair ferns. She placed that on top of a lace
buffet tablecloth between two blue candles, where the food
would later be served. She called out a cheery greeting to
Alexandra, who stood in the kitchen busily mashing a
dozen egg yolks with mayonnaise for deviled eggs, and
Dorsey, who blended cooked bay shrimp and cream with
tartar sauce, a hint of dry mustard and some fresh dill, for
pâté.

Their buffet was scheduled for 7:30 P.M., so it was with
a degree of surprise that they responded to the security
doorman's call at six.

"Hello," Dorsey said, pushing on the intercom talk button.

"There's a Mrs. Laser here," the doorman called up.

Dorsey glanced over at Shane, who stood nearby with a
scowl on her face.

"She's too early," Shane whispered, shrugging her shoulders. "I'm sorry."

"Hey, forget it!" Dorsey told her. "Tell her to come on up," she said into the intercom.

Shane stomped into the kitchen and threw a wet sponge onto the blue-tiled counter. "Damn! She's impossible. She's been here practically every day since I moved in."

Alexandra hugged Shane's tightened shoulder. "Forget it, will you? It's all right. Dorsey and I understand."

Three minutes later Simone was inside the apartment, setting down brown paper bags filled with food she had prepared and taking charge of the household.

"I brought you some of my three-color Jell-O molds," she said, shuffling by them toward the refrigerator. "Everybody raves about them. And some chopped liver too."

She began rearranging the food, the settings, the flowers and candles, and an embarrassed Shane looked as if she could crawl into a hole.

"Just leave her alone," Alexandra whispered to Shane. "It's just a buffet."

When Simone seemed satisfied with every detail, she washed her hands and began to put things in their place. Then she cleaned the kitchen counters, grabbed her paper sacks and headed for the front door, where she said goodbye.

"Where are you going, Ma?" a surprised Shane asked. "The party's going to start in about an hour."

Simone stared at the floor. "I can't stay," she answered. "I have a lot of things to do. I just wanted to give you kids a hand, that's all."

As the girls tried convincing her to stay, Simone stood folding the paper bags she had brought. When she finished, she wished them luck and with a long, lingering glance around the apartment, left.

"Can you believe her?" Shane said as the door closed behind Simone. "She has to put her two cents into everything I do."

"Five cents," Alexandra corrected. "Inflation."

Shane didn't laugh.

"C'mon, Shaney babe," Dorsey said, trying to get her friend to lighten up. "Your mother means well."

"No, she doesn't!" Shane protested. "She just wants to make me feel lousy—to show me how inadequate I am."

"Well, it's too late to argue about it now," Dorsey remarked. "It's almost party time."

At seven-thirty Dorsey put some soft-rock records on the stereo. At seven-forty the first guests began to arrive: a few company members and Joshua, the pianist, carrying a Spanish guitar under his arm.

The apartment looked lovely, so festive and gay with colorful flowers and flickering candles, and the girls were filled with pride at their accomplishment. The lace-covered buffet table was now laden with lovely things to eat— monkey bread, cold sliced breast of turkey, assorted cheeses, fresh pasta salad, a variety of cream dips, shrimp pâté and deviled eggs. Even Simone's offerings were on the table.

For liquid refreshments they had concocted a delicious cold punch of pink champagne and pineapple juice, red rosé wine and sparkling club soda, all mixed with ice, fresh orange slices, and red cherries speared with pineapple chunks. By eight o'clock the party was in full swing. Except for the arrivals of Julia, Richard Caligari and Senator Thomas Childs, everyone was there.

At eight-fifteen promptly, the phone rang and Dorsey, almost as if she had been anticipating the call, picked it up. "City morgue," she said, forcing a smile.

"Hi, hon! Just wanted to apologize for not being able to make it tonight."

Dorsey's throat tightened at the sound of her father's voice. "Where the heck are you?"

"In California," Senator Childs answered.

Deandra, Dorsey thought. Goddamn fucking Deandra. "Why? What happened?" She dragged the telephone into her bedroom for some privacy and sat on her bed, swallowing the tears burning behind her eyes.

"Deandra's mother took a turn for the worse last night and I caught a direct Pam Am flight from London to L.A."

Anger, resentment and jealousy built steadily inside her, and she found release by tapping her foot on the floor. "So when will I see you?"

"Maybe next week," Senator Childs answered. "We'll see. I'll call you."

When she hung up the phone, Dorsey bitterly recalled all the times in her life her father had disappointed her. She was ready to throw herself across the bed and cry, but the bedroom door swung open and Shane entered. As she'd done a thousand times before, Dorsey swallowed her tears and hid her real feelings.

"Who was that?" Shane asked.

"My dad," Dorsey replied heroically. She turned away from Shane's searching green eyes and stared out the window.

"Out saving the world again, is he?"

Dorsey smiled. "Sure. Something like that. He can't make it."

Shane leaned over and kissed the top of Dorsey's blond head. "It'll be all right," she soothed her friend. "Caligari's here. The party's just beginning. Come out and have some fun."

"Sure," Dorsey said. "No problem. Just give me a few seconds to fix my lipstick."

When Shane left the room, Dorsey opened the top drawer of her dresser. She closed her eyes and plunged a hand into her crystal bowl, selecting at random a handful of pills. She swallowed them all without seeing what they were, wondering how they were going to make her feel. It didn't matter anyway. Anything had to be better than the way she was feeling right now. Fixing her lip gloss, she opened the door to the hallway, forced a smile and went back to the party.

The party was in full swing as Alexandra ladled punch

into a glass held aloft by Richard Caligari's strong hand. The man was gorgeous, handsome enough to grace the cover of *Gentleman's Quarterly*, she thought, or a movie screen, with his tan neck and broad shoulders draped in deep wine silk, those hard buns and thigh muscles covered in black gabardine and a black cashmere jacket and a paisley silk pocket handkerchief. All gorgeous!

"Can I get you something else?" Alexandra asked.

"Thanks, not right now," Caligari replied. He touched her shoulder, leaned toward her and spoke above the spirited din of two dozen lively people. "I can get something later."

Alexandra flushed with warmth at his touch. She felt dizzy as his Cartier cologne drifted toward her nostrils and knotted her stomach. Yes, she thought, as they headed toward the crowded living room. She was afraid to admit it, to face it, but she was developing more than a crush on the dance master, and *that* was one scary prospect.

By nine o'clock Dorsey had a dry mouth, wet palms, irregular heart palpitations and a rush of blood from her head to her ankles. As panic seized her, as anxiety and fear overwhelmed her, she rushed from a thousand laughing faces into the safety of her bedroom. There she slammed the door and swallowed a handful of tranquilizers.

Inside her bathroom she sat on the commode with the door locked and her head bowed and throbbing between her legs, almost paralyzed as she broke into a cold sweat. Ten minutes later the tranquilizers calmed her and she returned to the party still a bit dazed, searching the rooms for Shane.

When Shane opened the front door, she stood frozen. All heads swiveled in the direction of Julia Romanov.

Dressed in a black and white harlequin beaded Halston pants suit with a black fox Fendi jacket and diamond earrings, she was the center of attention. Shane gulped something that sounded like hello, then Alexandra took charge, introducing Julia and her escort, Vidal Genero, to everyone. She left the dance master for last.

"Mother, this is Mr. Caligari," Alexandra said.

Julia approached him, batted her sparkling blue eyes and extended her diamond-studded fingers. "How do you do," she said as though they were meeting for the first time. "I've heard so much about you."

"My pleasure," Richard Caligari said, bowing his head and kissing her hand in European fashion.

Alexandra's throat constricted with envy as a simmering jealousy sent her reeling into the security of the kitchen.

When Julia introduced Vidal, Caligari's remark startled her.

"I believe we've met before," Caligari said, shaking Vidal's hand vigorously. "Several years ago, in London."

Vidal searched his memory, then smiled as if embarrassed. "Of course," he answered. "I'd completely forgotten. It's good to see you again."

When they were alone in a corner of the room, Julia pressed Vidal for the details.

"I met him briefly nine years ago," Vidal admitted. "He wasn't the rage he is now, so it simply slipped my mind." Then he filled his glass with champagne punch and swallowed it all in one gulp.

Alone in her bedroom, sulking, Alexandra swallowed a full glass of punch. She stuffed a huge turkey sandwich into her mouth along with Simone's Jell-O, followed by a pint of Häagen-Dazs peach ice cream.

"We're a hit!" Dorsey said as she stumbled into the room, giggling like an idiot.

"So how come I'm depressed?" Alexandra asked. She spooned more ice cream into her mouth.

"That's *tooooo* easy," Dorsey replied, trying to keep her balance. "Your pretty mother's got the hots for your hero, and he's making goo-goo eyes at her."

* * *

Julia's eyes were fastened on Caligari as Joshua handed him the guitar and begged him to play. But the dance master needed little coaxing. The moment he embraced the old Goya instrument, the moment his slender fingers strummed the minor chords with some haunting Gypsy melody, a crowd gathered.

Julia perched on a chair and listened, gazing at his silky black hair, which tumbled in soft waves across his wide forehead, studying his dreamy black eyes which smoldered with intense passion. She felt a sweeping rush of tension grip her muscles, a peculiar tingling which drifted from her spine to the tip of her toes.

He was riveting, handsome, fascinating, mysterious, and the harder she tried to tear her eyes away and look at something else, the more difficult it became. She was drawn to the way he cradled the guitar against his chest, the way his fingers fluttered across the strings, the way his mouth and tongue ruminated on the lengthy trills and deep bass passages. And when their eyes met for a brief instant at the conclusion of his song, Julia felt the blood warm her cheeks.

Caligari's eyes closed on the image of Julia as he finished playing. There was utter silence, followed by a round of hearty applause which the dance master acknowledged with a smile. He pressed the guitar back into Joshua's hands and after refusing requests for an encore, headed toward the buffet table for refreshments.

He stood nibbling cold turkey and was pouring himself a glass of punch when a sudden swirl of perfume surrounded him. A gentle voice purred behind his ear.

"May I?"

He turned and without thinking, surrendered his cup of punch. "You may," he said, ladling himself another. "Can I offer you something else?"

"Thank you, no," Julia replied.

There was an awkward silence, then simultaneously each asked the same trivial question about the weather and both laughed as their words collided. The ice between them had been broken.

"How's Alexandra doing?" Julia asked as she placed her lips around the cup and sipped.

"Fine," he answered. He could not keep himself from drifting off into her blue eyes or trying to imagine what her satin hair would feel like against his lips.

The rest of their conversation centered on such inane topics as the effects of vitamin B-6, the best restaurant in Chinatown and baseball. As time flew by, Caligari realized his heart was pounding like a schoolboy's and his muscles were involuntarily clenching at each of her gestures.

He made a conscious effort to relax his breathing but soon found himself mesmerized by the candlelight halo surrounding her silky brown hair. And as she drained her punch, he recalled that black olive she had toyed with at their luncheon, because she was teasing him once again, this time with a ripe, red cherry from the punch.

Suddenly, without warning, she reached across and brushed lint from his shoulder. The touch of her hand sent chills through his body. He had not responded this way to a woman in a very long time and it unnerved him. In a few minutes he was in a cold sweat and asked her permission to remove his jacket.

"Of course," Julia said.

Her flesh awakened as she stared at his body—arm and chest muscles outlined through wine-colored silk, the deep natural tan of his Gypsy heritage boldly displayed by his open shirt. She felt dizzy standing next to him, feeling his body heat radiate toward her like the shock waves of an earthquake. Quickly she swallowed the rest of her drink and held the cup out for more.

The music in the room changed suddenly from the driving beat of Billy Idol to an old romantic Nat "King" Cole ballad, and Caligari asked Julia to dance.

"Dance? With you? But I'm not very good," she said, setting her cup down and following his lead.

"Don't worry, I'll show you," he told her.

She felt his warm fingers curl around hers and sucked in her breath as he led her past the buffet table to a quiet corner. When he swung her around and pulled her in his arms, she fit easily into the waiting contours of his body. Neither said a word as they swayed, but Julia noticed her own breathing align with his in a chorus of soft exhalations.

He held her gently at first, like a delicate bird. Then, as the music played, his grip tightened. She felt his strong arm curve around her waist, felt his palm press against the small of her back as he pulled her closer.

She reached up and curved her fingers around the nape of his neck. He was irresistible, and many times she had to remind herself not to hold him too tightly or breathe too close to his ear. They were business partners and nothing more. But, oh, the feel of him. And just as she surrendered to his beckoning body, there was a tap on his shoulder as Vidal cut in.

From a corner of the room, Paige McDowell jealously watched the love of her life dance with the beautiful Julia Romanov, and it hurt. She knew that look in his eyes. Once upon a time he'd had it just for her. Now everything had changed. In the years since their divorce, she'd tried desperately to exorcise him from her brain but his image continued to live there, tonight more strongly than ever.

She would leave eventually, she knew, try to survive without him. Either that, she'd decided, or she would just go crazy. Then a curious thought came to her. She hadn't thought of it in years. What might have happened to their relationship had she told him the truth three months before their divorce. Perhaps things would have changed if he had known, she thought. Perhaps they would still be together.

Mark Parsons and Rory Dalby huddled in a corner with Seth Pollace, drinking punch. Rory had spiked their cups with vodka and they were feeling no pain. Now, as they watched the crowd fawn over the dance master, Mark complained bitterly about the tongue-lashing he'd received in class this morning.

"Did you hear the way he yelled at me today? Shit! Who the hell does he think he is, Balanchine?"

"You're too sensitive," Seth told him as he lit a cigarette. "Just do it the way he wants and quit screwin' around."

"And you're fucked!" Mark answered. "Just wait till it's your turn to dance with the prima ballerina." The reference was to Paige. "Then tell me how you feel. She's a tub of lard. Feels like dead weight when I lift her."

"I've lifted her before," Seth said. "Felt fine to me. Like a butterfly."

"Shit!" Rory said. "You both sound like a couple of assholes. So she had a bad day. So what! She's still gorgeous to look at. I know a dozen guys who'd give their right arm to dance with her."

Mark laughed. "If they gave their right arm, what would they lift her with?"

Rory snickered. Seth just grinned his reservations.

"The man's an asshole besides," Mark said. "Pussy-whipped all the way. Just look at him operate over there."

"Quit complaining!" Seth said. "When was the last time you had an opportunity to go to Europe and dance with someone like Paige."

"*If* we get to Europe, you mean," Mark said.

"Don't listen to him, Seth," Rory said. "He gets a few drinks and likes to sound off."

"Shit! No big deal. I've been to Europe dozens of times," Mark sneered. "My family has country homes in London and outside Paris. I can go anytime I want to."

"Well, go then!" Seth said, disgusted. Then he moved from the group to dance with Dorsey.

"Guy's a jerk!" Mark said.

"He's okay," Rory said. "You've just had one too many. You know how you get."

"I don't know," Mark said. "But I do get the feeling

Caligari's just using me. That he's getting ready to dump
me. And it's just a matter of time."

"More like your goofy imagination," Rory insisted.
"Working overtime."

By midnight, people were beginning to drift off and by
1 A.M. everyone had gone. The party had been a success,
the girls agreed as they cleared away glasses and emptied
food trays, yet later each lay in bed with thoughts of failure.

Alexandra had scrapped her diet because of Julia and in
her diary expressed her disappointment at Caligari's behavior. She could not believe in her wildest imagination that
the famed choreographer would even speak to her mother,
let alone find her interesting. From a "10," in her opinion
the dance master had gone down to a "6."

Shane felt humiliated, annoyed at her mother's unwel-
come visits. But she was also sad that Simone had not
stayed to enjoy herself. Of course she knew the reason
why. It was always the same with Simone. Embarrassment,
shame at her leg. And it would haunt her even more at a
party filled with ballet dancers.

For Dorsey it had been another exercise in familial futil-
ity. But this disappointment had been the straw to break the
camel's back. There would be no next time for him, she
thought, drifting off to a troubled sleep. Never again! Not
for him or anyone else. Then again, what did it matter? In
a few weeks they'd be leaving for the Hamptons to rehearse for their European tour. Maybe she could forget him
there. Build a new and better life for herself in ballet, in
performing.

Chapter 20

      As the warm spring days dwindled and the hot summer months approached, Caligari outlined his plans for the company. Everyone was ecstatic. During July and August, while the city steeped in a heavy, sweltering heat, the company would stay cool in the Hamptons at a large oceanside mansion, preparing for the European tour.

During his solitary evenings, Caligari had created a new ballet for Paige and was also contemplating some solo work for Shane and Dorsey. Nothing was said about Alexandra.

"Wait until we get to the Hamptons," Dorsey reassured her. "He'll do something special for you. You'll see."

A disappointed Alexandra spent half her time crying, the other half trying to please Caligari—neither of which helped or satisfied her.

Two days before they were scheduled to leave for Long Island, they were granted time off to shop for and pack personal things. Paige McDowell prepared a list of suggestions to bring along and they fanned out across the city to buy them.

Dorsey, Shane and Alexandra spent the day purchasing new pink tights and black leotards—standard class uniform—and half a dozen pairs each of satin toeshoes which would barely constitute a six weeks' supply. Caligari would buy the others.

Then came the special touches every female dancer tries

to find: unusual hair ribbons and flowers, extraordinary belts or scarfs and colorful rehearsal clothes to make her look unique and pretty, apart from the rest.

Then the toeshoe rituals began.

At home Dorsey pulled the shank nail out of each shoe and scored the undersides with a special claw knife so they'd be less slippery. Then she set the arches very high to make her foot look prettier.

Alexandra closed hers in and out of a doorjamb until they were soft and pliable. Then she sewed an extra bit of elastic to fit across her ankles for security.

Shane's ritual was one Simone had taught her: a cross between the two her roommates used, except for some elaborate cross-stitching sewed on the shoes' points to make them last longer.

Besides the other purchases, each bought extra pink satin lacing ribbons, stage as well as street makeup and clear Future floor wax to bake their toeshoes in for when they grew too flexible to support them.

It was 10 P.M. Time to relax. They were exhausted from all the preparations and were now sitting on Dorsey's king-sized bed in their nightclothes, waiting to smoke a joint she was rolling.

"I've never smoked one before," Shane admitted.

"Well, I have," Alexandra said. "But it didn't do anything."

Dorsey licked the tissue papers with her tongue and expertly twirled the cigarette between her two fingers. "Don't worry," she said. "This grass is primo stuff—two hundred bucks a lid, guaranteed to blow you both away."

She lit the skinny cigarette, inhaled the smoke into her lungs and held her breath. Then she passed it to Shane as she exhaled. Shane coughed on the first drag as the smoke attacked her lungs. Alexandra puffed as though she had smoked the stuff all her life. Within ten minutes, time had ground to a halt as all three giggled at each other's comments, finding instant and profound humor in everything they uttered.

"I'm going to Brooklyn to say good-bye to my mother tomorrow," Shane boasted with her tongue glued to her palate. "Then it's five whole months rehearsing and touring Europe without her checking on my every move. Five beautiful months without her nagging."

"Oh, she's not so bad," Alexandra said. "Not as bad as mine, anyway."

"Foo! You're just jealous," Dorsey said, directing her remark toward Alexandra. The cigarette had relaxed more than Dorsey's body. It had also loosened her sharp tongue. "You just didn't like the way your hero danced with her at our party."

"That's not true," Alexandra said defensively. "Besides, Julia's not Caligari's type anyway. He was just being courteous."

"Jeez!" Dorsey exclaimed, slapping a hand on the bed. "Wouldn't Caligari make a neat stepfather?"

Alexandra's eyes widened first in disbelief, then in indignation. "Are you crazy? My mother and Richard Caligari? Ugh! That's like . . . like Gandhi marrying Francesca Adair."

"Speaking of Francesca, I read she was in Japan or someplace, following Kremorkin around the world." Dorsey's words sounded like a tape recorder at slow speed.

"Isn't she gorgeous?" Shane said.

"Maybe she'll marry Ilya and become your cousin or something."

"God forbid," Alexandra said. "One asshole in the family's enough."

"Adair is not an asshole. She's a cunt. There's a big difference," Dorsey said.

"Oh, you're both jealous of her," Shane said. "She's beautiful and a talented actress too."

"Not half as talented as my mother, may she rest in peace. She was the only woman I ever knew who liked a drink before cocktails. Christ! Now, there was a real nag."

"No, no, no, no," Shane chimed in. "You've both met her. Simone's brought nagging to a high art form."

"Hey," Alexandra said to Dorsey. "Why don't we get your dad to pass a new law against mothers who nag excessively? Like maybe exile them to some faraway island."

"No way," Dorsey said. "You'd never find a place big enough to take all those *mothers*."

They laughed at each other's jokes, then Shane said, "I hope I never nag my kids that way."

Dorsey glanced from her to Alexandra, then back again. "You gonna have kids?" she asked with disgust.

"Sure!" Shane said. "Aren't you?"

"Not unless they can find a way for me to have them outside my body."

"You'll change your mind," Shane continued. "Just wait till your biological clock runs down."

"By that time so will his biological *cock*," Dorsey continued. "Then it won't matter."

Laughing with tears in her eyes, Alexandra reminded them of the late hour and the girls retired to bed.

The following day, Alexandra said good-bye to Julia and Birdie. Julia hinted then that she might take the cruise she had previously canceled during the same time the company would appear in Europe. "Perhaps I'll see you in Paris," she said as Alexandra squirmed.

At home Dorsey relented and tried to reach her father by phone so she could at least have a last lunch date with him before leaving the city. But the Senator had already flown to France for an emergency NATO meeting, leaving a message with his secretary that he'd return in ten days and would contact Dorsey at her Hampton residence then. As a peace offering, he'd sent a huge bouquet of roses for good luck, along with his love.

Shane Laser took the steamy subway to Simone's apartment in Brooklyn so she could tell her mother a proper good-bye. And it was there she received the shock of her life.

Chapter 21

"What do you mean you're coming with us?"

"I've got a job as a seamstress with the ballet company," Simone said, rushing about to pack. "I'm going with you tomorrow."

Shane wanted to scream, to beat her head and hands against the walls in protest. "How? When?" was all she could say.

"Remember the day you auditioned?"

Shane nodded.

"Well, there was an ad for a costumer on the bulletin board. I pulled it off so no one else could see it and a week later I applied." Simone continued shuffling about the room as she spoke, folding and stuffing her things into a shabby suitcase. "At first they weren't sure they could afford me. Then they must have had a windfall or something 'cause three weeks ago Paige McDowell called and hired me herself."

"Why didn't you tell me before?" Shane demanded.

Simone paused and studied her daughter. "I wasn't sure I'd go at first. I signed a lease. Had to find someone to sublet the new apartment first. You know—so the rent would be paid. Then a few days ago, this nice young couple rented." Simone studied Shane's face. "What's the matter? Aren't you glad I'm going?"

"Sure. Sure," Shane lied. "Of course I'm glad. Why shouldn't I be?"

"She's coming along with us!" Shane screamed, tossing her hands into the air and throwing things around her bedroom in a frenzied search for her hairbrush. "She has a job with the company as a seamstress. My God! Can you believe it?"

A surprised Alexandra and Dorsey did their best to console and soothe her, to offer support and advice.

"Hey, it's not the end of the world," Dorsey told her. "Everything will be fine. Besides, we'll be with you, remember? One for all and all that shit."

Locating the brush, Shane sat on her bed yanking her long coppery hair with a vengeance, jerking the knots and tangles through the thick boar bristles. "But you don't know her like I do," she continued complaining. "She'll tell me what to wear and how to stand on stage and what to eat and how to go to the bathroom and which friends are doing what behind my back. I won't have a minute's peace with her around." Her tender scalp glowed a bright crimson at her self-inflicted rage.

Dorsey snatched the brush from Shane's nervous hands and eased it soothingly through Shane's long mane. "But this time you'll stand up to her."

"Yes," Alexandra said. She hugged the shaking Shane. "This is the most important time of your life, and you can't let your mother spoil it for you, no matter what."

"Yeah, sure. That's real easy for you to say," Shane whined. "Your mother's not going with us."

Alexandra smirked. "If I know Julia, she'll find some way to put her two cents in. You'll see. She'll show up one morning with all her diamonds and furs, and everybody will hop, skip and jump to please her."

In the midst of the discussion no one noticed Dorsey's attention begin to wane. Her gaze wandered off as she let Shane's hairbrush drop from her hands, to land soundlessly on the bed. And then she sat transfixed for a while, as if she were a million miles away. Shane finally nudged Alexandra as together they watched Dorsey rise from the bed and leave.

Both girls stared dumbfounded at Dorsey's silent exit, then at each other as Dorsey closed the door behind her.

"Has she been smoking any stuff?" Alexandra asked.

"No," Shane replied.

"Pills?"

"Who knows?"

"Was it something I said?" Alexandra whispered.

A light went on in Shane's head. "Something we both said, maybe." She paused. "How insensitive. Her mother's dead and we're always complaining about ours."

BOOK TWO

The Rehearsal

Chapter 22

At 9 A.M., two air-conditioned buses parked in front of the theater, opened their stainless-steel doors and swallowed whole all members of the Caligari Ballet Company, including the dance master himself, Paige, Joshua, Simone, and several new staff persons that had recently been hired. Within half an hour everyone's luggage was squeezed firmly into the buses' bellies and when the doors were finally closed, the group applauded.

Some dancers relaxed, shut their eyes and snuggled against one another in the comfortable chairs to get extra sleep. Others waited excitedly for the city's tall buildings to recede from view.

As the buses pulled out on the first leg of their 105-mile journey to the Hamptons, the humid air already smelled rancid. It was good to be leaving the city. In another hour the sidewalks would start to sizzle and it would be difficult to breathe. Kids in the ghettos would uncap fireplugs and romp naked through the rushing water while the ice cream men would sell everything but ice. Before the day was over, tons of egg creams and soda pop would slide down dry, thirsty throats and tempers would flare. One more time New York City would become a living, breathing inferno.

"Six weeks in the Hamptons," someone shrieked as they entered the Queens Midtown Tunnel.

"Six weeks of torture, you mean," Mark muttered under his breath.

On the long journey to the island, they sang raucous songs and chatted like magpies, wildly speculating on what the Hampton estate would look like.

"A palace," one girl declared.

"Mishagothic," another guessed, laughing.

"Early Bordello," came a giggle from the rear.

"Disneyland!" shrieked another.

They drank iced coffee and tea from thermos bottles, ate apples and sucked oranges. They peeled hard-boiled eggs but swallowed only the yolks. A few smoked cigarettes over the nagging protests of others, but as the city's concrete began to vanish and its strident voice grew still and silent, a greener, sweeter air surrounded them and everyone relaxed.

Attitudes changed as they passed through Hicksville, Plainview, Patchogue and Eastport, each town bringing them closer to their destination. Young faces beamed at the beauty of Shinnecock Hills, Water Mill and finally Bridgehampton, where their real joy and excitement emerged.

As they approached their destination, Caligari rose from his seat and stood near the driver, pointing out a tiny pebbled road which cut sharply to the right around Georgica Pond. There, he led the driver to another road lined with giant windswept treees which curved through a maze of hedges that led to a huge mansion.

Everyone gawked from the windows as the buses halted. The house was enormous, made of hand-hewn stone and stained-glass windows, with large wings on either side. Tall trees stood everywhere, along with mimosa, pampas grass, sweetheart ivy and rambling pink roses. Along the roadway red geraniums held hands with purple peonies, daisies and Charlie hoppers while an old-fashioned swing built for four swung gently back and forth, squeaking in a briny wind.

When the luggage had been unloaded, Caligari walked up the front steps of the mansion. He cupped his mouth and called the group to order. "Attention, everyone, please!" he said, clapping his hands loudly. Within seconds all eyes and ears were upon him as the attentive crowd stood restlessly quiet, waiting for the dance master to speak.

"Your rooms are numbered, ready and waiting," he told them, "and as soon as the household help has shown you to your quarters, join me for a short assembly in the ballroom before lunch."

Everyone scrambled to follow his wishes, and after half an hour they were back, sitting cross-legged on the wooden floor of the large ocean-fronted room, waiting for Caligari to address them.

The grand ballroom was stately, like something from *Gone With the Wind,* and except for mirror-covered walls, a black grand piano, some portable ballet barres and several comfortable chairs, it was totally devoid of furniture.

Caligari walked about, touching individuals as he passed. "As you can see, the house we're in is splendid, and I want to remind each of you that we're guests here. The household staff is employed to take care of the property and not to do errands or make your beds or wash the rings from your bathtubs. But there *are* some special accommodations.

"Your meals will be served thrice daily in the main kitchen, which will be open twenty-four hours a day. So please don't take food to your bedrooms. And there are laundry facilities located in a nearby cottage." He paused a moment, walked to the front of the room, then quickly turned around. "I want you to know how much I'm looking forward to the European tour, and I expect each of you to be down here early tomorrow morning dressed and ready to work. For now, take the day off and get settled—do anything you like." He smiled. "Within reason, of course."

When Caligari was through speaking, everyone fled to the kitchen for cold chicken and tossed green salad. Finished, they fanned out across the four-acre estate to explore

the grounds. Dorsey and Alexandra ran down a steep in-
cline over some sand dunes toward the ocean, while
Shane, who had never been to the Hamptons before, opted
for a shady, tree-lined side of the estate where a family of
crested bluejays had taken up residence.

She rested on the grass under the branches of a large old
tree, listening to the birds shriek. So absorbed in the
beauty, she was amazed to suddenly see a foot dart out
from an upper-story window and grope for a nearby tree
branch. Startled at first, she hid behind a bush to watch as
the one leg was followed by another, then a torso, then a
head—which when fully emerged became an energetic
young boy.

"Hey, you!" Shane called just before he dropped to the
ground. "What do you think you're doing?" The moment
the child heard her, he scampered away and Shane's extreme sense of justice called her to arms. Quickly she ran
after the intruder, leaping hedges, a white picket fence and
some sand dunes, heading toward the ocean, where she
saw the boy trip over something and fall. That "something"
turned out to be a handsome young man sunning on a
terry-cloth towel.

He thrust an arm out and grabbed the boy's leg. "Hey,
Tommy," the young man said, holding the squirming child.
"Where's the fire?"

Shane reached them and caught her breath. Then she
launched into questions of her own. "What's the matter
with you?" she shouted. "Don't you know nice people
don't climb into other people's houses? What were you
doing up there?"

The child kept his mouth closed but slid his hands slyly
behind his back as if to hide something.

"And what's behind your back?" Shane asked, ap-
proaching.

"Nothing!" the boy barked. He shifted his position as
she came toward him.

Shane reached behind and snatched what he was hiding
in his hands. "Why, you sneaky little thief!" she said, star-

ing at one of her tiny crystal figurines. "I ought to call the police and have you arrested."

Just as the young man was getting a better grip on him, the boy broke loose, scattering a flock of seagulls as he ran down the beach.

"Come back, Tommy," the young man called after him. "You'll have to face the music sooner or later." His words were useless. In a few seconds the boy was gone.

"Sorry," the young man said to Shane. "I tried my best." He extended a hand. "Tilden Bradshaw Kane, but my friends call me Brad."

The moment their eyes met, sparks ignited. "Shane Laser," she said, aware he was still holding her hand. "I'm here with a ballet group. We're renting that old stone mansion, and I caught the little thief in the act." She withdrew her hand, but her fingers still tingled.

"He's not really a thief," Brad said. "Just mischievous, that's all."

She showed him the figurine. "Like I said before, a thief."

Brad ran a hand through his sun-bleached hair. "Well, don't worry about him. He'll never do it again. I promise."

Shane stared at the handsome stranger with the bronzed body, at his dazzling smile, at his pale blue eyes which changed from moment to moment like the ocean waves.

"I'm not worried about him doing it again," Shane said. "But somebody should speak to his parents about this."

"Well, I will," Brad said. "Tonight."

"I'm serious!" Shane insisted.

"I am too," Brad assured her. "And I will. The little thief's my brother."

"He's gorgeous!" Shane sighed at their usual bedtime powwow. "Tall, handsome, with a million-dollar smile. God! I can't get him out of my mind." Shane's green eyes were glowing in the soft lamplight of the large room where three equidistant cots had been placed for sleeping.

"He's a lawyer and he's going to run for Congress some-day and then the Senate."

Dorsey's back went up instantly. "Christ, Shaney babe! Take my advice and stay away. Dump him now before it's too late."

Both Alexandra and Shane stared at Dorsey in surprise.

"Why?" Shane asked. "What do you mean?"

"It's simple," Dorsey said. "Men who are interested in public life don't make good husbands. That's all."

"For heaven's sake, Dorsey," Alexandra said. "Just be-cause your dad stood you up for lunch and didn't show up at our party is no reason to put Shane's new friend down."

"Oh, yes, it is," Dorsey continued emphatically. "Fore-warned is forearmed and we made a pact to help one an-other, so I'm following through." She sneered. "I know all about people like this T. Bradshaw Kane, and it's not just the broken lunch dates and the no-show at our party; it's the kind of lives they're forced to lead and their families be damned. No! I'd never marry anyone who had his eye on public office. And I'd counsel any of my friends likewise."

Alone in her tiny room, listening to the surf beat against the shore, Simone lay in her bed resting and thinking. She was almost happy; glad to be with her Shane again, glad she would be there to make sure no one took advantage of her little baby. Now, at last, it was all beginning to happen, all the sacrifices finally beginning to pay off.

They were both earning nice steady salaries, and when the tour started there would be some extras and a generous per diem. If things continued to work this way, she could put aside a nice little nest egg for the future, should any-thing unforeseen occur.

Besides all that, she had earned a few dollars in the apartment transaction. But best of all, their trail would now be cold again and that's what really mattered.

She'd taken care of everything else, leaving word with the new tenants who had sublet her apartment to forward all mail in care of General Delivery. She'd shut off the telephone so no one could trace them that way. All along, she'd seen to it that no stone had been left unturned, and it was good to feel a measure of personal security. Because the important thing was that Shane never, ever learn the truth. She had given her daughter everything she'd never had. And in giving everything to Shane, she felt young again, whole, perfect and complete.

Chapter 23

At 7 A.M. the following morning, Caligari trod the crashing surf thinking excitedly of the work ahead of him. The day had begun like the color gray, with a sad wind, with the white waves rolling in then breaking into a thousand shades of blue along the shoreline.

Gone were the neon lights of the city; gone were the people, the persistent honking of cars and buses, the filthy litter of 42nd Street, the drummer beating out his brains for a little change near Central Park, the constant motion of a city simultaneously dying and being born. He missed none of it.

Now, here in this sea swept paradise in the Hamptons, where a hundred years ago peaceful Indians sang their sacred love songs to the earth, sea and sky, he walked the grounds checking the heated Olympic-size swimming pool, the Swedish sauna, the oversized Italian-tiled Jacuzzi, the steam room and tennis courts, coming finally to understand and realize that the beautiful Julia Romanov—no, the *very generous* Julia Romanov—had not only granted but exceeded his wildest wishes and dreams.

At 8:30 A.M., after a light breakfast of bran and fruit, Shane followed Dorsey and Alexandra to the center of the main ballroom, where six portable barres had been arranged. She took her place with the others, stretching her body, chatting absently with Seth as everyone waited eagerly for Caligari to enter and begin.

She'd slept like a baby last night thinking about Brad, thinking about whether or not he would call her on the telephone as he'd promised, having dreams of a first romance with him. Then Joshua suddenly struck the first piano chord and her attention turned toward the dance master and the matters at hand.

It was almost 9 A.M. when Caligari removed his wristwatch and placed it on the piano. "Today begins the first official day of our professional lives together," he said to the class. "And I want you to know how excited I am at that prospect." He noted the beaming, smiling faces as he stood there. He could almost hear the eager heartbeats pounding inside their chests.

"From now on we're on a twenty-four-hour-daily crusade. Twenty-four hours of thinking, eating, sleeping and dreaming ballet with no room for any outside interference."

Shane swallowed a lump in her throat thinking of Brad.

Alexandra swore off junk food again.

Dorsey beamed.

Mark nudged Rory.

"I expect you ladies," Caligari went on, "to toughen up. To take *all* your classes en pointe." He continued in spite of the grunts and groans, which he had anticipated.

"Please remove any lamb's wool from the insides of your toeshoes as well. There's no way for your feet to make contact with the floor with three inches of cotton batting stuffed inside your shoes." With that, he nodded toward Joshua and tapped out the rhythm for pliés with his pointer.

"Down, two, three, four.

"Up, two, three, four.

"Watch your arms, please!"

He strolled through the barres, touching his pointer to

knees that were not aligned over toes, to bad turnouts which would produce stressed joints and to badly curved backs. In a few minutes leg warmers drooped down thighs and ankles and beads of sweat glistened on hard-working bodies.

They looked like a sharp group, he thought as they continued. A fine crop of young dancers he knew would develop nicely as they went along. And because of that, they would meet the challenge of his demanding choreography.

By nine-thirty the compulsory warm-up was concluded and everyone cleared away the portable barres so they could stretch their legs on the floors and walls before starting adagio.

For adagio, Caligari divided the class into four groups of five, tossing off a series of difficult combinations, and by nine-fifty, everyone's leg warmers were soggy with perspiration. But the real work was yet to come.

At ten-fifteen they began jumps, then turns, running diagonally across the length of the room. "Piqué turns," Caligari barked as the piano pounded. "One, two, three, four."

Each dancer crossed from one corner of the room to the other, spinning on a single toe to the rhythm of Caligari's pointer rapping the floor. As each dancer reached the opposite end of the room, he or she fell sharply to a presentation fourth-position pose only to hurry to the back of the line again.

Over and over they spun, then they began jetés, leaping in high splits one after the other, like rats on a treadmill, until Caligari was satisfied.

As she leaped high in the air toward a corner of the room and landed on her soles, Alexandra felt her old blisters open up and scrape against the wooden insides of her toeshoes. Without the protection of the lamb's wool, the already thin tissue was beginning to rub, to peel away from her knuckles, and she dreaded the moment when she would remove her shoes to deal with the bleeding, raw skin. But she couldn't think about it now. She had to concentrate on the steps.

Leaping up and coming down, she smiled at Caligari, but inside her brain choice expletives blinked on and off like nasty little neon signs. But like the others, she would tolerate it all, and valiantly. Pity the poor dancer who couldn't handle a few damned blisters, she thought. That would be the least of it.

Before the day was over, there would be knees popping, rib cages tearing, backs spraining, and pinched nerves for everyone. Standard stuff that always went with the territory. But, damn him. Damn Caligari for making her take the lamb's wool from her shoes. But bless him too, because deep in her heart she also knew it would make her feet stronger, and in the end because of that she would become a better dancer.

At eleven-thirty Caligari broke the class into two factions. For the women it would be a class in pointe work. For the men a lecture and demonstration on the difficult art of partnering. Paige would attend to the ladies while Caligari presided over the latter. Then they would join together after lunch for rehearsal.

Proud of their bodies, so magnificently honed and shaped by their dedicated years of building strength, young male dancers were always shocked to learn that it was the female who was the focal point of everything, that it was she who most balletomanes came to worship and that their own function was sometimes little more than a crane or a backdrop for all the ballerina's presentations.

So it was with careful attention to their egos that Caligari first explained, then reminded the male members of his company that the first order of business was to pay strict attention to that aspect of their performance before considering any move from corps dancer to soloist to principal.

"Your first job is to make her look lithe and lovely," he

told them. "To follow her line, to find her center and support her, to learn and discover everything there is to know about her. And you can't do that unless you know how her body works."

There were expected titters from some corners of the room, particularly from the older gay boys, but Caligari ignored them. He understood their feelings, their frustrations, and he intended to reward them in his own way. He had plans for all these young men to become as important as his female dancers could ever hope to be, and he would prove that to them with his new choreography.

"No, Mark, no!" Caligari scolded. "Your shoulders are too stiff and you're not giving that plié enough oomph! Without a deep plié, you can't push off to a high leap."

Mark gritted his teeth, glanced at Rory, then at the floor. He had the feeling Caligari was picking on him and it really pissed him off.

"I'm doing the best I can," he called. Then he grabbed his leg warmers from the barre and left the room.

At twelve o'clock they broke for a lunch of cottage cheese, fruit, yogurt, vitamins and protein shakes. Then came a short rest and back to work. But not before Shane Laser received a a bouquet of red roses from Brad sent by special delivery.

"Who sent them?" Simone demanded when they were alone.

"Nobody important," Shane answered, trying to look unimpressed. "Some guy I met on the beach yesterday."

"Unimportant people do not send roses," Simone insisted. "What does he want?"

"Nothing," Shane answered. She wanted to smell the flowers, to cradle them in her arms, but she couldn't. Not as long as Simone was watching her.

"He's got a *lot* of nerve," Simone continued harping. "He doesn't even know you."

"Well, it doesn't matter, Mom. And if you'll excuse me, I'll put them in a vase."

Alone in the kitchen, Shane read the note that accompanied the flowers.

Hi gorgeous. How about brunch? lunch? dinner? tomorrow? I'll even settle for breakfast—if it's not too early in the A.M. Brad

Rehearsal began officially at 1 P.M., and while some dancers stretched their muscles for a short warm-up, others sat on the floor pasting Band-Aids on their open sores. Again and again Caligari pushed them, and although Shane worked hard, she could barely think of anything except those gorgeous red roses and Brad's invitation to dine. Yet she tried to forget it, to keep her mind riveted on her work.

It was important to concentrate on timing and count while executing lifts. To focus on difficult spins and high jumps. She'd known many dancers who had spoken of injuries they'd suffered trying to fight gravity while their heads were in the clouds. She did not wish to become another casualty. Yet the instant her partner Seth's hand gripped her waist in a series of supported lifts, her mind automatically drifted.

Seth's hands suddenly became Brad's, and a rather ordinary piece of reality turned into an extraordinary experience.

She was transformed into a princess; he, a prince who had come to rescue her from the wicked witch. He kissed her hand and begged her to come away with him, but she shyly refused. He led her to his far-off kingdom and together they soared through the air. Their bodies blended and her long, feather-light leap into his arms was breathtaking. Then he kneeled to beg her hand in marriage and she could barely contain her happiness as she accepted.

"Shane?

"Shane!"

Shane looked up from her arabesque pose.

"That was lovely," Caligari said. Everyone applauded.

Shane looked around. She was embarrassed as every eye stared in her direction. She realized then that she'd had more than her head in the clouds. She had put her soul up there and it had soared. She always wanted to recall that feeling.

Throughout the day the dance master worked them again and again, teaching steps, perfecting technique, polishing their head and arm movements, over and over improving their skills until at five o'clock he reluctantly let them go.

A few minutes after their dismissal, the strong smell of healing ointment filled the house as everyone attended to their battle wounds. After that, a quick rush to the laundry, where three washing machines and dryers ran constantly. Some dancers soaked their bones in the precious warmth of a waning sunshine by reclining on the beach. Others massaged away their aches and pains. At dinner there was steak, baked potato, carrots and spinach, but no dessert. Then Caligari treated them to a video movie.

By nine o'clock the house grew quiet. It was time for bed. But not before Mark and Rory entered the bedroom of the three girls.

"What's this?" Mark teased.

He was holding one of Shane's crystal figurines, and she snatched it from his hands.

"You're a little too nosy to suit my taste," she told him. Then Dorsey scooted both boys out and shut the door.

Alone in the bathroom, Alexandra wrote the following in her diary:

> *Shane got roses today and all of Mr. C's atten-*
> *tion. Lost four pounds but I won't be happy*
> *until HE notices me and gives me something*

special to do. P.S. I've almost forgiven him for dancing with Julia.

A.

"Mark and Rory have to go," Paige said firmly as they sat alone in the living room.

Caligari had to agree. The two young men he'd hired to cover his tracks when he'd accepted Julia's offer had not lived up to his hopes.

"It'll be tough on them," he said. "But of course, you're right."

Paige stared at him. "Shall I dismiss them or will you?"

Caligari didn't answer.

"I'll tell them tomorrow," she said finally. "Before class."

She headed for the door. "Oh—one more thing."

Caligari's eyes met hers. He knew exactly what was coming.

"The Romanov girl."

"No!" he said. "She stays. I've taken a liking to her."

"Yes," Paige said. "So I've noticed."

Chapter 24

Rory and Mark's dismissal stimulated fear. Each member of the company thought he or she was next.

For Rory and Mark, the resentment and anger was vocalized only moments before they left.

"I've worked like a damned dog for you," Rory screamed at Paige.

"Don't you dare yell at her," Caligari demanded. "The decision wasn't hers. It was mine."

"Don't hand me that!" Mark intervened loudly. A blue vein in his forehead burgeoned and snaked toward his left eye. "The old girl's beginning to lose it and she's blaming us."

Caligari grabbed Mark by the collar and led him toward the door. "Face it!" the dance master said when he let him go. "You were not up to par. You couldn't hack it!"

"You'll pay for this humiliation," Mark yelled at Paige from the front steps.

Rory tried to calm him, but it was no use.

"One of these days I'll prove how lousy you really are."

As their taxi sped down the winding pebble road, Caligari felt like garbage. He hadn't counted on this happening. At least not this way. But who was he kidding? He had used them for his own purposes and he knew they would eventually get hurt. To sacrifice his own ass, to keep his secret about Alexandra from Paige, he had chosen those two as sacrificial lambs.

They were having lunch in the kitchen.

"So that's how it ends," Seth said to Alexandra, Shane and Dorsey.

He was referring to Mark and Rory and the bad feelings their dismissal had engendered.

"For some people," Shane said. "Just for some."

"Don't you worry about it," Dorsey reassured Seth. She patted Alexandra's shoulder as she spoke. "They both deserved it. Especially Mark. What a punk! He hardly worked at all."

"I don't know," Seth continued. "Who's next?"

"Not you," Dorsey told him. "Not anyone at this table. We're all terrific." She paused. "Besides, Mark is a spoiled rich kid. He'll probably come to Paris and heckle us when we perform."

"Who said?" Seth asked.

"He did," Dorsey replied. "He threatened to come and embarrass us all."

Chapter 25

The next days were ones of feverish prepara-
tion. Caligari, working in a private cottage at the edge of
the grounds, spent his time exploring and listening to New
Wave music done on computers and synthesizers.

In the main house Paige conferred with costume, set and
light designers, who arrived intermittently. When they
weren't rehearsing, every dancer submitted to a ritual of
body measurements by the seamstresses.

When the hot tub wasn't in use, the sauna was kept
busy, and when the pool was empty, the steam room was
filled. It was therefore a minor miracle that Shane Laser
found any time to enjoy a picnic with her new suitor, Brad
Kane.

"The roses you sent were beautiful," she told him on a
sunny Sunday afternoon at the beach.

"Roses suit you," Brad said as he opened a white wicker
picnic basket.

Shane sat next to him on a red-and-white-checkered
cloth as he unpacked the food. She noted his muscular
arms and immaculate fingers, the way he squinted in the
sun, glancing at her with a glint in his turquoise eyes.

"I stopped at Dean and DeLuca's for some special stuff,"
Brad said. "But I'm not sure any of it's right. I mean, I
don't know what sort of stuff you dancers eat."

Shane laughed. "Whatever we can get our hands on."

"Good," Brad said. He smiled broadly. "That's how I like my women—lean, mean and hungry."

It was noon and the sun was brilliant, high in a pale blue sky, with a gentle breeze singing its lone sweet song across the deserted sand dunes. Some of Shane's loose coppery hair whooshed across her face, and Brad reached across to brush the strands from her eyes. His hand lingered on the contour of her cheekbone, and in that moment Shane knew her first real taste of sexual desire.

In her professional life many young men had touched and held her body in the most intimate ways: waist, crotch, breasts, buttocks, thighs. But that had been different, part of a dancer's routine. In reality, she had never known a young man's intimate touch, his kiss or caress. She had never even dated. Yet in her daydreams, she had always fashioned some marvelous romance.

He would be handsome, tall, witty, even a little shy, but always a gentleman, and he would love her so much and so passionately that no one would understand. He'd bring her roses and precious gifts, and after they'd marry they'd spend their lives in a state of eternal bliss. So even though this moment was brand-new, it somehow seemed familiar.

As Brad opened the wicker basket and spread out the food, she gasped. On top, packed in crushed ice, was real Scottish salmon, Osetra caviar with toast and whipped cream cheese. Beneath that was a tray of greens, cold dill chicken, Maroilles cheese and pumpkin tortellini drenched in walnut sauce.

For sweets, there were jars of Paul Corcellet jams and Carr's biscuits, along with freshly baked cheese cake, blackberries and a chilled bottle of 1966 French Krug. Besides all that, a bouquet of wild flowers which he placed at her feet.

Shane was overwhelmed. "It's so lovely! I don't know what to say."

"Here," Brad said, smiling smugly, as though he'd known he'd done well. "Let me help you."

He removed some white Wedgwood china from the picnic basket with sterling-silver cutlery and white Irish linen napkins. He fixed a plate for Shane and she attacked all of it with a dancer's voracious appetite. Everything was delicious, all new to her palate, and Brad smiled as she ate. He was attentive, filling her glass with champagne, her head with stories about his favorite Uncle George.

"I had this Christmas party to go to when I was seventeen," he told her. "We'd just moved here and my parents were out of town. Well, I didn't want to go, but my Uncle George found out and hit the roof. He took me to this fancy store to buy a new suit because the party was one of those cotillion affairs. You know—white gloves, fancy shoes, and he thought I should go and make friends. God, was I scared."

Shane smiled at that.

"The night before, I tried everything on and I looked great," he boasted. "Except for my scruffy shoes. But it was too late to buy any. So Uncle George got this bright idea I should wear his—and by God, they fit.

"Next day, half an hour before the party, I put on my new stuff and went looking for the shoes. But no deal. I couldn't find them. Then I went looking for Uncle George. No deal again. He'd gone to the city.

"I called him on the phone to ask where he'd put the damn things and there was this long silence, then his silly giggle. Poor old George! He forgot. He took them with him that day to wear to dinner, and I was stuck with this new suit and my old gray Nikes." Brad laughed. "I looked like a nerd, but I went anyway."

Shane laughed too. "Never mind poor old George," she said. "Poor old *you!*"

They were silent for a while, watching a few colorful sailboats in the distance, when a sudden gust of wind flipped the edge of the checkered cloth across Shane's legs. As Brad reached out to straighten it, his fingers touched her sun-warmed thigh. Her skin tingled and she thought she'd leap out of her skin.

"Speaking of shoes," Brad told her, "why don't you take off your shoes and socks and get some sun on your feet?"

Shane giggled. "I don't think you'd like seeing my feet."

His brow creased. "Why? What's wrong with them? Leprosy?"

"Close enough," she said.

"Well, I'm a big boy. I think I can take it."

He began undoing the buckles of her shoes, but her firm grip soon displaced his fingers.

"This has to be done carefully," she said, slowly unbuckling her sandals. "And be prepared for a shock."

When her socks were removed and Brad finally saw her feet, Shane thought he'd lose his lunch. "I warned you," she said.

He stared at raw blisters, angry red bunions, thick calluses, malformed bones and took a deep breath. "No problem," he said, swallowing hard. Then he lifted her right foot and kissed the arch.

Dorsey called Alexandra over to the window. "Can you beat that? He's actually kissing her foot. Be still, my anxious heart!"

"How sweet," Alexandra sighed.

"I wonder if she's still a virgin," Dorsey mused.

Alexandra coughed. "Some of us are *actually* saving it."

Dorsey threw a pillow at Alexandra's head. "The first thing you'd better learn is that it doesn't pay to save anything you don't get interest on."

Richard Caligari had been staring out his window for the last half hour, watching Shane and her new companion play on the beach. He didn't like what he was seeing. Damn! There was no room in the life of a serious dancer for love or romance. No room at all. Oh, he didn't mind their having casual sex or even fleeting passions. That was acceptable, even good for a dancer's emotional growth as an artist. But he would not tolerate the insipid romantic dawdlings of his youthful charges without his express permission.

He saw his dancers as empty blackboards, clean slates just waiting for him to make *his* mark on. Not somebody else's. No, he would have to do something to distract the girl, and he would have to do it soon.

A scowling Simone parted the curtains and watched her daughter. All morning long she'd not had a moment's peace, sewing lace, pinning tulle and sizing satin. All morning long she had sorted costumes and toeshoes, cataloguing them, setting them in place so when the tour started dancers could find what they needed. It was not exactly what she had been hired for. She had signed on as seamstress and designer, not wardrobe mistress. But she would never complain to anyone. Telling Caligari to go suck eggs would satisfy nothing. She could not risk losing her job and having to return to Brooklyn. She had to be close to Shane—now more than ever.

Look at him, she thought, peering out through the curtains. Look at that cocky little bastard kissing my kid's foot. What the hell did he care? Did he know how hard Shane had worked to get here? Did he care that she, Simone, had sacrificed everything to help her in the process? Well, she had news for him. Big news! She'd let him play his little game for a while, but in the end, when it really counted, she would win like always.

Chapter 26

"I think we need to talk," Simone said to Caligari. "Alone."

He followed her to a corner of the living room and waited till she sat down. What, he wondered, did she have on her mind?

"I'm worried about Shane," Simone said.

"She's doing fine," Caligari told her.

"Not her dancing. That guy she's been seeing. It's not good for her. I thought you'd want to say something to her about it."

He paused, looked at her face. "I've thought about it already," he said. "Not to worry."

Dressed in pink tights and black leotards, Alexandra descended the long winding staircase behind the closed ballroom where Caligari was teaching. She would be late again, but she didn't care. Even after what happened to Mark and Rory.

Since they'd come to the mansion, though Caligari had been polite, he'd barely noticed her. He had given her *nothing* of importance to dance and that depressed her. In the past when depression hit her, she'd eat too much or sleep too late. And today had been one of those mornings.

Before joining the others, she stopped by the kitchen for

a bite of toast and a sip of coffee, wondering what kind of excuse to give the dance master. She hoped he wouldn't stop teaching, as he once had, to rant and rave, to lecture everyone on the importance of being prompt. Then again, what the heck! Some attention, even if it was lousy, was better than none at all.

She sat near the kitchen greenhouse window, sipping fresh orange juice, absently scanning the front pages of the *New York Times* when an article on Senator Thomas Childs caught her eye. She studied the caption under his photo, wondering if Dorsey had seen it, wondering how she would handle the news. What a mess. Poor Dorsey. Things in her friend's personal life had gone badly enough, and now this.

She ripped out the article and shoved it into her ballet bag. She would show it to Dorsey at lunchtime before anyone had a chance to really hurt her with it, she decided. Better she find out from a friend than a stranger.

Caligari was furious when Alexandra entered his classroom, but he continued working. It was more important to ignore than reprimand her, to continue with the momentum and not waste time scolding or berating her. Besides that, he didn't want to bring her to Paige's attention because of Mark and Rory. So while Alexandra did pliés in a corner of the room, Caligari clapped his hands to the rhythm of Joshua's piano chords, counting and correcting each dancer as he walked among them.

Tap, tap, tap.

"Don't bend your wrist that way, Shane. It's important not to break the line of your arm. And relax your shoulders."

Tap, tap, tap.

"Chest out, head up and smile, Seth. Nobody cares about your silly bursitis or your bad back. They've paid twenty or more hard-earned dollars to see you soar. They can go to an emergency room for free to see what you're doing."

Tap, tap, tap.

"Project, for God's sake! And you—those bourrées are ghastly. You should be able to glide across the room holding a quarter between your thighs."

When the combinations were over, the dance master covered every mirror in the room, and the students gaped at each other in surprise and confusion. Without a mirror, a dancer couldn't function. Without checking his image, he could neither see his line nor correct his mistakes.

"There are no mirrors on stage," Caligari told them all, plying the last cloth. "So learn how to sense and feel the right positions with your brain, to know in your mind when something is wrong." And for the rest of the day the mirrors remained covered.

As he continued to ignore her, Alexandra felt Caligari's silent anger pierce her skin, felt his ire more directly than if he had taken the time to read her the riot act. Nothing hurt more than being ignored. It was like being a nonentity, as if she didn't count or matter. And coming from him, it hurt twice as much because she cared deeply. Because, more than she could admit, she still needed to please him and gain his love.

"We'll be working on a new ballet today," Caligari announced. Everyone watched as he walked to Shane's side, leading her to the room's center. "And we'll try *you* in the first lead." Eyes of green envy glowed from every corner of the room, a reaction he had anticipated, particularly from Paige, who stood simmering in a corner. He wasn't surprised.

Dancers always reacted jealously whenever choices were made. It sometimes made them dance better. But he'd had good reasons for choosing Shane and to his way of thinking they were sound ones. And he hadn't done it for Simone. He'd had it in mind ever since he'd seen Shane dance with Seth.

For Shane's partner he used Seth, that tall, attractive

young man with dimples, laughing blue eyes and black hair which fell across his forehead. The boy's classical training had been formidable and he danced with the raw bravado of Fernando Bujones, a dancer Caligari admired.

"This is an ensemble piece, a story ballet," Caligari told them. "It's the tale of a famous matador who forsakes his childhood sweetheart for a wicked temptress he encounters in the bullring. When the temptress leaves him, his confidence leaves too, and without his confidence he's gored. Later, on his deathbed, his first love redeems him just before he dies."

As each dancer was assigned a part, others were told to understudy the lead roles, should illness or injury occur. Dorsey was to understudy Shane. And once again, Alexandra was relegated to the corps.

The news of Caligari's choosing Shane came to Simone just as she was packing toeshoes and costumes, and she was ecstatic. He had done it at last! She quickly finished her chores, then took a break so she could peer into the rehearsal hall doors and watch.

"There will be little music in this ballet," Caligari told everyone. "You will provide the background by clapping very intricate Spanish rhythms of point and counterpoint with your hands." He demonstrated a sample staccato pattern, which everyone tried.

"For the love duet, which we will work on this morning, there will a Spanish guitar. While in the bullring, we'll hear a lone trumpet."

There were "oohs" and "aahs" from every corner of the room as Caligari again demonstrated the lively hand rhythms. Then he began choreographing the love duet as Joshua played the sad guitar melody.

Shane felt Caligari's arm encircle her waist, felt his groin press against her buttocks, and as he demonstrated, a shock ran through her. It was all too much. Something extraordinary was beginning to happen to her body, and she was confused and excited.

"The ballet begins with the matador praying to La Virgen de la Macareña," Caligari continued. "It's high noon and he kisses his sweetheart, then heads for the bullring. The lone trumpet marks his entrance, and as he fights the bull, everyone surrounds him with boisterous hand rhythms. Then suddenly the bull becomes the temptress—we'll call her Fate if you like—and it's here the matador becomes enamored of her charms. He quickly forgets who he is and what he must do. Then Fate takes over and he's mortally wounded."

He began to create the ballet on Shane. A slow, beautiful adagio filled with exquisite lifts, a sexy and suggestive pas de deux. Shane melted as Caligari lifted her over his head, then brought her down to rest in his arms.

"You'll wear a low-cut black chiffon costume cut high above your thighs," Caligari said. "With a beautiful red rose the size of a grapefruit on top of your head. The stage lights will shimmer blue for the duet, then red in the ring, where all your movements will be sharp and devastating, calculated to charm, captivate, then destroy him."

They worked that way all afternoon and without question, excitement continued to mount. Each dancer brought to his or her role an enthusiasm, a special quality only he or she possessed. And by 6 P.M. Caligari finally called it a day. Everyone collapsed from exhaustion except Shane. She was preparing for another date with T. Bradshaw Kane.

Inside her bedroom, Paige McDowell placed her hands on her hips and paced. What nerve! What gall! That lousy, ungrateful son of a bitch had given that magnificent ballet to a child with the emotions of a flea. Damn him, she fumed.

She kicked the wall as she passed, wondering what the hell was wrong with him, yet knowing in her heart what he was really up to. Well, who did he think he was kidding?

She knew what was going on. After all, she'd been there herself when he'd interfered with *her* private life just as he was trying to do with Shane. But that wasn't the only point. She had decided long ago, watching Margot Fonteyn hop around the stage in her forties, that she would hang it all up at thirty-five. It was horrible to see. She didn't want to end up as a dancing memory. She needed that ballet to go out in a blaze of glory, while she still had the strength to hack it. She wanted to be remembered as strong and able, not weak and wimpy.

Well, she wasn't going to tolerate it. No way! That ballet had been created for her. Christ! She could taste it. And before the evening was finished, it would belong to her or else!

Dorsey was depressed about not getting the role of Fate in Caligari's new ballet. After all, her feet were more beautiful than Shane's could ever hope to be and certainly a lot more fleet. Then she reminded herself that Shane was a friend, a roomie, her Shaney babe, and they had made a pact, hadn't they? One for all and all for one? But when Alexandra handed her that news article, she almost fainted, and was now in a local bar tying one on.

Chapter 27

T. Bradshaw Kane sat in his Rolls-Royce limousine, clutching long-stemmed red roses and a very faint heart. He had a longing, a secret passion for the girl. No. It was more than passion—it was love. But he was afraid to admit it.

Well, of course he was. Who wouldn't be? At least with the plans he'd made for his future, or rather, the plans his father had made. Shane just didn't fit in. She was an entertainer, too young, too poor, too Jewish, whatever that meant. Well, of course he knew what it meant. His father had said it often enough.

"They're pushy, son, loud and aggressive."

Funny thing was, those characteristics best described his father. But that wasn't the issue. Besides, Shane wasn't loud and aggressive anyway. She was soft and sweet and demure, like his mother.

Well. Tough luck, Daddy dear. He liked her. No, he loved her. Wrong again! He both liked and loved her. And she'd make a really great congressman's wife as soon as she gave up this silly ballet stuff.

As Shane watched the magnificent white Rolls drive along the dirt road, she nearly lost her footing. Terrific! She could see the headline in the *National Enquirer*:

BALLERINA ON EVE OF BIG SUCCESS
FALLS LIKE KLUTZ
ON OLD PEBBLE ROAD AND GIVES UP CAREER

What a story. One for the books. But it *was* an awesome automobile.

As the car parked, she waited patiently. Dressed in a simple ice-green frock Dorsey had loaned her and wearing her own white pumps, lace gloves and small purse, she carried Alexandra's expensive pearls draped around her throat.

She was nervous, happy, excited, her feelings colliding all at once. And why shouldn't she feel happy? Brad was terrific, handsome, rich, and best of all, he liked *her*. What's more, she not only liked all these feelings, she reveled in them.

When the chauffeur came to her side, he tipped his visored hat and opened the door. Inside, Brad welcomed her with an armful of long-stemmed roses and a tiny velvet box.

On a tattered stool in a dark and dusty tavern, Dorsey gulped another drink. Not counting the brandy she'd had after first discovering the news, this one made five.

All night long she'd avoided the local yokels who'd sidled up to her barstool with their phony offers of solace and companionship. She knew what they really wanted was her body. Nobody cared about her. Nobody really gave a damn. Then as the bar was closing, the drinks slammed into her head all at once and out of extreme loneliness, drunkenness and melancholy she'd decided to allow one of the jerks to join her.

"Buy you a drink?" he dribbled.

"Yeah, sure," Dorsey slurred.

The guy was zonked, about thirty-five, rocking back and

forth on his stool as one of his eyes blinked a millisecond slower than the other. He smiled at Dorsey as he toasted her health and a jagged tongue peeked out from a gap between two yellow front teeth.

"What's happenin', little lady?" he asked.

"Gonna have a baby," she spit out, slapping the bar for a refill.

"Hey, no kiddin'," the guy said, extending a feeble hand. "Lossa luck."

"Not me, you silly ass. My father."

He pounded the bar with a weak fist. "No shit! Firs' time I ever heard of a pregnant guy."

Dorsey ignored his stupidity. "Hey!" she shouted to the bartender. "Gimme 'nother drink."

The bartender, a tall thin man whose pumpkin head rested on a celery-stalk neck, slowly wiped the counter. "Sorry, lady, closing time."

"Hey," the guy said, waking from a two-second sleep. "How 'bout we go to your place?"

"Don't have no place," Dorsey said. She lay her head on the countertop and closed her eyes. "Don't have nothin'."

"Then how 'bout my place?" He slid off his stool and teetered, trying to wink his eye. "Round the corner."

Dorsey studied two images of him. "Nope. Going to the city. Got to score."

He laughed. "The city! You crazy? You can't drive in your condition. Don't you know you're drunk?"

"No problem," Dorsey said. She stood up and tried to walk. "I can still hitch."

It was nine-thirty. Shane and Brad had enjoyed a magnificent eight-course dinner at Rénaud's, a very posh, very private restaurant serving only those patrons in possession of their unlisted phone number. Now they were heading toward Brad's private cottage, located off the east end of his family's huge estate, where iced champagne waited near a blazing fire.

Shane was heady with the joy of all that had happened: joining an important dance company, moving out on her own, getting the lead in Caligari's new ballet today. And now Brad. It was all a magnificent dream.

Brad's warm, protective arm curved around her shoulder as she rested against him. She listened to his heart as it beat next to hers and felt the contours of his chest against her cheek. And she was beginning to feel *that* special way again: warm, elated, dizzy—the way Caligari had made her feel this afternoon at rehearsal.

Simone quivered with rage.

She had gone to Paige's room to make a last-minute adjustment on the ballerina's costume when she'd heard them arguing. And she would not have snooped except that Shane's name had come up in the context of the heated discussion. Because of that, she put her ear to the closed door and listened.

"How could you have done that to me?" Paige demanded. "How could you have humiliated me that way?"

"I don't know what you're talking about," Caligari replied.

"Don't hand me that. You know perfectly well what I'm talking about. You gave *my* ballet to a kid who can't even blow her own nose."

Paige's costume twisted in Simone's sweaty hands. Can't blow her own nose?! Who the hell did this old broad think she was anyway? Pavlova?

"You must think I'm a fool," Caligari said. "I gave that ballet to Shane because she's talented, and deserves it. Not for any other reason."

"Don't lie to me!" Paige exploded. "You gave that ballet to her because she's seeing some guy who lives down the road and you don't like the idea of her getting involved. We both know what you're trying to do.

"Well, let me tell you something, Richard. There isn't a

kid out there who wouldn't kiss your feet or worship at your shrine, but I'm not one of them. I'm a thirty-five-year-old prima ballerina who knows she's on her way out, and when I do go, it better be in a blaze of glory. You owe me! For many reasons. Now, that particular ballet belongs to me and we both know it. So I either get it or you go to Europe without me."

Simone was livid. She waited for Caligari to tell the bitch off, to say something, *anything*. But his total silence sickened her and she finally had to leave.

Scurrying down the hallway, she cursed Caligari for his cowardly weakness and damned Paige for her selfish jealousy.

Well, Simone thought, opening the door to the fitting room, we'll see about her. If Caligari goes back on his word, if he takes the ballet from Shane, Simone would make Paige's life miserable. She'd get even with that bitch somehow, even if it killed her, even if it killed them both.

Chapter 28

It was warm when the Rolls pulled alongside Brad's cottage, located far beyond his parents' estate. The air smelled of sweet jasmine, and a yellow midnight moon gently rolled the tide along the shore. They had decided to skip the confines of the cottage, to take a blanket with their champagne and lie out on the beach under an inky blue sky and watch the stars.

Brad led Shane along the cool sand dunes, stopping at a small private cove where the ocean waves sighed against the shoreline. There, he spread the blanket and fell to his knees, pulling Shane down beside him. They sat huddled together without speaking, just watching the ocean's ebb and flow, holding hands and sipping champagne.

"Some gorgeous night," Brad said, leaning his body against hers.

"Yes," Shane agreed. "It's so beautiful."

The champagne had gone to her head and she was feeling gay and free as a bird until a strange rustling noise behind them startled her for a moment. But Brad's strong arm across her back quickly reassured. "Hey, it's nothing," he said. "Just somebody's cat or dog out for a late romp on the beach." Comforted and relaxed once again, she returned to the warmth and certainty of his affection.

Brad nuzzled Shane's long, billowing hair. Then he

kissed her cheek. She felt a chill through her body as his lips lightly brushed against her ear. She swore to herself then that as long as she lived, she'd never wash that spot again.

She'd been amazed at the secrets they'd revealed, the things they'd told one another during dinner, as if they'd shared an eternity and could confide their most cherished dreams without fear. It felt strange at first, like standing naked in the glaring spotlight, exposed to scrutiny, vulnerable and defenseless. And though she wanted to trust him, a part of her rebelled. As with all things in her life, she sensed an inherent peril in this adventure.

Long ago, she had made a commitment to Simone, to herself, to ballet, and now she was caught in the competitive grasp of Brad's loving power. Apprehensive at these new and potent feelings, she knew that both Brad and ballet would be equally fierce in their demands and *that* was unsettling. What would happen to her life if he really became a part of it? What things would change?

Before she could finish her champagne, Brad whisked the glass from her hand and with his lips pressed against hers, he slowly explored the interior regions of her mouth. His kiss was warm, liquid, sensitive and when he drew away, she was fully aroused, trembling all over. His masculine fragrance clung to her nostrils, and the tempo of her heart registered the depths of her desire.

"You're beautiful, Shane," Brad whispered in her ear. "Prettier than any girl I've ever known."

Shane smiled as she inhaled him. She had never thought of herself as pretty, much less beautiful.

Brad's arm encircled her body, his fingers wound through her long, gleaming hair, and with a single fluid motion they fell breathless together in a passionate embrace. She lay crushed beneath him as he kissed her, feeling protected by his muscled torso.

Swept away, she could hardly breathe at his strength, at the strong waves of desire that flooded and weakened her body along with her resolve. For a long time she clung passively to him until something inside her burst and she responded with her own fiery passion. She opened her mouth wide to his kisses. She wrapped her arms around him and tore the buttons off his shirt. It was then she knew how much she really wanted him, that she would go wherever he was leading.

He drew away and, gazing at her glowing green eyes and moonlit hair, slowly unbuttoned the lacy bodice. She waited as he reached inside and with confident warm hands caressed and massaged the roundness of her breasts. He bent and kissed each of them, licked them with the tip of his tongue, sucking ever so gently one rosy nipple, nibbling the other. Everything inside her melted at the feeling, and she drew his head closer to her bosom while her fingernails raked along his back.

Brad must have experienced fear at her wild awakening and he pulled away.

"Let's take a swim," he said, standing. "I think we both need some cooling off."

"Can't," Shane replied dreamily. "No bathing suit."

Brad's laughter rippled out to sea. "You ever skinny-dip?"

"No," she said.

In a flash Brad's shirt was off. "Come on," he coaxed, continuing to undress. "Take off your stuff and let's go."

As though she had done it a thousand times before, Shane undressed. It wasn't difficult. Ballet had taught her to be proud of her body, to bear her carriage well. In a few seconds she was naked and they were off—two iridescent bodies dashing toward the sea, plunging into the dark, salty water, with their innocent laughter echoing above the waves.

Together they swam, splashing each other like children at play. They were giggling and teasing when Brad suddenly seized her waist and pulled her sharply against him.

She felt his organ swell against her leg, erect and mysterious. And as they bobbed up and down in the cool water, he kissed her face and neck.

She waited with a pounding heart, with every nerve in her body alive and straining toward him. His mouth teased her nipples while his fingers reached below to caress the lips of her mound.

"I'm going to have you, Shane," he whispered. "I'm going to take you here, right now on this beach and make love to you."

Shane hugged him to her chest, kissed the wet ringlets that spun from his head and dripped water onto her skin. "Yes, yes," she answered, mad with her own excitement. "I want you, too."

Brad carried her out, fell beside her on the damp sand near the shoreline. He covered her face and neck with kisses, caressed the insides of her thighs as the surf rolled over them. Shane was burning inside from her own heat, luminescent outside from the moonlight, drunk on him, giddy and high, floating in anticipation.

"Oh, Brad, Brad. I've never been with anyone before," she murmured. "I feel afraid."

"I know," he whispered back.

His hands were everywhere, touching her hips, her belly, the soft hairs of her mound. And as his lips and tongue kissed their way toward her inner thighs, she closed her eyes and moaned. She was lost to it all, clinging rapturously, responding to his every move.

She felt no chill as the waves covered and caressed them, nothing but a steady warmth which surrounded her, which continued to grow inside like a fire until he grasped her hips and in one deep thrust, entered.

At first she choked at the pain, then she relaxed. She opened her legs wide and clung to his shoulders while his buttocks rose and fell. Soon she arched her back and, kissing his neck, joined him in the rhythm. She closed her eyes as the pain left and the pleasure took its place. And then she came, a shooting star in a moonlit dream, no longer a child, no longer a virgin, and the feelings they shared had been everything she'd dreamed of and more.

* * *

Dorsey wakened at 3 A.M. She had mung in her mouth, a head as heavy as a watermelon and a herd of buffalo running through her ears. Worse than that, she couldn't remember where she was. Then the bed shifted and she recognized the drunken body lying next to her. She leaped out quickly and in a flash recalled the tavern and their encounter. Then she remembered all the drinks she had had.

She looked around her, disbelieving, nearly gagging on her next breath. The room smelled like a toilet, littered and dirty, strewn with old pizza boxes, empty beer cans and stale cigarette smoke. Jeez! What a mess. She searched his things for a cigarette and found a pack on his dresser. She lifted it, lit one and in the flash of the matchlight noticed the photograph of an infant among his things. That's when she realized how she had come to be here in the first place.

Her heart plunged suddenly, like an elevator with a snapped pulley, and holding a hand across her mouth to keep from screaming, she crouched naked on the floor and wept.

Alone in her room, Alexandra wrote the following in her diary.

> *He gave Shane a magnificent ballet today and I was so jealous I could have died. But I love Shane and I'm happy for her too. It's strange to feel that way—jealous and happy at the same time.*
>
> *Oh why, God, why? If you didn't want me to dance, why did you burn it so deep inside me? Why did I struggle to lose ten pounds? Why did you give me a strong body and so much desire? Will I ever realize my dream?*

A.

By the time she finished, her tears made the ink on the pages run. She soon slammed the book closed and buried her head in a pillow.

When Shane returned to the house, it was long after curfew. She crept up the staircase to her bedroom, avoiding a confrontation with Simone. Then, holding a flashlight, she sat with Dorsey and Alexandra, telling them what had happened.

"It didn't hurt?" Dorsey asked.

"Only a little. But then it felt good."

"Typical dancer," Dorsey said, laughing. "The kid loves pain."

Alexandra noted Shane's new locket and said so.

"It's eighteen-karat gold," Shane told them both. "Brad said it once belonged to his grandmother."

"This *is* beginning to sound serious," Dorsey remarked.

Shane beamed a half smile. "He gave me this too," she said.

Opening another package, she showed a tiny piece of delicate spun glass in the shape of a ballet slipper and told them both the story of Brad's thieving little brother.

"It's so beautiful," Alexandra said.

Shane placed the tiny slipper on her dresser next to the other crystal figurines she had brought with her to the Hamptons.

"So when's the wedding?" Dorsey asked.

Shane shrugged. "That's a little premature, isn't it?"

"Any kids?" Alexandra asked.

Shane shrugged again.

"And what happens to the career?" Dorsey said.

"Hey, I'm a dancer," Shane told her. "I'll *always* be a dancer. Why should that change if I get married and have kids?"

Dorsey's voice climbed in register as she answered. "Because he's got political ambitions, that's why, Shaney babe. Because a man with political ambitions needs a dutiful wife and a bunch of kids to look good on TV. But you and your kids'll never see him. Of all the people in the world who should never have kids, it's those *goddamn, fucking politicians!*"

"Okay!" Alexandra mediated. "That's enough." She glanced at Shane as if to apologize for Dorsey's outburst. "Now let's hit the hay. We've got a big day ahead of us."

Chapter 29

In the morning Shane came to breakfast on the tail end of a magnificent dream. Five minutes later she walked right into a nightmare. Simone cornered her at the kitchen counter, where Shane had ordered a poached egg, wheat toast and coffee.

"Where the hell have you been all weekend?" Simone asked through clenched teeth. "I've been worried sick."

At her mother's tone, Shane's stomach began to churn. "I went out with Brad." Her voice was placating. "I told you. Remember?"

"No, I don't remember anything of the kind."

Of course she didn't remember, Shane thought. How could she? Simone never listened. She was too busy talking or giving advice. "But I told you on Friday at lunch while we were sitting at that table over there."

Simone's gaze rested suddenly on Shane's throat. Her eyes grew cold as ice. Shane realized Simone was staring at her new locket.

"Where'd that come from?" Simone growled. She reached for the locket, lifted it from Shane's neck, turning it back to front.

Shane took a deep breath to muster her courage. "Brad gave it to me," she said all at once. "Saturday night."

"Piece of crap," Simone snarled as she let the locket fall.

Shane felt a pain in her gut as the locket returned to her skin. "It's not crap. It's beautiful," she said, caressing it.

"What the hell do you know about beautiful!" It was a statement, not a question.

Shane was about to answer when breakfast arrived.

She reached a hand for the tray, but Simone beat her to it. Her mother studied the tray's contents contemptuously, then motioned to the cook. "Take it back," she ordered, banging it on the counter. "The egg's overdone and the toast is cold." She turned back to Shane. "And you, young lady—sit down! Over there where we can talk. I've got something important to tell you."

Caligari came to class Monday morning with a heavy heart. Ever since his encounter with Paige he'd been in a terrible state. And the reasons were obvious. Paige's demands would have to be met—certainly for now. There was no other way; at least no easy way. It was a bitter pill but it had to be swallowed.

Yet everything inside him screamed out to say no. To tell her to get lost, that nobody talked to him the way she did, that no one made such demands. But the damned woman had not only been right about some of his reasons for giving Shane the ballet, she'd hit other personal nails on the head, leaving him defenseless.

Besides that, without Paige's support, right now he had no damned company. And that was the plain truth. She was the backbone of the coming tour in Europe. Every ballet he'd ever done was recorded in her memory. Only *she* could dance all the roles and teach them to the others. Without her cooperation the tour could fall apart. And he wasn't about to let that happen. But it was still blackmail. Plain and simple blackmail.

Well, no matter. He had to make the change, and now. So coming down the staircase, he didn't feel so well. He felt even worse when he entered the rehearsal hall and saw Shane standing at the barre. He could tell by the frightened look in her eyes that somehow she already knew.

* * *

Simone listened at a crack in the door. She was determined to hear what the dance master was going to say. Did the wimp have enough balls to stand up to the strutting prima ballerina? she wondered. But it wasn't the only thing on her mind. There was this Brad jerk, for instance. He was much more dangerous to Shane in the long run. She could cope with a bitch like Paige, could make her life miserable. But a guy like Brad could make Shane change the course of her whole life.

Simone would have to put a stop to him, and soon. But how? She pressed her ear closer to the door as Caligari began. And as his lips formed the words she hoped she would never hear, she felt her knees shake like jelly.

When rehearsal was over, Shane burst through the doors and ran past Simone with Dorsey and Alexandra close behind. Inside her room she fell on the bed and sobbed like a baby. Dorsey and Alexandra comforted her but nothing helped. It had happened so quickly, just as Simone had told her. Much as she hated to admit it, her mother had been right.

"C'mon, Shaney babe," Dorsey said, kissing Shane's cheek. "These things happen. You've got to learn to accept it."

Shane kept sobbing. Sure, she thought. Easy to say. Caligari hadn't taken the role from *her*.

When Shane didn't respond to Dorsey, Alexandra tried reasoning. "C'mon, Shane. He gave the role to Paige because he expanded it. That's all. What other reason could there be?"

Shane straightened up. "Ask Simone!" she declared.

A full chorus sounded. "Simone?!"

"Yes," Shane said. "She told me this was going to happen, but I didn't believe her."

"Jeez!" Dorsey said, handing Shane a tissue. "You know

your mother's goofy paranoia. She'd say anything to get you all riled up."

"No," Shane said. "Not this time. She knew before Caligari made the announcement. She said he was taking it away because Paige was jealous."

"If you ask me," Alexandra offered, "it's more likely your mom's upset about Brad, and she's talking to Caligari about it."

Shane blew her nose. "Do you think it's possible? I mean she went bonkers when she saw the locket this morning."

"Good point," Dorsey said. "Now that I think about it, Caligari gave us that nutty lecture about ballet and romance the day after you and Brad had lunch together. You could be right, Alex."

"Well, screw them both," Shane said, getting up from her bed. "Paige is human and she can't always dance the damn role. One of these days she's going to get sick or break a leg. And when she does, I'll get a crack at it."

"That's the spirit!" Alexandra said.

"Way to go!" Dorsey agreed.

The letter arrived by special delivery, and had a local postmark with no return address. Caligari opened it and removed the sheet of paper. The writing was small, irregular, like that of a child, but the message was clear in its meaning.

"You're going to pay for what you've done. You'll see."

That was it. He worried about it for a while, then dismissed it. A crank. Nothing more. Rory, Mark—it could be anyone he'd discharged, including dancers from another tour. But he had other things to think about so he tore the letter up. In a few days he had forgotten about it.

Chapter 30

Vidal Genero was growing restless. He had been like this for the last four months. Though he and Julia had spent time together traveling, enjoying New York City, meeting interesting people, he still yearned to be back on stage and in the limelight.

Two years go he had been the toast of London, hailed as the new Mikhail Baryshnikov, a dancer with a bold imagination and a stage presence few dancers could command. Then it all came crashing down around his ears.

In rehearsal one afternoon he'd slipped and fallen, and the cartilage in his knee ruptured. He felt total devastation at first, then a paralyzing immobility.

There were few options to his dilemma.

"Take the cartilage out," one doctor had said.

"Leave it in and give up dancing," another had counseled.

For Vidal, there could be just one solution. He would have the painful surgery, rest, then put his life back together again somehow.

Since the last operation more than a year ago, he'd spent time taking class, learning to live with the constant pain, believing that one day, no matter how much it hurt to dance, he would make a comeback. And he felt that way now, more than ever.

So when Julia asked him how he'd like to spend the coming weekend, he'd suggested they drive out to the Hamptons to visit Alexandra. But what he really wanted was to observe the Caligari Ballet Company in action.

Vidal's curious request had come as a shock to Julia. How odd, she thought. Why would he want to go there? Though Vidal and Alexandra had been friends and were even sharing a profession, they had never really been close. Yet the thought of visiting intrigued her. Of course, why not go? Why not visit and try to build a better relationship with Alexandra? She certainly wanted that to happen. And then she realized, she would also see the dance master, and that intrigued her too.

Simone had dialed the telephone number quickly.
"Kane residence," came the response.
"Mr. Kane, please," Simone said.
"Senior or Junior?"
"Junior."
"And whom shall I say is calling?"
"The name is Laser. Mrs. Laser."
That's how the initial conversation had begun. Now she was sitting in a small restaurant in East Hampton, waiting to meet the elusive young man, to talk to him about his intentions toward Shane. All this without Shane's knowledge or permission.

She noticed him immediately, and knew who he was the moment he entered the room. He was tall, good-looking and confident, the way rich people always are—like they own the world or something. She waved and waited as he came to her table and introduced himself.

"I thought Shane would be here too," he said, sitting down.

"I thought it would be better if the two of us talked first," Simone said. "I hope you don't mind."

Brad said nothing and Simone knew his nonanswer was really an answer.

A waitress took their lunch orders—green salad with bay shrimp for Simone, stuffed avocado for Brad.

"It's nice to meet you," Brad said.

"Likewise," Simone answered.

She quickly got to the point. "I understand you and Shane are sort of serious about each other."

"I haven't popped the question, if that's what you mean, but I am considering it."

My God! She'd been right all along, she thought. Thank heaven he was at least being honest.

"Then this conversation is a lot more important than I realized," Simone told him.

"Oh?" Brad asked. "How so?"

The waitress returned with their food, and Simone dug in. "Because," she said between bites, "I don't think you understand anything about the life of a ballet dancer. I wanted to make sure you did."

"Shane's explained some of it," Brad said confidently.

Simone studied him. "Perhaps. But there's something else to consider, Mr. Kane," she said, letting her fork rest on top of the greens. "Something more important."

Brad's eyes met hers in a standoff. "Oh? And what is that?"

"I'll be frank with you," Simone continued. "Shane's Jewish."

Brad smiled. "I know that. What difference does it make?"

"It won't sit well with an East Hampton constituency, for one thing."

Brad smiled again. "I beg to differ with that," he said. "In fact, it could help."

"But there are other things besides that, Mr. Kane," she said, realizing she was not scaring this idiot with the last bit of news. "Things I'm unable to tell you now, except for this. Should you marry her and run for Congress—and Shane says you will—be prepared for some problems should they start looking into Shane's background."

"I don't understand," Brad said.

Simone enjoyed the puzzled look on the young man's face. Not so haughty now, are you, mister, she thought. Now that your career could be in jeopardy. "You don't have to understand," she said. "Just believe what I tell you. Be prepared for some real problems."

"She's crazy! She's only saying that to make you stop seeing me," Shane told Brad the following day. "There's nothing in my background except poverty, and that's no disgrace."

"But she made it sound so damned sinister, for God's sake," Brad continued.

"Well, who are you going to believe? Her or me?"

Brad kissed Shane's pert little nose. "Guess I don't have much choice, do I? But why is she doing it? I mean, she's your mother."

"That's easy," Shane told him. "She's spent every dime on my career. Every waking moment of her life has gone toward that end, and she doesn't want you taking me off course. Her course, I might add. She's put her whole life into me. You have to keep that in mind when you talk to her."

Brad was silent for a moment. "But how *do* you feel about it?" he asked. "Your career, I mean."

Shane searched her mind for an answer. "I don't know. I've never really thought about it. Ballet is everything to me. I wouldn't know what else to do with my life."

Brad's eyes twinkled. "Well, you could marry me, you know."

Shane kissed him. "I could, but how would that change ballet or what I am?"

"Well, you'd be Mrs. T. Bradshaw Kane, for one thing."

"Shane Kane," she giggled. "It would look cute on a marquee."

When Alexandra saw the limo pull up, she called Dorsey and Shane to the window. "What did I tell you? There she is. Madame Got-rocks herself."

They watched Julia and Vidal exit the Rolls, walk up the stone steps of the main house, then disappear into the mansion.

"I wonder what she's got up her sleeve," Alexandra said to the others.

"You're so paranoid," Dorsey exclaimed. "She's just coming to visit you."

"Yeah!" Shane chimed in. "You're lucky. At least she's not trying to interfere with your private life like mine is."

After a short visit with Alexandra, Julia and Vidal were invited by Caligari to relax on some comfortable chairs and observe the company. They were only one week away from their first European tour and everyone was excited. Caligari clapped his hands loudly as the group assembled and took positions to rehearse a classical fugue they were to perform on tour. But before that, he made an announcement.

"We have visitors today, boys and girls. You all remember Julia Romanov—Alexandra's mother—and her friend, Vidal Genero, from the London Ballet."

Their presence was acknowledged by soft applause, then Caligari nodded and Joshua played a chord on the piano.

There were lifts, leaps, turns, spins—choreography Vidal had never seen before—and it was exhilarating to him. Dorsey Childs' footwork was startling. Shane Laser's spins were breathtaking. Seth Pollace's leaps defied gravity. Even Alexandra looked slim and tough, with the prettiest penché arabesque he had ever seen.

Jesus, Vidal thought as he watched them dance to Caligari's pounding. This is what he'd been born for. This is what had been missing from his life all these months. And he knew without question, no matter what, he would have it once again.

After Julia and Vidal returned to the city, it was difficult for Caligari to even eat dinner. He sat in the dining room contemplating his problems—a musical score that hadn't been finished, lighting effects that hadn't been working, costume fittings that were driving him to drink and distraction—but he still couldn't stop thinking about Julia. What on earth was happening to him?

Julia.

He felt his groin stir, and he knew he had to leave the room quickly before the others could see. He was still in his tight black leotards, wearing his dancer's belt—a small G-string that would quickly give him away. He stood carefully, holding a newspaper flush across his hips. Then, without speaking to anyone, he hurried from dinner and fled to his room.

Shane was preparing to meet Brad for a late dinner, and Dorsey was teasing her again.

"Shane Kane. Sounds weird."

A pillow landed on Dorsey's head. "Not any weirder than Horsey Dorsey," Shane replied.

When they both left the room, Alexandra scribbled in her diary:

> *Julia and Vidal were here today and I'm depressed. Caligari gave me nothing except a small solo which he thinks we might have to cut when we get to Paris. SHIT! If he does that, I'm definitely going to quit this company. Then I can join Mother and Vidal on their European cruise. Anything has to be better than this.*
>
> *A.*

BOOK THREE

The Tour

Chapter 31

The day they were to leave for Paris arrived. Up to the last moment Caligari kept them busy rehearsing, and there was precious little time to pack.

While Alexandra cursed an extra pound she'd gained, Shane wrapped her tiny pieces of crystal in tissue paper.

"Do you always take those things everywhere you go?" Dorsey asked.

"Sure! For good luck," Shane defended. "Just like your crocheted slippers." She wrapped the last figurine. "I can't dance without them." She paused and hugged a pillow. "Especially my new glass slipper from Brad."

That's when she realized it was missing.

"Why, that sneaky little thief!" Shane said, slamming a fist on her suitcase. "That little bastard took it again."

"Took what?" Alexandra asked. "Who?"

"Brad's little brother," Shane said. "He must have climbed in here sometime when we were away and taken it. Damn him!"

Prior to leaving, Caligari and Paige were still offering each other assurances that they would be well received in Europe, suppressing any lingering fears of failure.

The ballets were all superb. This was a talented, healthy

and exciting young group. They had been well rehearsed, properly financed, endowed with the best that money could buy. There was little to be concerned about.

Unlike other companies which usually left their dancers to fend for themselves and cared only about schedules and body count when the curtain rose, Caligari had supervised all diets and activities, determined all play and sleeping schedules. And except for Shane's and Dorsey's singular transgressions against curfew one night, for which they both apologized, everything had run smoothly and was still in his grasp. There was every reason to believe they would achieve great success in Europe.

Moreover, though he had pushed his dancers to the limit, the work had not exhausted, but strengthened them. They were fully prepared for what lay ahead. So it was incumbent upon both him and Paige to look confident and relaxed, to set a good example. Most of all he had to keep the contagious smell of fear from everyone's nostrils.

At 6:45 P.M. they boarded a chartered jet at Kennedy Airport. The air-conditioned plane was a welcome relief from the heat. Shane, Dorsey and Alexandra sat near a wing, holding hands as the screaming engines revved and they taxied toward the runway. Each had her own private thoughts.

Shane's centered on what Simone had told Brad at their luncheon. At one point she'd even contemplated confronting her mother about it. But after mulling it over awhile, she changed her mind. It would be a waste of time. Simone was a master ot twisting things. No matter what Shane would say, Simone would have an answer.

Dorsey sat with a raging headache. Except for last night she'd been sleeping badly, taking more uppers and downers than usual. She dreaded Paris only because her father would be there with Deandra, and she would have to smile for the paparazzi who followed the flamboyant Senator about. He'd be in Paris on government business, and when he attended her performance—which he would because it was good for his image—he'd play the dutiful father. And she hated going through all that.

Alexandra noticed Shane falling asleep with her head against the window. She was glad for that. The night before, Shane had had another nightmare and it had taken all her strength to comfort and keep the girl quiet. This time she'd had no help from Dorsey, who'd slept deeply through it all.

Though Alexandra loved her two new friends, she was jealous of the principal roles they'd been given. She didn't like being an understudy, or just dancing in the corps. More than once it crossed her mind to quit as soon as they'd finished their Paris engagement. It wasn't sour grapes, she'd decided, but the new realization that she just *had* to be first to survive. And in Europe she might find a small ensemble company to give her that opportunity.

Chapter 32

Their jet landed at Orly Airport at 7:45 A.M. It was drizzling as the sleepy group boarded luxury buses which took them north by way of the Autoroute toward the city. At first everyone slept, but as the sun peeked through streaking clouds along the Left Bank, all eyes strained to see.

To Caligari, Paris was the most glorious city in the world. And he had traveled the globe. Each time he saw the Seine, the cathedrals, or walked the tree-lined Champs Élysées, his heart beat a little faster.

In Paris he found a peculiar harmony of contradictions, a city that was ornate yet uncluttered, complex but simple in its beauty. And he admired the people and loved the food. Most of all, Paris was Romance, a beguiling enchantress stirring his blood, his imagination, and each time he came to her bosom he dreamed of falling in love.

Their house in Neuilly was huge, with an eighteenth-century beaux arts facade of carved gray stone and dark wood trim. It was set on a small slope of green lawn that faced northward to the Seine, and behind it lay the Bois de Boulogne. It was four stories high, with leaded glass windows, ornate wrought-iron balconies and an astonishing frame of tall green trees and carefully clipped hedges.

Inside the lobby were high arches, polished walnut paneling and a main salon that featured apricot silk walls and coffered ceilings. Soft and commodious sofas and armchairs, upholstered in brown and apricot velour, were intimately arranged near a large marble fireplace, while crystal chandeliers gleamed from every ceiling.

As at the Hampton estate, all accommodations had been previously arranged, and Dorsey, Alexandra and Shane headed up the winding walnut staircase to the third floor. There they found three sunny-yellow beds and a bath. Double French doors which opened from the bedroom onto a balcony and a view of the Seine. Within minutes they were unpacked and in bed for a nap.

Resting in his room, Caligari searched an American newspaper for announcements of his arrival. As she had promised, Julia had run large ads. They were tastefully done and well placed and he was pleased. Even the theater columns, though filled with items on Francesca Adair's current visit, were buzzing about Caligari's arrival also.

On another page, there was a photo of Senator Childs and President Francois Mitterrand shaking hands. And beneath that was a photo of the beautiful Julia Romanov and her escort, Vidal Genero, at her exclusive apartment on the Avenue Foch, here for a short visit before leaving on a cruise along the Riviera.

Reading on, Caligari chuckled.

His company had arrived on the heels of the Bolshoi Ballet's last days in Paris, and he wondered if Julia had planned things that way on purpose. No, he decided. She'd done everything in her power to help, not hinder. It was just a coincidence. Besides, his company was quite unlike the Bolshoi—more classically pure than dramatic. He'd let Paris choose between their totally different styles.

After a light lunch, while his company members rested at Neuilly, Caligari and his stage manager made a fast trip to inspect the theater. Although he had once performed at the charming Théâtre de la Cité, located on the Right Bank near the busy Place du Châtelet, it was necessary now to check the facilities. He had to make sure that the stage floor would be easy to dance on, that it wouldn't be slippery or nicked—either way a dangerous situation.

He was therefore astounded to find, when he arrived, the very finest accommodations.

The stage was gorgeous—clean as a whistle, with ample space and dressing rooms for all his dancers. The whole theater sparkled inside and out, as it had recently been refurbished with materials similar to those Julia Romanov had used for the Caligari Company's New York City home. Seeing it, he was relieved and pleased.

That same night, as the Caligari Ballet Company slept peacefully, two bold young men crept through a maze of doors and windows, down a dozen elevators and up a thousand steps. They were sweating profusely, with their racing heartbeats always one step ahead of their legs. They crawled through small spaces and basements, brushing away spiderwebs, trying their best to keep from being seen. They would spend the night in a rathole if necessary, whatever it took to accomplish their ends.

Chapter 33

In her luxurious apartment on Avenue Foch, Julia Romanov rested on a red silk settee with a member of her secretarial staff. Together, they were sorting out all the invitations she'd received since her plane had landed at Orly.

Everyone begged her presence at their parties: the Maharanee of Khartoon, with her two eligible sons; the Duke and Duchess of Claymore; Lady Caroline Moret; and Madame Paranger with her inept ambassador husband, who were hosting a party for Senator Thomas Childs and his guest, the famous American actress Francesca Adair.

"They say she's slept with every important male ballet dancer in the world," Julia's secretary, Elise, said.

Julia smiled. Perhaps.

There would be feasts, she knew, magnificent banquets crawling with fascinating people and the kind of stimulating conversation she always enjoyed: on art, literature, theater and politics. And she would have attended all of them except for two things: she would try to see her cousin Ilya one more time, then attend to the startling announcement her loving Vidal had made.

He had dropped his little bombshell on her two hours before they landed. "I have something to tell you," he'd told her. "It's time I got back to work."

With those words, she saw herself lonely again and the feeling of being isolated haunted her. Alone was the one place Julia Romanov never wanted to be.

On the arm of Vidal Genero, she felt young, attractive, secure, the envy of every woman at every party she attended. Besides that, as a *premier danseur* from London, Vidal carried his own fame. To lose such a "hot property" could keep her away from the important action, at least for a while. Nobody liked a beautiful fifth wheel at a dinner party.

She couldn't imagine taking a cruise alone, or even living alone. Without a companion to share things, where was the fun of life? And Vidal had brought her great pleasure. Even though she wanted him to be happy, she hated the thought of losing him more. Then an idea enticed her, and as she played with it in her mind, she heard Vidal bound up the white marble staircase and enter her bedroom. He told her it was important, that Alexandra was waiting on the telephone.

Chapter 34

It was the morning of their first dress rehearsal and everyone was nervous. Class had been over for an hour and the dancers stood quietly on stage as the lighting director and stage manager fussed with their props, lights and backdrops. Since Caligari was a man who detested clutter, who liked his choreography to stand on its own merits, all props and backdrops were kept simple. Yet the details and kinks still had to be worked out.

Backstage, posted on the callboard were the lineups. Each girl was expected to know the other female roles, while each boy was expected to know the men's. Shane and Dorsey were to understudy Paige's role of Fate. Meanwhile, Alexandra, who was still relegated to the corps, had finally gotten the nerve to make her move. Then Caligari called for a quick run-through, and as Joshua pounded the piano everyone continued with the work.

In the theater lobby as the company rehearsed on stage, members of French television, along with newspaper journalists and paparazzi, waited to interview the daughter of the flamboyant Senator Childs. The intrusion rankled Caligari at first, and as he moved to evict them from the premises, a breathless Paige cornered him on a ramp which led from the stage down to the orchestra.

"Don't be too hasty," she whispered in his ear. "We can use them to our own advantage."

"How?" Caligari asked.

"Tell them to interview Dorsey here on stage and *we'll* get the publicity." Her smile was cunning. "I see packed houses because of her. The situation's a natural."

Ten minutes later Caligari permitted them to take photos of Dorsey dancing with the company, while Paige supervised the interviews.

It was important not to be seen, and the two young men had been quiet, still as death itself, for hours. But now they were finally beginning to relax, to feel a little better. It would soon be over, they knew. Just a little more patience, a little more time. And to keep from going mad, they shared jokes with one another while keeping their minds fixed on the time, and on what they were about to do.

Chapter 35

The excitement in the hours before opening night was both terrifying and glorious. Like horses on derby day, they were all on a razor's edge. Some dancers grew quiet, while others discharged energy in a dozen different ways. Some responded with chills, diarrhea and vomiting.

On stage, Caligari calmly made last-minute changes in the angle of a spotlight while a wardrobe mistress altered tutus to fit the weight some ballerinas had lost in the last hours.

Outside the theater, publicity people checked the marquee and the one-sheets inserted in glass cages on either side of the theater. They made last-minute checks with the box office. Happily, they confirmed the sold-out status of the entire week of performances, thanks to Julia's ads, Caligari's notoriety and the stories on Dorsey Childs.

Arriving by the hour were boxes of Swiss chocolates, trays of freshly sliced fruit—bananas, melons, strawberries, kiwi slices, large succulent blackberries—and baskets of flowers sent by friends and well-wishers.

Inside the dressing rooms, dancers exchanged traditional *"merde"* gifts, small tokens of affection to convey love and good wishes.

Paige was nervous, screaming at Seth, then at a stagehand whom she later fired. Then, two hours before curtain time, Caligari worked with her and Seth on a tricky lift which had developed a timing problem.

"Hold her tightly, Seth," Caligari demanded. "But not too tightly. You want to control her body but not inhibit it." He watched them do it again. "No, goddammit! Keep your eyes *on* her. Find her balance point before you move."

Seth sulked away to his dressing room before they could try it again.

Some dancers ran up from the downstairs dressing rooms, checking and rechecking the wings to make sure no new piece of scenery or prop would inhibit their exits or entrances. Seamstresses still worked on newly snared costumes, confirming their numerical place in the correct order of appearance. And two hours before curtain time, the makeup rituals began.

Alexandra sat at a table between Dorsey and Shane in the brilliant glare of their tri-mirrored dressing room, doing what she had been trained to do since the age of nine, when she had appeared in her first "Nutcracker."

She applied Max Factor's Fair panstick to her face and throat for that all-important white, procelain pallor. Then she added the darker tones to create a thin nose, cheek hollows, a peaked forehead and a well-defined chin line. Following that were the highlights—a flat white base under her eyes and above her cheekbones to claim the light's attention, and over that, tons of white powder on her face, arms, shoulders, chest and back.

With stage makeup it is the eyes ballerinas pay the most attention to, and of all the dancers in the company, Alexandra's eyes were the biggest and most compelling. Especially now, with her weight at 105 pounds, they seemed even larger and more magnetic.

On her eyelids she used white highlight, with brown streaks in the crease. She darkened and elongated her eyebrows in an upward sweep and lined the rim of her lids with black eyeliner. She pasted long black lashes over her own, and as the glue dried, she blushed her cheeks and painted her lips with bright red lipstick.

She combed her hair in the regulation bun for the first classical fugue, using Elmer's glue to keep stray hairs in place. Last of all came huge rhinestone earrings to frame her face. Finished, she smiled at her reflection, pleased with her doll-like image.

"Twenty minutes to curtain," came the call throughout the doors and hallways. "Twenty minutes."

While some dancers nervously adjusted their toeshoes, flexing their arches, testing and restesting the strength of the ribbons and thin plastic bands on their ankles, others rode the elevators to the stage for a short warm-up. In the wings there were hugs and kisses with whispers of "break a leg" or *"merde,"* a French word meaning "shit," used by dancers around the world for "good luck."

Backstage, after vomiting for the fourth time, Dorsey finally calmed and stretched her legs against a wall, one heel on the floor, the other toe pointed to the ceiling, with her forehead touching her kneecap. Shane dipped into slow splits on the floor and flexed her arches. Near Shane, Alexandra did very deep, slow pliés, while in an obscure corner, Paige shook loose the muscles of her arms and legs, pacing back and forth like a caged tiger. Caligari moved among them, a calming influence, bestowing confidence, shoulder pats and gentle hugs as everyone bristled, waiting nervously for the orchestral downbeat.

Outside it was bedlam. The streets were a mélange of traffic, taxis and limousines, with beautiful people lining the lobby of the brilliantly lit, fountain-fronted theater. Among the first-nighters were Senator Childs, with his young, blond wife, Deandra; Francesca Adair, the famous American actress and balletomane; and Julia Romanov, with her escort, Vidal Genero.

Tossing her curtain of shiny straight shoulder-length hair to the side, Julia was a show-stopper dressed in a black Geoffrey Beene layered organdy dress, banded in black lace with a tight matte jersey bodice. Over her shoulders, a classic dark sable. She wore huge diamond earrings and a matching necklace of seventy blue-white five-carat stones that glittered as brilliantly as her shocking blue eyes. On the arm of Vidal, who was dressed in a leather tuxedo copied from one he had seen on the artist Erté, they were a paparazzo's dream.

Peeking from a small hole in the curtain, Dorsey suddenly yelled, "Look! Isn't that Rory and Mark?"

"Where?" Seth demanded.

She called out the section of the theater, but Seth shook his head. "You're seeing things," he said and continued warming up.

After looking again, Dorsey wasn't so sure.

Chapter 36

A hush fell over the crowd as the orchestra ceased its tuning and the huge crystal chandelier slowly dimmed. And Julia, sitting in her center-aisle seat, folded her program and waited for the curtain to rise. Somebody coughed, then polite applause began as a single spotlight followed the orchestra leader to the podium.

"I think the Rothschilds are here," somebody murmured.

"And Princess Stephanie."

Backstage came the downbeat as each dancer took his or her position behind the curtain.

"Full house," somebody called from the wings.

"Shh!" Caligari scolded.

The entire company stood in fourth position, arms in front, chests high, heads pulled to the ceiling, hearts pounding, concentrating, banishing and denying fear. Then the red velvet curtains slowly lifted to reveal a black and terrifying abyss.

The dancers looked spectacular—the women in white tulle, romantic tutus with crowns of blue flowers for their hair. The men in pale blue tights and royal-blue jackets.

In the wings Caligari watched them, his thoughts at first poetic. Go, little fledgings, he thought. Then the poetry left and the craftsman took over. Damn that girl, he thought, she's not counting properly! No, Seth, no! Don't pull her too close. God, they looked awful, he thought. Ruining his ballet.

Alexandra counted as she spun, "One, two, three, four; two, two, three, four." She arched her foot, tensed her calf muscle and never felt stronger in her life. This was what she had been born for, this special moment here on stage, warmed by the lights, buoyant and ethereal, a floating bubble in a loving breeze.

In the audience Vidal caught his breath. He couldn't believe his eyes. He nudged Julia as Alexandra leaped across the stage. "Look at her," he whispered. "Look at her elevation. I can't believe it!"

A lady in front turned her head in Vidal's direction and Julia nudged him to silence.

Vidal settled back and watched the rest of the fugue, a magnificent piece set to Bach which commanded his full attention. And the more he watched, the more his muscles twitched. He could do the leap better, he thought, and with more aplomb. And that lift should be higher, with more bravado.

The dancers whirled point and counterpoint to the quick melodic passages. Then came the adagio, as Seth and Paige claimed center stage. It was lovely—arabesque penchés and romantic lifts across the stage from one wing to the other—and Seth partnered Paige brilliantly. Then the corps took over with changements and chaînes turns as Paige and Seth exited to the wings to catch their breath.

Doubled over and gasping for air, the dancers let the wardrobe mistresses pat sweat from their arms, foreheads and shoulders. Then the performance smile was plastered on their faces once again as they prepared for the next entrance.

* * *

Watching Alexandra dance, Julia dismissed the girl's anxious phone call prior to performance. She was taken back more than eleven years to the time when Alexandra first told her she wanted to be a ballerina.

The child had been home from school on Christmas vacation, and Birdie had taken her to Lincoln Center to see the New York City Ballet. She was enthralled with the experience, as though God Himself had wrapped her in His arms and planted an unshakable dream in her heart.

"Oh, Mommy, you should have seen their white lace dresses," she said, prancing. *"So pretty. Oh, Mommy. I want to dance just like that when I grow up."* As she talked, she imitated the poses, the coltish legs and arms stretching out, and as she fell, Julia had to keep from laughing.

Now, in this theater, Julia wasn't laughing anymore. Instead she nearly wept. Oh, Alexandra. If only things had been different, she thought. If only she could have been more of a mother.

Applause burst forth like a torrent at the fugue's conclusion. Backstage, some dancers gasped for air while others changed costume for the next number.

Then came the intermission.

In the lobby as Julia chatted with several friends, Vidal noticed a familiar young man waving at him.

"Excuse me for a moment," he said to Julia. "There's someone I haven't seen in a while."

Five minutes later the lights began flashing, a small bell chimed and the crowd returned to their seats.

When the curtain rose, the company began again with a New Wave ballet danced to synthesizers. Then there was another ensemble piece done to a Japanese koto. At the end of the performance, the company assembled for bows while flowers and applause rained down on everyone. Then the curtains parted for solo bows.

                                * * *

Alexandra watched with hunger as the curtains parted
and Paige passed gracefully through. She felt her stomach
sink as roses were delivered on stage and Paige, accepting
them, customarily kissed and presented one to her partner.
Plain as day, Alexandra saw herself in Paige's place, and it
was then she knew she'd made the right decision.

When the lights came up at the program's conclusion,
Vidal begged a raging headache. He told Julia he would
return to the hotel and rest. She would have gone with him,
but an invitation to join the company's celebration had
been extended. As Vidal hailed a taxi, Julia settled into her
Bentley limousine. But on her way to the party she saw the
dance master walking alone on a darkened street and called
out to him.

Chapter 37

Before he saw the Bentley, Caligari heard the melodious voice call out. When the limousine pulled up to the sidewalk and Julia waved hello, he smiled.

"Hi," she said.

"Hi, yourself," he replied.

"Come on, I'll give you a lift to the celebration."

He shook his head. "Thanks, but I won't be going. I'd just keep the kids from having a good time."

"Then let me buy you dinner," Julia offered. "It'll give me a chance to thank you, to tell you how wonderful it all was."

Her words were appealing; he needed the compliment as well as the company. "Funny," he said. "I've been meaning to thank you too."

Entering and sitting beside her, his arousal was immediate, urgent, strong, and he was grateful for the long trench coat that concealed his desire.

"Thank me for what?" Julia asked.

"For what?! For everything," he said. "For giving me the chance to do what I've always dreamed of."

"Can't think of money better spent," she said.

He settled in his seat, aware of her leg, which rested gently against his as though it belonged there naturally.

"So where can I take you?" Julia asked. "La Ripaille? Régine's? La Tour? Maxim's?"

"A quiet place," he said. "I've had enough crowds for one night."

She thought and then smiled. "I know just the place."

Fifteen minutes later, they were on an elevator inside the Plaza Athenée, one of Paris' most elegant and luxurious hotels.

"I keep a suite here all year round," Julia said as the elevator doors opened. "We can order dinner and relax in complete privacy."

She was meeting his needs once again, he thought. He couldn't think of a thing to say.

"Are you always this quiet and depressed after a performance?" she asked as she opened the front door to her suite.

"I'm really not depressed," he said. "A little low key, maybe. Recharging the batteries. Always thinking how I could have done things better."

She seemed to understand, he thought, gazing at her blue eyes and satin hair.

"Would it help if I said how beautiful everything was?"

"No, but tell me anyway."

He followed her inside and heard the door close. When the lamps clicked on, his eyes roamed the softly lit room.

Like her, it was lush, a large cream and gold suite decorated in the style of Louis XVI.

"You look exhausted," Julia told him, taking his coat. "Why don't you sit near the fireplace. I'll order some food and we'll make a nice fire." She paused on her way to the closet. "Maybe you'd like a nice hot shower? That always makes me feel better."

He breathed an overdue sigh of relief. "To tell you the truth, I'd love one."

While he showered, Julia lit a fire, arranged soft cushions on the lush gold carpet. With a sense of excitement, she ordered Petrossian caviar, Louis Roederer Cristal champagne, some fresh fruit, a pot of kona coffee and a bottle of Napoleon brandy. Then she wondered if he were really hungry and wanted a substantial meal instead. She knocked to ask, and at first touch the bathroom door opened. She watched through a small crack, fixated as the water cascaded down his dark naked body.

As he soaped in the cascading water, her eyes roamed his strong thighs and muscular buttocks, feasted on his small waist and hairless chest. She was mesmerized. He was gorgeous, sexy, all of him smooth, the color of sweet caramel candy.

His eyes remained closed as he washed, as though his bathing were some sort of meditation, and watching, she found herself unconsciously lifting the hem of her dress, roaming along her bare inner thighs, stroking lightly at the crotch of her black lace panties. She imagined herself lying next to him, naked, kneading his hips, his belly, his groin. Her bracelet soon snagged the black lace undergarment, and as a tiny sigh of longing escaped her lips, she moved quickly from the door, thankful he hadn't seen or heard.

Room service arrived a few minutes later and Julia arranged things near the warmth of the fireplace. Soon after, Caligari emerged from the bathroom wearing Vidal's robe, and she invited him to join her near the crackling fire.

"I didn't know what you'd like," she said as he dropped beside her on the carpet. "So I ordered caviar and champagne."

He settled back, resting his elbows and back on the large silk cushions, and scanned the array of food. *"Everything* looks delicious," he said, staring pointedly at her.

She filled a plate for him, feeling herself grow warm, as if she were being drawn like kindling into the dangerous fire of his dark Gypsy eyes. Then his gaze met hers in a head-on collision and a split second later she was pinned beneath his chest on the cushions.

As his mouth covered hers, a wild wind surrounded the hotel windows, sang out against the glass panes like a new hurricane. It whirled and swirled, taking everything in its path along with it. For her, the world ceased to exist. But she wasn't afraid. She was warm in his arms, shielded by his strength, rescued from the slings and arrows of those whose outrageous lives she touched in so many ways. She was in the eye of the storm, tranquil above the turmoil, dancing on the moon and playing with the stars.

"Julia, Julia," he breathed against her ear. "I've dreamed a thousand times of loving you this way."

She felt drunk at his whispered words and recalled clearly the savage hunger in his eyes when he'd first entered her car. All along she'd known it wasn't food he'd craved. Now she felt that way too. And so she yielded, melted, offering him her lips again and again, panting wildly as his fingers reached beneath to remove her garments.

Naked in the dancing firelight, she felt the dam inside her body shake and tremble at his touch, bursting finally as he kissed her breasts, tumbling over her in great torrents of feeling. It was glorious! Love! Surrender! Freedom! Everything she'd been searching for all her life. Love! She could smell its elusive bouquet. It was inches from her grasp.

Unlike the very gentle Vidal, Caligari was fiery and demanding in his lovemaking, kissing every inch of her body, digging his fingers into her soft and willing flesh. She found herself moaning, drifting as their bodies entwined.

While his hands roamed the planes and curves of her body, snaking along the tender skin of her inner thighs, she ran her fingers through handfuls of his damp black hair. Spurred on by her eagerness, he sank his teeth into her arm, rolled over and lifted her above him. Her pink nipples fell gracefully, naturally to his tongue and lips.

With her head drawn back and her palms framing his head, she felt his finger knead one nipple, the tip of his tongue slowly circle the other; then he crushed her to him in a passionate embrace.

Lying tightly against him, she grew conscious of his massive thighs which pressed against hers, of his thick mat of pubic hair, of his fully erect penis which leaped at the opening of her creamy slit. It was all happening so quickly. Swept away for the first time with any man, she felt totally wicked and abandoned herself to her wild desires.

Instead of being the follower, she eagerly pursued him, crouching down and taking the tip of him inside her mouth.

He was the first man she had ever kissed there, and the experience was exhilarating. She was surprised to find the skin so soft, so sweet to the taste. As she kissed him, she felt his organ throb and grow stronger, felt his hands and fingers along her lips and tongue as he helped guide her movements. It was all delicious, so new, and she felt a sense of power at controlling and stimulating his passion.

She wanted to experience everything and teased the tip with gentle bites and a darting tongue. She rubbed the shaft with gentle strokes, as if she had done it a thousand times. Loving him that way felt right, comfortable, as natural as kissing any other part of his body.

Moaning with pleasure, maddened by her impudence, he grabbed her shoulders and rolled her on her back. Her satin hair fanned out like a flower as she stared up at his face in the orange firelight, at the great black brooding eyes, at the long dark hair that tumbled down across his forehead. She sighed with longing at his moist, sensuous mouth which lay just inches from hers, sighed at the broad naked shoulders that gleamed all red and yellow heat above her in the flickering shadows. Her lips uttered her passion and she closed her eyes as his lips grazed hers in a tender kiss. She gave herself recklessly as the kiss, which started at her lips, moved across her cheek, down her neck, her breasts, her belly to her thighs.

As he exhaled his hot breath against her dark triangle, she shivered, relinquishing everything in a sigh of relief. She was limp, unable to move a muscle. Soon his lips and tongue sought the plump folds of her vagina, capturing the sensitive bud in his mouth.

Waves of heat radiated out from her groin as she spread her legs, fanned out across her body, from the top of her head to the tips of her toes. As he teased her with the steady rhythm of his tongue, the intense heat, the unbelievable pleasure made her body arch like a cat's.

She pushed his head closer, felt the perspiration drip down her forehead and into her satin hair. Where the dam once lived, a fire now raged, and she writhed beneath him, begging for deliverance, begging him to quench the flames.

He released her and for a moment their eyes met. "You're beautiful, Julia. My God! You're so beautiful."

The heat of his body against hers penetrated her skin and spread like wildfire through her veins. Then a steel rod drove the breath from her lungs as, with a low, deep moan, he lifted her buttocks, arched his hips upward and slowly entered.

At first he moved slowly, easily, watching her face. Then he dipped and let his tongue slide along the lines of her lips. She loved and reveled in the smell of him, swayed as he pumped, sucked him deeper inside with her muscles and let her tongue graze his. Where before two shadows had moved on the wall, there was now only one.

He thrust deeper, deeper in a place she had no name for, in and out, dripping wet with perspiration until she felt herself quicken. She let out a cry as she came.

He kissed her mouth, her eyes, her face, thrusting as it happened. He pulled her leg across his and buried his head in her neck. Then, with more precise timing, rotating his hips as he thrust, he climbed to his own ecstasy.

Sweat dropped from his hair onto her shoulders and mingled with hers. She heard him inhale sharply, then hold his breath. And as he thrust rapidly, his body suddenly froze and shuddered. She came again with him, feeling his warm semen spurt inside her. Then they collapsed together in a drenched heap on the floor.

Chapter 38

    While he slept on his side near the fireplace,
Julia ran a bubble bath. She stared at the image of her
naked body in the soft pink light of the boudoir, smiling
like a sated cat who had secretly slurped a whole dish of
cream. She leaned closer to her reflection to see her eyes.
The river of ice had melted and a soft dreamy blue peered
back at her.

    A miracle had finally happened and the experience had
been magical—as if some missing part of her had been
found and she was whole once again. It wasn't just the
orgasm, she knew, or even Caligari, that magnificent
beast. It was the feeling, a deep inner belief that she was
no longer different, she was a normal woman like all
the rest. More important, she believed the ghost of Giorgio
had finally been slain.

    Caligari wakened with a start and reached across the
mound of pillows to touch her arm, but she wasn't there.
Then he heard the sound of splashing water in the
bathroom. He sat up and, brushing back his thick black
hair, stretched his body. Inside the room the once-roaring
fire had dwindled to a few glowing embers, yet the suite
remained warm as toast.

    He tied a towel around his waist, took the tray of champagne, caviar and fresh fruit and carried it with him to the washroom, where he gently nudged the door open with his knee. He found her there, sitting in a steamy tub of jasmine-scented bubbles with her hair piled high on her head, looking beautiful.

"A little refreshment for madame," he said playfully.

"I thought I heard you rustling about," she said, laughing. "C'mon. Come in and join me."

Caligari set the tray of goodies on the broad base of a nearby marble table and moved toward the tub. He put his toe into the inviting water and purred. The temperature was warm and delicious, fit for a king. He tossed away his towel and edged down into the pool of sweet-smelling foam, where he stretched his long, muscular legs as far as they could go, easing his back against the opposite side of the tub to face her. "You're sleek, Julia, like a cat," he said, settling in. "Did anyone ever tell you that?"

"Not a soul." She sponged her shoulders with the foamy water and smiled as she continued, "I've been called a lot of things, and by a lot of people, but a sleek cat's not one of them."

Caligari pressed his strong legs against the sides of the tub while his toes gently teased her hips. It surprised him now how easy he felt in her presence.

He reached for the bottle of Dom Pérignon and poured two full glasses. He handed her one, and as they toasted each other he drank in the features of her beautiful face. She looked incredible in the low, pink light, he thought, especially her eyes, which were now so clear, so crystal-blue, like the ocean as it shimmers with the sun's last rays. Looking at her made him suddenly swell and he knew it was just a matter of time before he'd make love to her again.

He finished his champagne and placed his glass on the nearby marble table. He took the crystal dish of caviar and, reaching inside, drew out a finger full of black roe. Slowly, seductively, he licked it all clean, making noises of satisfaction as she watched him.

"Share?" he asked, spearing another finger full and offering it to her.

She nodded and sat up, with her small, perfect breasts bobbing above the bubbles toward him.

He pulled the roe closer to himself, beckoning, teasing her. "C'mon," he said. "Slide over here and get it."

Laughing, she inched toward him in a swish of water, placing her empty champagne glass on the tub's lip. Then, perched on her knees with her lips parted and a wicked glint in her eye, she snatched his hand and sucked the finger clean.

Every single nerve in his body jumped, came alive at her touch, as though he had plugged himself into a wall socket and pulled the switch. He grabbed her and pulled her to his lips, kissing her with every ounce of passion in his body.

Their breathing grew intense, as though they had just run the hundred-yard dash together and won.

Then, unable to restrain himself any longer, he took her again in the tub, with the warm water cleansing and surrounding them like the sac of a newborn baby.

Later, in the soft light of a new dawn, they rested on the silken sheets of the bed, coiled in each other's arms. He felt warm and comfortable as her long fingers stroked the corded muscles of his chest. He felt content, happy beyond his wildest dreams. A deep hole in his being had been filled. After eluding him for so long, love had charged in and challenged him, and he felt like a king whose once-lost empire had now been reclaimed.

Together, in low, romantic tones, yet hesitating in such new and dangerous territory, they shared the most intimate details of their past lives, trusted one another with their fragile hopes and dreams.

Love makes you so strong and able, he thought as he told her of his mother and his life as a child. Love makes you so frightened and vulnerable, she thought as she told him of Giorgio and her mother, Tatiana.

They kissed each other's faces and hands between words, giggled, stroked, caressed, inhaled each other's now-familiar scents. He studied her eyes in the low light and tried again to get a fix on the color, but it still eluded him. She let her fingers wade in the sea of long dark hair that covered his forehead in a tumble of black velvet waves.

It was this way with them for hours; touching, feeling close, complete, whole, so very satisfied as they talked. And they talked endlessly for hours about everything, and all the barriers between them fell easily away as the truths of their lives tumbled in a waterfall of sharing. All the years of suffering, of loneliness, of searching, of finding and loving false prophets had brought them to this room, to this place, to this moment in time.

"The first time I laid eyes on you, I nearly threw you on that Oriental rug and made love to you," he told her.

She chuckled wickedly. "I wish you had. We've wasted so much time."

He lifted her chin and grinned. "Baloney, my dear! You'd have sent me up on charges just like that." He snapped his fingers.

They laughed, tumbling beneath the covers where they shared more kisses and tender embraces. Then they lay in each other's arms, wondering again.

"Anticipate any problems when you get home?" he asked, nuzzling her forehead.

She looked up at him. "You mean Vidal?"

"Yes."

"Of course not," she said with a grin. "I do as I like." She settled back in his arms again. "Oh, Richard, I feel happy tonight. I have so many feelings I've never felt before. So many new and wonderful things. I feel like a schoolgirl."

"Mmmmmm," he agreed.

She sat up giggling. "No. I don't only mean us and what happened here tonight. I mean the ballet too. It's as if I've been given a second chance with Alexandra."

"Alexandra?"

"Yes," Julia said. "She looked so wonderful. So happy on that stage. I can't tell you how good it made me feel."

"She has improved," he agreed. "But she still has a long way to go."

Julia raised an eyebrow. "Then she hasn't talked to you? You don't know how she really feels, do you?"

"I'm not sure I understand," he said.

"She called me sometime before the performance," Julia said. "She wants to leave the company."

Caligari stared at her in amazement. "I don't understand. Why? Why would she say a thing like that? I've been good to her. I've always taken care of her."

"Oh, she's acknowledged that. But you cut a small solo she had in your Spanish ballet, and she says you're not using her enough."

"Well, I will," he told her. "Eventually. When she's ready. When the time is right."

Her maternal instinct came quickly alive as Julia's hands left his body. She stared at him, her back as straight as a ramrod. "I don't think you're listening to me, Richard. You've *got* to use her for something. Give her a break. I certainly hate to remind you, but she *is* the reason I invested in you in the first place."

He hugged her and laughed. "You once told me you liked candor, Julia. So let's not kid ourselves. You did that just as much for yourself as Alexandra."

Julia's eyes blazed with fury. "What the hell do you mean by that remark?"

"Hey," he said, kissing her forehead, "let's not do this to one another right now, okay? Tonight's been magic, a healing to me. I haven't felt this good in years."

She pulled away from him. "I'm afraid 'right now' is perfect," she said. "It's *time* Alex did something more than be a backdrop for Paige McDowell. At the very least, she should have a chance to understudy some solo part. In that fugue, for instance."

"You promised not to interfere in the creative process,

Julia," Caligari scolded. "That was part of the original deal."

"The deal, Mr. Caligari," Julia said angrily, "was *always* in terms of Alexandra's needs." She hesitated. "And I'm afraid if she leaves the company before the year is over, that escape clause applies."

They had started the discussion holding one another. Now they were on either side of the bed. "I beg to differ," he said. "The document I signed says it applies *only* if she learns who's backing me, and there's no chance of *that* happening."

Julia tossed aside the covers and left the bed. "No, maestro," she said, dressing herself quickly. "You'd better call your lawyer and have him read the fine print. No Alexandra, no money! That's the bottom line."

"Where are you going?" he yelled.

"Home," she said, putting on her sable.

"Back to Genero?"

"Yes, if it's any of your business."

"Don't make a fool of yourself, Julia. The guy is using you," he shouted, rising. His eyes blazed with jealousy.

She turned and glared at him. "You mean like you're using me?"

"That's different!"

"Yes, it is. When you're on the receiving end."

Two seconds later she slammed the door.

It was late at night and Simone lay weeping. All her life she'd waited for a moment like this and now she couldn't even share it with Shane. Damn them! Damn everything and everybody for what had happened to her.

Long ago she thought she'd have been a better dancer than her daughter, but after tonight, after seeing Shane in that solo, she realized the truth. Shane was pure magic and Simone would finally have to put that tired old myth to bed. She would never have been as beautiful. Never in a million years.

Of course, she was happy for Shane, thrilled to pieces.

Well, maybe just a tad jealous. But that kind of feeling was normal, she knew. After all, it hurt a lot not to be able to go to a lousy party, to celebrate the occasion with your own kid.

After all, she had done everything in her power for Shane's success. And she needed, wanted to be part of things—a full part of Shane's life, to be exact. But to dress up, to try and hide that ugly, withered leg, to drag herself up a flight of stairs, to sit on a chair in some crowded room and watch a bunch of healthy young dancers would only remind her of how tired she was, how worn, old and ragged. And then she would think of what her life might have been like if it hadn't been for *him*, for them, for what happened when Shane was just an innocent baby.

After the party, Shane ran to her mother's bedroom. It was late, but a light still beamed under Simone's door. She knocked softly and waited.

"Who's there?" Simone asked.

"It's me, Mom."

When Simone opened the door, Shane could see she'd been crying. She kissed her mother's cheek and tried to hug her. "Why didn't you come to the party?"

"Too tired," Simone said, closing the door and moving away from Shane's touch. "Another time, maybe."

Shane knew it was useless to argue. Simone discussed only what she chose to. "So?" She paused. "How was I? Did you watch me?"

"Is the Pope Catholic?" Simone said. She dragged herself back to bed. "Of course I watched you. You were the best. As soon as that Paige bitch breaks a leg—God willing—they'll throw flowers at *you*. My God! Your extensions were beautiful. Your arms were gorgeous. Plisetskaya in her prime was a duck compared to you."

Shane squeezed her mother's hand for the compliment. If Simone was anything at all, it was truthful. "I got your *merde* gift too," she said.

Simone's eyes lit up, then just as quickly dimmed again. "I had a feeling you wouldn't like it."

"Like it? I loved it! I took it to the party with me and showed everyone. They all said they'd never seen a prettier piece of crystal."

Chapter 39

The call that wakened Julia at 9:30 A.M. the following morning was similar to the one which wakened Senator Thomas Childs and his guest, the American actress Francesca Adair.

"This is the American Embassy, Madame Romanov. It's a matter of the utmost importance that you be here within the hour. And please. Inform no one we've called."

On stage at the theater, 10 A.M. class commenced on schedule. Everyone felt confident but very tired. The reviews had been incredible. Every Parisian newspaper, every tabloid, every television and radio journalist had deemed Caligari an innovator, the "brightest light on ballet's horizon." As a result, the theater's management requested that the company stay one more week, but the dance master declined. He firmly believed in the old adage "Keep 'em wanting more."

Besides that, even if he wanted to he couldn't change the company's itinerary. Rome was a week away, then the premiere of "Patrins" at London's Royal Festival Hall.

"One, two, three, four." Caligari rapped the pointer as Joshua played the piano. "Deep pliés, please."

Several dancers groaned. One winced and hobbled away.

"I know you're tired," Caligari told them. "We all are. But there are still some rough spots we have to cover." He looked at them through steely eyes and tried not to think of Julia. "No matter how glorious the papers say we are."

When class was over, he asked Alexandra to join him in the darkened orchestra.

"I've been watching you," he told her. His throat muscles involuntarily clenched as he swallowed. "You've lost a lot of weight and you've been working like a demon. Because of that, I'm going to give you some responsibility to go with the new image."

He was handling the situation well, he thought. And most of what he was telling her was true.

Alexandra smiled. For a moment he thought there were tears in her eyes, but it was too dark to see.

He actually liked the girl at the same time he hated Julia for what she was forcing him to do. But he would take whatever she dished out, for now. Until the gala, anyway. After that, he would be through with her, with everyone who had ever tried to hurt or take advantage of him. Never again would he permit anyone to interfere with his work. And that included Paige. After the Christmas Gala, nothing would ever come between him and his art again.

He said it quickly. "I want you to join the others who are understudying Paige in 'Patrins.' Learn it!"

Alexandra gasped. "But Mr. Caligari, it's, it's . . ."

"It's all right," he said, taking her hand. "You'll be splendid. I'll give you some private classes and we'll work it out. Don't worry—you'll be fine. Maybe even ready in time for the New York gala."

In the Bentley on her way to the American Embassy, Julia swallowed her tears. She had waited a lifetime to meet someone special, to fall in love. And it had finally happened. Damn Caligari! Damn all men!

She hadn't expected it to happen this way. All at once, so quickly. And with *him*, of all people. All her life, love had eluded her. Now, in the space of four hours, she'd managed to find then lose it. Why? Why had she behaved like a shrew? The man was an artist. He was sensitive and distinguished, not a fool. Who the devil did she think she was?

Then the bitterness returned, the alienation she'd felt when he'd mocked her, when she'd left him last night.

No! She wasn't thinking right. It was the other way around. Who did *he* think *he* was? Telling her Alexandra wasn't ready. Why, the kid looked smashing. Anyone with eyes could see. And if she couldn't help her own daughter, who in the hell would?

Well, screw him, she thought. Let him work his damned frustrations out elsewhere. She'd made her demands known, and if he knew what was good for him he'd follow through—or else! Still, in spite of her anger and rage, in spite of her enmity, a part of her felt desolate. If there truly was only one man for every woman, she'd blown it, and now her future looked bleak.

When the telephone suddenly rang backstage, a lighting technician answered. He left the phone dangling and walked on stage, calling for Shane. "Hurry up, honey," he prodded her. "It's long distance."

Two seconds later Shane was standing in the wings, holding the receiver to her ear and listening to Brad's voice.

"I miss you, dammit," he told her.

Shane laughed. "I miss you too. Oh, Brad, our performance was fantastic last night. You should have been here. And the flowers you sent were so beautiful. Thanks."

"Never mind all that," he said. "When are you coming home?"

"As soon as the tour is over. You know that." Shane shifted the receiver to her other ear and rubbed a sore muscle in her thigh.

"But I can't wait that long, Shane. I miss you. And," he paused, "and I'm asking you to marry me."

"Oh, Brad," she said. Her heart raced wildly as she contemplated his question. "You're kidding, of course."

"I am not! I mean it. I'm crazy about you, you numbskull."

"Oh, I love you too, Brad. But marriage—well, that's such a serious step. Something we should talk about first. I mean what about my career?"

"You won't need it anymore," he said, totally dismissing her question. "I'll buy you a big house in the Hamptons and we'll have six terrific kids."

She laughed again. "Now I know you're kidding. Well, aren't you?"

When he answered, his voice was low and without humor. "No, I'm not, Shane. I've never been more serious in my life. And if you don't come back soon, I'll fly out there and drag you home to prove it."

It was useless to argue, so she changed the subject instead. "Hey, what about my pretty crystal slipper?" she asked. "Did you ask Tom to give it back?"

"I already told you the kid didn't take it."

"I don't believe him," Shane said.

"Think what you like," he told her. "But Tom left for summer camp the day after we met on the beach. He wasn't even around when I gave it to you. Try looking a little harder. Maybe you misplaced it." He paused. "Very clever, Shane! You managed to take me off course, but it won't do any good. So I'll say it again. I love you. I want to marry you, and the minute you get back we're going to make wedding plans." He threw her a kiss, then the line was filled with static and they said good-bye.

Alone in the wings, Shane contemplated the phone call. If Tom hadn't taken her crystal slipper, who had? More important, if she said yes to Brad's marriage proposal, what would happen to her career? To her life? To all of Simone's dreams? But what if she lost him? Afraid to speculate any further, she returned to class, aware for the first time in her life she was trembling all over.

* * *

When Julia finally arrived at Avenue Gabriel, she was startled at the number of paparazzi and French police surrounding the American Embassy. The air was charged with electricity, with a strange excitement, as though something important had happened. She'd been summoned before by the embassy, but it had usually been in regard to her business dealings. This time, however, the call had been so secretive, and she was concerned as well as curious.

Half a block away, she left the Bentley in the dense traffic and walked toward the gate, where she was jostled by a huge crowd of reporters. Then, outside the wrought-iron fence surrounding the compound, her identification was checked, and after a thorough search of her belongings she was given permission to enter.

After a few minutes, Julia was taken up the carpeted staircase to a large office, where Control Officer Edmund McCall, a stocky man with balding brown hair that had recently been transplanted in a V of soft plugs above his forehead, greeted her with a firm handshake. He introduced her to Senator Thomas Childs and the American actress Francesca Adair, then to Monsieur François Gibert, a representative from the United Nations' High Commission for Refugees.

"Thank you for coming," Control Officer McCall said, returning to his place behind a large desk near a flag of the United States. "We're in need of your assistance."

"Of course," Julia said. "I'll do whatever I can."

Mr. McCall offered her the comfort of a brown leather chair situated in front of his desk. Then he sat and nodded in the direction of a steel door which two Marines stood guarding. At his gesture, a Marine pressed a button which caused the steel door to disappear into a side wall. Opening, it revealed the figures of two young men—one dark with a medium build, the other tall with long blond hair. Julia recognized the blond one instantly.

The moment they entered the room Julia gasped.

"Ilya!" she cried, rising and extending her arms to receive him. "My God! I've been desperately trying to reach you." She held him tightly in her arms until he collapsed at her feet, sobbing, telling his story of escape from the ballet in broken but fairly good English.

"Yuri and I—we leave company two days ago," he said as they helped him up and into a chair. "We climb through attic of theater then hide there two days. It was horrible! Please, Julia, you will help? I must leave. Must to go to America."

Julia squeezed his hand tightly. "Yes, yes. I'll help you, Ilya," she said. "I'll do everything I can."

She glanced at the control officer. "What happens next, Mr. McCall? Can he come home with me to New York City?"

McCall glanced quickly at Gibert, then back at Julia. "Ordinarily we try our best to internationalize these defections by referring such cases to the United Nations High Commission, of which Mr. Gibert is a member. And it's worked for Mr. Gregorsky here," he said, referring to the young man with Ilya. "They've had luck finding him a place and a position in England where he has some friends."

"But since you're a relative of Mr. Kremorkin's and America is his first choice of destination, our embassy will do what we can to help. But we'll need your total cooperation."

"Just tell me what to do," Julia told him.

"Mr. Kremorkin will need your sponsorship. By that, we mean a permanent residence in the United States and the promise of work in his field of endeavor. Are you prepared to provide those things?"

Julia looked into Ilya's red-rimmed hazel eyes. "I'll do whatever it takes," she said without wavering.

Senator Childs broke in, "The next few weeks won't be easy, Miss Romanov," he told her. "Expect the KGB to harass him—to follow Ilya, and you and members of your family. They'll do everything they can to get him to change his mind and go back. His defection's going to be an embarrassment to them."

"The best thing," McCall added, "would be for you both to fly back to New York City with the Senator by military transport and wait out the next few weeks in your apartment. Eventually they'll accept it and just give up. Now, if you're unable to provide work for Mr. Kremorkin, Miss Adair has graciously offered him a job."

"Yes," Francesca said, crossing her long, sexy legs. "I'm preparing a new movie around the first of the year and Ilya will be perfect in a co-starring role."

Outside, the paparazzi screamed for acknowledgment. By this time everyone knew that two dancers had defected from the Bolshoi Ballet, but no one knew exactly who they were. For Ilya Kremorkin, just a few short hours after a U.S. debriefing, his identity would finally be revealed and his dreams of freedom, of dancing in the West, would be realized. When the press conference began, he took his place with his friend Yuri at the bank of microphones, between Julia Romanov and Edmund McCall, to answer questions. But in all the excitement he failed to see the hungry, delicious glow in Francesca Adair's pretty eyes.

Chapter 40

Sitting at her bedroom window in the last moments of a dazzling sunset, Alexandra gazed past huge green trees, across the grounds at an old bridge which spanned the stately Seine. She marveled at its ancient beauty, savored its peaceful and quiet serenity.

Suddenly a small boat, alive with laughter and people, passed slowly under the bridge. In its wake, luminous waves undulated toward shore, reflecting the sun's last rays like the facets of a fiery topaz. This was Paris—old but young, simple yet romantic—and she would miss it.

Soon they would be leaving for Rome, and she reached for her diary, wanting to capture her last impressions.

Dear Diary,
Where do I begin? Julia and Vidal flew back to New York with Ilya, Dorsey's father, and Francesca Adair. (She's prettier in person.) The whole world is buzzing about Ilya's defection. Headlines everywhere. We're very distant cousins on Tati's side but I've never met him. The only thing I remember is how upset Julia was when she got back from Paris about eight years ago. Ilya performed Spartacus then and they couldn't spend five seconds alone without the KGB breathing down their

necks. God bless America. Dumb communists! Someone should tell them the harder you hold someone the more they want to leave.

Shane had another nightmare last night. Screamed like a baby. Tati told me dreams tell important things. I wonder what's really going on in Shane's mind. Lately she spends time with her mother, which blows me away. She used to call her the "old bat." Now they're like peas in a pod.

Dorsey's been acting weird too. But I think I know why. She binges on French food, then takes laxatives and some horrible medicine that makes her throw up. Acts real goofy sometimes too. I think the pills are starting to get to her.

Now for some good news: Ta-da! Lost fifteen pounds and am taking daily private lessons with Mr. C. It all started right after we opened in Paris, just when I was going to quit. Finally! A part in "Patrins."

Why he chose me, I can't say, but I trust him. He wouldn't give me the time of day if he didn't think I had talent. Now, for sure, I know I was meant to be a star.

Oh, well. Onward and upward—or is it southward?—to Rome.

On Thursday the company reached Rome's Leonardo da Vinci Airport following a smooth two-hour plane ride from Paris. The welcoming weather was warm and sunny, and after a pleasant bus trip south along the Appian Way, they reached their luxurious villa, which was located above Lake Albano in the peaceful green Alban Hills not far from Castel Gandolfo, the Pope's summer residence.

Everything went as scheduled on opening night at Teatro del Caracalla in Via Viminale, opposite the Termini Station, and the Italian reviews were as splendid as those they had received in Paris.

On their off hours most company members rested their weary bones, but when Alexandra wasn't working privately with Caligari, she joined Dorsey and Shane in an exploration of the Eternal City.

They rode in small horse-drawn carriages called *carrozzelle* and sipped espresso in the cafes along the Via del Corso. They went shopping on the Via Veneto and bought *merde* gifts on the Piazza del Popolo. They threw coins in Trevi Fountain and walked through the Trastevere visiting its quaint old shops.

After performances, they stuffed themselves with *calzone*—real Italian pizza—and *abbacchio,* lamb smothered in white wine, with fettucine; and for dessert, delicious gelato. Then ten short days later they were packing once again, leaving for London to complete the last leg of their tour.

Chapter 41

When the company arrived in London they were exhausted. They would be premiering "Patrins," the company's new Spanish Ballet, at the Royal Festival Hall. Everyone was excited.

Their lodgings, located in a London suburb called Barnes, were once again indulgent and generous: An eighteenth-century manor house with bow windows and wrought-iron grillwork, surrounded by old weeping willow trees and an enormous pond filled with ducks, geese and swans.

Inside the house, the furnishings were pure Victorian, heavy pieces inclined to intimidate and confine—Belter tables, polished brass, brocade curtains, ornate red velvet couches, wing chairs and a faded Duncan Phyfe mahogany piano. But the bedrooms were delightfully warm, with lace coverlets, Austrian puffs, Georgian silver, and except for some older staff members who groaned about the hard beds, there were few complaints.

Every day at 9 A.M., the company would leave Barnes and ride by bus to merge with the rhythm of London's heartbeat. They would travel across the Thames River to King's Road, continue around the south end of St. James's Park, pass Trafalgar Square and over Waterloo Bridge.

There, in a garden complex of buildings on the South Bank side, stood the Royal Festival Hall.

Once again Caligari was pleased with what Julia had provided. She might have been a demanding bitch, but she certainly wasn't cheap! The stage floor was perfect, and the acoustics, so important to the texture of "Patrins"' success—was a musician's dream.

They took class as usual, stretching their muscles to the limit, massaging each other's bones, sweating like pigs, careful most of all to avoid injury. And so far, they had been extremely lucky. No one had fallen or slipped. No ballerina had been dropped. There had been no pulled muscles, cracked ribs or torn ligaments. No broken toes or infections—not even a groin strain—and his male dancers had done their heroic share. Everyone hoped their luck would continue.

Simone spent time in the theater wings watching Caligari teach Alexandra the finer points of Spanish port de bras, or "carriage of the arms," so vital to the look of "Patrins." While watching, she would try to look busy, but anyone with eyes or imagination could tell that what she saw made her seethe.

For weeks she'd tried to convince Shane to work harder, to capture Caligari's attention any way she could. But Shane had at her core a basically timid personality. Simone tried to point out how both Dorsey and Alexandra were being treated differently, and Simone attributed that special treatment to their parents' wealth and imposing power. Shane naturally disagreed. But it was obvious to Simone she'd been right, and the taste of her truth was like bile in her mouth.

The day before opening-night performance, Alexandra, Shane, Dorsey and Seth stood in their costumes watching Caligari make some last-minute changes in "Patrins." It was a dress rehearsal and everyone knew the dance master was nervous. It wasn't unusual. A premiere was not an everyday occurrence. Even though Caligari was a strong choreographer, he was still an artist, sensitive and vulnerable to judgment like anyone else. But it was Paige and her red satin shoes that held everyone's attention.

"Look at her," Seth snickered. "She thinks she's Moira Shearer in *The Red Shoes*. He's changed that damned lift a dozen times to suit her." He crossed his arms over his chest and leaned against a wall. "Probably make me look like a fool when he's finished."

"Oh, don't be silly," Shane told him. "He has to accommodate her weaknesses. You're young and strong. You can handle things better than she can."

"He should've never taken the ballet away from you, Shane," Seth remarked again. "You did it best."

"Thanks," Shane replied. "And one of these days I'll have an opportunity to dance it." She paused and glanced nervously at her roommates. "And so will you, Alex, and you too, Dorsey."

"Sure," Dorsey said, laughing. "When and *if* Paige breaks a leg."

"Shit!" Seth said, kicking a shoe rack with Paige's name on it. "She'll never break a leg. Old dancers like her know how to fake it. The audience will think she's doing handstands, but I'll be the one making her look good. I'll do the work and she'll get the glory."

"Seth!" Shane scolded. "What's the matter with you? Where's your company spirit?"

"Fuck company spirit! Mark and Rory were right about them both," he said and quickly sauntered off stage.

A few minutes later Paige tripped. She screamed at a stagehand who had moved a rosin box from one corner of the stage to another. "How the hell can you be so stupid?!" she yelled. "Don't ever do that again!"

The man hurled his mug of tea against the wall, shatterng it, and stormed off stage.

"You're fired!" Caligari called after him. "Pick up your pay and don't come back."

Sometime around 9 P.M. a shadowy figure crept unobserved through the theater walkways, through the wings and past the one guard who sat sleeping on a cot near the sideboard.

The figure soon found the object of its desire—a pair of red satin toeshoes, and within seconds the deed had been accomplished. Walking quickly away, the smiling figure left. All that remained was the havoc to come.

Chapter 42

It was the night of the premiere. "Patrins" would be performed and judged, with its fate tossed into the capricious lap of posterity. Caligari's pride in his creation balanced on the fulcrum of fear. He loved the work but hated the scrutiny.

What would they say about him and his ballet? he thought, pacing backstage before performance. How would his work, his company be received? Would the audience understand and appreciate the intricate hand rhythms, the passionate shouts and impressions of *duende*, or possession? And would the virtuoso guitarists, Gypsy masters he'd summoned from Spain, give them everything they'd expected?

When creating any new work, Caligari saw himself as a matchmaker, with his dancers the bride and his chosen music the groom. And tonight more than anything, he wanted his new ballet to yield harmony, love, appreciation and respect—the perfect marriage.

Backstage held the usual hysteria, fear and excitement that always reigned on opening night. But a premiere also brought with it a special insanity, an overwhelming state of excess.

Stagehands scurried back and forth, fixing, hauling,

doing what had to be done. Towel-draped dancers lined along the walkways, stretched each other's legs, moaning, groaning, shaking loose, breathing each other's rarefied but stale air, holding each other's sweaty hands in comfort. There was ventilating, hyperventilating, crying and a strange laughter that would soon turn to tears.

Sitting on the floor, Alexandra calmly curled Band-Aids over her pinky toes while Dorsey crunched her pointe shoes in a large rosin box. She had taken a bad spill that same afternoon and wanted to be totally sure of her footing. Shane stood near Simone, who was busy checking a roster, arranging costume changes and new shoes for the dancers' easy access.

Outside, the audience was in great spirits, exceeding all attendance records. Caligari's company had had great publicity coming on the heels of their previously successful appearances. As notorious theater lovers, Londoners would not be outdone by the likes of Paris and Rome.

The night was clear, as glittering black as the limousines which dispatched their precious cargo in front of the theater. And all day long there had been rumors that the Prince and Princess of Wales would attend. That news brought the paparazzi out in droves and made the already exciting occasion that much more magnificent. The cream of London's fashionable society paraded their furs, jewels and gowns, each anxious to see the dancer master's premier effort, each one secretly hoping to be seen in the company of Their Royal Highnesses, Prince Charles and Princess Diana.

Minutes before the performance, Paige stood alone in a corner near a large trunk, shaking loose her legs and arms like a sprinter before an Olympic run. She was meticulous, a classical Virgo who insisted on having all her costumes arranged beforehand and in perfect numerical order. There was a special rack for her things only, with a particular order for the three separate pairs of pointe shoes she would both wear and destroy during this single ballet.

In the first act, her softly arched pink satin shoes would easily hold her, then a tighter, sturdier shoe would be used for Act Two. For Act Three, where Fate entices and destroys the matador, she had the hard, red satin pointe shoes with a heightened arch. They were bent slightly at the heel so her fouettés—thirty-two fast and furious turns on one pointe in one place—would hold her as steady as a spinning top.

Tonight she was especially nervous. Unknown to Caligari, two weeks ago she had decided to quit, to hang up her shoes after the tour. And she had chosen this ballet as her own special swan song. For that reason alone, she would give it everything she had, including her blood.

Going out gracefully was important to her. She had seen it all before. The older ballerina in a young company, fighting the competition to keep it all together. Fonteyn, Ulanova, even the beautiful Makarova, who only danced selected roles.

In their prime no one could touch them. But as the years flew by, their bodies could no longer respond to the rigorous demands of class, of touring, of performing.

Their feet were no longer quick, their balances difficult, their spins and leaps so lacking in power it hurt her artistic senses to watch.

She didn't want to finish that way. She didn't want to make a fool of herself or be remembered for roles gone by. Most of all, she didn't want her audience watching her but seeing a memory.

Behind the curtain, against a sunburst backdrop, Paige and Seth took center-stage positions as the wing lights were still being adjusted. On stage, just moments before the orchestra conductor headed for the podium, a murmur of acknowledgment rose as members of the Royal Family took their seats. All eyes were riveted on the beautiful Princess Diana, whose low-cut dress of black matte jersey would no doubt create sensational morning headlines. Then the chandeliers dimmed, and once again the curtain lifted to the blinding glare of spotlights and *that* terrifying darkness.

Just as the curtains parted, Paige smiled. She had Vaseline on her teeth to keep her lips from sticking to them. The audience paid a good deal of money to see her sparkle and she would not disappoint them.

She felt her heart pound in her chest, felt the adrenaline shoot through her veins like a blood-hot bullet. Yet she also sensed their affection. They were rooting for her success and she damn well knew it. When an audience gave like that, it was tempting to please them totally, tempting to deliver not only her physical presence but her soul as well.

She danced wistfully at first, with a series of gentle balances around Seth's innocent Matador. Then Act One was over and she ran off stage to change.

As Act Two began, she continued with slow turns, quiet lifts, her body borne across the stage on Seth's shoulders like a great bird of paradise, light as a feather. She felt the guitar strings shiver and vibrate through the pores of her skin, felt the warmth of the lights caress her body. She was doing it well, and it all felt good.

Caligari watched Paige from the darkened shadows of the wings, mesmerized by her stage presence. Tonight she might not have had youth on her side, but she certainly had drama, poise, fire, beauty and control. She knew exactly who she was and what she was doing.

Her head was a tear-drop pearl gleaming on her long white neck. Her arms were billowing black chiffon. She had the strength of ten men in her limbs, and in arabesque her ankles flared up and out like the graceful arches of a beautiful bridge.

She balanced perfectly at every point, creating one sensational pause after another, taking incredible chances like a young neophyte. She had the fire of the Black Swan, the youthful charm of the Bluebird. Caligari couldn't believe his eyes. She was putting her whole life into this one ballet, and he steadied himself against the wall to keep from being swept away.

At the end of Act Two Paige ran quickly off stage and into the wings. There, she collapsed on the floor and gasped for air. Simone fanned her with a damp towel as she gulped mouthfuls while the rest of the company took their places on stage for the opening of Act Three.

Revived, Paige undressed and wiped her sweat-drenched body with a dry towel, with one ear tuned to her cue. She moved swiftly, rubbing her swollen toes with anesthetic ointment, then she fastened her tiny black chiffon costume and pinned the bright orange rose on top of her head.

With her costume on and her makeup checked, she slipped into the red satin pointe shoes, tying them tightly at her ankles. Then one, two, three, four, came her cue and without a single moment to flex her arches or test her pointes, she took a mouthful of air and flew on stage in a breathtaking leap.

The audience screamed as she landed like a butterfly, then continued across the stage, jumping higher with each new jeté. They gasped as she began a series of fast chaîne turns along the brink of the proscenium. How it thrilled her to hear them collectively hold their breath, then exhale like one organism. She was not only circling the edge of destiny, she had fire in her veins. Tonight she would go out, not in a blaze of glory, but in a goddamned conflagration!

Then came the pas de deux and again she knocked them flat. She felt her strong body glow like a string of white pearls in Seth's dark embrace, felt her spirit soar as she flirted and teased, balanced only by Seth's kiss. Then her toes began their usual third-act rebellion—red-hot burning needles beneath her toenails. There's no time to worry, she thought, and pushed it all away.

A true professional, able from years of training to endure unbearable torture, she ignored the pain and continued.

Smile and sparkle.

She did pas de chât, a delicate step of the cat, bourrées,

so light and breezy she appeared to be moving on a con-
veyer belt. Her huge orange rose stood out against the blue
background, the black chiffon skirt whispering along her
pink tights, the black lace fan clasped in her hand, poised
on her hip in a pert gesture. Then the sad wail of the trumpet marked the beginning of her most stunning undertak-
ing.

Suddenly, a horrible pain!

Ignore it. Smile and sparkle.

Her legs felt tired, heavy, like mounds of dry sand as
red-hot needles seared past her ankles and shot through her
calves.

Pain. Unbelievable pain.

Smile and sparkle.

Not now! She had no time for it. Not now! Not now!
She had thirty-two fouettés to perform, and by God she
would do them all!

Pain. Unbearable pain.

Smile and sparkle.

To the sound of castanets, to the clapping of intricate
hand rhythms, she stood front center, fourth position, and
began the rond de jambe.

Smile and sparkle.

Spinning on her left leg, her right foot whipped out and
around with her arms turning, then rounded in front. Her
left toe spun on a single spot on the floor. Within seconds a
stabbing pain carved and ground her flesh as if she were
hamburger.

Head to the light and smile.

One, two, one, two—spot the balcony.

Feedback, good.

Smile and sparkle.

One, two; one, two.

She felt her thighs grow heavier with each spin, felt her
toes drench in a sticky sweat. But the spotlight was warm,
and this night was hers. Nothing would keep it from being
the greatest.

Almost there.

Smile and sparkle.

Thirty-one, thirty-two.

Applause!

It felt wonderful as they stood up and cheered, and without thinking she began an encore—a whole new set of fouettés. Nothing in the world could beat the feeling of love and adoration the audience was giving. Nothing! She was born for this, a hungry newborn babe sucking at a full, sweet breast.

Up, down, around—twenty, twenty-one, twenty-two.

Pain.

Smile and sparkle.

Twenty-six, twenty-seven.

Breathe. Smile and sparkle.

She ignored her agony as the audience gripped their chairs and hung from the rafters, as they leaped from their seats screaming. But she knew something terrible was happening. One more moment and her leg would rupture.

Smile. They loved her.

Breathe. Thirty-one, thirty-two. They adored her.

She finished with a standing ovation and the applause was a deafening din. It was the proudest moment of her life as she took her bows. Then the curtain closed, and when Seth let go of her hand, it hit her all at once and she collapsed.

Chapter 43

Caligari saw Paige drop and ran on stage. He lifted her from the floor and charged through the stunned crowd of dancers. "Move! Coming through!" he yelled. "Out of my way!" He ran with her limp body in his arms to her room, where he put her down on a chaise lounge, then closed the door on a hundred peering and stupefied faces. It was then he noticed his hands and realized how bloody they both were. He grabbed the telephone and screamed for the stage manager.

"Emergency!" he yelled. "Get a doctor!" Then he turned his attention back to reviving Paige.

He smacked circulation into her bloodless face and hands, trying to force her to consciousness. After a few moments she finally began to moan and roll her head.

"Paige. Paige. What happened?" he cried.

She gestured with a limp hand for a glass of water, and Caligari poured some from a pitcher. While he held her head she struggled to drink, but after two sips she fell back against the chaise, exhausted. She tried to speak, to tell him, but her voice was a whisper. And as her eyes closed involuntarily, he covered her with a blanket and continued to reassure her.

"It's all right, Paige. Don't worry. A doctor's on the way."

The sight of her lying there made him sick to his stomach, and a primitive fear nearly overwhelmed him as he unlaced her red satin toe shoes. What he saw when he removed them made his blood run cold.

The cloth of her tights was in shambles, stuck with clotted chunks of raw bloody tissue. Her mutilated toes were a dancer's nightmare, and he almost retched as he peeled away the fabric, but he stayed calm for her sake.

Waiting, he was like a small child again, fearful, feeling powerless, reciting the only prayer he recalled from his youth. "Hail Mary, full of grace. Blessed be the fruit of thy womb." There was a knock on the door, and a quick entry by Dr. Frank Mortimer of Middlesex Hospital brought him back to the present.

As Dr. Mortimer entered, Caligari saw the myriad faces straining outside. Everyone was concerned and puzzled. But there was no time to explain, and he closed the door on their curiosity and concern.

"I came as fast as I could," Dr. Mortimer said, placing his black bag on the floor beside Paige. "Tell me what happened?"

Caligari told him everything. How Paige had danced, then collapsed and fainted. He told how he had carried her to the dressing room and removed her shoes. "It's not unusual for a dancer's feet to bleed," Caligari explained. "But this is ridiculous."

"Let's have a go," the small and rotund doctor said as he adjusted his wire spectacles.

Paige was beginning to waken as Dr. Mortimer examined her feet, and the pain she experienced at his touch was excruciating, like dull, rusty nails scraping skin from her bones. She winced as he cut her tights at the knees and removed the fabric from her legs. She nearly leaped from the chaise as his fingers pored over her injury in bright light beneath a magnifying glass.

"Can you give me a bit more detail about what happened, Miss McDowell?" he asked, preparing a shot of Novocaine.

"I don't really know," she said. "I felt pretty good until Act Three, about half an hour ago. Then I rubbed some Nupercainal ointment on my toes—like I always do to deaden the pain. You see, I had all these difficult turns to do. . . ." She was getting off track and quickly returned to the explanation. "So I went on stage and danced full-out, but by the end of the last set of spins I thought I felt knives in my shoes."

"You're not far off," Dr. Mortimer said, snapping off the bright light. "You've got bits of glass in your toes."

"Glass?!" Caligari and Paige said simultaneously.

"Glass," he repeated.

At the hospital they gave Paige a strong shot for pain, soaked her feet in a betadine solution, removed the glass slivers and treated her for infection. Then Dr. Mortimer asked the one question both Paige and Caligari had been terrified to consider.

"Any idea how the glass found its way inside your shoes?"

Before Caligari could reply, Paige instinctively took control. She knew the dance master would speak truthfully, whereas her good business sense, her calm-headed rational would prevail. At this point the integrity of the company was paramount. Who did it to her, if it was deliberate, was not as important as what would happen next. There'd be plenty of time to ask the "Who?" question later.

Her mind focused more on the bad publicity the incident would generate, and once again she became the consummate performer laughing a bit theatrically as she quickly responded.

"I can see you know nothing about ballet, Dr. Mortimer. These things do happen. We use a good deal of spun glass in all our backdrops—it's fireproof, you understand—and I can think of a dozen ways glass slivers could accidentally get inside my shoes." She emphasized the word "accidentally" and forced a smile.

Dr. Mortimer raised an eyebrow as if to say he knew the difference between spun glass and glass slivers, then he responded, "And what do I tell the press, madam? They're clamoring out there for some *reasonable* answers."

Paige thought for a moment. "Well, glass does sound dramatic, don't you think? And there is the question of doctor-patient confidentiality."

He nodded his understanding.

"Let's just say exhaustion," she told him. "It's certainly true. And it's more fitting for a ballerina my age."

Dr. Mortimer gestured in agreement. Then he gathered his things and left.

When the door closed behind Dr. Mortimer, Paige collapsed, sobbing in Caligari's arms. He cradled her, rocked her like a baby, smoothed her long hair and soothed her with tender words. Her performance had been a miracle, and he wanted her to know that. But the other facts were obvious: someone had tried to hurt her, for whatever reason, and Caligari was determined to find out who.

"Who'll dance the role?" Caligari asked her, and she whispered the name in his ear.

"You're something else, Paige," he said. "Courageous and brave, but besides that, once again you saved my ass."

"Oh, don't be so smug, Richard," she said. "I did it for myself."

Her remark surprised him. "I don't understand," he said.

She drew away from him—black mascara was tracking down her white cheeks—and lay down with her long dark hair spilling across the white pillow like black ribbons. "Do you think for one minute I want the press in here prying, asking me all their stupid questions? Not on your life! No, I'm not that dumb. I know what someone tried to do to me. But tonight was *my* night, my *last* night, and I don't ever want anyone to recall it with distaste. No. I want them to remember this as a night when a screaming audience begged me to take another bow, not as the night some malcontent tried to cripple me."

"Wait a minute. What do you mean your *last* night."

She turned her head away and blinked her eyes. "I mean I'm through, hanging up the shoes, Richard. It's all over."

Tears spilled from her eyes and rolled down her cheeks. She wiped them with the back of her hand as he touched her shoulder. He couldn't believe what he was hearing and dismissed it as something said in the heat of the moment.

"But I don't understand, Paige. Dr. Mortimer said you'll be as good as new. That all you need is a few months to heal."

"A few months away from work when you're nineteen or twenty is bad enough," she said, wiping her nose. "At thirty-five, it's a goddamned death sentence. Don't waste your time, Richard. I've made up my mind."

Caligari stood up, nearly knocking over his chair. "I won't listen to this crap, Paige. You're a strong dancer. More capable now . . ."

She held her ears. "Don't!" she shouted. "I don't want to hear it anymore. No more reprieves. No more! I'm going to teach, to try and make a new life for myself. Maybe get married, even have a baby. There's still time for that."

"A baby?" he said, keeping his voice in check. "You're not the type. You wouldn't know what to do with one."

She stared at him through solemn eyes. "It shows how little you know me, Richard." The sedative Dr. Mortimer had given her was taking effect, and as her words began to slur, the truth barreled down on him.

"I love children," Paige continued. "I've always loved them. But you don't have to worry, Richard. Even if I marry and have a baby, I'll still continue working with you. Not just for the welfare of the company but out of my own selfish needs."

"What are you talking about?" he contradicted her. "You don't have a selfish bone in your body."

He leaned to hug her, but she pushed him away. "My God," she said. "We've known each other a lifetime, but you don't know a thing about me. Well, take a good look, Richard. I am selfish. Selfish enough to even commit murder for you." She sat up, trembling all over.

He reached for her again.

"No," she continued, pushing his hand away. "Don't touch me. Let me finish, because if I don't say it now I never will."

He held his breath and waited.

"One year after we were married I got pregnant."

He stared at her as if she really were a stranger. His body was rigid, his eyes blindly dilated, his hands trembling.

"Don't look at me like that, for God's sake. I had no choice. You had just given me the lead role in 'Appassionata' and I wasn't about to let anything get in my way. Not even a baby. Not even *your* baby. I was going to the top, Richard. With you. So, I had"—she broke —"an abortion."

He was numb, paralyzed, cold and unresponsive as she fell against the pillow sobbing. "Just think, Richard," she said as she began to wind down. "We would have had a child—a grown son. A wonderful ... little boy ... just like ..."

Then her voice trailed off as she drifted into sleep.

Sitting alone in his room at the Barnes manor house, everything hit him at once. Paige wanting to leave. Dancers in his company so angry, so desperate to be acknowledged that they put glass in a prima ballerina's toeshoes! And now this. The knowledge that he and Paige would have had a child sent chills down his spine.

He put his head in his hands and began to weep tears that sprang from the deepest part of him. He had not cried this way since his youth long ago, since his mother and father, since he had walked the streets of New York City so hungry he would have killed for a single crust of bread. A baby boy, he thought, conjuring an image. *His* baby boy.

So what had the great dance master accomplished with all his talent? His God-given creativity? The answers were blemished and unclear. Then a soft knock at his door brought him back to his senses.

He stood up, wiped the tears from his face and brushed back his hair. He opened the door and found Dorsey standing there like a frightened puppy with her tail between her legs.

"They said you wanted to see me," she said. "But I can come back another time."

"No," Caligari told her as she started to leave. "We have to talk. Paige chose you to dance her part in 'Patrins' tomorrow." He paused. "Until she recovers from exhaustion."

Chapter 44

It was late when Dorsey returned to her room after Caligari's eleventh-hour summons. Both Shane and Alexandra stood waiting for her arrival with bated breath.

"What happened?" Alexandra asked as the three huddled together on Dorsey's bed. "What did he say?"

Dorsey had stars in her eyes as well as tears. "He wants me to dance Paige's role in 'Patrins.' Jeez! Can you believe it?"

"Of course," Alexandra said. "You're great! You *should* do it."

"Yes," Shane agreed, hugging her.

"I don't know," Dorsey said. She sighed with a trace of self-doubt. "I mean, maybe I'm not ready."

"Nonsense!" Alexandra said. "You're not only ready, you'll knock 'em dead."

A slow, digesting silence followed, then Shane asked the one question poised on everyone's tongue. "Did he say what really happened to her?"

Dorsey shook her head. "Not a word. He's sticking to the exhaustion bit."

"How stupid," Alexandra said. "We all saw the blood. Paige's feet were awful."

"What about the silent treatment we're supposed to give to the press?" Shane said. "It's all so confusing."

"Well, you read the memo like everyone else," Dorsey reminded them. "All press questions about Paige are to be referred back to him."

"Hey! I'm sorry for Paige," Alexandra said, breaking the solemn mood. "But Dorsey has the role now and *that* calls for a celebration."

"Right!" Shane agreed.

Dorsey searched one girl's face, then the other's as tears filled the corners of her eyes. "You mean neither of you is angry . . . or jealous?"

"Me?" Alexandra asked.

"Jealous?" Shane reiterated.

Then in a hail of demented laughter, they leaped on Dorsey and attacked her with pillows.

Later in Simone's bedroom Shane sobbed like a baby. "How come he didn't pick me?" she sniffled. "I mean I love Dorsey, Ma, but I'm just as good as she is." Her fist hit the pillow. "So how come?"

"So how come?" Simone's voice repeated. "I'll tell you how come. She's got connections, that's how come. Look who her father is."

Simone stroked Shane's brow, slowly brushing the long coppery hair away from her daughter's eyes, feeling her own blood turn to ice in her veins. All the work she'd done, the plans she'd made and look how miserable her Shane was feeling.

"Don't you worry, honey. As long as I'm alive you'll get your chance to show 'em. This isn't the end of the line, you know. It's just a matter of time before Dorsey blows it."

Shane blew her nose and stared at her mother. "What do you mean, Ma?"

"What do I mean! What do I mean!" Her words mocked Shane's.

"Didn't I tell you that Paige would break a leg one of these days?"

"So?"

"So," Simone said, smiling. "So it happened, didn't it?"

"What's that got to do with Dorsey?"

"So something's gonna happen to her too. It's just a matter of time. Mark my words."

"What exactly do you mean?" Shane asked.

"It's no secret, Shane. Everyone knows. Dorsey's goofy, a doper," Simone told her. "I don't give her another six months to live, let alone dance."

Shane's eyes glowed like green neon at Simone's remark. "What are you saying, Ma? Dorsey's my friend."

"What I'm saying is, I've known a few people like her in my lifetime." Simone had a faraway look in her eyes as she spoke, as if she were in another time and place. "Every doper lives on borrowed time, and sooner or later she's gonna do what they all do."

"What's that?"

"Take the wrong pill at the wrong time and either wind up dead, cut up or in a loony bin. I don't care how good a dancer she is. She'll be finished. End of report!"

She tickled Shane's chin and kissed her forehead. "And when that happens, my little baby, you'll be the one."

The following night, the moment the curtain rose on "Patrins" and Dorsey began to dance, the crowd sat transfixed. She had them in her palm—wild, loose, free, with an abandon that gave the role a new and different light. She was Carmen, the Pietá, Madonna and Child, fire and ice, a devil, an angel, some gorgeous ethereal creature whose feet never touched the ground.

Unlike Paige, she wore her long hair loose and it fluttered against the dark background like a thousand luxurious strands of gold, each one catching and reflecting the orange stage lights as if her skull were in flames.

Her long, long limbs, the short torso, the perfectly formed head and procelain face, her lyrical arms, which were free yet always aligned, her breathtaking balances, her haughty attitude, all surprised and stunned not only the crowd but Caligari as well. The role had possessed her, and

she was no longer Dorsey Childs but a strange sun creature, a flaming comet who had granted these insignificant
earthbound mortals who sat mesmerized, watching her, a
simultaneous glimpse of both heaven and hell.

When she'd finished, they were screaming, "Brava!
Brava!" leaping from their seats, throwing roses, carnations and baby's breath at her feet. She had fifteen curtain
calls with accolades the company hadn't seen since last
performing three years ago in San Francisco.

In the morning it was all over London, all over Europe,
all over America and the whole world: The publicity Paige
had predicted Dorsey would generate had come to pass.

Last night an older star had shone brilliantly. Tonight a
new one was rising and her name was Dorsey Childs.

After the performance, it was a backstage circus. The
hounds had caught the scent of success, and the hunt was
on. Calls flooded the switchboard. "Sixty Minutes," *People*
magazine, *Paris Match, Time, Newsweek, Elle, Vogue,* all
of them wanting to interview the talented young woman
who everyone said had wings on her feet. And just as
Paige had predicted, they were not only interested in her
dancing. That she was the daughter of the flamboyant
United States Senator Thomas Childs made her all that
much more interesting copy.

Paige clicked off the television set. It was the morning
after Dorsey's triumph and she'd had just about enough of
London's clamoring for the girl. If she was to believe what
they all said, the child had made history. Oh, well, she
thought. Here today, gone tomorrow. Out of sight, out of
mind. Yesterday it had been her; today it was Dorsey.

She was happy for the girl but disappointed for herself.
She had so much wanted the world to remember her own
portrayal of Fate. Now she would take second place. With
all this hoopla, they would hardly recall her performance at
all. They'd always remember Dorsey's. So her blaze had

fizzled, doused not by a shower but a deluge. She'd never had a chance.

A nurse brought her tea and she drank it with disinterest while her mind simmered with so much unfinished business. How would she cope? Could she make it? Was she really serious about never dancing again? And how had Richard taken not only her pronouncement of that, but her abortion as well?

And she pondered other questions, like who had given Richard the money for the theater and tour? But most of all, she wanted to know who the hell had tried to cripple her!

BOOK FOUR

The Gala

Chapter 45

In New York City the blazing summer heat succumbed to October's chill and the soothing green of Central Park was replaced by autumn's flaming colors: bold orange, crisp brown, deep wine.

Julia sat with Ilya Kremorkin in her Fifth Avenue penthouse apartment, sharing a late breakfast near the terrace window. She was enjoying the magnificent view when Ilya switched on the color TV, which drew her attention from the calming spectacle below to the commotion on the set.

Richard Caligari and his entourage of dancers had just landed at Kennedy Airport, where they were besieged by a sea of reporters. Julia watched the handsome dance master handle their questions with finesse.

"We've heard rumors that Miss McDowell miscarried on stage."

Julia held her breath as she waited for his answer, but an irritated Ilya clicked the sound off as quickly as he had turned it on. Now she was left high and dry for Caligari's answer.

"What's wrong, Ilya?" she asked him.

"Dancers," he said. "Is hard for me to look."

Two seconds later the telephone rang and Ilya was once again and with great reluctance speaking to the Russian authorities. As usual his face turned blood-red as his fingers gripped the phone. He listened, he pleaded, he argued, then he slammed the receiver on the hook and ran upstairs.

Julia followed after, taking the small elevator to his room, where she knocked and waited at his door.

When he invited her in, she sat by his bedside and reached for his hand. Her action opened a floodgate of emotion and tears.

"Ilya," she said softly. "Why do you talk to them if they upset you so? It isn't necessary."

He wiped the tears from his pale face, kissed both her wrists passionately, then turned on his side away from her gaze. "They know me," he said. "They know my life." His voice caught deep in his throat. "I can't take any more, Julia. I must to work, to forget."

She brushed the long blond hair that fell around his shoulders. "Don't worry," she told him. "You'll work, and soon. I promise."

Francesca Adair was a one-woman dream factory, the desire of every red-blooded male and the envy of every woman. And why not? She had it all. She was a rich, beautiful, famous woman with platinum hair and large brown eyes and a weakness for famous male ballet dancers.

Wickedly buxom, she worshipped at their shrines, following them around the world wherever they appeared, demanding audience which she always received. To date, none had ever refused her. Except for Ilya. But her problem with him had been politics, and now it was clear sailing.

Rock stars had their groupies—pretty young things who'd eagerly spread their nubile legs, young girls who needed to experience, however vicariously, some piece of the musical magic so they could fill some void, heal some self-inflicted wound, feed some imaginary hunger. It was that way with Francesca too.

But she hardly needed the dancer's spotlight. She had her own piece of that little rock. However, there were other things ballet dancers could provide, important things she both envied and admired. Their physical prowess, for examples, their ability to cope. Their perfection, their dedication, and most important of all, the respect, the deference society people paid them. By standing in their company, she hoped their prestige would rub off on her.

Abandoned as a tiny child, then thrust into the cloying arms of a devious, unscrupulous couple who saw the cute little tyke as a meal ticket, Frances Adams was carefully tended like a slot machine that would provide the big Hollywood payoff.

From the age of eight, she wanted ballet lessons, but they discouraged it. They needed "quick" money, and in an uncertain environment a child always obeys. So at the age of nine, before she could experience life and made decisions, Frances Adams became Francesca Adair, commercial actress, abandoning *her* dream in favor of *theirs*.

"You have no grace, darling," they would discourage her. "And your back is crooked."

Francesca always believed them. Drummed into her head continuously were a thousand and one similar excuses until the thrice-told lie gained a power of its own. Then, like a teetering snowball on a mountaintop, it rolled downhill, gaining momentum, gaining enough strength and mass to finally bury her.

By the time the snow had melted, a vixen with the morals of a flea emerged.

"You have to sleep with the nice man, honey," they would tell her. "And the nice lady too."

So vulnerable and afraid of being discarded, she believed what they had told her, even basked in their approving smiles. An unwanted child, she took love wherever she could find it. Then she accidentally discovered they were stealing her blind, taking her hard-earned money to pay for the career of their latest find.

So at the age of twenty-four, preceding a terrible five-year court battle where her whole sordid life was revealed to the world, she made her final break with them and began a bid for the restoration of her soul.

And for the last four years, part of that restoration included being seen in the company of the elite, being close to and worshipping what she could never become: respectable, dignified, honorable.

She idolized, adored and admired them, placed them on pedestals. And like some kind of drug, she swallowed their esteemed company, pushed their prominence into her veins. And whenever or wherever the likes of an Ilya Kremorkin appeared, Francesca Adair was never far behind.

Caligari trudged up the staircase to his SoHo apartment. He was exhausted from the tour, from the long journey across the Atlantic, tired of the intrigue, of the games people had been playing.

He'd been hounded everywhere by the press. Everyone wanted to know what had *really* happened to Paige McDowell. There'd been so much speculation and from so many sources, with each prying journalist hoping to uncover the truth by printing the lie. And that annoyed him. Why did the public's "right to know," he wondered, supersede not only the truth, but *his* need for peace?

And as the cancer grew, it infected even him. The crazy notion that perhaps Paige might have put glass in her own shoes in a bid for his affection had crossed his mind more than once. And that unnerved him.

Inside the apartment he switched on the lights, looked around at the vast, familiar surroundings and threw his luggage to the floor. No matter what else he was feeling, it felt good to be home.

He ripped off his clothes, took a hot shower and shampooed his hair. Then he toweled dry, put on a black velour robe and turned on his telephone message machine to listen to his calls.

"Hi Mr. C," his cleaning lady chirped. "The vacuum cleaner's on the fritz, so the floors are a bit dusty. Don't worry, I'll have it fixed in a jiffy. See you on Wednesday."

Several calls from domestic and foreign journalists followed that one, each wanting to set up an appointment for a private interview. One asked which "conglomerate" was backing him, and he flinched as he contemplated the fallout from that little bomb should it be uncovered and dropped.

The gala was just a heartbeat away, and he desperately needed it to showcase his company in New York City. All the reviews, the accolades from Europe were one thing. Having hometown acceptability, which translated into dependable financial support for the company's future life, was another.

The gala—he was almost there. The realization of his cherished dreams would culminate in that event, and he looked forward to it like a child. A whole life devoted to this single experience, and it was about to happen. It was the single most important thing to his future success. But without Julia's backing and support for it, he'd be back to square one.

He poured water for himself as the calls continued.

His lawyer wanted information on the tour. Then two callers hung up. Then someone called about a mixup at his bank over a withdrawal. Then there was a call from Vidal Genero, which completely surprised him.

"I hope you're not the type to hold grudges, Mr. Caligari," he said sincerely. "I'd like very much to audition for you. Please return my call when you have a few moments."

Caligari chuckled with gusto as he pondered the young man's request. He wondered if Vidal had discussed it with Julia. Then he wondered if Vidal knew about his own relationship with the blue-eyed witch. Absurd, he thought, pacing. What relationship? They had none.

Well, no matter. Caligari could use a strong dancer like Genero *if* the young man was in shape; and he certainly held no grudges. Whatever Genero had done long ago had been his own business. And in the long run, he had done Caligari a big favor.

Just as he made a note to call Vidal, Julia's voice came purring on the line and the warm, liquid tones made him shiver.

"I'd like very much to talk with you, Richard. Please call me when you arrive."

So, he thought, the beautiful and beguiling witch had finally come to her senses. She realized how much they really meant to one another and wanted to apologize. Well, he'd let her, by God. Then he'd throw her on that fancy cashmere rug in her Trump Tower apartment and make love to her till she screamed for mercy. She'd never again need the likes of a Vidal Genero for excitement, or any other man for that matter.

Chapter 46

The same day they'd arrived home, Simone checked into a cheap motel. In the morning she began her search for a new apartment in New York City. She wanted her baby back home with her, and now that she'd saved some money from the tour, she could do it. Thank God! She didn't want Shane in the company of that doper, Dorsey Childs, another minute.

Besides that, she couldn't go home to Brooklyn. Much too risky. The letter she'd received care of General Delivery had certainly proved that. No matter what else happened, she and Shane had to steer clear of trouble. Then, if she could figure a way to get rid of this Brad jerk, they'd be home free. Maybe Caligari could help her in that matter. She would talk to him and see.

Changing! Everything was changing.

Caligari had given the company three days off, calling an early morning class for Monday. When that day arrived, Alexandra, Shane and Dorsey hurried about the apartment, determined not to be late and risk his formidable wrath.

Each girl knew without question that the stakes were now higher, that they were no longer silly little corps dancers, that they had grown, that they were stronger, more determined, physically fit, ready to take on any as-

signment with some new ingredients added to their once
naive personalities—like competition, for example, and
ambition. Ever since Paige's "accident" every female
dancer knew she was being studied, scrutinized and evalu-
ated with new eyes. They were now, as never before, up
against each other to fill the injured prima ballerina's
shoes. And Dorsey wondered if, because of that, the days
of the Three Musketeers were finally over.

No one had told them Paige would be permanently out
of commission. But certain rumors of her retirement continued to persist, and each soloist secretly coveted all her
leading roles. And even if she mended in a month, anyone
with an ounce of intelligence knew she was simply too old
to get back in shape for gala time.

"Where the hell are my new tights?" Shane screamed.

"On your stupid legs," Dorsey hollered back.

"Stop shouting, both of you," Alexandra shouted. "It's
time to go."

Changing! Everything was changing.

In class that same morning, everyone seemed rested,
ready for the next round. In spite of the press hovering
outside the studio offices, clamoring for interviews with
Dorsey, everything continued as usual. Except for one new
addition—Vidal Genero.

After receiving his message a few days ago, Caligari had
returned Vidal's call, inviting him to join class, thinking he
would then determine from Vidal's performance whether
the young man was in shape and therefore acceptable to the
company.

Lined up at the wall, hands clasping the barre, everyone
prepared for action as Joshua played the first melody on the
piano. Caligari kept his eyes focused mainly on Vidal as
the pliés began.

"First position—down, two, three, four."

As Caligari watched them, it still nagged at his mind that
one of his students could possibly be the culprit. That one
among them had deliberately put glass slivers in Paige's

shoes. His eyes scanned the line as he nominated then eliminated each individual face.

Dorsey. Too light-headed. No!

Shane. Too innocent and naive. No!

Alexandra. Hardly! Much too much integrity. No!

Then his eyes fell on Seth. A bit frustrated at Paige's demands but still a gentleman. No! Well, maybe. No again! Then he wondered if it could have been someone outside the company. But who? Better to forget, concentrate on class. He clapped his hands. "Center floor everyone; groups of six," he said, then he waited for them to assemble.

Watching Vidal again, Caligari was impressed. The young man was good, strong and classically trained. Even with that Ace bandage wrapped around his knee, he danced full-out. *His* kind of dancer—a young man with guts. If his "center floor" proved as strong as his barre, he would certainly hire him.

He recalled that first time he'd laid eyes on Vidal a long time ago, and smiled. Then he caught himself and realized the young man was also Julia's friend. Friend? Who was he kidding? The man had been Julia's lover—maybe he still was. Oh, what the hell! The way she'd behaved, they deserved one another. Yet he was seized with a burning jealousy as he watched Vidal dance. Musn't let it get in the way, he thought. He had plans. Interesting plans for his dear, dear Julia.

When her private phong rang early that evening, Julia was afraid to answer. It would be the media, she knew, the KGB, or perhaps that rat, Richard Caligari. Whoever it was, it would mean some kind of confrontation and she was not in the mood for games. But with Birdie out shopping and Ilya upstairs taking class, she reluctantly picked up the phone and was temporarily relieved to find that it was Francesca Adair.

"Hello," came the actress' sultry voice.

"Hello, Miss Adair," Julia replied.

"Call me Francesca, please," she said. "And how's our Ilya?"

Our Ilya? What nerve! "He's fine," Julia replied. "Considering."

"I'm returning his call. Is he there?"

"Yes," Julia replied. "He's here."

There was a pause. "I see," Francesca said. "May I speak with him, then?"

"Of course. But he's taking class right now. I'll have him call you the minute he finishes."

When Julia hung up, the telephone rang again. This time it was ABC News calling Ilya for an interview. She declined for him, just as she had with CBS and NBC half an hour ago, then hung up. When the phone rang once more, she was in a fit of pique and her voice held a sharp and cutting edge.

"I'm returning your call," Caligari said.

The moment she heard him she was smothered in desire. Then reality closed in. "Sorry to be rude," she apologized, "but the press has been dogging Ilya ever since we left Paris."

"I understand," he said.

They were civil to one another as she asked him to meet her the following evening and he agreed.

When Shane and Dorsey left class to have dinner, they found Brad outside cooling his heels near his limousine. Shane excused herself, telling Dorsey she'd see her later, then joined Brad inside the car.

"Where've you been?" he asked, hugging her tightly. "I've missed you. Been calling you all weekend."

Shane clung to him, realizing she'd missed him more than she cared to admit. "We took the phone off the hook. With everyone calling, it was impossible to get any rest."

Brad rapped the partition between himself and the driver. "The Waldorf," he said.

Shane looked at him and questioned the reason for their destination.

"Dad keeps a suite there," he said. "Don't worry. We'll have a nice quiet dinner, then a visit." His voice became serious. "We have to talk, Shane. There are things we have to settle."

Simone stood in an upper-story window and watched Brad's limousine drive away. Damn him! She had to think of something to discourage him, to get him out of Shane's life for good. Her other plan to frighten him away had obviously not worked. She needed to do something else. Maybe *now* was the time to approach Caligari.

Alexandra thrust her way through a sea of reporters and took her mother's private elevator to the penthouse apartment. The moment she opened the door, Birdie hugged and kissed her. "Let me look at you," Birdie said joyfully. She stepped back. "God Almighty, can you believe it? As thin as a rail."

Alex turned round and round, absorbing the admiration and affection like a sponge. "Didn't I tell you I would do it? Didn't I?" She kissed Birdie's cheek.

A few moments later Julia joined them. "Welcome home, Alex," she said, kissing the girl's cheek. "You're looking very nice."

"Nice? She looks fantastic!" Birdie sang. Then as though the cook sensed herself an intruder, she made gestures toward something left undone in the kitchen and left.

After a few moments of self-conscious chatter, Alexandra's eyes searched the surroundings. "Where is he?" she whispered. "I'm dying to see him."

"He's upstairs, working," Julia whispered back.

"Can I go?"

"Of course. He's anxious to meet you. And remember, Alex. We're all he has left in the world."

* * *

It was clear neither Shane nor Alexandra would be coming home tonight. Dorsey put the groceries away, removed her tights and leotards, washed them in the sink, then took a nice hot shower. It was good to be alone for a change.

Standing naked, she stared at herself in the mirror. Same girl, same face, same eyes, same body. Yet everything was changing. The idea of being a star was scary. She wondered how Gelsey Kirkland must have felt when it happened to her.

She telephoned her father to talk about it but was put on hold. She needed advice, someone to help her sort things out, make some sense of it all. After five minutes of waiting, of being shuffled from office to office, she hung up, irritated, frustrated, slamming the phone with a bang.

She lit a joint to relax. Ten minutes later she felt depressed and took two Dexedrines. Then a wild insatiable hunger seized her. She remembered what was in the refrigerator: cold chicken, potato salad, cole slaw and a fresh loaf of French bread with creamy butter. Her mouth watered as she contemplated the food. Soon she was out of control. A few seconds later she was in the kitchen, piling her plate with enough food for five people. She could hardly wait to be seated at the table.

As she walked, she stuffed her mouth like an animal, as if another creature was lurking behind a door waiting to steal her food. Chicken wings were torn greedily from breast sockets. Greasy fingers scooped slaw, mayonnaise and potatoes into her mouth. All this plus a container of milk with a small strawberry shortcake were devoured within the space of ten minutes, and she was still hungry.

She tore into chicken legs and thighs with Dijon mustard. A pint of butter pecan ice cream. A jar of cashews. Food, glorious food. She was shaking all over, crazed, as she licked it from her plate, sucked it from her palate, picked it from the cavities of her teeth.

Then fifteen minutes after she'd devoured everything,

guilt overwhelmed her and she ran to the toliet, pushing two fingers down her throat to throw it up.

Leaning over the toliet and heaving her guts up, acid and gas burned her stomach and throat. She was hot, sweating like a pig, feeling herself growing fatter and uglier by the minute. She could feel the fat swelling her body, alive and multiplying, a fungus that would swallow her alive.

Finished heaving, she took a laxative, then an enema. Not satisfied, she ran around the house like a chicken with its head cut off, exercising, exorcising, doing jumping jacks until she lost count. Then she fell on the floor, too exhausted to breathe.

Brad and Shane made love, and once again she felt safe and cherished. Then Brad called room service and ordered dinner. Afterward they drank tea and talked.

"I love you, Shane. I want to marry you. But I won't be put off any longer."

Shane started to explain but realized she was stuttering. "You, you're n . . . not being fair, Brad."

"I don't understand. You love me, don't you?"

"Of course I do."

"Then there's no problem," Brad said.

"But there is!" She found herself trembling, afraid as she answered.

"Name one," he challenged.

"I'm a dancer, Brad. I can't, I *won't* give it up."

Brad was silent. Then as though he were arguing a case in court, he began to rationalize. "You're twenty, Shane. Think about it. How long do you ballet dancers last if you don't injure yourselves first?" He answered the question before she could. "You've got fifteen good years. What happens after that?"

"It doesn't matter," she countered. "I'll cross that bridge when I come to it."

He reached out and held her again. "God, Shane. I'm offering you everything important—love, marriage, a home, family, the real things, the only things that matter, all the things you've never had."

She pushed away. "But I can have both. Why are you making me choose?"

"Because two careers in one household won't work," he said, rising. "Don't you understand? The feelings we share come once in a lifetime. You've got to recognize that. You have to realize how much that means. Think of the life we could have together."

She knew she cared for him deeply. But she couldn't shake her feelings, her own notions about what *she* wanted. And then there was Simone.

"But what about my mother?" she asked. "She's worked hard all her life for my success. I can't just throw it all away."

He whirled. "Are *you* dancing or is *she*?" he yelled.

Her body, her whole being quaked with every word. And worse, she was more confused than ever.

Alex spent the night at Julia's penthouse. Before going to bed, she wrote in her diary:

> *Dear Diary*
>
> *Met Ilya today. He's so sweet. Watched him work out and I've never seen such perfection. Even if he comes from the schmaltzy Bolshoi, he looks like one of those line drawings in a textbook; perfect alignment, perfect structure, perfect control. As if God created his body just to dance.*
>
> *He worked with me for a while and I loved it. He showed me stuff no one ever did before. Now I can do a tour jeté with more height and a straighter back. "All in plié," he says. His accent is so cute.*
>
> *He made a pass at me, I think. But he's going*

out tonight with Francesca Adair and I don't think Julia likes it one bit. But hell, we can't all do what Julia likes.

Love, Alex

Chapter 47

The moment he saw her he felt himself rise. She did things to his body and brain that no woman had ever done before. But then the coldness of her voice cut sharply through his warm skin and almost froze his insides.

"We have things to discuss, Richard. Important things. Come in."

She closed the door to her Trump Tower apartment and he watched her walk. The long torso and shapely legs. The royal-blue velvet suit with a white silk shirt. Pearls at her throat not half as white as her teeth. And that royal blue, so pale compared to the color of her eyes.

He followed, sat on the couch near her, accepting her offer of white wine. He'd need it, he thought, from the way things were going. From that look in her eyes. God, why couldn't he stop wanting to touch her?

He stretched his long legs in black trousers and adjusted his black cashmere turtleneck and Harris tweed jacket. He felt warm as he waited for her to begin. He knew she was struggling, just as he was.

She poured wine into crystal glasses, keeping her eyes fixed on what she was doing. "I'm pleased at the changes in Alexandra," she said, handing him a glass.

He nodded, picturing the last time they'd shared wine together. He'd given her everything then, including his heart. I have to be careful, he thought. Can't make the same mistake twice. But still, he searched for an opening, for a softening of her voice as a cue.

"Thanks. I'm happy to hear you say that," he answered, leaning back. "Alexandra's been a great student. She has real potential, and eventually she'll have an opportunity to show it."

The silence that followed was difficult. He was working against himself. One more moment and he'd sweep her into his arms. Then those feelings quickly subsided as she broke the spell once again.

"And just when do you suppose that opportunity will come?"

He studied her. He must be cautious. "Soon." He paused. "When she's ready."

"Do you think she'll be ready by gala time?"

He sipped his wine as she did, but her question hung there. "If you insist," he said. He hoped she would smile with him, but she didn't.

"I do!" she said. Her blue eyes sparked. "I certainly do insist."

Her attitude was haughty and cold. She reminded him with that remark that she still held the purse strings. So that was the way she wanted things. Well, he would not only tie pretty bows for her, he'd tangle her up so tightly she'd trip on her cute little ass.

"Your wish? My command," he said, now realizing what his only options were. "And I have just the partner for her." He visualized it in his mind as he said it. Vidal and Alexandra in a comic pas de deux. The critics would have a field day. And the laugh would be on Julia.

"Really!" Julia said. "And who would that be?"

"Vidal Genero."

The haughty and cold attitude disappeared. Perplexity took its place.

"I'm afraid I don't understand," she said. Where there were sparks, an icy fire now glowed.

"Vidal's joined my company." He sipped his wine, eyeing her. "It *was* your idea, wasn't it?"

She stammered. "Yes, of course," she said.

Just as he thought. Vidal hadn't discussed it with her at all, and she didn't seem too pleased.

She poured more wine for herself. A clear signal. Fortification, he thought. She offered him another glass but he refused.

"That's a lovely idea, Richard," she countered. "But I have a better partner for Alex, a more worthy one."

Caligari sat up like a soldier. What the hell was she up to now? He put his glass to his lips. "And who might that be?" He tilted his head back to drink the remnants.

She didn't blink an eyelash as her words spilled out quickly. "My cousin, Ilya Kremorkin."

He nearly choked on the liquid. "You can't be serious, Julia."

She stared at him, long and hard. "Oh, but I am. Dead serious."

How stupid! He should have seen it coming. Kremorkin had to work and she *was* his cousin. He stood up, walked to the window, turned swiftly around. He felt the large blue vein in his neck throb as he fought for the right words, then the appropriate voice in which to deliver them. "Listen to me, Julia. I've done everything you've ever asked. Every single thing. But this time you're pushing too far."

"Please, Richard. It's distasteful for me to remind you. . . ."

"Stop!" he said. "I don't need another of your reminders. But we've been here before, you and I, and Ilya Kremorkin is where I draw the line. He's a fine dancer but unacceptable to me."

"Do you want to explain that? Or do I take it as your final answer?"

Caligari's patience had reached the breaking point. Yet it was important that she understand. "You may dabble in art, Julia, but dance is life and death for me. Ilya's a star and there's no room for that in an ensemble company. His dramatic style belongs to the Bolshoi, not the clean, classical lines I've worked hard to establish. That's what I'm about, who I am, and nothing's gonna change it. Not even you."

"You're talking nonsense. Ilya can adapt. He's an artist. Just give him a chance—that's all I'm asking."

"It's not that easy, Julia."

He was afraid of the look in her eyes as she stood up and placed her glass on the table. "Then we have nothing more to discuss," she said.

He was surprised at her easy capitulation. Maybe he'd read her wrong. Maybe she'd only been testing him. "All right," he said. "See you at the gala."

He turned to leave, unaware that her eyes were burning holes in his back. Then he heard her make the one pronoucement he never wanted to hear.

"If Ilya doesn't dance for you, there will be no gala."

His first instinct was to grab her by the throat, to throttle her. But instead he stayed calm. "No more jokes, Julia. I don't find that remark funny."

She didn't move a muscle. "I'm not trying to be funny," she said. "And this is no joke."

He continued his tightrope walk to the door, hoping she'd laugh or recant. But she never said a word. So he turned the knob slowly and opened the door without looking back. When she added nothing further, he knew he had some hard thinking ahead. He was so close to his dream he could taste it, and she was taking the feast away.

"I suppose you have another deadline to impose."

"Yes," she said. "Tomorrow morning."

The instant the door slammed, she fell against it, beat her fists and let the tears spill from her eyes down her cheeks. Once again she'd driven him away. And once again she knew the reason why. Fear. Plain and simple fear. Most of this exchange had nothing to do with Ilya. It was self-inflicted sabotage.

She was afraid—afraid of getting close, afraid of loving, afraid to commit. And it hurt. It felt goddamned lousy and she wished there was some way to change what had just happened between them. If only she could take it all back.

Oh, why, why hadn't she been easier with his pride? He was a sensitive man. She knew that. She damn well knew that! But what about that miscarriage Paige McDowell was reported to have suffered? If he loved *her*, why was he still screwing Paige?

She stumbled her way to her bedroom, threw herself on the bed, aware once again that the ghost of Giorgio had never died. It had all been an illusion, a dream. Giorgio was alive—alive and well, still very much at her side.

Chapter 48

When Caligari left Julia's apartment, he took a taxi to Paige's Greenwich Village address. He wanted to visit her, to see how she'd been doing. But he wasn't going to delude himself either. Once again, he needed her sympathy, her advice. More than anyone, she would understand his feelings. And she would help him with some answers, or pose the right questions.

And if she couldn't provide him with those things, she'd at least offer the warmth of her friendship and company, which he needed even more desperately. Right now, he didn't want to be alone.

As he drove through the city, he sat back and closed his eyes. He saw visions of Julia and tried to understand how he could possibly care for such an intractable woman. Moreover, how could he have trusted her with his heart? She was overbearing, strong, a little like him, and that thought made him uneasy. On the one hand, he admired the lengths to which she had gone to give Alexandra a chance at a dream. On the other, he knew her romantic feelings for Vidal had played some part in her initial decision. But he also distrusted his own reasoning. He had a feeling about her. Deep down, he felt Julia was really fighting for her life, and in some strange, convoluted way it had come down to butting heads with him.

She had given him the professional opportunity of a lifetime, for which he was grateful. She had opened his heart to immense personal achievement and satisfaction, to longing and desire—feelings long dormant in his life. But she had also pulled the rug out from under him. And if position in life was really everything, he was now on the floor with very bruised buns, and it didn't feel so hot.

Now, parked in front of Paige's Greenwich Village apartment, Caligari paid the cabbie and took the stone steps two at a time. He buzzed the door and waited for Paige's response, which came instantly. Inside the hallway, he walked to the second floor and knocked, waiting for Paige to open so he could hug her, make some kind of human connection. He was glad when she opened the door and greeted him warmly.

Inside Paige's living room, she served him iced tea, hobbling about on her bandaged feet with some degree of ease. He was proud of her adjustment. She'd done quite well, he thought, considering everything that had happened. There was not the slightest sound of rancor in her voice as she joined him on her Casa Bella pink silk couch, which lay between two pink and white striped seashell wing chairs near a clear glass table laden with flowers.

"The bouquet you sent today is especially lovely," Paige said, referring to some nearby long-stemmed pink roses sipping water in a Waterford crystal vase. He had sent them to her this morning, just as he had every day since the London incident.

"They suit you," he said.

After a bit of small talk, for which he was grateful, Paige helped him open the door to his real reasons for being there. Dear Paige. Always making things easier for him. Damn! Why couldn't he love *her* instead of Julia? But Paige only inspired friendship and warmth, while Julia made him come alive.

"Now," Paige said, setting her legs up on a hassock. "Tell me why you're *really* here."

He laughed a little at her ability to read him, placed his glass on the table and told her as clearly as he could without giving anything about Julia away. "Ilya Kremorkin wants to dance with our company. The conglomerate backing us insists we hire him. But I'm at the point where I'm ready to chuck it—the whole enchilada—tell them to get lost. I just wanted you to say I was doing the right thing."

"I can't tell you that," she said. "In fact, I think it's a great idea."

He could hardly believe his ears. "Paige! What the heck are you talking about?"

"I'm talking about Kremorkin. He's beautiful! What on earth's the problem?"

"God," he said. "I don't understand. You're the last person in the world I thought I'd have to explain things to. Of course he's beautiful. Dynamic, in fact. But he belongs at the Bolshoi, not in my company. It would be like stuffing an apple in a cherry pie. It just doesn't fit."

"Mmmmm," she mused. "Apple surprise. I'll bet if it's served right it would taste delicious."

"Oh, for God's sake, Paige, be serious."

"I *am* being serious, Richard. Kremorkin's a great catch. If you'd look at it properly, you'd see he's a godsend. Here's the perfect opportunity for you to get rid of Julia's influence once and for all."

He was dumbfounded. She had known all along, perhaps, and he wondered how. . . .

"Oh, don't look so shocked, for goodness sake. I'm not an idiot, you know. I've had an inkling about Julia as benefactor for a long time. You just put the capper on it tonight when you came here with the news about Ilya. Two and two have always made four.

"Of course I was suspicious when you brought Alexandra into the company. Then, when I tried to get rid of her and you vehemently objected, I thought that was fishy too. So I sat back and watched Julia wind you up and turn you down for a while and I knew I was on the right track.

Then, with Ilya being forced down your throat, I no longer had any doubts.

"But let's not get off the issue here. You think you have a problem and I think it's a blessing. Ilya is celebrated, a marvelous curiosity. Wherever he chooses to dance, the crowds will line up three deep. Groupies, balletomanes, everyone will be waiting to see what the golden boy can do."

"And what happens when that curiosity dies down?"

"It won't," Paige said confidently. "As long as Ilya performs, New Yorkers will be there, eating him up alive. All you'll have to do is sit back and count the money. Then you'll have all the backing you'll ever need for a world-class company, and this time without any outside interference." She laughed. "In a curious way, Julia's cousin will actually rescue you from her clutches. He'll actually wind up liberating you." She giggled again. "Oh, smile, Richard. Julia's doing you one hell of a favor, only she doesn't know it."

He thought about that for a while and was tempted to agree. Paige, as always, was making good sense. But the personal stuff between him and Julia was still in the way. If he capitulated, Julia would think him weak, a wimp, and he didn't want that either. No, he thought. Before taking that Russian in, he would try another way.

"I'm going to call Senator Childs one more time," he said, getting up to leave, "and see what he can do. And Paige," he paused. "Keep Julia's backing under your hat. That was our deal. If Alexandra finds out her mother bought her a place in the company, we'll lose the gala. Without the gala, we have nothing. No theater, no school, nothing. I don't have to tell you what it means to me."

Paige took his hand and patted it. "Some of us lose sometimes, Richard," she said, blinking her eyes quickly. "But it doesn't matter. We live, and we go on. So don't be foolish. Take the offer. It's a sound business move, good for the company."

* * *

At home Caligari telephoned Senator Childs, but the Senator wasn't in. Ten minutes later he returned Caligari's phone call.

"I need help," Caligari explained. "Funds are running out again, I could use some financial assistance. Any chance of your intervening for us with government help at this time?

"It's worse than ever, I'm sorry to say," Senator Childs told him. "Especially now that Dorsey's made headlines. With her picture plastered on the covers of those news magazines, there'd be no end to the questions they'd ask if someone found out I tried pulling strings. All my European negotiations would be ridiculed, Mr. Caligari. And I'd lose my credibility and effectiveness. I'm sorry, but I have to beg off again." He paused. "There is one thing, however."

"What's that?"

"Long ago I promised you a party, and there's nothing to prevent me from arranging that. Maybe you can find your angel there. I have some very rich friends, as I once told you. And there are favors owed me."

They left it that way, with a party planned for the following week. But Caligari knew it wasn't enough. He could do only one thing in the meantime, and that was to tell Julia he'd accept Ilya into his company. Then he'd pray that the contacts he'd make at Senator Childs' party, would prove fruitful so he could tell Julia to take a hike.

When Julia hung up after speaking with Caligari, she felt sick to her stomach. It hadn't pleased her in the least to push the sensitive and creative man into a corner. Everything inside her screamed out to call him back, to apologize, to explain, to change what was happening between them, but a stronger urge pulled her in another direction. She sensed it had something to do with her own survival, which she couldn't understand, and also her inability to give in, to admit she was wrong, to get close. Most of all, she knew it was about her fear of loving.

Chapter 49

Ilya Kremorkin had been in the headlines ever since his New York City arrival, and he was beginning to grow accustomed to it. But the morning his limousine parked at the door to Caligari's theater, he was greeted by a three-ring circus.

The media lined the streets, studio exits and entrances. Reporters hung from fire escapes with cameras, microphones and tape recorders, screaming his name, begging him to respond. But Ilya said nothing. Instead, he flashed his world-famous boyish grin, and with the help of a fierce bald-headed bodyguard Julia had hired, pushed his way through the sea of human madness.

When he walked into the huge rehearsal hall, his fellow dancers, along with Richard Caligari, stopped what they were doing and applauded. Ilya acknowledged their respect with a bow, and after pausing to inspect the premises, dropped his ballet bag in a corner. Then he removed his sweater and took a place at the end of the barre, behind Dorsey.

"Welcome to our company," Caligari said sincerely.

The Russian eased his feet into a perfect first position, grabbed the barre, nodded and said, "To be here, sir, is for me *great* privilege."

* * *

Caligari stood by the mirror and watched Ilya work. The boy was fascinating, beautiful to observe, bold and heroic, with a strong back, the hallmark of any Bolshoi artist. But he was far too dramatic for the company's classical image, and Caligari would have to work with him on a more simple line, on follow through, with particular emphasis on his flowery arms.

There were differences in style that Caligari appreciated, differences Ilya would have to eventually change to fit in. But Caligari was no longer worried. Ever since his talk with Paige, he had come to her way of thinking. Judging by what was going on outside with the press, Kremorkin would certainly bring the crowds in.

As the class progressed, Caligari noticed that Kremorkin watched the others instead of trying to lead. That pleased the dance master greatly. It was the mark of a true professional. To observe, to examine, to contemplate, to study, proved not only an intelligent mind, but a total lack of temperament. And temperament was a quality Caligari never tolerated in anyone.

For the class in pas de deux, the dance master paired Ilya with Dorsey and the moment they began to move together he realized something extraordinary was happening. He couldn't take his eyes away. They were amazing together—electrifying: There were twenty students leaping, spinning, dancing their hearts out, but everyone else paled in comparison, became little more than a blur.

Dorsey smiled as Ilya lifted her high in the air. His hands were strong. He was confident, firm and very aware. She couldn't believe her good fortune. Every ballerina in the world would kill to be in her toe shoes. His palms were dry and warm, without any calluses, and he smelled masculine and spicy. His shoulder-length blond hair was a bit darker than hers, with natural streaks of gold and platinum, and his deep-set hazel eyes were as riveting as a pair could be.

As their bodies touched, she felt her heart leap to her throat, her mouth grow dry. It was an instant response, a visceral high, one she usually got from drugs but never from a man. Men had always been commodities to her, rising, falling like the stock market, to be bought or sold as their value to her increased or changed. But something told her this was blue-chip stuff on the upswing, to be coveted and held on to at all costs.

She leaned against him as the music started, felt his strong hands grip her waist and take total command. She was a ship lost at sea and he was the captain. Every inch of her body was understood as they sailed into unknown waters.

In a matter of minutes they were both drenched, chests heaving, sweat mingling, their bodies in the sort of intimate union even husbands and wives rarely experience. His arms extended between her thighs as she flew on his shoulders, and her backside slid down his chest, then pressed hard against the firmness of his groin. The lift again. His mouth was close to hers as he hoisted then released her. The soft arabesque continued as his fingers wound around her hips, then rested at the curve of her breast. Buttocks and thighs rubbed, caressing. His mouth was at her nipples, then at her ear. It was just like making love and she knew if it continued, she would come.

"Come with me," Ilya whispered to Dorsey at the conclusion of class.

She smiled, knowing exactly what he wanted. She wanted it too. "How do we get out of here without everyone seeing us?" she whispered back.

"I meet you," he said. He wrote an address on a piece of paper and gave it to her. "One hour. Please. I don't like late." Then he walked away, shook Caligari's hand and left, flipping the keys to Julia's Trump Tower apartment.

As Ilya left class, Caligari called Alexandra and Vidal aside. "I'm going to make a new pas de deux on you," he told them. He hardly noticed how excited they both seemed at that prospect. He was thinking only of how much he wanted to embarrass Julia.

He could see her smiling in the gala audience—covered in chinchilla, dressed in some designer gown with all her jewels—a public humiliation. All of it her own doing. She'd sit there watching her boyfriend along with her beautiful young daughter bounce around the stage like imbeciles. And he could make them look really silly if he chose to. The idea of getting back at her that way intrigued him, but there was also Alexandra to consider. The girl was beginning to look good, to show some real promise. And she'd worked honestly and hard to achieve it. He would have to decide how to get his revenge on Julia without hurting Alexandra in the process.

Simone ached for revenge as she watched Caligari work with Alexandra and Vidal Genero. She was bitter and angry as she clenched her fists. But anger was a familiar emotion. She was used to it, had in fact come to call it her friend. Anger had helped her survive when she had nothing, when she and Shane had been alone. Anger was like second nature to her. And as it fed her psyche, it became fuel, a propellant. Caligari was being unfair and it bugged the hell out of her. First Dorsey, now Alexandra. When would it be Shane's turn?

Shane and Seth watched the dance master work with Alexandra and Vidal.

"What gives?" Seth said. "This guy walks in and just takes over. I bust my ass for six months and what the hell do I get? A secondary role with a ballerina who's on her way out, then another with a rising star. Who do they think Dorsey is? Peter Pan? Shit! I should get credit. I was the one who carried her across that stage."

He looked at Shane. "I told you Mark and Rory were right. And what about you? You dance circles around Alex. I know you're pissed, so why the hell don't you say something to him?"

But Shane said nothing. She just stood there trembling, watching Caligari make a new ballet on Alexandra and Vidal.

Dorsey showered in the dressing room. She dressed in tight stone-washed jeans, a gold cable-knit sweater and custom-made black Gucci boots with a matching leather jacket. She was excited about seeing Ilya, thinking about peeling off his clothes and running her fingers down his tight stomach muscles, slowly, very slowly. Yum!

She brushed her blond hair, pinned it on top of her head with a tortoiseshell comb and hung banana-bunch earrings from her ears for a bit of punk levity. Outside she dodged reporters who waited to talk to her and quickly hailed a passing taxi. Inside she sat back while her imagination ran wild.

She could feel the juices flowing. All the important juices, anyway. What a deal! Ilya Kremorkin wanting her. Her!

She shut her eyes to the life of the city and imagined him at the door waiting for her, a gleaming Russian god with smooth skin. She thought of the wild things he would do to her and shivered. Ten minutes later she was at the address he'd given her. She went past security, up the elevator and was soon at the front door, which was flanked by a body-guard.

Before she knew what had hit her, the door opened and Ilya snatched her inside. Then without words, with his huge hazel eyes riveted to her face, he kicked the door shut. With his arms framing her neck like bookends, he pressed her against the wall.

His lips were hungry, demanding as his tongue forged its way deep into her mouth. She yielded instantly, felt herself go limp just for a moment. Then as her strength returned, she grabbed his neck and shoulders and let her hands ride his broad back to rest on the bones of his tiny hips. When her fingernails raked his buttocks, he scooped her up-

and carried her to the fireplace. There, he threw her on a fur rug near a raging fire.

She was excited beyond reason, breathless as he pulled off her sweater, snapped the buttons of her shirt and ripped her panties in two. Then he let his robe fall from his shoulders.

His body was evenly bronzed, smelling of musk, of danger and excitement, but it was the look in his eyes that made her dizzy. He was all sinew, a sun-drenched god of muscle and strength. She closed her eyes as his tongue teased and licked her breasts, as the pink buds grew hard and glossy. She moaned at the intense pain and pleasure, but that only excited him. From that moment on they were in sexual combat.

He wedged open her legs, and while his middle finger plunged inside the wet vaginal folds, his thumb gently massaged her clitoris. Her belly rose and fell with each of his movements. Her hips swayed to every pleasurable sensation. Then he mounted her and pushed himself inside.

He was huge and long, like a bull in heat—and as his buttocks rose and fell, he licked her breasts. She gripped him as he pumped, felt her flesh come alive with his turbulence and speed. A burning volcano shot from her cunt through her belly and rose like molten lava to the top of her skull.

He growled, howled, made sounds she'd never heard before. Then he stopped suddenly, grimaced and drew himself halfway out.

She felt him throb inside her, felt his organ grow longer, wider, filling her like a living entity. A few minutes later she was pulling his arms, scratching his back with her nails and begging him to finish.

As he pushed in and pumped again, they watched each other—two wild animals in a timeless moment of raging passion, savages clinging to each other as if the world were going to end and they were both damned to hell. He was on top, she was on top. They were sliding and pulling, pumping and rolling over and over. They grasped everything and anything they could lay their hands on for satisfaction. And then she screamed. And that brought his screams. And together they came, howling, falling, drenched, on the rug, spoon fashion.

Simone threw down the spoon she was holding and buttered Shane's bread. The sharp knife she used brought back terrible memories, but she chose to ignore them. There were more important things to take care of, like convincing her daughter that she was right.

"Didn't I tell you about those two girls?" she said. "I was right, wasn't I?" She put the bread on a plate and put the plate on the table in front of her dazed daughter's eyes.

"Well, don't you worry, honey," she said, rubbing between the girl's shoulder blades. "I'll take care of everything. Don't you even give them a second thought."

"I don't know, Ma," Shane said. "Maybe I'm fooling myself. Maybe I'm just no good."

Simone bristled. "Don't you ever say that again! Never! Understand? Alexandra is the spoiled daughter of a very rich woman and Dorsey is a hophead kid with a big-shot father. Today—that's what really counts. It's time you learned about life anyway. It isn't fair. It never has been and it never will be. You've got to take it by the horns and swing it until you get what you want. It's the only way, baby. Ask me—I know!"

"Well, I don't know," Shane said. "Besides, Brad tells me . . ."

"Brad, Shmad," Simone interrupted. "How many times do I have to tell you to forget him, that he's after one thing and one thing only—to ruin you. To get you to do things his way. Sure he'll marry you—with a lot of ifs. *If* his mother likes you. *If* his father likes you. *If* his brother likes you. *If* you convert to *his* religion. *If* you give up your career.

"Well, that's not my idea of a happy relationship. So forget about him. You have only one thing to work on and that's the solo Caligari gave you for the gala. That's what you have to pay attention to. That's where your future is. When the critics see you dance, you'll get the break you really deserve. Then we'll see who makes it." She kissed the girl's cheek. "There's an old saying, Shane," she said. "The cream always rises to the top. And that's what you are, baby. Cream."

She poured cream in her coffee as Ilya dressed.

"I have, how you say, appointment," he said. "We do again, no?"

"Yes," Dorsey told him, sipping the liquid. "Again, again and again and again and again."

He sat down beside her. "Please, to write for me your name and telephone on piece of paper."

Dorsey did as he asked and gave it to him with a kiss. "In case you don't know, you've already met my father," she said as he read it. "In Paris. Remember?"

A flicker of fear glowed in Ilya's eyes at the sight of the last name, and Dorsey, aware of his strong reaction, tried to reassure him. "Hey, take it easy," she told him. "You're in America, not Russia. What we do is *our* business, not my father's. She put her clothes on.

"But your father, he help me to escape. Be very angry. Maybe send me back if I am with you."

"Oh, don't be ridiculous!" Dorsey said. "We're in the same ballet company. We see each other every day. It's so simple. I'll just tell Daddy we're dating, that's all. Besides, he wouldn't even care."

He stared at her. "Dating. What is this dating?"

"You know, like going out together. Having lunch, dinner, going to a movie." She laughed lasciviously. "Making love." She lay back down with her legs spread-eagled.

"Yes," he said. "I like all these things." Ilya leaned down and kissed her nose; they were twin black profiles against an orange fire. Then she pushed away, buttoned her jacket and ran a brush through her hair. When she'd finished dressing, he walked her to the door.

"See you tomorrow," she said. "In class."

"Yes," he said, tickling her neck with his fingertip. "Class. Tomorrow."

He opened the door, said good-bye and shut it. Then he lifted a telephone and with a grin on his face, dialed Francesca Adair.

At home Alexandra finished writing in her diary, then tucked it under her pillow.

"Where's Shane tonight?" Dorsey asked, entering Alexandra's bedroom.

"With her mother," Alexandra said. "Where else?"

"Again? Jeez! You know we're going to lose her."

"Who knows," Alexandra remarked. "And where the heck have *you* been? You're glowing like Day-Glo paint."

Dorsey grinned. "I've been to London to visit the Queen."

"Anyone I know?"

"I plead the fifth."

"In that case, I'll take my shower."

When Alexandra went into the bathroom, an overwhelming compulsion seized Dorsey and she lifted the pillow to read Alexandra's diary. Alex was Ilya's cousin, she thought, rationalizing what she was about to do. And she wanted to know everything she could about him.

She lifted the pillow, picked up the book and turned to the back pages. What she saw made her angry as hell.

"Ilya made a pass at me, I think." Bullshit!

"Francesca had a date with Ilya." Bullshit!

"Dorsey's too thin." Bullshit!

Jealous! They were all jealous. What did they know. Ilya had made love to her tonight. Real and passionate love. And unlike Alex, she could tell the difference between a pass and real affection.

And *"too thin"*—that was just another bit of envy. She

was gorgeous. Absolutely gorgeous and they all knew it. Oh, well. What the hell did any of it matter? She was becoming a star, beginning to pay fame's price of jealousy, envy, perhaps even isolation, if it came down to it. But none of that mattered. She had Ilya, and nothing could compare to what had happened between them. She knew that as well as she knew anything. Ilya loved her and she loved him.

Chapter 50

Dance came naturally to Ilya Kremorkin. As naturally as walking. One leg would simply follow the other, then his arms and head would balance everything else. Born in Chimka, a small thriving city on the outskirts of Moscow, his mother died in childbirth, while his father, a career army man, blamed the boy for the loss of his beautiful wife.

When Papa could no longer stand the sight of him, Ilya was sent away to live with Tante Kyra, an adoring aunt who not only raised, but spoiled him. And spoil him she did. Nothing on the face of the earth was good enough for the boy. When there was no meat to be found, Tante Kyra seduced the butcher and there was *pirozhki* with rich sour cream on the table. When others could not find sugar or honey, Tante Kyra debauched the dairy man and made honey mousse smothered in fresh whipped cream. Nothing was beyond her reach if it meant pleasing Ilya. A sly old woman with a mischievous grin, she thought the sun rose and set with him, that the boy had only to ask to receive.

On his ninth birthday, Tante Kyra took Ilya to the Bolshoi Theater to see "Giselle," and with that single experience, his future was sealed. It was like a miracle, and at home he couldn't stop talking about the occasion. He lectured, preached, remembered and imitated every leap, jump, spin, turn. Then he begged Tante Kyra to enroll him in the local dance academy, and she agreed.

From the moment he walked into class, the teachers were astonished. Ilya had total control of his perfect body, and they were enthusiastic about his youthful and athletic prowess. For seven years he studied there. Then, with a wish to experience something of the material world, he joined a touring company traveling to South America, Australia and Turkey, where he quickly developed an appetite for freedom.

At eighteen he returned home, and after passing the difficult Director's Barre Test, joined the Bolshoi Ballet. Immediately, he was placed under the tutelage of a Russian dance master who had once trained at the impressive Vaganova School. From there it was just a matter of time before the talented, tall young man was propelled through the corps to soloist, then on to principal dancer, where at age twenty-three he was named *danseur noble*, and given the title Honored Artist of the U.S.S.R.

Six months later he would have no peace.

While on tour in London, Ilya met his cousin Julia, who took him to see George Balanchine's New York City Ballet Company. From that moment on, his beautiful *Ruskaya dusha* no longer belonged to the Soviet Union. His Russian soul was now haunted, thunderstruck at such modern choreography. He wanted an opportunity to dance these new forms. He was bored, tired of interpreting the old-fashioned repertoire of "Don Quixote," "Swan Lake" and "Giselle." He needed new and exciting ways to express himself, to communicate his feelings.

Alone at night, he walked the floor, imitated what he had seen on that London stage and, like his predecessors before him, Nureyev, Panov, Baryshnikov and Godunov, he grew ultimately determined to one day defect. And on the last day of their current Paris engagement, he and his friend Yuri slipped away and asked for asylum.

* * *

Francesca Adair and Ilya Kremorkin were together. To the uneducated eye, they might have been locked in a duel for life, but they weren't. They were making love. Between them, it had been previously agreed that nothing would be denied or forbidden, that they would give themselves to each other without reservation.

This encounter, which followed Ilya's seduction of Dorsey, began frantically in the back seat of Francesca's Rolls-Royce limousine and was finishing now at the actress' Sutton Place apartment amid an array of extraordinary sexual devices and paraphernalia.

Francesca begged to be tied up, then ravished, and Ilya complied. She pleaded for humiliation and domination and he obliged. She demanded that he punish and kick her while she lay tied to the bed in the most degrading position. In a desperate need to experience her most bizarre sexual fantasies, she had unleashed a wild man, a closet deviant whose own needs would far exceed her own.

Lying together on black satin sheets, he teased her breasts to the rhythmic snap of a leather strap. Over and over he hit her chest until the nipples swelled and the soft tissue cracked and peeled. Waves of pain mixed with feelings of pleasure as she abandoned herself to his wild imagination, moaning, pulling the leather thongs that bound her. And for her, the fun was just beginning.

For Ilya it was like tearing the wings off flies—delicious!

Francesca reveled in the pain, delighted at being whipped, bitten and scratched. Pain made her feel alive. She enjoyed the vibrators deep in her anus, loved having her genitals pinched. She adored the hot, melted wax poured on her skin, then ripped away.

And it continued that way until Ilya's erection became unbearable, until his testicles were so heavy with liquid, he ripped her bonds, rolled her on her belly and entered from behind.

And just as he controlled her pain, he also controlled her pleasure.

With all his strength he rammed her, flashing a wicked grin as he pumped. Then the charge left his testicles and he withdrew to let the jet stream fly across her back. She arched upward to experience the warmth. Then she dropped to the bed, exhausted with joy.

Chapter 51

In the days and nights that followed, Ilya and Dorsey were seen wherever the lights of New York City glittered: at the theater, dining, dancing. They had become a national pastime, appearing on network television, radio talk shows, giving interviews to worldwide newspapers and magazines. Why and how Ilya had defected was certainly intriguing. But it was that special touch, the little Cinderella romance blossoming between the Russian hero who'd left his chains behind and the all-American girl whose father had rescued him, that strummed the public's heart strings.

In the evenings they dined at Lutèce, La Caravelle, Tré Scalini; at the newest, most trendy places. They held court at La Côte Basque and P. J. Clarke's. They danced till closing at Régine's and applauded Bobby Short at the elegant Cafe Carlyle.

But in the mornings, both Ilya and Dorsey were in class, working, preparing for the Christmas Gala, and Caligari began to notice then respect in Ilya a determination and a dedication to dancing he had not seen displayed in anyone since he himself had been drawn to New York City many years ago.

The young Russian, already a superstar in Europe, Asia and South America, had settled like putty in Caligari's hands, submerging himself in purely classical techniques. He accepted direction easily, allowing the dance master's power to filter through, to take hold and fertilize with the intent that he would ultimately bloom in the company's image. And Caligari was greatly pleased.

While the media fawned over Dorsey and Ilya, Caligari focused his attention on Alexandra and Vidal. Day after day, night after night he worked with them in preparation for a television special he'd been asked to participate in.

The ten-minute spot for a PBS telethon had been initially designed for Ilya and Dorsey, even though Caligari had previously declined to offer their talents. He was afraid that Ilya and Dorsey would have too much exposure, and he didn't want that to happen. He wanted their first performance as partners to be live, at the Christmas Gala. By using Ilya and Dorsey as the gala pièce de résistance, he was bound to insure not only a packed house on opening night, but worldwide publicity as well.

Eventually, and with Paige's encouragement, he had agreed to the PBS telethon, but decided to use Alexandra and Vidal instead.

With so much attention from the dance master, Alexandra had begun to bloom, and Caligari more than once caught himself inwardly smiling at how beautiful she and Vidal were beginning to look together. So much for revenge, he thought, watching them glide across the stage. So much for his anger at Julia. Watching them dance, he knew he would have to find another outlet.

But then Caligari's enthusiasm for Alexandra and Vidal was totally misunderstood, misinterpreted by everyone else in the company. And as usual, the jealous gossip mongers began to spread their poison.

"He's just trying to keep Ilya and Dorsey in their places," Seth whispered to Shane, watching Alexandra and Vidal work.

"He ought to. They're becoming tiresome and vulgar," Shane whispered back, agreeing with the remark.

"Oh, you're both just jealous!" a corps member told both of them. "You wish Caligari were giving *you* all that attention instead."

Neither of them answered. Then the day of the PBS telethon arrived.

Everyone gathered in the dressing room to wish them good luck and watch the final fitting on Alexandra's costume. Shane, Dorsey, Paige, Seth—they were all there. A pale romantic delight, the tutu was held by spaghetti straps with a pearl-studded satin band that cut across Alexandra's bustline, flaring out to her knees in yards of see-through fabric.

"It's gorgeous," Dorsey told her as Simone pinned the straps.

"It's beautiful," Shane said.

"Ouch!" Alexandra screamed as Simone accidentally stuck her with a pin.

Simone apologized.

When Simone finished pinning Alexandra's costume, she worked on Vidal's. Then, hand sewn, they were hung on racks and packed for transport.

One hour before the telethon, Alexandra sat in her dressing room in a blue silk Chinese dressing gown, applying her makeup. Seth stopped by to wish her good luck, accompanied by a surly Mark who had since become Seth's lover. Then Dorsey and Shane came by.

Vidal came down to wish her *merde* and to present her with a small bouquet of flowers. She hugged him and apologized for not having had time to buy him something. Then, in a gesture of respect and affection, she selected one pink rose from the bouquet, kissed the velvet petals and handed it to him.

"I'll press it," he said, kissing her cheek. "I'll press it in that book of poems you once gave me."

"Break a leg," she called as he headed for the door.

"You too," he said. Then he threw her a kiss.

* * *

Ten minutes before curtain, Alexandra zipped up her costume and tied up her toeshoes, dipping the satin backs in a sink full of water so the heels would cling to her feet. Then, followed by Vidal, she walked out toward the television stage, where they warmed up, holding on to a couple of chairs.

The coast-to-coast telethon would be going out live, and *that* produced great nervous energy. Unlike tape, where mistakes could easily be changed and cut, this was for real. Going live meant no second chance to do things over.

Consequently, Alexandra was nervous as she waited, feeling her heart race and her hands grow clammy. This was the moment she'd waited for all her life, her first important role. So much counted on doing well, and she couldn't help but wonder what would happen if she failed. Then Vidal, with his English cool, calmed her in a dozen ways.

He rubbed her bare shoulders as they waited in the darkened wings, he whispered encouragement in her ear and by the time their names were called, her hands were warm as toast.

Two minutes later the last guests, a string quartet, came offstage, and while the PBS host made a short appeal for money, Alexandra and Vidal took their places in front of the television cameras.

Lights!
Camera!
Action!
Smile!

The moment the spotlight caressed Alexandra's face, she grew calm and tranquil, with her mind focused on the dance. Then the music began and Vidal, supporting her first in a beautiful attitude, *sur la pointe*, lifted her triumphantly above his head in a pose so majestic Alexandra thought she'd entered heaven. But the moment he let her down, it felt more like hell. Something sharp was stuck inside her costume.

It was hard enough to dance "Romeo and Juliet" live in cramped quarters on a nicked and slippery floor, but to have needles or pins pricking her skin was a horror. Each step, each lift became a fearful agony of human roulette, a dark terror of being stabbed, all balanced by Alexandra's deep need to do well. They were live, coast to coast, representing the ballet company in its first prime-time exposure. So much was riding on her performance.

But Alexandra's bravery took hold. She ignored the intermittent stabs to her breasts, spikes to her buttocks, stings to her back, and though each lift, each spin felt like knives piercing her body, she managed to rise above the pain.

And they were gorgeous—two figures spinning like polished white marble against a black velvet backdrop. They were lovers. Romeo and Juliet. A dream brought to life— she, a dazzling white swallow pursued by a streak of light. They were love and desire, ignited and dazzling.

Ten minutes later it was all over, and after taking an obligatory bow, Alexandra rushed to her dressing room. Within seconds she'd removed her costume to find bloody spots all across her body.

She grabbed her damp costume, opened the fabric and examined every inch. What she found in the seams made her angry as hell. Pins! Pins and needles!

She dressed, wondering if someone had done it on purpose! She swore to tell Caligari about it, but when he knocked on the door and entered, she soon changed her mind. It could have been an oversight and Shane was still her friend. If Simone had made such an error, Caligari might dismiss her. And Alexandra didn't want that responsibility. So, instead of telling him, she basked in the glow of the dance master's warm compliments and was delighted when Julia telephoned to congratulate her. Like other times in her life, Alexandra had risen above adversity and was proud of that accomplishment.

Chapter 52

On the night of Senator Childs' party, Caligari dressed in a midnight-blue Bill Blass suit and a white-on-white custom silk shirt, with a butter-cup yellow silk knit tie. Although the party was being held in his honor, he paid scant attention to his clothes. He had other things on his mind, important things which concerned not only certain members of his company, but the Christmas Gala as well. Foremost in his thoughts was the future of Alexandra Romanov.

Ever since she and Vidal had performed in that PBS telethon, he wanted to create something special for her to perform; something extraordinary, where all her talents could be showcased. God! All this time he had underestimated her ability.

There were such possibilities in the girl, and in Vidal too. Possibilities he had never dreamed of. That excited him. Discovering raw talent was like detecting a new spectral color, unearthing a species of plant never before seen or finding the cure to some terrible disease.

At the same time, he worried about Ilya and Dorsey.

They'd been spending too much time together, he thought, and that disturbed him. Under other circumstances he might have encouraged their emotional attachment, just as he had between other dancers, particularly those show-

ing little depth in their performance. But for certain performers, closeness could be toxic, like poison, draining
them of their vital energy and displacing the all-important
focus of their lives. That's what he thought had been happening to Dorsey, and he wanted to correct it.

In that regard Ilya was also linked to Francesca Adair, a
woman whose reputation as a human barracuda preceded
her. He didn't like that relationship either and felt the actress would be a liability to Ilya's career, not only for the
Russian dancer's acceptance by Americans, but for Dorsey's sake as well. Pitted against Adair, the Senator's fragile daughter would be swallowed alive.

And then there was Shane. Simone had come to him
with her concern for the girl, and he had agreed to speak
with her regarding her romance with Brad Kane. He understood Simone's feelings: about how easily a beautiful
and talented dancer could be lost to the clever wiles of
what appeared to be love. But every serious dancer had to
make a choice—Shane included. Yet he also understood.
In trying circumstances, people reach for comforting
things. And nothing promises comfort more than love. Or
what appears as love.

Almost ready, Caligari brushed his black hair, which had
grown long down the nape of his neck, and loosened his
tie. He thought perhaps he should have had a haircut. Then
the chauffeured limousine he'd ordered arrived, and throwing a plaid Burberry scarf and a navy cashmere coat over
his shoulders, he left to pick up Paige.

The moment Shane left her mother's room, Simone removed the thermometer from her mouth and touched it to
the glass of warm tea near her bed. A few seconds later she
popped it back inside her mouth and waited. She wanted to
make her temperature seem higher than normal. She was
determined to keep Shane at home, concerned for *her* welfare and away from Senator Childs' party. Ever since she
had seen *that* car, the one with the California license plates

parked outside Caligari's new studio, she'd kept her eyes on *all* of Shane's comings and goings. Although she couldn't be sure, she still feared the worst. If she was right, something from their past was about to destroy their future.

Though she could hardly prevent the inevitable, she could certainly forestall it. In so doing, she would choose not only *her* time, but *her* place as well. The last thing she wanted was for Shane to get hurt, to learn the truth. But they couldn't keep on running. So if things were about to burst wide open, she wanted to be there when they did.

"Fresh orange juice, Ma," Shane said, entering Simone's bedroom. Simone nodded, waiting for the girl to remove the thermometer from her mouth. It lent a nice touch to the charade, she thought. Mother permitting daughter to play mother.

"Is it high?" Simone asked, waiting for Shane's reaction.

"Mmm! About a hundred," Shane answered. The girl shook the thermometer vigorously and washed and returned it to its container. Then she lifted Simone's bedside telephone.

"What are you doing?" Simone asked, as if she didn't know.

"I'm calling Brad," Shane answered. "I'm not going to the Senator's party. Your temperature's too high for me to leave."

"Where's Shane tonight?" Alexandra asked Dorsey as she dressed hurriedly.

"With Simone. Where else?" Dorsey replied. She lay on a bed, turning page after page of a weekly tabloid. Then she noticed a photograph of Francesca Adair with Ilya Kremorkin and her temperature rose instantly.

"She's coming to the party, isn't she?" Alexandra asked.

Before Dorsey answered, she plunged an angry fingernail through the photograph, splitting one of Francesca's pretty eyes in two.

* * *

Senator Thomas Revere Childs had had his eye on the White House from the day he was born. At least that's what his father had always said. Like Franklin Delano Roosevelt before him, the Senator had come from a clever political family with a long history of public service, and according to Papa Childs, Thomas would continue the tradition. Thomas Childs never had a choice.

After graduating in the top ten percent of his class at Harvard Law School, he traveled extensively. Then, when he was twenty-eight, his father, a past ambassador to Brazil, began grooming him officially.

The young man was made to attend all state functions where a mixture of American public servants, including the President, current and past cabinet members, international bankers, congressmen and senators, mingled with high-ranking foreign diplomats.

Each night Ambassador Childs would prepare a dossier on certain guests, with instructions for Thomas to study and recall. Included were the most intimate details of their private lives. From the likes of his father, he learned whose wife wore which special perfume, and what gentleman sponsored whose extremist organizations. He also learned and remembered their hobbies, their interests, even their pet peeves. Most of all, he knew who was sleeping with whom.

Later on, it would all pay off when favors of support were needed. Later he would make the private information a stepping stone to his career. But he would soon learn that though the name of the game was always power, one could easily get caught in one's own web.

When he married Louise Baeydeker, the daughter of a blue-ribbon Fortune Five Hundred family, everything seemed to fit, and he continued to keep his eye on the presidency. But terrible things happened on his way to that dream.

His wife's alcoholism, exacerbated by her loneliness and feelings of insecurity, was the first of these to crush him.

Then another, more horrifying nightmare caused him, in the end, to have to settle for less.

Less makeup, Julia thought as she dressed leisurely for Senator Child's party. She had spent the day at Elizabeth Arden's and her skin was pink and moist. She didn't need any artificial help.

She slipped on an off-the-shoulder Chiari red taffeta gown, a cabochon ruby and diamond necklace with dangling cabochon ruby and diamond earrings, then piled her satin hair on top of her head, pinning it all with a large diamond clip. After grabbing a full-length white Fendi mink, which for some odd reason made her think of Richard Caligari, she waited for Vidal to arrive.

Caligari arrived just as the party was beginning, and Senator Childs introduced him immediately to those who he thought could be of help. And when the Senator noted Francesca Adair standing at the buffet table with an arm around Ilya Kremorkin's waist, he poked Caligari and snickered, "Next to Julia Romanov, she's your best bet— the most influential and richest of the lot. Besides that, she loves them." The Senator winked conspiratorially as he downed another neat Scotch. "And from what I hear on the Hill, I'm told they love her too."

"I can't wait for the baby to come," a very pregnant Deandra Childs said as she offered Julia and Vidal champagne.

Julia accepted.

Vidal declined.

And while he headed toward the bar for something stronger, Julia explored the downstairs portion of the two-story mansion.

The whole house said "welcome," and as she wandered, she allowed herself the pleasure of drinking it all in. Mirrored walls and lacquered ceilings gave an illusion of great space. Reflected light from the marble fireplace and clever

indirect lighting bounced brilliance from crystal wall
sconces and English silver out to a huge terrace where the
view below showed a forest of blinking lights. And scattered everywhere and underscored by gorgeous Aubusson
rugs were large, wine velvet sofas and chairs.

At the buffet table, Julia smiled at the enticing array.
How diplomatic, she thought. Even the food held no favor-
itism.

The finest black caviar was stuffed into bleached white
eggshells and stood next to dilled meatballs, moussaka and
Egyptian bean salad heaped on frozen romaine lettuce.
And there was *plaky* from Armenia and mushrooms stuffed
with snails, Chilean *empadas*, sherried shrimp, Russian
pirozhki, with a huge galantine of turkey and pistachio
nuts, surrounded by an array of Spanish, Greek and Italian
olives.

Julia spread some galantine on a biscuit, took an egg-
shell of beluga, then made her way back to a seat in the
living room.

The moment she settled onto the wine velvet sofa, she
noticed Richard Caligari standing with Paige McDowell
and Deandra Childs. It made her lose her taste for food.
Seeing Paige next to the obviously pregnant Deandra reminded her of that newscast which had reported Paige's
possible miscarriage, reminded her of many things, and
she put her plate down, finished her champagne and gestured to the waiter for another.

As she drank, Julia noted a number of familiar faces in
the group. Francesca Adair was standing with Ilya, who
blew Julia a kiss. And the Vice President, with a contingent of CIA and FBI bodyguards, was there, along with
ambassadors from Finland, Brazil, Saudi Arabia and a host
of Hollywood celebrities, all of whom Julia knew well.

From New York society, there was Pamela Brookline,
whiskey heiress, with her handsome escort, Ian Hughes,
head of IBR Computer Corporation. Then there were Mr.
and Mrs. Robert Shayer, patrons of the arts. Off in a small
alcove near the door was pretty Caroline Jensen of the

famous cosmetic Jensens, laughing with William Sweet, a well-known South African diamond merchant. And from London, Sir John Fielding III stood with his wife, Lady Margaret Fielding, second cousin to her Royal Highness, Queen Elizabeth.

As he passed, Julia caught the roving eye of Count Marko Ignobile, president of Milan's largest banking dynasty, and waved hello to Stone Lawrence Jerome, dance critic of the *London Dance Log,* who was trying to interview a very reluctant Dorsey.

Then, seeing Caligari again, Julia wondered what the hell she was doing here in the first place, and wished she were somewhere else.

Dorsey avoided Stone Lawrence Jerome for the fourth time and made a beeline for Ilya Kremorkin. She pulled him from the clutches of Francesca Adair and with a caustic remark led him into the ballroom to dance.

"Why you are behaving like a child?" he asked her as they moved together to the slow and romantic music.

"Why you are behaving like a prick?" she replied, mocking his accent.

Ilya thought for a moment. "Prick? What means this word?" he asked.

She reached between his thighs as they danced and squeezed his mound.

"Ah!" he said, wincing, and pulling his bottom half away. "Is now quite clear."

It was clear to Richard Caligari. He would not find the financial backing he needed, at least not in this place. Nobody was responding. They all loved ballet, his ballets, but not enough to put their money where their mouths were. Then Senator Childs sidled up to him once again and prodded him toward Francesca Adair.

"Still think she's your best bet," the Senator whispered. He was three sheets to the wind, the dance master noted, not responsible anymore, and it made him angry. What a waste!

Caligari made a sour face at the suggestion.

"I think I understand," the Senator coughed. "But if I were in your place, I'd think twice about using her." He chuckled at his choice of words, then drifted off again.

Caligari wouldn't consider using her at all. She was everything he disliked in women: bawdy, loud and common. Besides that, he'd had enough problems handling Julia. He hardly needed another female dictator. And Francesca Adair was enough of a hindrance already. As they drifted aimlessly toward one another, he mustered the courage he needed to tell her what had been on his mind for a while.

"I've been meaning to talk with you about Ilya," he ventured.

Adair's eyebrows raised; the smoke from her long brown Sherman cigarette drifted by his nose. "And what about Ilya? she asked with a makeshift look of feminine indignation."

"I feel personally responsible for his professional future in this country, and the publicity he's been getting by running around with you can't help him win friends and influence people."

He listened to his own words and thought he sounded pompous and presumptuous. He tried to be more gentle and clear. "You know as well as I that Ilya's image as an artist is being distorted by the media. He's coming off like some kind of clown instead of the serious artist he really is."

Francesca stepped away from him. She flared her nostrils as though she were smelling rotten eggs. "And what has that to do with me?"

"Everything!" Caligari said. He held his breath until the smoke from her cigarette left the area around his nose. "I've read those articles in the tabloids. Articles about the both of you. And because of his affection for you and your friendship, I thought you might want to influence him in a more positive way."

Francesca's laughter was bawdy. "Ilya's a big boy, or haven't you noticed? He can make up his mind whether or not to continue seeing me. After all, he did leave Russia for more freedom. I can't imagine why he'd choose to give it up. And more important, why would anyone ask him to? Especially you."

"I don't think you're listening to me, Miss Adair," he insisted.

"Oh, but I am, Mr. Caligari," she countered. "I *am* listening. And you're coming in loud and clear. It's pretty obvious you don't want his image sullied by the likes of me."

"That's not it at all," Caligari persisted. "I'm only asking that you give him some time, an opportunity to make friends with the American public, a chance for them to witness his artistry before he becomes a silly playboy in their eyes. How will they ever learn to respect him, to take him seriously?"

"They'll take him seriously, Mr. Caligari. The moment he steps on stage and does his first tour en l'air. So if you'll excuse me," she said, blowing another thick cloud of smoke in his direction, "I have other people to do."

In the midst of the festive occasion, two sets of eyes met across the crowded room. It was a moment of recognition which soon turned into demanding sexual urgency, and in one quick instant two halves of a whole came together.

Self-consciously, the two drifted toward one another from the farthest corners of the room, circling first to test the frightening waters. Then, like a pair of gripping magnets, they met. One positive, one negative. A perfect match.

But there were too many faces of inquiry, far too much danger. So, silently they retired, quickly ascending the staircase together while their aching hearts raced in wild anticipation of things to come.

Upstairs, away from judgment, they found an empty, darkened room to be alone.

Sitting alone on the velvet couch and sipping a worthy champagne, Julia's eyes roamed the room. The many political and Hollywood dignitaries fawned over one another, gleaning, she thought, what each could do for the other. Actors and politicians were natural allies, she thought, and watching them operate was amusing.

Then it struck her that the familiar faces in the room had grown fewer. Except for Paige McDowell and Richard Caligari, who kept staring in her direction, there was no one she knew personally, and she wondered where everyone had gone: Vidal, Alexandra, Francesca Adair, Deandra, the Senator, Dorsey, and her cousin Ilya.

She looked across at the mantel clock, a beautiful eighteenth-century gold piece with an ormolu mounted case, and noted the late hour. She was growing tired, restless, self-conscious about Caligari's gaze. She would find Vidal, she decided, and they would leave.

She stood up, started a search for him through the crush and found Dorsey sitting alone in the game room.

"Hi ya," Dorsey sang, looking up. "Long time no see."

Julia greeted the girl, realizing she was high on something. Then and there she decided to speak to Alex about changing roommates. "Hello," Julia returned. "Have you seen Alex anywhere?"

Dorsey pondered the question. "Let's see," she said. "I think she went upstairs awhile ago. She wanted to see the bedrooms. C'mon, I'll take you."

Before Julia could say no, Dorsey had taken hold of her hand, guiding her toward the staircase.

As they moved, Julia thought she saw Caligari follow, but wouldn't turn around to see. She was afraid if their eyes met she would fall apart in his presence, and tonight she couldn't afford such a display.

At the top of the staircase, Dorsey's shoe came undone, and she sat down giggling in the middle of the floor trying to fix it. She waved Julia to go on without her, telling her that the rooms weren't locked, but Julia just waited.

Dorsey finally pulled off both her shoes, tossed them aside and, taking Julia by the arm, turned the first knob on a guest bedroom.

Finding it empty, she closed the door and continued down the hallway.

"That's my grandfather," Dorsey said as they passed a gallery of austere portraits hanging on the wall. She giggled as she reached out to tickle his beard. "And that's his wife, Meanie Jeanie, the college queenie."

She made a face at her grandmother's portrait just before she opened the next door and switched on the light. But this room was not empty.

With their trousers undone, with their genitals half exposed, Vidal and Senator Childs were leaning against a wall locked in a strong, sexual embrace.

A stunned Dorsey held her breath at the spectacle while Julia stood frozen in place.

As the men scrambled for decency, Caligari appeared from down the hall and shut the door. Two seconds later Dorsey fled along the hallway, hysterical, while Julia stayed paralyzed and speechless. Caligari tried comforting her, even tried to explain. He had expected an incident like this to happen long ago, had even thought he would enjoy Julia's misery at the discovery, but he felt only sympathy for her.

In the old days Vidal had courted a young male dancer in his newly formed ballet company. As a result, the dancer had lost sight of his career and had gone down the tubes. Caligari had had words with Vidal then, but it was useless. Now it was Julia who had to face the fact of Vidal's bisexuality.

Julia seemed to gain a sense of herself and what had happened. She left the room and ran down the staircase with Caligari following behind. He called out to her. He

wanted to help her understand and forgive. But by the time
he reached the elevator, the doors had closed. He was too
late.

For the rest of the evening, Senator Childs feigned illness and stayed secluded in his room. No one else had seen
what had happened, but when the guests had gone, Dorsey
and her father began a marathon of cruel accusations.

She was pitiless, showing her father no mercy, reminding him how *that* scene with Vidal had been so reminiscent
of the days before her mother's suicide.

Then the Senator attacked Dorsey, convincing her that
what she was saying was cold-blooded and untrue, just the
biproduct of her drug-distorted imagination and her anger
at his marriage to Deandra.

One hour after that fruitless confrontation, Deandra was
rushed to the hospital, bleeding from the uterus, with the
baby she longed for fighting for its life.

Chapter 53

For days after the party, Caligari waited for the walls to collapse, for the news media to uncover and report the story of Senator Childs. But that never happened. They reported nothing except Deandra Childs' unfortunate miscarriage.

He was saddened by that event, but otherwise glad for the Senator. People were entitled to do as they pleased with their private lives. Some, like the Senator, were compelled to do it in secret. But his concern was with Dorsey, who had not come to class and had not been seen for the last few days. He hoped it would pass, that the girl would understand, that she would forgive her father for his weakness, then get on with her own life.

He was concerned about Julia too, and about Vidal, who had skipped one class but had finally come to another. These were crucial times for his company, and he had to say something to his dancers about the dangers and pitfalls of their romantic liaisons.

Simone spotted them the moment she left the studio to run an errand. They were standing half a block away, leaning on an old blue car. God help her, where was Shane?!

She stepped back and hid behind the doorway so they couldn't see her, so she could look again to be sure she wasn't seeing things. But it only confirmed her worst fears. It was them all right—bold and big as life, as threatening to her and Shane's existence as they had always been.

Her mouth went dry as sand, her arms and legs grew heavy as lead. She had chills and goose bumps as big as eggs on every part of her body. Then a sharp pain crushed the inside of her chest.

None of it fazed her as she moved against the terrifying symptoms. Even if she were having a heart attack, she would have to find Shane before they did. But God help her if she couldn't!

On her way to the studio, Shane stopped at her apartment to pick up some things. She had been staying at Simone's new place for the last few weeks, and when she entered her apartment she began arguing with a very bewildered Alexandra.

"I said you could borrow my tights," Shane shouted. "You didn't have to steal them."

Alexandra stared at her friend in total disbelief. "Steal them?"

"Yes," Shane said. "They were here the other day, hanging on that shower rod, and now they're gone. If Dorsey's not around, that leaves you."

To prove Shane wrong, Alexandra checked the label on the tights she was wearing. She was embarrassed to find her friend was right. She stuck out her bottom lip and offered a shy pout. "Sorry. It was an honest mistake."

"Mistake?" Shane yelled again. "Is that what you call it?"

"What else?" Alexandra said. "If you wait a second, I'll take them off and give them back."

"Forget it," Shane said, stomping from the room. "You can keep the damn things. All I know is my mother was right. You and Dorsey—you're both spoiled rotten. You think you own the world." She grabbed her ballet bag and pulled open the door. "But you don't," she called from the hallway. Then she slammed it shut, leaving a baffled Alexandra behind.

An agitated Shane entered class through the side door. She was troubled, a nervous wreck. She had never talked to anyone that way in her life. Imagine, screaming at a friend. Screaming at Alexandra, whom she dearly loved.

Everything was changing too quickly. Everything was coming down around her ears. Simone was hovering more closely than ever, with her constant lectures and pressure for Shane to push harder in class, to succeed. Then Dorsey and Alexandra were blooming in Caligari's favor, moving ahead, leaving her behind. And she was just as talented as they. Everyone said so.

And Brad was pushing her into a relationship she actually wanted but wasn't ready to commit to. At least not at this point in her life. And certainly not as seriously as he. She was young, too inexperienced to consider marriage. She wanted to dance, to make something of her life.

And what were her chances for that? Even with the little solo Caligari had given her, the one Simone said would launch her come gala time—well, who could tell? She'd probably wind up ignored, lost in the hype surrounding Dorsey and Ilya. Damn! With all that, no one would know she existed.

She laced up her toeshoes and joined the others on stage for a short warm-up. Then Caligari cleared the area so he could work with her solo. But before that, he called her aside for a private chat.

As he spoke, her stomach churned. Each of his words brought waves of fear which made her legs shake and quiver.

"I've been meaning to speak with you, Shane," he said. "I haven't had a chance to tell you, but you've been growing beautifully as a dancer and I expect great things from you."

Shane forced a smile. Her heartbeat increased where it

should have quieted. Now she sensed something more coming.

"But I want to tell you a few things before we begin work this morning."

She was right! Her hands were clammy as she waited impatiently for what was to follow, noticing Simone gesturing at her in the wings. For a moment she wondered why her mother wasn't up in the sewing room, then turned her attention back to the dance master.

"I really don't want to interfere," Caligari said, "but if ballet is as important as I think it is to you, you must be aware that dance and romance are very uneasy companions. That is, unless they're handled properly. Like politics and religion, for example." He reached for her arm and she could sense his own discomfort with the issue. Her first thoughts were of Ilya nd Dorsey. Had he confronted them on this issue also? Her second thought was of Simone. Damn them all! Too many people were meddling in her life these days, and she hated it.

"I don't really want this to sound like a lecture," Caligari continued. "But I think you should ease up on seeing Brad for a while. At least until you've gained more . . ." He didn't finish but only smiled. "That's all I wanted to tell you. Now let's get to work."

He patted her cheek and left the stage for his seat in the darkened auditorium. She saw him sit, waiting for Joshua to begin. Then the sound of the piano chord started her spiral into hysteria.

As she danced, her hands grew wet with perspiration, water dripped from every pore of her body. Her head whirled with all the feelings and emotions she had been blocking for the last weeks. Worst of all, she kept falling off tempo, as if inattentive to the music. And the harder she tried, the worse it got.

Half a dozen times she stopped to gasp for air. She wondered if she were physically sick or something. Then voices screamed deep inside her ears. Layer on layer of noise rippled, pounded her brain like a jackhammer. She was awake in a living nightmare, and as she began a series of fast chaîne turns along the edge of the stage, soothing waves of darkness beckoned from the orchestra pit. Water, she thought—warm, cleansing water offering salvation.

She circled once, twice, three times, growing more frantic with each pirouette. Then, propelled by anxiety, by fear, by a hopeless confusion, she leaped from the edge of the stage with a scream and hurled herself into the pit.

Dorsey wakened abruptly. She was in a strange hotel, in a strange bedroom with a strange naked man, and she shook him awake. Then, gathering her senses, she tossed him and his clothes from the room with dire threats if he didn't quietly oblige. Quickly, she searched her purse for a stash of cocaine she had hidden in an old lipstick tube. Grateful to have it, she cut and drew four lines, which she quickly snorted. Now she was ready to face the world.

With cocaine she was invincible. Nothing could harm her. Nothing and no one could touch her. But she wanted Ilya. So she showered and dressed, combed her hair and put on makeup. Then she telephoned Ilya and begged him to meet her.

"Where you have been?" Ilya asked. "We are worried."

"I needed time off," she said. "No big deal."

She listened politely as he lectured about responsibility to him and ballet, about how important it was to rehearse together on a daily basis. But nothing was getting through. She wanted his arms around her, his lips pressed against hers. She wanted to ride a hansom cab through Central Park and dine at their favorite restaurants. All she could think about was touching him, having him love her and heal her wounds. She desperately needed him to erase the shame and degradation of her private life.

"Just meet me," she begged. "Now!"

"Okay," he finally agreed.

Then he gave her his new address, an apartment in the Eighties Julia had secured for him. Dorsey wrote it down and hung up, feeling as though a life sentence had just been commuted.

Shane had been lucky. She wakened in the hospital with no broken bones and no torn ligaments, just a nasty sprain and a tiny cut on her chin. And though she hurt—and the call had been a close one—a blessing had emerged. She had finally made up her mind.

No more Simone. No more Caligari. No more Brad. If she wanted to, she could toss her toeshoes in the garbage and forget about it. She would make her own decisions, do her own thinking from now on. And if it hadn't been for what happened next, her reasoning might have worked just fine.

Chapter 54

The moment she saw their car in the parking lot, Simone froze. The bastards had probably seen the ambulance, asked a few questions and followed Shane here. Shit! Now there was no turning back. Certainly no more running. She was about to face her worst nightmare, God help her.

She had left Shane alone for ten lousy minutes and they were probably in her room right now, spewing their garbage and confusing her baby. May they both rot in hell for what they had done. May they both not only rot, but burn for everything they had done. Poor Shane. So confused, and now this!

The door to Shane's room opened.

"Shane?"

A sleepy Shane didn't know them from Adam. The man was thin, bald, a bean pole with bug eyes and a three-day-old beard. The woman was short, stout and slovenly. At first Shane wondered if she was dreaming, if the sedative the nurse had given her an hour ago was making her see and hear things. Then she heard her name again and knew it wasn't a dream.

"Shane?"

Inside the elevator Simone listened to the gears grind, watched the numbers plod slowly by. Floor one, stop to load and unload. Floor two, stop to pick up. An old man on a gurney with a needle stuck in his arm. She remembered it so easily, recalled her own needle, her own gurney. The world looks different when you're on your back.

She felt empathy. She prayed, hoped that what she knew would happen wouldn't happen at all. That the car belonged to somebody else. That there was no connection.

Floor three. One more stop. Nails chewed and bitten to the quick. C'mon, c'mon. *Move it!*

Flour four. She was finally there, pushing her way out of the crowded elevator, heading straight for Shane's room.

Shane was startled when the man spoke.

"Shane, honey, we've come a long way to see you. We know it's a shock but we—we're your . . . real parents."

"Oh, no, you're not!" Simone shouted as she entered the room. She held the door. "Both of you get your butts out of here and don't come back. Ever!"

"No, Simone," the woman said. "It's no use. You're going to have to tell Shane the truth, and now."

A shivering Shane pulled the blanket to her neck and stared wild-eyed at the trio. What was happening? What were they talking about? What were they trying to do—make her crazy? "What is it, Ma?" she said. "Who are these people?"

Simone didn't answer, just picked up the telephone and warned she would call the police.

When they didn't move, she threatened them again. "If you aren't gone in five seconds, Sade, I'll have you arrested."

"Won't work," the man said. "Statute of limitations has run out. We're entitled to see our daughter."

"Maybe they've run out," Simone cautioned. "But unlike you, I haven't. Now I'm not up on your legal rights, and what's more, I don't give a damn. But if the cops get here and check your arms I bet you'll both spend some time in jail for using."

Two seconds later they were both gone.

"You'd better tell me, Ma," Shane said, still clutching the blanket. "You'd better tell me everything."

And Simone did.

"Twenty years ago that couple had a baby, only there were complications. The woman was addicted to heroin; so was the man. The little baby was born addicted too."

Simone fell on the bed and began to weep. "Oh, Shane, I prayed to God this wouldn't happen. I worked like a dog so you'd never know." Her tears ran openly now—great streams of water fell from her eyes.

As Simone told the story, Shane's thoughts were a chaotic jumble. She had never seen her mother like this before.

"The hospital cared for the baby until it was well. And when it stopped vomiting and sweating, when the shakes were gone, they gave her back to the parents, but on certain conditions. They were supposed to stay clean and never use drugs again. Of course that never happened. That woman you saw was the mother, my sister Sade. The husband was Gus." She paused and barely mumbled the rest. "And the baby was you."

In shock, all Shane's senses spiraled like a cyclone, like a haywire hurricane with no eye to the storm. But another part of her took over as she begged Simone to tell it all.

"I was just a kid, twenty, wet behind the ears when it happened. Nana and I lived in Manhattan then, and every day she begged me to go to Sade's to be sure you were being cared for. And I did." Simone stopped to blow her nose. "You were so cute," she sniffled. "But God—we worried day and night. If you've ever seen a heroin-addicted baby scream in withdrawal, then you've seen hell."

"Go on," Shane begged. "Please don't stop!"

"Well, I went to see you one day, as usual," Simone

continued, "right after a dress rehearsal at the City Center. I was supposed to dance a medley of Cole Porter tunes the following night for some Hollywood moguls. And I was excited. There was talk about sending me out to the Coast for a screen test and I was walking on air. Then everything just fell apart. I was still in my costume when I knocked on Sade's door but she didn't answer. So I barged my way in. I could hear you screaming all the way down the hall and I was scared. Gus could be an animal when he was high. When I got inside, I found him sprawled on the floor laughing, with Sade trying to burn you with a cigarette."

Shane felt his insides heave. She wiped tears from Simone's eyes, made her stop to drink some water, but begged her to continue.

"It was the worst thing I'd ever seen," Simone went on. Her voice caught in her throat. "I grabbed you from Sade's arms before she could burn you again, and I turned on the sink to let cold water run on your belly. Then the next thing I knew, Gus was behind me with a knife and everything went crazy.

"I was scared, Shane. I was about your age and I didn't know what to do. So I screamed and yelled, and when nobody came I kicked him with my feet to try and protect you." She stopped, shutting her eyes tightly. "The lousy son of a bitch caught me in the calf and . . ." She choked on the next words. "He cut my leg to ribbons." Her head drooped. "It never healed."

The last words brought Shane's arms around Simone's neck. She couldn't bear to see the pain. "Stop, Ma, please! No more!"

Simone held Shane tightly. It was the first time they had hugged in years. Together they sobbed like children. Then suddenly Simone drew away.

"I've been tough on you all these years, Shane, maybe out of fear, or anger. Who knows? Mostly, I didn't want you to find out about them. But to be honest I think a part of me wanted you to suffer for what happened to me that day. I actually think I made you dance to make up for what

I'd been cheated out of. But I don't really know the truth anymore. It's all mixed up in my mind.

"Later I fought for you in court, and they gave me temporary custody. So you were legally mine and not theirs. And when they left for California I was relieved. But I'll understand if you ever want to meet them."

Shane reached for her mother again, buried her face in Simone's neck and cried. Clutching each other, they remained that way until there were no more tears between them. And for the first time in her life, Shane was beginning to make some sense of things.

Chapter 55

      While Shane mended in the hospital, re-
hearsals for the gala continued. But when there was free
time, everyone came to visit her, to bring flowers, to give
love and support. Caligari came too, promising to keep
Shane's roles open if she was able to do them. She would
have ample time to recover and consider, the doctors had
told her, to get back in shape if she wanted to. It was up to
her.

    While Shane and Simone reconciled, Dorsey's relation-
ship with her father teetered on a jagged edge. Ever since
the party, they had barely spoken to one another. Aside
from his shame at what had happened with Vidal, the Senator had been devastated by his wife's miscarriage and was
keeping a very low profile. He had given up drinking, and
in the confines of his own home had decided it was time to
take Dorsey in hand and explain things more fully to her.

    But Dorsey was in her own world now, spending most of
her time with Ilya at his new apartment, helping him deco-
rate, giving him aid and comfort as though through him *she*
would find restoration. Together they made a charming
couple and the media still hounded them.

    In Hollywood the William Morris Agency sought to sign
them, and Caligari asked them to delay that decision. He

wanted the gala to be an artists' affair, not an audition for some television movie-of-the-week. Both had agreed.

Though rumors flew wildly about Ilya and Francesca Adair, Dorsey refused to believe them. Lies, he had told her. They were all lies made up to sell newspapers. Now it was two days since she'd seen him and she missed him badly. He'd had a cold and they had both agreed she would stay away for her own health. But on the third day Dorsey decided to bring him chicken soup and rang the downstairs bell to his apartment.

"Have still fever," he said on the intercom. "Is not good you come."

"Just for a minute," she insisted. "I brought some chicken soup. Pleeeease."

He let her up but only opened the door halfway. Then Dorsey barged past and headed for the kitchen. There she dropped her ballet bag on the floor and poured hot soup into a dish. "That's a matzoh ball," she told him as he studied the strange, round dumpling floating in the liquid. "It's supposed to have magic properties for colds, even if you're not Jewish."

She didn't notice how nervous he was as she fluffed the living room pillows and picked up some stray magazines to straighten up a bit. But then she headed for his bedroom, where the door was tightly closed, and he was clearly on edge.

"Not to go in please," he said, blocking her way. "Is big mess."

"Let me fix it then," she insisted, moving her hand toward the knob.

"*Nyet, Pajalsta!*" he said, trying to scoot her away. "I take nap now. You go, go, go."

Dorsey closed her palm over the knob, ignoring the words and gesture, and turned it halfway. Then she noted his pained expression of embarrassment, and she let the knob go. Blowing him a kiss, she headed for the front door.

On her way out, she watched him slip inside the bedroom and wave good-bye to her just before he disappeared. After opening the front door to leave, she saw some new keys sitting in an ashtray and tried the front door with one. When it worked, she called to ask if she could have it but he didn't answer. So she shrugged, slipped the key inside her pocket and shut the door.

Downstairs, seconds before stepping off the elevator, Dorsey realized she'd left her ballet bag in Ilya's kitchen. She heaved a sigh, pressed the elevator button again and waited for the door to close.

She rode the slow-moving vehicle upward, thinking of Ilya's soft skin, of his hard muscles, his lovemaking, his cock and her desperate need for his affection. And soon her lascivious thoughts were exciting her. Screw it, she thought. Cold and all, the minute she laid eyes on him, she would throw him on the bed and fuck him silly.

Leaving the elevator, she reached the door and knocked. No answer. Not a peep. Then she remembered she had the key and quietly pushed it in. Not wanting to wake him from his nap, she unlatched the lock and tiptoed in, going to the kitchen where she scooped up her ballet bag. She was about to tiptoe out when she noticed the door to his bedroom slightly ajar. Feeling hot and bothered, she licked her lips and decided then and there to jump him. What the hell, she thought. Can't get a cold giving a guy head.

She placed her bag on the floor and began a quiet trek to his bedroom. She hoped he was sleepy, dreamy, loose. That's the way she wanted him. Ready and willing, *unable* to resist. All he had to do was lie back. She would do the rest.

When she reached his bedroom door, she was ready, salivating like a baby with candy. She stopped and pushed the door open, but the distinct sounds of feminine laughter caught her totally off guard.

Television, she thought, smiling. Those stupid soap operas he loved to watch. But the laughter continued, and when she moved in closer and saw them, she froze like a chunk of ice.

Francesca Adair was going down on her lover!

Finding her voice, Dorsey screamed, picked up a Baccarat crystal vase and hurled it with a vengeance. It whizzed past their heads, hit the wall and shattered, raining down on their bodies like crushed ice. Then, like the vase, Dorsey shattered too.

Two hours later she wakened in a hospital straitjacket, sitting on the floor of a small windowless room with padded walls. In the distance someone was howling. It took her five seconds to realize the sound was coming from the depths of her own throat.

Chapter 56

Dorsey's father was at the hospital moments after the frantic phone call came. Two hours later he had her placed in a private drug treatment center near Chatauqua, under strict psychiatric supervision.

Her drugs were taken from her, and she was forced to dry out, cold turkey.

When the pills, cocaine and pot wore off, her nights were terrifying nightmares, her days a living hell, with vomiting, nausea, sensations of her brain shrinking, headaches so bad she thought her skull would explode.

She cried, she cursed. She begged God for salvation. But her mind stayed a steady strobe, flashing freeze-dried images dredged from the depths of her subconscious mind. At a million photos per second she had no peace.

But the healing process called for more than drying out, and she had daily visits with a psychiatrist.

Dr. Carla French, M.D., was a gentle woman who easily determined that the girl's drug problems were symptoms of all her deep-rooted terrors, of her anger and paranoid jealousies toward her father, her guilt at her mother's death. And though Dorsey tried hard to be heroic and joke her way through the whole ordeal, it was useless. After living so long in a state of such bitter disappointment and agony, everything floated to the surface and the demons that had long laid siege to her mind and body reared their ugly, naked heads. She had no choice now but to deal with them.

They started therapy, started working on her distorted self-image, on her bulimia, a name Dr. French had given to her "fear of getting fat." They talked about anorexia, her compulsive need to manipulate her total environment by controlling her intake of food. And they talked about her relationship with her father and also her deceased mother.

Then gradually the tiny, frightened child began to express itself.

"How are you feeling today, Dorsey?" Dr. French asked.

It was the sixth morning of her stay, and they were seated in Dr. French's bright and airy office on the far end of a row of country cottages located on eighty-five acres of magnificent rolling hills.

Dorsey stared out the window at the wintry landscape, wondering when they would give her the next tranquilizer.

"I'm, er, fine," she said, shivering.

Dr. French removed her frameless, blue-tinted glasses, stood up and walked around her desk to where Dorsey was sitting. She placed her spectacles on the table and sat on the edge of the wooden desk.

"Have you been cooperating with the nurses? Going on walks to the brook?"

"Yes," Dorsey said, feeling lightheaded.

"Good! Then we can really begin your therapy."

Everyone at the ballet company was shocked by Dorsey's breakdown. Especially Ilya. Every day new stories circulated about her demented state of mind. Crafty journalists would wait for Alexandra, Shane, Ilya, Seth, anyone who could shed light on Dorsey's condition. But no one would speak of it. They were her friends, after all.

And so the work continued without her. And the stories of her supposed "break" with Ilya dominated the tabloids.

Caligari was in a quandary of his own. He's lost Dorsey, and however temporarily, Shane. And though he sympathized, he began looking toward other members of his company with new eyes. He had to find another dancer who would respond quickly, one who could learn all of Dorsey's ballets. And again, Paige came through for him. Fully recovered from her dreadful experience in London, she was ready to put on her toeshoes again and get back in shape. She was, after all, a professional. Dancing was all she had ever wanted in life, except for Richard Caligari. There was enough time to retire at thirty-six or even thirty-seven.

As Shane grew stronger, as she and Simone faced their problems together, as they began to talk, to understand each other better, the girl's health began to improve. And on a sunny Saturday seven days after her "accident," she returned to class, ready once more to work with her colleagues.

Caligari was pleased for her as well as for himself, and the moment Shane walked into class she was surrounded by love and affection, which she sorely needed.

Immediately she was also asked to fill in for Dorsey. To dance with Ilya. And the two performers took to each other easily. No one spoke of the real reasons for Shane's hospitalization. Everyone believed the stories Simone had told.

"Shane was tired and fell into the orchestra pit," she said, and they all bought it. After all, it could have happened to anyone.

On the tenth day of Dorsey's hospitalization, a small breakthrough occurred. Dr. French had succeeded in getting Dorsey to reveal her anger. And as she faced the challenge, as each protective layer peeled away from her skin and she could tolerate some "light upon the darkness," bits and pieces of the story came tumbling out.

"Why do you keep asking me about my mother? I loved her, damn it! That's all."

Dr. French kept that blank look on her face. But to Dorsey it felt like eyes boring holes through her skull, as if the doctor could see things she didn't want her to.

"It's important for you to ventilate, Dorsey. You have to get things off your chest so you can get well."

"I am well, damn it. Look!" She stuck out her tongue in a gesture not meant for medical inspection.

Dr. French was quietly unmoved. "It doesn't help to be so antagonistic, young lady. They brought you here in a straitjacket, and if you don't get some help you'll stay in a mental straitjacket for the rest of your life. *I* care about you, even if you don't. And I'd like to help you recover."

"Oh, you're so full of shit!" Dorsey snarled. "All you doctors care about is yourselves. You're like all the other assholes I know. I'm just one more head for you to shrink. One more stupid guinea pig. So why don't you just let me go home."

Frustrated, Dr. French opened a file cabinet near her side. She removed a manila folder filled with Dorsey's papers and threw it on the desk. "You can't go home unless someone in this hospital releases you. And I'll do that only if you face your problems. And I mean *really* face them. If you don't like me, if you want to change doctors, that's okay. Fine! Here's your file. Choose another physician and get on with it. Just stop playing these silly games."

As the file landed on Dr. French's desk, a photo of Dorsey's mother scattered with the rest of the papers. Dorsey saw it and began to cry.

Although she empathized, Dr. French was also secretly delighted. They were the first real tears Dorsey had shed since coming to the hospital. And, noting her reaction, the psychiatrist seized upon the opportunity to really confront her. Deliberately, she pulled the photograph from the file and began baiting the girl.

"You said you loved her, didn't you?"

Dorsey didn't answer.

"I don't understand," Dr. French said. "She looks like a real bitch to me."

"No!" Dorsey said. "Yes!" she screamed. "But she was an alcoholic. She wasn't responsible for the things she did."

"Not responsible?" Dr. French said. "You mean like you?"

"Don't you twist my words around," Dorsey said. Her throat constricted as she continued. A band of ice tightened around her chest. The breakfast she had reluctantly eaten this morning heaved itself upward in long rolling spasms of nausea. She got up quickly and ran to the toilet. Doubled over the bowl, she threw her guts up. Then five minutes later they were at it again.

This time Dr. French showed a photograph of Senator Childs with his wife Deandra.

"Why are you doing this to me?" Dorsey cried when she saw the picture. "I can't handle it anymore."

"Then tell me!" Dr. French demanded. "Tell me everything. Let's get it over with once and for all."

Chapter 57

Though Shane and Ilya looked splendid together, though Alexandra and Vidal worked beautifully, though Paige was back and solidly at his side, Richard Caligari was at the end of his rope. They were ten days away from the gala and very little was going right. The corps looked god-awful. The new stage had developed bumps where some wood had buckled and had to be repaired. All the original music was still being scored, with emphasis on some irregular tempos, and the costumes were not fitting properly. And true to form, everyone was fighting with everyone else.

But none of what was happening was new to him. When creative juices flowed, when creative people assembled, though they were not really at cross purposes, it always seemed that way. Then Murphy's Law reared its ugly head. *Whatever can go wrong, will go wrong.* And by God, it did.

And it galled him that with all his other problems, some of the bills were not being paid on time and creditors were making daily calls to his offices. He knew Julia was playing games, and he would speak to her about it the moment he was free.

Tired, frustrated, he did what others do in the same circumstance. He took it out on the people around him.

After lashing out at Alexandra and Vidal for something
the dance master had already corrected in class, he lectured
everyone, accusing the whole company of being lazy, inattentive and uncaring. Then he slammed his pointer on the
floor and stormed from the stage. A few moments later
Alexandra followed after to apologize.

She quietly approached his office, thinking of what she
would tell him, of how she would ask his forgiveness. Perhaps he'd been right. Perhaps she hadn't been trying hard
enough. But three feet from his open doorway, she heard
his voice raised in anger and decided her apology would
have to wait.

As she turned to leave, she couldn't help but overhear
that his conversation concerned her. It made her stop and
do something she'd never done before—eavesdrop!

"I don't care how carefully you've been paying the bills,
Julia, or how long. A deal is a deal. I've kept my part of
the bargain, now you keep yours. Alexandra is doing well
and there's no damn reason to have creditors bother me
when bills are due. You're just being spiteful right now
because of Vidal, and I won't stand for it. Whatever he did
at the Senator's house is *his* business, not mine. And I
don't intend to fire him just because you say so.

Thunderstruck, Alexandra felt her blood boil, surge
through her brain and push against her skull. One more
second and her head would burst open, spurting blood
toward the ceiling in a great red fountain. My God! Julia
and Caligari, scheming together. They had been doing it all
along. How awful. How humiliating!

"Wait a minute," Caligari continued on the telephone.
"Go back a few steps. Vidal had nothing to do with our
original deal. Alexandra was the only consideration. Then
I made the stupid mistake of letting you force those other
demands down my throat. Well, I did your bidding then,
Julia, but no more. You're beginning to choke me."

He paused again.

"There was Ilya, for example. And Vidal, indirectly. I
think I did more than my share. So don't threaten me,

Julia, because two can play that game. And unless you want Alexandra to know everything, get the hell off my back. *And keep off!* Vidal stays or it's over. And this time I mean it!"

With tears burning her eyes, with her whole body trembling, Alexandra pushed her way through the open doorway and made her presence known.

"You're both wrong, Mr. Caligari," she said, trying to keep her composure. In shock, she grabbed the telephone from his hand. "Julia," she said, biting back her tears, "you've finally done it. This is your last bit of meddling in my life. The very last."

She looked daggers at the dance master. "As for you, Mr. Caligari. To hell with you too. To hell with you both for making a fool out of me. *I quit!* And I never want to see either of you again as long as I live."

Sobbing, she slammed the phone on the hook and ran from the theater.

In a quandary before, Caligari now wanted to shoot himself. A fine young girl had been hurt because of his damned ambition. He didn't know how, where or when he'd begun to change, but he no longer liked who he was. Most of all, he didn't know what to do about it.

Half an hour after the scene with Alexandra, he received the following telegram from Gregory Kingston, Julia Romanov's attorney.

> ALL FUNDS FOR CHRISTMAS GALA
> HAVE BEEN WITHDRAWN ACCORDING
> TO MAY CONTRACT. STOP. CLAUSE
> 12B, INITIALED BY YOU, IS NOW
> IN VIOLATION. STOP

He sat down, crumpling the telegram in his hands. Now it was really over. Now there would be no more quandaries, no more rope to hang himself with. War had been declared, and in a life-and-death struggle Caligari began reaching for straws. Alexandra aside, he needed money to present the gala. He needed money to save face. He needed money to prove himself. He needed money to take care of his "family." And there was just one person on the face of the earth he could go to for help. But he didn't want to do it; yet he knew he had no choice. He was still shaken, paralyzed by what had just happened and he sat on his chair to contemplate his dilemma.

Chapter 58

The breakthrough Dr. French thought Dorsey had made soon became little more than a scattered schizophrenia. The girl would come to her office every morning and float like a bubble waiting to burst. That way she could leave the earth without pain, she had told the physician. But in the meantime she was at least talking a little about her life, however negatively she recalled it. So Dr. French let her ramble, hoping that perhaps this new behavior would help give her the courage she needed to expose the rest.

"I think I'm going crazy," Dorsey said one day. "Well, aren't I?"

"Only if you want to," Dr. French told her. "Crazy is a choice you get to make. If you go crazy, you don't have to face life. It's up to you."

"Well, life hasn't been much fun for me," Dorsey said. "Not real life, anyway."

"How so?" Dr. French asked.

"Well, Mommy and Daddy were always fighting—mostly about me."

Dr. French noted the juvenile way she referred to her parents. "About you?" she repeated.

"Sure. Mommy was *always* jealous of me, and Daddy

loved . . ." She stopped, stared at Dr. French with glazed eyes.

"Go on," Dr. French urged her. "Who did he love?"

"Daddy loved *me*."

"Are you sure about that?"

Dorsey shifted her position, crossed one leg over the other, then back again. "Sure I'm sure." She sang the rest. "But he wouldn't be. He wouldn't love me if he knew the truth."

"And what truth is that?"

Dorsey threw her head back and laughed—the sound of a mad and deranged child. "Well, *I* did it," she said. "Don't you see? *I'm* the one who did it all."

Dr. French placed her elbows on the desk. "Did what?"

Dorsey leaned forward, whispering conspiratorially. "Promise you won't tell anyone?"

"Promise," Dr. French assured her. She held up one hand and crossed the other over her heart.

Dorsey continued her whisper. "I was the one," she hissed. "I stole Shane's crystal slipper. I crushed it with a hammer and put glass in Paige's toe shoes so she'd look like hell at the premiere. I took care of Alex too. With straight pins and needles in her costume. I even wrote a threatening letter to Mr. Caligari—just to scare him."

She giggled when she'd finished.

"Why did you do it?" Dr. French asked. "What did you hope to gain?"

Dorsey's features rearranged themselves into an angry glare. She almost left her seat in righteous indignation. "Well, I *had* to, dammit! Those fucking people were eating me alive, getting roles I should have had, dancing with partners I should have danced with, getting all Mr. Caligari's attention, when it was me who was the important one. Everyone knew it. Everybody said I should have been a star long ago. Seth, Mark, Rory."

"But that's what was beginning to happen for you, Dorsey. You're not thinking clearly. You can't blame those things on your friends. If you ask me, I think part of you was afraid. Afraid it was all going to happen, and it scared you. Success *can* be pretty scary. I think it's one reason you took drugs. So you could block out your fears and feelings."

Dorsey continued as if she hadn't heard a word. "Did you know we used to be the Three Musketeers?" she sobbed. "Me, Shane and Alex. And I still love them both. Especially my Shaney babe. In a lot of ways she's just like me." Now the tears flowed down her cheeks in long, dirty streaks.

"Why?" Dorsey squeaked in a reed-thin voice. "Why did I really do it?"

Dr. French came around the desk and put an arm over Dorsey's shoulder. "Drugs distort our perceptions of life, Dorsey. And I think you did those things as a result of paranoia, to protect yourself from something that was happening only in your mind. As the drugs acted on your brain's chemistry, your perception of reality changed. Certain things became distorted and very threatening. Now you can look at it, understand it and be free of the guilt. Now you can go to your friends and tell them the truth."

"No!" she screamed, drawing her knees up into a crouch. "I can't do that! They'll hate me."

The scene between Julia and Alexandra was a short, sweet horror.

"I can't believe you did it," Alexandra said, glaring at her mother. "You made a perfect fool out of me. In front of the whole world, you played with everything I care about."

"No. You're wrong, Alex! I did it *for* you. I wanted you to have the chance you should have had. I wanted to make up for all the things I've neglected to give you."

"Oh, don't make me laugh, Mother. You've never done anything strictly for my benefit in your whole life! Not unless you had something to gain from it."

Julia's voice was fierce as she answered. "That's not true!" she defended herself. "It takes two to tango, and many times I tried to get close to you but you refused."

"Close? Don't make me laugh! You don't know the meaning of the word. Close is trust, close is honesty, close is love and loyalty. I've never had *any* of that from you. Never! So I'm leaving. I'm leaving you and everything in this house for good."

Caligari felt like garbage and tried reaching Alexandra to apologize. But each time she heard his voice on the telephone, she'd hang up. He finally gave up trying and continued scratching for money so the gala could go on.

He had his troupe of dancers to think of. A waiting public. There were salaries to be paid. So many people depended on him. But how to find the money? Then one week before the gala, they were to be evicted for nonpayment of rent, and he sat in his office with his head between his knees, knowing there was a way, but fighting it nevertheless.

Chapter 59

"Tell me about your mother's death," Dr. French asked Dorsey.

The girl had progressed to lying on the office floor in a full fetal position, sometimes speaking like an infant. "Mama?" she said. "I tried helping her but it wasn't any good. 'Don't touch me,' she used to say. 'Don't ruin my hair, don't ruin my makeup, don't ruin my clothes.' Christ! She made me feel like shit, like a goddamn leper."

"But you told me she loved you," Dr. French offered. "You said that to me the other day."

"Oh, sure, she loved me," Dorsey said, rocking her body on the floor. "She loved me. She loved me."

"And what about your father? Didn't he love you too?"

Dorsey's body went straight, rigid, head to toe. "Daddy, Daddy. Yes, he loved me. But he loved someone else even more. Someone he wasn't supposed to love." She snickered. "But I saw them."

"Who? Who did you see?"

"John," Dorsey said. "I saw John."

"And who is John?"

She hesitated before she spoke. "A man, silly." She whispered her next words. "But don't tell Daddy I told you."

"And who is this John?" Dr. French urged.

"My mother's friend. He and my father were . . . shh . . . lovers. But don't tell Mommy I told you."

For a moment Dr. French was afraid to continue. She thought Dorsey was going through too many changes far too rapidly. Still, she pressed on. They were too close to the truths keeping Dorsey prisoner. "And how do you know they were lovers?"

"I watched them," Dorsey said, sticking her thumb in her mouth. "I watched them make love to one another. Just like Daddy did with Vidal."

"Is that why you think your mother killed herself?"

"No!" Dorsey screamed. "Yes! No! Yes! I don't know. God! Everything's all mixed up." She was agitated now, thrashing and rolling from one part of the room to the other.

The doctor fell on the floor and held her, staring into the girl's frightened eyes. "Tell me," she insisted. "Let it all come out."

And Dorsey did.

"I couldn't believe it!" she cried. "Daddy loved John more than me. I just couldn't believe it. He'd kiss him on the lips, the way he kissed Vidal. He'd hug him and they'd laugh together and run along the beach. Imagine. Two men! I see them all the time making passes at one another in the company. But not *my* father! Not him.

"But I saw and I knew. And Mommy knew too. Even the servants knew. So I made a plan to get him back."

"Plan? What kind of plan?" Dr. French asked.

Dorsey smiled. "Well, if I could get Daddy to love *me* instead of John, everything would be all right. Then Mommy would forgive him and we'd all be one big happy family again."

"So what did you do?" Dr. French asked. "How did you achieve your end?"

"Well, I didn't know how at first. But then it hit me. If I went to his room alone, I could fix things. So I did. I sneaked into his room. I crawled in beside him while he was sleeping in the guest room and I kissed him. Then . . . I touched his . . ." She stopped abruptly as Dr. French waited.

"Where? Where did you touch him?"

"Where! Where! Where!"

"Answer me, Dorsey! Get it off your chest."

Dorsey stayed silent, holding both hands over her mouth to keep the words from betraying her. Then it came rolling like thunder from her lips. "I touched his wee-wee, that's where," she screamed. "But Mommy switched on the lights and found us." Her body went rigid again.

"And then what happened?"

Suddenly Dorsey was out of control. She stood up and bounced off the walls like a pinball in a machine. "Mommy ran away, she ran away. She ran away and got a gun. Daddy and I ran after her, down the staircase, down the hall, but it was no use. It was no use. We heard the shots from the bottom step before we got into the room. Bang! Bang! Bang! Then we found her on the floor, all bloody with her skull smashed, with one eye hanging loose, and IT WAS ALL MY FAULT! *My fault. My fault. My fault.*"

Now Dr. French understood everything. Now she realized why Dorsey had tried to keep her body looking like a boy. No breasts, no periods, body hair. She needed and wanted her father's love so much, she was willing to do anything to get it.

She telephoned for a sedative, then held the shaking girl in her arms. Five minutes later Dorsey was asleep as they carried her to her room.

"I think she's going to be all right," Dr. French said to an assistant. "I think the worst is over."

"So you've come to ask for my help, Mr. Caligari. How interesting."

Francesca Adair flared her nostrils again as the dance master explained his situation. "And why should I help you, considering how rude you've been to me regarding my relationship with Ilya?"

"For the sake of art. For your own personal satisfaction. For Ilya, if that means anything."

He was appealing to the best and the worst in her, using everything in his power to make her see that what she could contribute was vital and important.

"I have twenty dancers who depend on me," he went on. "I have a crew of twenty men and women who have families to feed, with rent to pay. I offer you a partnership in this gala in exchange for a loan which I will repay as soon as receipts are counted. You can't lose any money on the deal. And I'll give you billing as executive artistic director, with your name above the program."

Francesca smoked her cigarette slowly, then stubbed the butt out in a Baccarat crystal ashtray. "Let me think about it," she said, yawning. "I'll get back to you."

It was then Caligari knew the audience was over. He just didn't know how the play had gone.

Chapter 60

When Dorsey wakened from the sedative Dr. French had given her, she was alone in her room with no restraints. It was the first time they had left her like that. But her mind was a fog, a blur, an opaque and blissful calm.

She got out of bed and wandered. She thought she was dreaming as she stared out the window of her room. A crested bluejay sat on the branch of a naked crabapple tree, staring back at her. At least she thought he was. Sweet little bird, she thought. She hoped he was warm.

In her daze, in her bewilderment she picked up a sweater and put it on. Then she picked up another to cover the bird. Quietly, carefully, she opened the door and scurried down the deserted hallway.

There was nobody there. Nobody to see her. Nobody to stop her. So she slipped out a fire door and ran down the path toward the crabapple tree to give the bird her sweater. But by the time she arrived he had already flown away.

Freedom! It sure felt good.

The crisp air smelled wonderful as she tucked the extra sweater under her arm and wandered down a familiar walkway toward a small rippling brook near a wooden section of the hospital. She had gone there frequently with Dr. French and talked. She liked it because of the sparkling clear water, because of the trees, the birds, the natural quiet. Most of all because the brook ran free.

Freedom!

Freedom from fear.

Freedom from anxiety.

Freedom from guilt and especially loneliness.

Reaching the brook, she climbed on a huge rock and sat listening to the rushing water, to the birds chirping in the trees. It was all so lovely. Whatever they had given her was better than any drug she had given herself. It was making her feel warm and wonderful.

And she needed that. All the days of her life had been so structured, so focused. Now in this place she had a measure of peace. No schedules or rehearsals, no sex-crazed unions of disenchantment, no binges or purges, no rejections, no starvation of her soul. All those years in ballet had been nothing more than a proving ground, and she had lost the game—whatever it was.

Yes, she needed to feel wonderful. She needed the peace and quiet. Most of all she needed to erase the images of her father, of her mother, of the blood, of that horrible night, of the guilt that flashed through her brain like a blood-sucking spirit.

Freedom.

Blood.

Freedom.

She stared at the tall blue pines that guided the brook, at the pinecones and acorns that scattered their remnants across the rocky ground, at the overcast gray sky that was winter bleak. All of it sad and lonely. Lonely like her future. She'd been responsible for her mother's death, she knew, and nothing on earth could change what had happened. Then she heard something flutter in the pine tree, and she wondered if it could be the bluejay.

She stood up and ran blindly with the sweater, calling

after him. Then suddenly she tripped on a rock and stumbled near the brook's edge. There she noticed something sparkle in the stream.

With her long blond hair like golden autumn leaves, with dirt gritty in her mouth, she plunged her hand into the icy water and pulled out a piece of jagged glass.

It was sharp, she noted as she sat up and dusted herself off. It was blue—the color of her eyes. Then she saw the blood running from her fingertips where she had cut herself.

Blood.

Freedom.

Blood.

How easy, she thought. Just a few simple cuts and it would be all over.

When Dr. French knocked on Dorsey's door, there was no response. She pushed a key into the latch and was surprised to find the door had not been locked. Inside, she was further shocked to find Dorsey missing from the room.

She checked the bathroom, then ran down the hallway, putting the staff on full alert. Soon everyone was searching the interior facilities. Ten minutes later Dr. French realized Dorsey wasn't anywhere inside the building. She organized a search party, and they fanned out across the grounds.

Francesca Adair reached for the telephone and dialed Richard Caligari's private number. When he came on the line, she gave him the news.

"I'm going to let you have what you need, Mr. Caligari —at least for now. My lawyers are working on the papers and will contact you in a few hours when they're drawn.

"But I warn you," she continued. "Stay out of my private life. Stay out of my relationship with Ilya. And most of all, stay away from me. I'm giving you this money for one purpose and for one purpose only. To please Ilya. For some strange reason he wants to dance for you. And I want whatever he does. That's all I have to say on the matter. You have my support for the gala and for the gala only. After that, you'll either sink or swim. And frankly, my dear, I hope you drown."

When they finally found Dorsey, she was unconscious, with her hands and fingers drenched in blood. Both her wrists were slashed to ribbons, gouged deeply with the sharp sliver of broken glass she had found in the brook. They wrapped her limp body in a blanket, rushed her inside, treated and infused her, tried to breathe life into what had been lifeless for so many years, but it was no use. At the age of twenty, on the brink of stardom, on the brink of discovering the truth, Dorsey Childs set herself free the only way she knew how.

Dorsey looked like a child in her coffin, a pewter box lined in soft white satin with a simple cross engraved on its case. In her arms were a Bible and the tiny white crocheted slippers she loved so much. Senator Childs, recognizing fully his own culpability, sobbed openly at the graveside with his handsome gray head buried in the palms of both his hands.

Everyone who had known her gathered at the casket to say prayers and toss flowers. Along with all her problems, Dorsey had had the gift of making people love her, of making them laugh. She had brought a special joy to each of their lives, and for one brief instant her light had burned so brightly.

Alexandra and Shane clutched each other, sobbing as the casket creaked its way into the deep ground. Richard Caligari kept Paige from faltering. Julia, in pain at her own strained relationship with Alexandra, stood alone in a corner, isolated from everyone. It was where she belonged, she thought, a commentary on the condition of her life.

For Ilya it was simple devastation. He believed she had done it because of him.

And the newspapers played everything to the hilt as some of the stories about Dorsey's problems began to leak.

And then it was over.

Time to go home, to think about their own lives, to pick up the pieces.

Chapter 61

Caligari had been calling Alexandra ever since Francesca's funds for the gala had come through. But each time the girl heard his voice she'd slam down the telephone.

Now he was in front of her apartment building, begging through the intercom to be let upstairs so he could explain.

"There's nothing to say, Mr. Caligari. There's no excuse for what you and my mother did. None at all."

"You're right, Alex. I know that now," he replied. "But at least let's talk about it. Give me a chance to apologize."

"Apology accepted," she said abruptly, then hung up.

Two seconds later Caligari was buzzing again, begging to be let in.

Alexandra finally relented.

"You can only stay a few minutes," she said, closing the front door and showing him into the living room. "I have things to do."

He walked inside, grateful for the opportunity to talk to her face to face. And he hoped and prayed that what he was about to say would have some real meaning for her. He took a seat on the couch and, in a small voice that sounded strange coming from him, said what he had to.

"I know you won't believe me, Alex, but I want to tell you how really talented you are."

She laughed in his face. "What did she promise you this time, Mr. Caligari? The moon?"

He hung his head in shame. "I deserved that," he told her. "But with all my heart, I mean what I'm saying. Right now you have what it takes to make it big—anywhere you decide to dance. Stuttgart, New York City Ballet, American Ballet Theater—they would all accept you in a minute based on what *you* can do, not on what Julia or I would tell them. You must believe me."

Alexandra's hands flew to her ears. "Lies!" she screamed. "All of it lies. Dorsey lived by a bunch of lies, and look what it got her. No, Mr. Caligari. I don't want to hear it anymore. Not from you or anyone else. So please go. Please get out of here!"

"Don't use Dorsey as an excuse," he said, standing his ground. "She lived in a world that had nothing to do with reality. No, Alex, I'm not leaving," he continued. "I'm not budging from this seat until you tell me you'll never give up dancing." His look was straight, unwavering. "I'm not going anywhere until you agree to either audition for someone else or—" He paused, then said in one breath, "Or come back and dance for me."

She was silent for a moment, as if the wind had been knocked from her sails. Then she launched into a tirade. "Dance? For you? Never! How could I ever trust you again? My God! The lies, the games you and Julia played were despicable. You bought and sold me like a side of beef. As if I were a prostitute or something."

Caligari hung his head. "You're wrong, Alex. If anyone was a prostitute around here, it was me. I'm the one who sacrificed principles—even if it was for some noble dream. I'm the one who lied and played games, and for that I deeply apologize. But one thing has nothing to do with the other. You're good, Alex. Damned good! And I couldn't stand it if you let your talent go to waste because of me. Somehow, some way, you've got to prove that to yourself.

"Sure, at first I didn't think you had it. There were so

many things working against you. But you had the one
thing, the most important quality it takes—commitment!
The harder I hit you, the harder you worked. Then Julia
began to push for you. She was the one who kept after me
to spend private time with you. She saw your talent the
first time in Paris, and ordered me to give you more things
to do. I fought her tooth and nail but she won."

Alexandra half smiled, as though none of what he'd said
had sunk in. "Yes," she said. "Julia's that way. She likes to
run things. Even got this fancy apartment for me and my
roommates." She laughed. "What a jerk I was. Oh," she
snickered, "and by the way, just in case you don't know
she came clean on everything, she told me how she bought
up your old building so you'd *have* to come to her for
financial help. Nice lady, huh?"

Caligari gritted his teeth at the news, but it didn't deter
him. He had come for other reasons. He was determined to
get Alexandra to hear and believe him—to make her get
on with her life.

"I don't care about that, Alex. I only care that a fine
dancer, a hard-working young woman like yourself
shouldn't throw away a future just to spite me and her
mother. I can't and I won't let that happen."

"Well, surprise, surprise. You and Julia have no say over
my life, Mr. Caligari. At least not anymore. So if you've
finished—please go. I have things to do."

He stood up reluctantly. He felt sick inside. There was
so much more he wanted to say, but he knew she wouldn't
listen. So he headed for the door like a dog with his tail
between his legs, and without looking back even once, he
left.

Chapter 62

Rehearsals for the Christmas Gala proceeded without a hitch. Ever since Francesca had given him the money, her word had held as good as gold. Everything had been paid for: taxes, rent, salaries, telephone, stagehands, costumers, musicians, seamstresses. Every part of the Caligari Ballet Company was now being taken care of.

And as the daily routines settled in, as he focused on the work and on accomplishing his goals, he tried not to think about the sacrifices he'd made, or the people he'd hurt in the process, or his feelings for Julia.

But he was taunted when the night closed its arms around him and whispered its lonely secrets in his ear. And it frightened him to contemplate a future without friends, without love, without family, without the warmth of human companionship. His soul ached for what had happened to Dorsey and for what he had done to Alexandra. Most of all, he'd come to learn that some dreams are not meant to come true. That God's time is not always Man's time.

The first call came a few days before the gala. An exhausted Caligari had fallen asleep in his apartment when the telephone suddenly rang. He was in a daze as he listened to the tape monitor on the answering machine and was astounded to hear Julia's voice. He came quickly awake as she spoke, but he steeled himself and never lifted the receiver.

"Richard," she cried. "Forgive me, please. Everything's gone wrong."

He was still hurt, still angry, and he hardly knew what to say to her. So he just listened to her pain, watching a light snowfall drift past the windowpanes of his SoHo apartment.

"There are so many things I want to tell you," she went on. "About myself, about what happened. But I offer no excuses. I can't. I don't even know what they are. I only know I was wrong in so many ways. If you'll only forgive me, that would help. That would mean so much. It would at least take some of the pain away. And I'm in so damn much pain these days."

He stayed silent, deciding whether or not to answer or switch off the volume. But he couldn't move. In some strange way, though a part of him still cared, he liked hearing her suffer.

"Oh, God, Richard. I know you're there! Answer! Speak to me. I'm a wreck. I can't sleep or eat a bite. I've lost Alex and now you, everything important, and I don't know how to deal with it. God, I'm so lost. Richard, please!"

His voice was like ice when he finally grabbed the receiver. "You dug your own grave, Julia. You did it all by yourself. You're your own worst enemy and I don't know how to help you change that."

"You're right," she cried. "It's all I've thought about day and night. But I want Alex back. I need her. And," she choked a little, "I need you too. But if I can't have that, for God's sake, at least say you forgive me."

He bit his bottom lip as he tried to explain. "*I* can forgive you, Julia," he said finally. "But that's not the problem. Can you forgive yourself?" And with that, he simply hung up.

After the phone call, he walked around the rooms of the SoHo flat, thinking about her. He knew he still loved her, for whatever reasons, and in a weaker moment he might have responded differently—hurt though he was. But too much had happened; too much water had passed under the bridge.

He sat on the sofa and was about to switch on the television set to watch the news when the phone rang again. This time he picked it up without first listening to the monitor. When he heard Alexandra's voice, butterflies lifted his stomach. He knew now, in a very small way, how Julia was really feeling. In these last days his guilt over Alexandra's quitting had nearly smothered him.

"I've decided perhaps you're right, Mr. Caligari," she said distinctly and with pride. "I *am* talented. And I *do* deserve to dance with a good company."

He was thrilled, deliriously happy to hear her say those words. Together he and Julia had caused all her pain. Now they could take pride in her development and success. Something good could still come of it all.

"I'm proud of you, Alex. You've risen above some pretty heavy stuff and you're doing the right thing. Do you want me to call some people at the New York City Ballet or ABT? I'm sure I can arrange an audition for you."

"You're meddling again," she said almost playfully. "But that won't be necessary."

His heart sank. He wanted to help her so desperately.

"I want to dance for *you*," she told him. "In the Christmas Gala—if it's not too late."

Chapter 63

On the eve of the gala no one slept. In the morning minds wandered, lips stuttered, eyes blinked wildly and random muscles grew taut and anxious. A light snow had fallen the previous night, but by noon the next day a warm sun had melted it away. Now it was sunny—cold but very clear.

At four o'clock the company began assembling on stage, warming up with a short class while the stagehands, artists, lighting directors and costumers moved among them, setting the stage.

In a state of sustained tension for days, Caligari knew what the critics could do to his dream if his company of dancers did not live up to their expectations. This time the stakes were really high. Higher than they had ever been before. And tonight all stops would be pulled out. Tonight he would be going all the way.

But if he failed, it would be his last hurrah, he'd decided. If he failed tonight, he would probably give up the dream and never think about it again. And what does a man have when he gives up his dreams, he wondered. And the answer came way too easily. Without his dreams, he cannot exist.

* * *

Backstage, Alexandra and Vidal tested the jump-lift again. Two days ago Vidal had sprained his calf muscle and he'd spent the last days with an Ace bandage wrapped tightly around it. For the performance tonight, he would have no support at all, and it caused him concern. But like a trouper, like all dancers, he said nothing about his fears and just held back a little to conserve his energy.

And who would he complain to anyway? Alexandra? Everyone had something to fret about tonight. Especially her. Why make it worse? From this moment on, it was in the lap of the gods. He only hoped they'd be benevolent.

Resting for a moment on a couch backstage, Shane rubbed Ilya's back with her thumb and forefinger—deep, penetrating motions to soothe the dancer's tense muscles. His first performance in America and it was terrifying. What if the people didn't like him? he thought. What would happen if he failed?

But it was always like that on opening night. Tension, fear, excitement, self-conscious laughter, frequent trips to the toilet, to the sink, to a private corner for prayer, for coffee, cigarettes, even pills.

Yet the *merde* gifts were exchanged as usual. And the flowers came, and the fruit, and the candy from well-wishers arrived hourly, accompanied by cards and telegrams filled with support, love and affection.

Outside, the night sparkled as the brightest of New York City's luminaries came to support, came to pass judgment, came to inaugurate the company. Dressed to the nines in minks, ermines, diamonds, pearls, rubies, million-dollar smiles and assorted Palm Beach tans, they were a magnificent group.

The glamorous Jacqueline Onassis and a handsome escort emerged from a Rolls-Royce limousine looking like a couple from the top of a wedding cake. The noble premier danseur Alexander Godunov, holding hands with the beautiful Jacqueline Bisset, walked ahead of Francesca Adair, who was strutting on the arm of her agent, Stephen Stillwell. And the Jensen heiress laughed broadly with Roman Reich, world renowned diamond merchant, as both rushed from the cold air into the warmth of the red velvet lobby.

Gleaming chauffeured Rolls-Royce limousines, Mercedes Benzes and stretch Cadillacs lined the streets. Parking in front of the brightly lit marquee, which glittered like a string of pearls across the throat of the busy theater, they discharged their expensive cargo.

And while the patrons rode the escalators to their balcony and box seats, while the touters pushed the elegant program souvenirs, while those who needed it drank champagne, while tuxedoed ushers and gowned usherettes directed people to their seats, the performers backstage stretched and warmed their muscles.

Paige stood alone in a dark corner meditating. Seth paced like a caged tiger ready to strike. And Alexandra and Vidal tried the lift just one more time.

"It's nothing," he assured her as they broke for a moment's rest. "Nothing at all." He was in fact lying. In great physical pain, he smiled and walked quickly away.

Striding to her seat, Francesca Adair tossed her head like a queen. She strutted among them like the belle of the ball, with her famous goose-egg diamond dangling from her throat, held by two strands of perfectly matched pearl-and-emerald beads. It complemented her flowing black Ungaro gown, which was covered by a full-length hooded mink cape.

And tonight, for a change, they would pay homage to her. It was only right. They were here, after all, at her express invitation: West Coast personalities, who bowed toward the east for cultural enlightenment. And East Coast cognoscenti, who loved to lead the way.

And they paid for their invitations with pure gold—up

to five thousand dollars a seat for some. But it was worth it. Besides being a privilege and an honor, it gave them an edge. In the morning they could tell those who could not attend that *they* had made a new cultural find, that *they* had been there when it had all happened, in the midst of the newest, the brightest that New York City had to offer. And who could resist being part of that?

In the orchestra pit, a cacophony of shrill sounds arose as musicians ran scales to fine-tune their violins, violas, trumpets, drums, flutes and cellos.

"Give me an A."

Then the call came backstage.

"Places everyone. Ten minutes to curtain!"

In the audience the crystal chandeliers slowly dimmed, and as the crowd settled in and grew silent, the red velvet curtain began to rise.

Flex the arch and pose. *There is no pain.*

Where's my light? *There is no fear.*

Breathe deeply. *There is no failure.*

Five, six, seven, eight. *Smile.*

In the darkened theater Julia Romanov slipped quietly into her seat just as the lights went out. She had come late deliberately so no one would see her, so no one would stop her with their aimless bits of chatter, which tonight she had no taste for. No. Tonight she had come to see Alexandra dance, to witness the birth of Caligari's success, something she felt entitled to see. No matter what had happened between them, she had played a part in the scheme of things. Some of tonight's joy belonged to her, and she wanted to claim it.

As she opened the red and gold engraved program and noted Alexandra's name, then Richard Caligari's, she took a deep, agonizing breath and swallowed the tears. A sharp pain rose between her breasts as she contemplated all that had happened. She pressed it down for relief, realizing that because of her actions she had alienated the two most important people in her life. No, it was much worse than that. She had driven them completely away. It was her fault, she knew. But it was over. Better to forget and watch.

As the curtain rose, she adjusted the folds of her peacock-blue Dior velvet gown and the dark sable coat behind her until she was comfortable. Then she watched a single spot follow the conductor to the podium. Then came the downbeat as the on-stage guitars began to hum.

The opening ballet was a great success: Paige and Seth with ten company dancers clapping and performing Caligari's celebrated "Patrins." Fifteen minutes later a mesmerized audience loudly cheered. Then the curtain fell and Vidal and Alexandra settled into position for Caligari's premiere of "Dracula," the story of a lonely man doomed to wander the earth in search of a redemptive, true love.

Behind the curtain Vidal waited as Caligari's newly commissioned score began. A haunting violin solo, it spoke poems of a man's tragic loneliness and need. Vidal swung his red satin cape around his black body suit and began the sad choreographic lamentation Caligari had created for him.

Soon the full string section began an overlay of lush and romantic melodies, and as the dance continued, Vidal swayed his loneliness to a melancholy mode.

After a few minutes Alexandra bourréed toward him, and meeting together, they drifted across the stage like soft fog across a new moon. He held her waist as she posed in arabesque, then attitude, and lifted and carried her high on his shoulders before letting her down to glide about the stage like a gyro. Spin after spin, cutting sharply from chainé to piqué turns, her long dark hair flew wildly about. Then preparation for the jump-lift began, only this time Vidal prayed his leg would hold.

Chapter 64

Alexandra moved toward him slowly, unaware of his pain. One beautiful leg followed the other in perfect bourrées. Then, turning, and with a long run, with a deep plié and perfect confidence in him, she flew like a bird into his waiting arms.

As she balanced high on his shoulders, she felt his thighs shiver, as though she were too heavy for him. For a few seconds she worried, then she realized he was steady and she relaxed. Coming down, she pointed her foot, flexed her thigh, calf, ankle and arch. She felt her toes all crammed inside their pink satin prisons. Vidal smiled at her and she knew, as she balanced on her left leg with the right one stretched out behind, they had passed the halfway mark. One more lift to go.

Slowly, to the deep tones of the viola, she engaged Vidal, and in her youthful presence Dracula's hope for redemption returned. The dark blue backdrop, the brilliant lights made a lush palette for the red satin cape Vidal twirled about Alexandra's romantic startling white chiffon tutu. Then came the next lift as she leaped into his arms again.

He thought his legs would give way as he caught and carried her. It was a shock, a horrible, crushing pain in his calf. He could barely carry his own weight, let alone hers. But there was no choice, only a heroic commitment. So he smiled as he lifted and displayed her and tried to think of pleasant things. But as he bit back the tears of agony, he recalled what Dr. Mills had told him.

Ten minutes before curtain he had begged the physician for a shot of novocaine for his leg. But the doctor had refused. "You're a fool," Dr. Mills had said. "Nothing's worth risking permanent injury. Even this. If you can't do the job, just cancel. There'll always be another time. But if you tear the cartilage tonight, it's all over."

But he couldn't cancel. It was unthinkable. This was the chance of a lifetime. They were all outside waiting to be entertained, waiting to get their money's worth, their pound of flesh. Besides that, all the younger dancers were watching him, hoping he'd fall. And Julia was most likely in the audience, hoping he'd make a fool of himself. And then there were the critics, waiting to criticize. But it was more than that, he knew. He desperately needed the love, the adoration, the applause. Needed it like a drug.

Smile! he thought. Hold your head up and smile. If only he could get through this one.

Setting her down, he let the pain wash over him in sickening waves, but like the great Northwestern wind, he held it all steady. It was all right, he knew. Now he was home free.

Dressed in his Yves St. Laurent tuxedo, Caligari watched them from the wings, marveling at Alexandra's beautiful legs, so long and straight, so flexible at the arches they gave her movement a fluid and feline grace. Oh, she was something special, he knew, a dancer they would speak of for years to come. If he'd done nothing else in his life, he had helped to shape a brilliant career. That alone was worth something, an extraordinary accomplishment.

* * *

Last night a dream had come to him. And as he watched them dance, he recalled it now so vividly. It had been dark then, and he'd been alone in a forest of fog, frightened and lost. He cried out for someone, anyone, but nobody answered. Then a feminine vision appeared.

"Can you help me find my way?" he asked. "I'm cold and hungry."

"But I came before," the vision had said. "You turned me away. Now I cannot help you."

Then the fog surrounded the vision like a shroud, and it soon disappeared. He'd wakened from that dream in a cold sweat, and he hadn't been able to shake the peculiar feelings. What did it all mean? he wondered. What did it all mean?

A cone of light followed the duo, followed Alexandra and Vidal across the stage. Together they were romantic, challenging each other with sensual gestures. The two were ageless, Edwardian, like the brilliant facets of a well-cut diamond. There was something wild in Alexandra, something so utterly fearless, it was thrilling to observe. It showed in the flourish of her sure hand and her proud head —the stage presence and courage.

Every light bounced from her slender body and scattered outward like a thousand stars. She was in another world, projecting an inward light of her own. Together they ignited flames and passion, and as the audience pressed forward in their seats, as they held their breath, Caligari felt his heart flutter like a schoolboy. This was a moment he had prayed for all his life. And now it was real.

At the end of their performance, everyone in the audience rose and cheered. Everyone except Julia. She ran to the ladies' room, where she locked herself in a stall and cried. She had no right to be in the theater, she thought, no right to listen to the thunderous applause outside or take pleasure in any of Alexandra's or Caligari's achievements. She had been a hindrance from the very beginning, suckingthe life out of everyone's dreams. Still, deep inside a part of her felt intensely proud. What had begun as a selfish act, aimed only at pleasing hemself, was destined now to become a New York City institution.

As Alexandra and Vidal finished and left the stage, they kissed Shane and Ilya, who passed by to take their positions for a New Wave ballet—an experimental and futuristic offering. Simone stood in a corner watching with tear-filled eyes. She was happy, sad, filled with emotions she hadn't experienced in years. Her heart ached for all that had happened, for all the years she had pushed Shane to fulfill her own dead dreams, and she hoped she had not destroyed the girl's spirit. She wanted Shane to pick up the pieces of her life, to make herself happy. Ballet be damned, if that's what was necessary for Shane to fulfill herself.

But tonight belonged to them both, no matter what. And unlike Simone, Shane would at least know she was capable and talented enough to make it.

As the first curtain came down at the end of the gala, the glittering audience leaped from their seats with a boisterous clatter. Cries of "Bravo" vaulted from the balconies, the box seats, the orchestra. Even the musicians applauded. Garlands of flowers rained down on stage, scattered and tossed with love from every corner of the auditorium. Roses, carnations, violets, all strung with delicate satin ribbons were tossed with love at the feet of the performers.

Then the second, third, fourth, fifth curtain came down, and as the roaring continued, the stagehands parted the long velvet folds so the soloists could pass through for bows.

As each artist came on stage, there was a deafening clamor. Then the audience screamed for Caligari to appear.

And when he finally came out, the applause rose uproariously, nearly shattering the crystal chandelier and lifting the gold-domed rooftop.

And then the performance was all over. Left only for the critics to praise or pick apart.

Chapter 65

After the performance, everyone hurried backstage to congratulate the company. They all wanted to be there, to meet the stars, to touch and see them, to be sure they were real.

Even for those who had seen it all before, this new young company was a revelation. Shane and Ilya, Paige and Seth, Alexandra and Vidal, Caligari and the entire company were brilliant, all beautiful, all ready for a celebration they deserved.

A party had been planned at Tootsie's to toast the company's success, to honor the dogged determination of one man who had had a dream and who now stood alone on a darkened stage in an empty theater trying to fathom what it would all mean in the morning and how his life would change.

Which of his dancers would leave him, for example, and which ones would stay and help the company grow? He didn't know the answers to those questions, but he did know one thing for sure. Never again would he sacrifice his principles or capitulate to anyone. Never again would a single human being tell him how to run his life, especially his career. From now on, no matter what was at stake, he would go it alone.

* * *

Alone in the wings, Alexandra watched Caligari move on the dimly lit stage. She knew they had both done well, and she wanted to say thanks, to give him the credit he really deserved.

Dressed for the party in a red silk Halston dress, with her hair a crown of flowered curls, she cradled her bouquet of roses in her arms, waiting for a moment to be sure the dance master was not in the midst of creative thought. And standing there, she realized what an extraordinary man he really was and the long, long way she had come since April.

She had gone from a romantic crush on him to feelings of anger, then contempt. Now she had come to respect and admire him. And though she still loved him, it was as an artist, a mentor, someone who had given her the most unique opportunity she had ever had. Had it not been for Richard Caligari, she would not be standing tall today.

Suddenly her face flushed as she realized he had spotted her.

"Alexandra?"

"Yes." She moved toward him in small, hesitating steps. "I wanted to give you something before I left for the party."

She felt flushed as she reached his side and removed a long-stemmed American beauty rose and offered it to him. "For you," she said. "For all your help. Without you, I'd never have made it."

Caligari took the rose she offered and lifted her chin. "Don't kid yourself, Alex. Don't ever sell yourself short. You did this alone. I had nothing to do with it. You had the one quality, the single most important quality any artist needs to make it, and that's determination. Nobody gave you that. All I did, and with your mother's help I might add, was to shine you on."

"Thanks for the compliment," Julia said, moving from the shadow of the wings. "I know I don't belong here, but I had to come backstage and congratulate you both."

Julia's eyes were glistening as she said her short piece, then she turned to leave.

"Wait," Alexandra called, running after her. "I have something to say to you too, Mother."

As Julia waited, Alexandra pulled another rose from the bouquet and gave it to her. "This one's for you, Mom. A remembrance."

Julia hesitated and gazed deep into her daughter's eyes, experiencing the deep humiliation Alexandra had once felt.

"I mean it," Alexandra insisted.

Julia reached out slowly, then recoiled. "No," she said. "I can't! I don't deserve it." Then she turned on her heels and fled.

As Shane ran to her dressing room to change, she thought of Dorsey, of the beautiful legacy her friend had left her when she died. She stopped for a moment, leaned against the wall as the sadness held her, then continued on her way. It was an amazing memory, all sad and soft and strangely warm. She had danced all of Dorsey's roles, and now she recalled the love in their relationship and all the wise things Dorsey had taught her. In some strange way, Shane had decided that by doing these things, she had kept Dorsey's memory alive.

Inside her dressing room, Shane changed her clothes. Dressed, she searched for her mother.

Ten minutes later she found Simone crying, sitting in a dark, deserted dressing room.

"Hey," Shane said, lifting Simone's chin and kissing her cheek. "Where have you been all night? I've looked all over for you."

Simone turned her face toward the wall. "I had some stuff to finish," she said. "Go on to the party. I'll join you there later."

Shane switched on the lights and closed the door. "Oh, no, you don't! Not this time, Mother. This time you're coming with me."

Simone stared at her daughter with tears in her eyes.

"Two weeks ago I was about to throw my shoes in the ash can along with Brad," Shane said. "But I've changed my mind. For now, there'll be no wedding. But no ash can, either, I might add. Now that I'm in this company, I'm going all the way to the top. What I want to know is whether or not you're coming with me."

Choked with tears, unable to speak, Simone's head nodded a passionate yes.

"Good," Shane said. She hugged her mother, then drew away. "Here," she said, handing Simone the full bouquet of roses. "I think these really belong to you. Now get dressed, Simone baby, in something nice and sexy! We're going to party."

Sitting in the back of a black Lincoln limousine, Richard Caligari rode with Paige to join the others at Tootsie's. He should have been happier at the achievement of his dreams but he wasn't. There was something missing. Tonight he'd done everything he'd ever hoped to do. But there was no one special to share it with. And that made him sad. What is success without sharing, without love? he wondered. Success was important and necessary, but now it gave him a solitary and very lonely feeling.

As they drove through the night, he gazed at the glittering Christmas decorations all around him. Christmas. It was a season he loved, bringing hope and joy with the new year, making memories of the old year fade. And then suddenly he was experiencing déjà vu—Paris all over again. Only this time *he* was in the car and *she* was walking.

He felt Paige poke him with her elbow. "Go on," she said wistfully. "Go after her before you regret it."

"No," he said, shaking his head vigorously. "No way."

As the car passed Julia by, Caligari crossed his arms against his body, kept his head from swiveling, kept his eyes from seeing her face as he passed. Then his heart started pounding and he remembered that awful, depressing dream. It suddenly came clear. One chance. He had only once chance.

He told the driver to stop, kissed Paige on the cheek and reached for the door handle.

And when the door slammed shut behind him, he ran after her, calling her name.

"Julia! Julia! Wait for me."

At the sound of her name, at the sight of him running toward her, Julia stood paralyzed, like a frightened deer caught in the glare of oncoming headlights. She quickly wiped the tears from the corners of her eyes and turned her face closer to the shadows.

She wished her heart would stop pounding. She wanted to speak without stuttering, but now it hardly mattered. He was at her side—warm, strong, holding her, covering her mouth with a long and passionate kiss.

"No," he whispered as she tried to say something. "Don't talk! Don't say a word. Let's just walk together, the way we did in Paris."